Darcy's Tale

Volume III

The Way Home

By

Stanley Michael Hurd

Publisher: Stanley M. Hurd

First paperback edition, published 2014.

ISBN 13 978-09910382-2-0

Cover design: J. E. Hurd

My thanks to the many readers whose encouragement has seen me through those times when an author inevitably doubts his or her ability and worth; without the inspiration of your praise, and the burden of my obligation to you, this might not have been completed, and certainly would not have been half as carefully crafted.

One special thank you is due my friend Janet Rutter, whose standards of excellence and execution are far beyond my own; I always feel her looking over my shoulder, unfailingly polite in the face of the most egregious errors, and uncannily correct in all her comments.

Thank you, one and all.

To Miss Jane Austen, with sincere thanks.

FOREWORD

Darcy's Tale has been presented in three volumes, as was the original *Pride and Prejudice* 200 years earlier; this has been done both for reasons of historical accuracy and because the story naturally divides itself into three major sections.

For those interested in such matters, the series is set in 1799-1800, rather than the more commonly accepted 1811-1812, for arcane reasons only Austen scholars would trouble themselves with.

The Correspondence section is included as a secondary view of the story, primarily from the viewpoint of Darcy and Georgiana, and is intended to be read after completing the story; the letters contained therein form a more condensed, personal, and yet somehow stately version of the events that occurred when Darcy and his sister were apart. Their letters are not requisite to the story — or, rather, where they are, they are included in the main text. The reader is invited to take this alternate route through the story at his or her discretion.

Volume III

Chapter One

*D*arcy's wretchedness was not soon to release him, and his scene with Elizabeth ruled his thoughts completely in the days following his return from Kent; he could find no diversion, neither place nor pursuit, which could offer relief. All his accustomed self-command was gone, and as much as he wished never to think on the matter again, he was unable to think of his proposal and its sequel less than constantly: whether seated in his library or straying through the haunts of London, he was never free of the events in Hunsford Parsonage. Trapped in a mortification of spirit compounded of anger, shame, and a bleak melancholy, he nevertheless found himself still plagued by the ideal of love now denied him. In spite of every thing, Elizabeth had been so nearly the embodiment of that ideal — how he could expect to find any one better suited to him, he could not imagine; he had to remind himself very often of her manner in refusing him, to keep from regretting her. These conflicting thoughts and sentiments hung heavily on him throughout the weary hours, leading his mind in a futile vagary that never arrived at any conclusion; his harrowed and disorderly emotions making him unsuited to idleness, he drifted about as aimlessly as his thoughts: through the house, or out into London's streets, and the days and nights passed.

Having once made the mistake of admitting his sister into his private struggles, he would never allow himself to do it again, on this subject most especially. She had moved back to her own establishment in Davies Street directly after his return from Kent, but she visited almost daily; whenever she was about the house he was most diligent to hide how he felt from her. In those first days, he was wont to become careless in his appearance, until one morning, when Perkins had been adjusting his cravat, he had tried to wave his hands away; Perkins had said quietly: "Your sister will be here this morning, Sir; she will notice." This was the only exchange that passed between them on the subject, but from that point forward Darcy was more attentive to preserve appearances. Keeping his sister from knowing that he was in any way suffering became his guiding principle; her happiness became nearly his sole purpose and objective; and, as she was so often about, he was required to be conscientious in maintaining his ways.

He had his duties to attend to, and, more from habit than any sense of purpose, he pursued his daily affairs; but even they had lost their power to shield him from the tumult of his emotions. It occurred to him to wonder at the fact that hearts, when broken, do not fail of their purpose; of all things fine and fragile, why should this one in particular be spared from all natural consequences, and endure when it ought to perish? But there he was, still in his customary place, going about his customary activities, with neither cause nor desire to do so—yet somehow unable to stop.

His friend Bingley was a boon, as he could always count on a welcome from him; but even seeing that good gentleman was not without its freight of distress, as Darcy could not but associate his friend with certain of the scenes that night at Hunsford. Bingley, too, he kept in ignorance of all that had transpired: he could not speak to him of either his injuries or his anger, and, gathering the fox to his bosom, he had only to suffer in solitude the daily gnawing away of his self-regard, and his future hopes.

Those truest friends of the spurned, anger and pride, stood always ready to his side, and in them lay his one sure source of energy and will. When needed, he would enter into their embrace in order to stir himself to action, scourging his lethargy and despair and driving them down; but they were dangerous companions, as his anger was like to break free and overwhelm him, forcing him to absent himself from company for long periods until he might regain his self-control.

In the low and enervated state which followed such fits of wrath, he began to apprehend how his striking out at Wickham that night with Elizabeth had caused him to say things he now wished he might have back. As ever, in his anger lay the seeds of remorse and shame, and never more so than in this instance: his comments regarding her family had been deplorable, and ought never to have been spoken—no matter how true they might have been. And then, in light of her refusal—and the fact that she had shared none of his concerns on the subject of misalliances—he cursed his want of control, knowing he had made himself look a vain, posturing fool in front of her. Never had he been more mistaken, nor could he imagine a more humiliating point on which to be so. Each time he reached this point in his thoughts, however, he would again fall prey to his anger, both at her, for her uncaring rejection, and at himself, for having put himself in such a position—and the thing would repeat itself.

At such times, out of an exigent need to divert his thoughts, he would often send a message to Bingley, or simply run up to Manchester Square himself, and carry his friend off to White's for an afternoon of cards—listening to others talk, losing himself in the play and whatever conversation there was to be had. Even this was not entirely free from aggravation, as he would at times perceive certain of the other members looking his way and speaking behind their hands, letting him know that his encounter with Miss Chesterton had yet to lose interest among that set in Society whose lives revolved around such things.

Late one morning, some two weeks after his return, Darcy was restlessly drifting about his silent library; a footman appearing at the door provided him with a letter which more than succeeded in distracting his thoughts; it was an express, with the man waiting for a return. The letter, from his cousin, Colonel Fitzwilliam, was as follows:

Clereford
6:00 p.m., Monday, May 12, —

Darcy,

I write to apply to you for a kindness: my mother has not reacted at all well to the news I brought of my assignment in Italy, and has grown so insistent and immoderate in her representations of the thoughtless imprudence of the idea, that your uncle and I are at our wits' end. She has been speaking of Georgiana and yourself, and I cannot but think that the two of you might be of material relief in dealing with her distress. I am hoping therefore that you and she can see your way clear to coming to Clereford, that you might aid in helping your aunt to see reason, and that our dear Georgiana might assist and support her in this difficult time. My father desires I should add his hopes for your soonest assent and arrival.

I am very much aware that you have concerns of your own at present, but I hope you will be able to find it in you to satisfy our faith in your compliance; I trust to your being sensible that I would not make this request lightly, to guide your decision.

With confidence in a return at your earliest convenience, I remain,

Your obedient &c.

Col. Edmund Fitzwilliam

Spectemur agendo

Darcy immediately approved this application; he would have done so, even had his cousin's letter not been couched in such pressing language. Without stopping to think, or to realise how neatly it would meet his own need for diversion, he wrote back a brief note, stating that he and Georgiana would arrive in Hampshire as soon as might be, and hopefully the very morning following. His sister had stopped at Grosvenor Square that day after her morning calls; seeking her, he found her reading in the front drawing-room. "Dearest," he said, "the Colonel has written to say we are needed at Clereford; do you have anything in hand that would prevent us from leaving?"

"No, Fitzwilliam, nothing: what is wrong? Is any one unwell?"

"No, not precisely; my aunt is exceedingly distressed at the thought of Colonel Fitzwilliam's assignment in Italy: both the Colonel and Uncle Jonathan would like us to be there, to be of comfort to her."

"Oh—oh, dear! Of course—can we leave immediately?"

"I had hoped we might. Take only what you will need for to-morrow; you can have Goodwin send most of your things on."

"For only to-morrow I have what I need here, I believe; I shall go up, now, to be sure," said his sister, hastily leaving the room; Darcy picked up the book she had left behind, that she might have it if wanted: it was entitled *Evelina*, by a Miss Frances Burney, with whose works Darcy was unfamiliar. Tucking it under his arm, he then rang for Goodwin and gave him his instructions. It was well short of two hours later when they made their way out of Grosvenor Square and skirted the Park headed west.

He had tucked the letter into Georgiana's book and now handed both to her that she might peruse the letter; she thanked him for the book and read the letter with care. As they passed the outskirts of London and into the countryside, they could not but conjecture as to the state of affairs that must exist at Clereford, which would call for their presence.

"I cannot imagine what can be going on," began Darcy. "What can my aunt be doing that would so disturb the Colonel?"

"He has been home a fortnight," Georgiana observed. "I should have thought that sufficient time to talk through almost any disagreement; but my cousin indicated that she was become 'immoderate'; what could he mean?"

Darcy could only shake his head. "Insistent I can well believe—even imperious; but on what point? That the Colonel must go is beyond contestation, and what else could be at issue? And my uncle, surely, knows better than we can how best to manage any such dispute."

"I can only think there must be some misunderstanding," Georgiana said.

"It must be that," Darcy agreed. "And I can believe that each might become so fixed in their positions as to invest the matter with more import than it actually merits; or it may be owing to some other point of contention altogether, and is being fought out on this point instead. We must tread carefully in the beginning, until we learn what is truly behind it all." While this did not end their conjectures, as may well be imagined, in their discussion they found little of substance to add through the rest of the afternoon's travels. Spending the night in Basingstoke and rising early, they reached Andover before noon the next day, and turned south on the old Roman road the four miles to Clereford.

Clereford Manor was a striking building, some parts of it quite ancient, whilst others were more recent, but all so thoroughly and properly blended as to make the whole an object of delicate grace and stately elegance. The drive through the Park was extensive and delightful, leading through gentle sun-lit dells and deep hangars of shaggy hardwoods, giving eventually onto an expansive lawn, which led in turn to a small formal garden just about the front entrance-way. There was throughout a dignity and elegance that spoke of generations of taste, discrimination, and refinement.

On arriving they were informed that Her Ladyship had kept to her rooms that morning; this intelligence was given to them in the muted tones of a house in bereavement. "Do you go to my aunt and see what may be done to comfort and condole with her," Darcy told his sister in a low voice, "Be not alarmed if she should appear distraught, and remember: try not to let her colour your judgement just yet; we have no real knowledge of what is going forward, and until we do, we must not commit to any decided partiality in the dispute. I shall see what Edmund and my uncle have to say."

Colonel Fitzwilliam just then appearing at the top of the stairs, Darcy and Georgiana stepped forward to meet him, but Lord Andover emerged from the library at the same moment and beckoned to them all. After hushed greetings and quick embraces, Georgiana hastened up the stairs.

Closing the library door quietly behind the three of them, Darcy's uncle, his gratitude evident on his face, motioned him to a chair. Taking his seat, Darcy spread his hands and looked enquiringly at his uncle, as one who would ask, "What on Earth is this all about?"

"Darcy," his uncle began in a low voice, shaking his head, "Edmund's mother has set herself utterly against this commission of his on the continent. She doesn't eat, and I doubt she has slept six hours in as many days; she is making herself very unwell. She has forbidden Edmund to leave; she has written to friends, the mothers of men in Parliament and the War Office, asking them to bring their influence to bear; she has all but forbidden *me* from leaving Clereford."

While this confirmed some of Darcy's surmises, it only heightened his confusion. "But what can she hope to gain in taking up such a position?" he asked.

"I am sure I do not know," replied His Lordship. "At first I thought it no more than a mother's natural fear for her son, but I was wrong, apparently; now when I ask her, she will only glare at me; she does not even hit my shoulder any more," said he in a worried tone, "and that has never happened in all the years we have been married."

"What can have brought on such an extremity of feeling?" Darcy asked.

"You shall hear for yourself, I am certain," supplied Colonel Fitzwilliam. "But the gist of it is that she has lost her first son to politics — she refuses to lose her second to war."

Darcy considered this and found his opinion divided; his uncle, watching his face, correctly interpreted the ambivalence of his expression. "Looked at from her point of view, she is not wrong," he acknowledged. "That is the difficult part. We are faced, not with an hysterical woman, but with an exceedingly determined one."

"The real issue, Darcy," said the Colonel, "is that I should have been in London this last week and more. There is a great deal to study before I go over, and the situation, apparently, is changing daily. We had thought there to be no pressing urgency, but the Russians have called Field Marshall Suvorov back to take on a new campaign, and Bonaparte has not been seen in Paris for a fortnight, opening the possibility that he has gone to take command of the French forces in Italy. That leaves the Austrians by themselves in Italy with a great deal too many open questions floating about. I *must* get to Whitehall! My only hope is that Mother will hear this better from you; at this point, she is not even speaking to Father and me."

Rising to his feet, Darcy nodded. "Georgiana has gone to my aunt, and I shall see what might be done as soon as I can see her." He left the library, and, sending word through Her Ladyship's maid that he waited on her convenience, he went up himself, and settled into his rooms. He had yet to receive a summons from his aunt before dinner, and she was not to come down; as Georgiana remained with her aunt, it was only the three gentlemen at table.

Lord Andover greeted him warmly as he entered the dining-room; his cousin nodded to him, but did not speak: his gloomy countenance was enough to tell Darcy how he chafed under the delay of another full day gone, and nothing forward.

Once the customary questions of weather and roads were attended to, his uncle opened the topic that had brought Darcy to Clereford: "Have you had any word yet from Georgiana?"

"Not a syllable," he stated.

His cousin made a noise of disgust. "How long am I to be tied here by the leg, Father?" he demanded in frustration. "You know what is at stake!"

"Be calm, Edmund," his father admonished, holding a reassuring hand up to him. "There is yet time enough; I have heard from Secretary Dundas this very afternoon— he assures me that the situation is stable enough at the War Office that another day or two is of no great moment."

"Not to him, perhaps, but it is to me!" said the Colonel heatedly. "How must I look, to have my mother holding me by her apron strings?"

"Dundas knows your mother well," replied his father, "and I have his assurance on the matter: this will not reflect on you; he is aware that you stay by my request. I have told you before: this has more to do with me than you; your mother has long resented how much of my time has been devoted to duties which she thinks might just as well be done by some one else."

"You will forgive me, Father, but I cannot help but believe it has more to do with George, blast him!" Colonel Fitzwilliam grumbled. "If he had not turned out to be such a wastrel, chasing around after Fox, she would not be so obtrusive when it comes to *my* aspirations!"

His father nodded at this. "Perhaps there is some truth in that, but these points have been long argued, and are now little felt; but she will come around, Edmund, I am certain of it; she must listen to reason, and soon; should she not, you will still be in London on Saturday." Father and son exchanged a look of understanding and agreement, and the matter was dropt.

For his part, Darcy wondered that things had reached such a pass that his uncle and cousin were prepared to circumvent his aunt's wishes, passing over her most strident objections, in what seemed to him a rather callous fashion. He could only imagine what arguments had passed before his arrival that would have admitted such behaviour in a family he knew to be as close-knit as any.

Chapter Two

*A*s Georgiana did not leave her aunt's rooms until very late, and went straight to her bed, Darcy did not see her before morning. She came down to breakfast, however, and he had an opportunity to gain some insight as to his aunt's state of mind.

"Here you are!" cried he with forced cheerfulness. "You look fit enough; did you sleep?"

"Well enough. I am hungry, though," she replied, yawning deeply. "Oh! —Forgive me, Fitzwilliam." Given how sleepy her eyes were still, Darcy guessed that she had not risen until nearly breakfast-time.

"How is my aunt?" he asked.

"Quite honestly, I do not know," said Georgiana, clearly troubled. "If she slept last night, I did not see it: it was well past midnight when she insisted I retire. I have never seen her thus, Fitzwilliam; I am exceedingly worried about her."

"Did she say much?"

Georgiana shook her head. "Very little, in fact; she kissed me when I came in, and said how glad she was to see me; she asked how I was, and about the journey and so on; but she hardly seemed to listen, and asked the same things again more than once. She did not seem able to let go my hand, Fitzwilliam," Georgiana said, looking very worried. "When I asked what was troubling her, she would only shake her head and ask after the roads. Twice, she dozed off, still holding my hand, but when I stirred, she woke instantly. From time to time she would ask a question about my reading, or my playing; for the most part, were it not for her silence, and her hand keeping mine, I should have thought there was nothing wrong at all. " She looked up at her brother: "She will be well, will she not? She looks so weak!"

Darcy sighed; the problem was so complex on the one hand, yet so simple on the other: the ties of love cut deep, when the pressures of the world were applied to them. Love, Darcy reflected, even familial love, caused so much pain, so much trouble and distress—but how to say that to a girl not yet sixteen? "I am sure she will be," he tried to reassure her. "I only hope the Colonel will keep well in Italy; if he returns soon, and whole, her recovery will, I trust, be complete."

"He will though, will not he?" asked Georgiana, distressed by the sudden apparition of injury.

Darcy wished he could offer her assurance on that point, but as he felt none, he could give none: "In all honesty, Dearest, I cannot say; he goes to war. He is as able, quick-witted, and dextrous as any one I know, but I do not trust his eagerness: he feels a great need to distinguish himself, which may lead him into harm's way."

"Then my aunt is right?" Georgiana asked, alarmed.

"She is not wrong," Darcy admitted, repeating his uncle's assessment. "But she must realise she cannot succeed; that is what puzzles me: the Colonel is not a child, to stay or to go at his mother's bidding; he must and *will* follow his own path."

"But if he should be wounded! Fitzwilliam, what if he should be...gravely injured? How could she bear it? How could we all?"

Darcy shook his head uncertainly. "We can but trust his abilities and luck will hold, Dearest, and stand ready to support our family, no matter the outcome." Georgiana looked as if she would have argued the point, had not her respect for her brother been too great for her to oppose him.

When breakfast was over, Georgiana went back to her aunt; shortly thereafter she came to find him, to say that she was come down, and awaited him in the summer drawing-room. The two of them entered to find their aunt sitting composedly, her hands folded in her lap; she wore a shawl, though the weather was warm; Darcy gave her his compliments, and kissed her cheek. While Lady Andover appeared outwardly calm, a determined set of her jaw told him that she meant to carry her point, and that she suspected he was there to dissuade her; on his part, he was not altogether certain what he *was* there for: whether he ought to persuade her, or oppose her, or simply listen to her. He did not like what her face showed him: the eyes were dark and hollow, and the cheeks were thin; there was an unhealthful pallor about her that spoke of a body close to failing under the demands of an implacable will; yet there was something behind her eyes that spoke more of despair than determination.

"So," she began, carefully smoothing the folds of cloth covering her lap, "are you come to prevail upon me, Darcy?"

"I am here, I hope, to listen to you, Aunt," he replied, his concern evident in his voice.

With a sniff the lady said, "That will be a novelty. I presume you have been informed of what has transpired?"

"Somewhat," he allowed with caution. "From what I gather, you have set yourself against the Colonel's going to Italy, on the grounds that you have already lost too much to the needs of the nation."

"Nearer the mark than I should have expected," said she. "Not but what I could say more on the subject."

"Of course," Darcy agreed. "But, my dear aunt," said he in a tone of gentle bewilderment, "there must be more to this; I do not understand: he is a man grown, and must follow his chosen course; how can you hope to succeed in opposing so what must be seen as his duty, as well as his desire?"

The deep unhappiness Lady Andover felt suddenly expressed itself on her face; —"Do not speak to me of *du-*

ty!" she said angrily. "And, pray tell—why do men's duties so often coincide so perfectly with their desires? A desire, an inclination, a woman might argue with; but let a man lay claim to duty, and all objection must fall before it." Georgiana, her face reflecting her distress at such heated speech, excused herself quietly and left the room. Darcy looked from her to his aunt with concern, and was confounded.

"What is it, Aunt—what is it, truly?" he asked, his accent filled with all the apprehension and alarm he felt at seeing her so distraught. "There must be more to this than you are saying. I know you must realise that Edmund's interests lie in the direction you oppose: he will distinguish himself, surely; he may even fall in the way of a title, with a bit of luck."

"And he may also simply fall, never to rise! Why will no one else see this?" she cried indignantly.

"I know full well he might," Darcy admitted frankly. "He is too eager for achievement; and in war, all his abilities will not save him, if his luck abandons him." He did not say it cruelly, but merely as a statement of fact, in accord with her own.

For a moment, she looked at him with an angry expression, but when he continued to look at her with concern and patience, without seeking to quarrel with her, her eyes fell, sorrow replacing the anger in them.

"Oh, Darcy," said she in a voice that barely restrained the tears behind it, "the thing of it is, it hardly matters, one way or another, do you see? —it is not just Edmund falling in battle I fear: even if all goes according to the fullest extent of his hopes, in his gain lies my ruin. If he succeeds—I will say, rather, *when* he succeeds—I shall lose him, as surely as though he had fallen; either way I shall lose him." She paused for a moment to regain mastery of herself, then said: "You are right: he will leave me. I have known it in my heart all along, I suppose." An even deeper sadness entered her eyes, and she went on,

"But all my boys are lost to me, and I cannot bear it. I had already lost my husband and my first-born to politics, and now I am losing my last dear one to war—it is too much. I will not...I cannot...oh, Fitzwilliam, I am so tired."

Darcy was mystified, confused by what she was saying; shaking his head, he asked: "Dear, *dear* Aunt Eleanor, how have you lost your husband? The two of you are amongst the most devoted couples I know."

She looked up into his face, as though weighing her words. "Yes, perhaps you are right, but it was so different when we were young, living here at Clereford; we were hardly ever apart...well, of course that could never have lasted, but still...I am very proud of him, you know, and it means so much to him...but these days, we only come here once or twice in a twelvemonth—and he hasn't gone riding with me since we were at Pemberley, for your father's funeral."

Her eyes softening, she said, "And George...my sweet Georgie...he was *such* a dear child, Darcy—you can have no idea! Edmund was always so serious, such a thinking boy, but Georgie laughed from sun up till sun down." Her eyes hardened, and she said, "Then that man Fox got hold of him; George wanted so much to be like his father, but of course, he has not his father's brain for policy, and so now—now, he is what he is. But still, I had Edmund; his career was not always so demanding, and he was there when needed, always considerate, and, in his way, affectionate. But then he became fixed on that wretched Corsican, and that marked my end."

She looked into Darcy's worried face, and shook her head. "I know I shall lose this battle—in truth, I already have: he has been gone for months—longer—his whole being focused on Bonaparte; Edmund is lost to me, just like his father and brother before him, and I am alone: that is my fate—but I would have some one know what I feel; I regret it must be you, and not one of the three on whom I have most claim."

Darcy thought this over, his eyes reflecting the disturbance of his mind. "I shall not speak to that last, Aunt, except to say I am honoured to be of use to you; but as to the Colonel—you have raised a strong man, and an intelligent one, possessed of no little initiative: surely this is something to be proud of, is not it? If he is not to use his strength, to what purpose was it given him? As a man, it must surely be better for him to do what he can, and pursue whatever accomplishment he is capable of, than to be one of London's many useless gentlemen. He has made his choice: as greatly as I might wish, for your sake, that I did not, I must confess I feel it were better for him to go than to stay." At his point, his aunt looked at him pensively, and her shoulders fell; Darcy could see she felt his argument; and by an almost unconscious nod of her head, it appeared to him that these thoughts were not altogether new to her. He went on: "I do hope you can find it in you to release him, Aunt, for you are making yourself unwell; it pains us all to see you so, and my uncle not the least." He looked at her in all sympathy, tracing the lines of sorrow at the corners of her mouth and eyes. He was moved to say, "But I hope you will believe me: you are *not* alone: you are greatly loved by all your family. I shall stay with you; shall I? —Georgiana and I, we shall both stay here at Clereford, until we can hear that the Colonel is arrived safely, and the situation is in hand."

The lady looked at him gratefully. "I would appreciate that, Fitzwilliam, very much; you are a dear boy—have I said that before?"

Darcy smiled. "Yes, I believe you may have. My dear aunt, you must know that you may rely on your family, as we have always been able to rely on you; I have reason to know that one of the most important functions a family performs is to sustain its members in misfortune; we shall be here, Georgiana and I, for as long as you need us."

His aunt gently squeezed his arm by way of expressing her gratitude.

Darcy sat by her side without speaking for a while, then asked: "Aunt, why have you told *me* this?"

"Georgiana is too young to burden with such matters," she replied, lifting her head and drawing a deep breath—the first in some time, it seemed. "Edmund and his father stopped hearing me almost from the very first, but *you* listen when a woman speaks, and think before you answer," she continued. "It is a most charming thing in a man—your cousin and your uncle might both benefit from your example—no, that is my anger talking. But also, Darcy, because some day soon you will marry," at this, a momentary pang passed across Darcy's face, which his aunt noticed; but, as he did not speak, she let it pass: "and you should know what a wife and mother feels; moreover...well, moreover, because you have enough of your father in you to care."

After waiting a brief moment for him to reply, she stood, and Darcy did, too; as she passed him towards the door, he asked, "What would you have me do, Aunt?"

The lady paused, then, with a sorrowful look, she told him: "Tell them I have given over my objections; but make sure Edmund understands, Darcy. I shall speak with him again, perhaps, before he goes, but he will hear it better from you, I doubt not; I am only his mother: you are his friend, and very nearly a brother to him: from you it will hold neither censure nor judgement. And would you send Georgiana to me? I find I am terribly fatigued, of a sudden."

Chapter Three

*D*arcy helped Georgiana escort his aunt carefully up stairs to her chambers before seeking his male relations; finding them together on the terrace, taking in the morning sun, he told them: "I have spoken with my aunt: I believe it will be well. She has gone back up; Georgiana is with her, and will help her to rest, I hope."

"What does she say?" asked his uncle.

"She wishes you to know she has given over her opposition: the Colonel is released."

"But what of her objections?"

"She understands the arguments against them, I believe; in truth, she probably always has. But this was important to her."

"Is that all?" demanded Colonel Fitzwilliam with some heat. "Just like that, and she concedes? Would that I had written you sooner, Darcy. Well, I, for one, shall not tarry to wonder: I shall begin packing immediately, lest she change her mind again"

"But, Darcy," asked his uncle, "how were you able to bring about such a sudden change of heart?"

"I shall need to reflect on what I have heard, if I may, before I answer," he said, not having decided just how to explain the matter. "But I am not altogether convinced it *was* sudden, really; more than anything, or so it presently seems to me, she simply wanted some one to listen to her." The other two looked at each other for a moment, and a marked consciousness crossed their features. Darcy excused himself and went up to his own chambers for a period of reflection. It troubled him to realise that his aunt and uncle, whom he had believed to be almost as devoted and happy a couple as had been his own parents, could have come to such a pass—so deep a schism—so late in their life together. He worried at this for a while, until, looking out the window, he spied his sister walking out into the shrubbery; he went out to her to hear about their aunt. Catching up to her where she walked along one of the many crossing paths, he stepped up to walk along beside her. "Is she well?" he asked.

"She has lain down," Georgiana replied. "I believe she has gone to sleep."

Darcy breathed a sigh of relief. "That is glad news, indeed. It relieves my mind a great deal."

They walked in silence for a bit, then Georgiana asked, "Fitzwilliam, is all well?"

"I have hopes that it will be, now," he answered.

"No...I meant, with you," Georgiana said hesitantly. "My aunt asked very particularly if you were quite well; she seemed concerned."

"I am well," he assured her, although he was conscious that what he said was less than the complete truth. But his health was with him, that was true enough, and he did *endeavour* to be well; further, as his sister could not benefit from the knowledge of his struggles, nor would he derive any benefit from her knowing of them, it was better that the true state of affairs be left unsaid.

"Really?" said she. "I, too, have thought perhaps you had something on your mind of late. It is not...are you still troubled by what took place in Hertfordshire?"

He looked down at her; with a shake of his head, he said, "No, Hertfordshire is not at issue, truly; but you know I will not dissemble: yes, there has been something on my mind of late, but it is not something I feel at liberty to discuss. This, unfortunately, must occur from time to time; I do try, and I shall try, to keep such things from your notice, and you may be assured that, for such as affect you, I shall certainly give you fullest information whenever I may properly do so. I realise this is less than satisfactory, Dearest, but I trust that you will admit the necessity, and forgive me." Georgiana, of course, nodded her acquiescence, though she looked at him thoughtfully; they continued their stroll, speaking rather of the day and the weather, and, when these topics of inexhaustible interest failed, of the affairs of their relations.

Eventually Darcy, looking at some clouds gathering in the west, said: "I shall go back in; I wish to speak with the Colonel. It threatens rain, Dearest; do keep an eye on the weather."

Going in, Darcy found that his cousin was in his apartments; he found him busily selecting and laying out a number of personal items to have with him on his journey: books, a carefully folded map, writing materials, and the like. He looked up as Darcy knocked at the open door. "What news? Is all well?" he asked apprehensively.

"Rest assured, Edmund, all is well; there has been no change, and my aunt is asleep."

His cousin looked relieved, and went back to his work. "I cannot tell you how anxious I am to be gone; at every moment I anticipate receiving word that the plans have returned to *status quo ante*."

"No, I think you are safe, there," Darcy said. "But, Edders, I need to pass along some things your mother told me. Primarily—and these are my impressions, not her words—she feels that all three of you are lost to her: that she is completely bereft and abandoned. And, if I may offer an opinion on so close a family matter, she is not wrong. I find no fault with any one of you, you understand, it is only that your lives are pulling you in different directions at present, and she feels it exceedingly, as it is her lot to be the only one to remain behind. Secondly, I believe she felt a little put upon, as both you and my uncle were so strongly opposed to her: forgive me—again, I find no fault on either side, and am only offering my observations for consideration, not opprobrium."

"Of course, Dirks—do not trouble yourself over that; but what you tell me *is* troubling." He slowly let his things drop from his hands, evidently thinking hard. Looking up, he said, "I fear that, in my eagerness for this assignment, I have lost sight of some things nearer home. Will you excuse me?" So saying, he went to his writing desk, and drew out a sheaf of paper.

Chapter Four

*T*he Colonel left the following morning: the family all turned out to see him off. His mother embraced him most tenderly before he mounted, his missive to her obviously having effected a rapprochement between them. Darcy and Georgiana settled in for an extended stay; early in the first week of June they received the Colonel's last letter written in England, posted from Dover just before he sailed for the port city of Genoa. It affected Lady Andover very much, and she was in low spirits for several days. Now came the period of waiting: it would be a month at the very least before they might have word of the Colonel's arrival. During that interval, Lord Andover made several trips to London, but could glean no serviceable news concerning the Italian campaign; Darcy did have the pleasure of seeing his aunt and uncle reconcile — having given his uncle the hint that perhaps a ride together in the countryside around Clereford would not go amiss — and also of seeing his aunt regain somewhat of her former strength, although her careworn features bore evidence that her fears persisted.

But where his own difficulties were concerned, as the days passed Darcy found his thoughts lingering on Elizabeth more and more often with regret, rather than anger; he remembered her many claims to worth and virtue, and began to overlook the manner of her rejection of his proposal; while he did this more often than he realised, whenever he did catch himself at it he would heatedly reprimand himself for the weakness of his resolve, and dwell on his causes for anger with her for as long as necessary to restore order to the state of his emotions.

He instituted a daily constitutional, taking his aunt out for a walk each afternoon, in the shrubbery when the weather threatened, or for longer walks into the park when fine, in hopes the exercise would be of benefit, and that she might find his company soothing. Often Georgiana would accompany them, and on occasion His Lordship would make a point of taking Darcy's place. Darcy benefitted from these outings too, for they gave him a welcome respite from his own thoughts.

On one such stroll, Darcy and his aunt were by themselves, taking their ease under a spreading tree in the park as relief from the heat of the sun; Darcy, looking out over the countryside and, noting a similarity to the countryside near Meryton, unconsciously allowed his thoughts to drift once again in the direction of Elizabeth.

His aunt broke in on his musings: "Who is she, Darcy?"

Darcy looked at her in surprise. "To whom do you refer, Aunt?"

"This girl you keep sighing over—who is she? Is it the one from Hertfordshire, or some one in Town you have as yet failed to mention? I do you the courtesy of believing it is not Miss Bingley."

"Pardon me, Aunt, but I was not 'sighing over' any one, I assure you," replied he with dignity.

The lady scoffed. "Men always suppose that they can so perfectly disguise their feelings," said she, "but in fact, you are none of you any more guarded than puppies; you may be able to regulate your features, but you reveal your thoughts with your every breath, to any one who takes the trouble to look. So, my question stands: who is she?"

"Really, Aunt, you must not ask such things," Darcy insisted.

"Only one pleasant thing accompanies age, Darcy—the prerogative of speaking one's mind: saying whatever one wishes, to whomever one wishes. Come now, this dodging about will not avail you." She set her hands on her hips and faced him squarely. "It *is* the Hertfordshire girl, is not it?"

"If I say it is, will you let it be?"

She pretended to give it consideration. "To be perfectly honest, I fear that is highly doubtful," she told him after a moment, a hint of mockery in her tone. "No, I see no hope at all." She looked at him more seriously: "Darcy—I saw the look upon your face when your marrying was mentioned between us, when first you came to Clereford. Unhappiness recognises its fellows, my dear, and I recognised yours; I have been waiting for you to mention it, but you are determined, it seems, to languish about and brood without the help of your relations."

Seeing that she would not relent, he offered her his arm and gestured forward along the path. They resumed their stroll, and he said, "What would you have me say? That I fell in love with the wrong lady? That I made a complete fool of myself? That every thought of her carries with it a heavy charge of disgrace, and even, may I say, anger? Very well: all that, and more." A thought occurring to him, he added, "But Aunt, Georgiana must not know of this; she was greatly affected by even the transitory hope of a sister, and I would not have her regrets reawakened."

Lady Andover nodded her understanding. She said, "But that was not anger I saw just now, nor when I first made mention; are you sure that is all there is to it?"

Although it pained him to admit it, after a pause Darcy allowed: "No, I know it is not, but that is only because I am an utter fool. There was a great deal I hoped for, at one point, but I fear that is all in the past."

"Tell me what happened," she said, patting his arm comfortingly.

And so Darcy related the history, with as much honesty and detachment as he could, starting in Hertfordshire and then into Kent, not forgetting to describe his actions in the matter of Bingley and Elizabeth's sister; he finished with his proposal at Hunsford. Lady Andover listened in silence for the most part, occasionally asking for more information on this point or that.

At his conclusion, he found his aunt staring at him in wonder and consternation. "You dear, sweet idiot," said the lady, not unkindly, but quite distinctly. Darcy looked at her, startled at this less than muted response to the chronicle of his trials of the heart.

"I beg your pardon?" he demanded.

"Not mine, but certainly your Elizabeth's, and more than likely your friend Bingley's," she said reprovingly.

"What can you mean, Aunt?"

"Dear *child*—have you listened to yourself? What possessed you to explain—in great detail, apparently—how completely she would dishonour you and your family, were you to deign to admit her into it? Is that your idea of a proper proposal? Is that how you would seek to endear yourself to some one? Heavens above!"

"But I only spoke the truth," he protested, "as she must have known it, herself; I believed it only right to assure her that I had considered it, too, and it was of no consequence."

"Oh, Darcy!" cried his aunt. "You told a lady of some standing—in her own country, of course, but still, a gentlewoman by any standard—that to marry her would be a degradation? You imagined that she would feel unworthy of you? So unworthy that she would need to be persuaded to accept your magnanimous offer of protection from the consequences of her unworthiness, before the more respectable members of Society? How uncommonly generous of you!"

In all his previous deliberations, his anger and mortification had largely held Darcy back from considering the affair from Elizabeth's point of view; now, his aunt's words brought to him a new perspective on the matter: perhaps he *had* placed too much emphasis on that aspect, in his attempt to persuade her that it would be well; — had he?

As this first, probing tendril of uncertainly took hold, it grew apace; he came with shocking rapidity to see his entire proposal, from the moment he walked into the drawing-room of the Parsonage till he fled into the night, as one long, wilfully insolent and wholly astounding exhibition of arrogance and presumption; indeed, each moment, and nearly every expression, seemed an attempt to surpass the last for ill-bred effrontery. Knowing now that Elizabeth despised him, and had not the least interest in marrying him, he was forced to examine their exceedingly animated discussion from her position. His memory, unfortunately reliable always, supplied him with a completely accurate and excruciatingly painful transcript of the proceedings, as it must have appeared to her.

"So evident a design of offending and insulting me..." — her first salvo. Weighing his expressions of devotion and esteem, or what he had intended as such, his words now took on a very different tenor: "...the demands of character and judgement always stood opposed to inclination," he had said. God in Heaven! he railed at himself, why not simply slap her? Could he have been more offensive?

"You cannot deny that you have been the principal, if not the only means of dividing them from each other..." — the second volley. Even at the time, in London with Bingley, he recalled hoping Elizabeth might never know of his interference; fate had, once again, made him its jape. Of course Elizabeth would despise him for an interfering, officious scoundrel: how should she not? And what had he done? Heaped coals on the fire with his affectation of unconcern. The wonder was how Elizabeth had managed to maintain her grip on civility; and he now recognised that, even in such trying circumstances, she had spoken only the truth as it was known to her at the time, without exaggeration or distortion, just as he hoped he would have. To realise this was to see her perfections yet more clearly, and how thoroughly he had destroyed any chance he might have had with her.

"Your character was unfolded in the recital which I received many months ago from Mr. Wickham..." — this was the final round, the one that had loosed his tongue and released that torrent of wounded primacy which had sealed the tomb holding all his prospects of happiness. Here was the foundation for all the rest: he had expected her to understand and accept, to take his part, solely on the strength of his character — yet he had shown her little enough to value in it; and certainly, given what he now understood of her views, she had small cause to take his part on any point whatsoever. Prior to his letter, what had he ever done that might have informed Elizabeth on his character, or Wickham's? And, given his behaviour throughout their acquaintance, why should she not have shown a preference for Wickham? Perhaps, had she had the knowledge he had provided in his letter available to her at the time, especially as regarded Wickham, she might have seen her way to believing him; but surely not as things had then stood. Darcy quite nearly writhed in discomfort as these things became clear to him.

Looking further back, all the way to that first evening at the Meryton assembly, he saw nothing in his behaviour but an endless succession of slights and discourtesy, if not necessarily towards her, certainly towards all her neighbours and relations. She may even have overheard his disobliging comment to Bingley concerning herself ("...almost from the first moments of our acquaintance...") — Heaven help him, had she? If she had...dear God above! — he was in an agony of shame at the mere possibility. But even had she not, his behaviour that night was calculated to offend the society of Meryton much more than it had been to recommend him to their notice — distant, judgemental, and ill-tempered, it was rather intended to disrupt and unsettle their society, than become part of it: the very height of incivility. "Had you behaved in a more gentleman-like manner…" Would he ever be free of the torment of that phrase, after this? *Such a fine gentleman was he!* —had he not gone to her in the full expectation of her acceptance, if only she might be led to rely on his assurances that *he*, as her husband and champion, would help her face down her detractors among the "better" elements of Society? How she must *despise* him! She would never see him again, that was certain—nor could he blame her.

Finally, working his way back again through his proposal, his embarrassment was such that he was almost mad with self-loathing. Impossible to imagine, that he could have said so much in so little time that could redound so to his discredit. On reaching this point in his introspections, which had not, in fact, required too very many steps along their path, he actually groaned out loud.

His aunt, who had been walking by his side in silence while Darcy laboured through these recollections and recriminations, now peered up at him sympathetically: "You begin to see it, do you?"

Unable to answer, Darcy could only nod despondently. After walking a little further, and another consideration obtruding on his internal reproaches, he asked, "You do not blame me for having made the offer?"

"Overmastering passions overmaster us," the lady replied, a hint of sadness in her tone. "That's how you know what they are. There is no fighting them."

The truth of this struck Darcy with force; looking back over the six weeks that had passed since Hunsford, he recognised that in spite of all his anger and shame, Elizabeth had never truly been supplanted in his estimation and in his heart; notwithstanding the wounds he had suffered, his estimation for her continued unabated, and she remained his standard of perfection in women. This insight carried him neatly out of his mortification, to sink him directly beneath a torrent of pain and loss. "But, then—what does one do now, Aunt?" he asked in subdued tones. "Having been overmastered, I find myself alone still—the lady despises me." All his sorrow and regret from the aftermath of his proposal descended upon him, and he was sore-pressed to keep his aunt from seeing how low he was taken.

"Dear Fitzwilliam," she said, laying a condoling hand on his arm and shaking her head, "the future is closed to us; were it not, life would be insupportable, as only uncertainty admits of hope." She considered silently a while as they walked. "There is no worthy answer to your question," she said at length. "Perhaps the classics hold an answer as good as any: time, and a journey. Take your friend and go—go abroad, or go north, or west; your uncle and I shall care for Georgiana."

"There is no cure in distance or travel," he said unhappily. He knew full well that his troubles would follow him, wherever he might contrive to go.

"No—no cure," allowed Lady Andover. "Only distraction, so that time, the one true cure, can pass more readily."

Chapter Five

*T*hat this was little spoken of between them
thereafter, is not to be taken as saying it was
little thought of, by either party. But Lady Andover had enough respect for her nephew's heart and head
to leave him to find his way through by himself, that evidently being how he preferred it; and, being not without
cares herself, she was more often occupied with her apprehensions concerning her nearer relation.

On his part, Darcy' reflections were more clamorous
and self-critical over the ensuing weeks than at any other
time in his life. Not an hour could pass without his wishing he might simply wrest the memories of Kent from
him forever; or better, go back and re-make the past. "In a
more gentleman-like manner" became an echoing litany
in his mind: each incident, each recollection of his behaviour in both Meryton and Hunsford, concluded inevitably
with this thought, scourging him endlessly with humiliation and remorse. At every point he had shown himself to
be every thing he abhorred, and now he could barely face
himself in the mirror.

Well, Elizabeth had given him to know her disdain,
in sufficient and not unjustified reprisal; thinking on the
matter more deeply still, he now could only imagine that
the women he had known in London must have felt
much the same as Elizabeth had, but had forborne to
speak, out of an excess of civility, if not out of pure, un-
sullied avarice.

The one beneficial effect of his trials was that they
gave him a new, more sympathetic view of how Georgiana must have suffered, when her dearest hopes were
torn away from her; he knew now what it meant to see a

future dispossessed of hope and joy; he determined he must do more for her pleasure in future.

But for himself he felt only contempt; there was nothing wise or worthy to be salvaged from his humiliation and anguish. The only wise thing that he could see to do, now it was too late, now that he had betrayed his deepest feelings and Elizabeth was lost to him, was simply to close his heart from that time forward, and neither seek nor expect love to enter his life again. He could not but recognise that much, even most, of his pain had been self-inflicted; yet it was that very knowledge that convinced him that he was unsuited for love, as it had been his own unconscionable assurance, presumption, and disregard for others that left him so little room for consolation. Georgiana had never wronged or slighted another in seeking love, as he had: his offenses were as natural to him as her virtue was to her. The inescapable conclusion was that he was simply not meant to form a true and lasting bond with any member of the other sex; and, with all the mistaken feelings, pain, and misunderstanding that love brought to every one he knew, there could be nothing to regret in letting it go. So he told himself, many times over; eventually, he came to allow it to be true.

Given this conclusion, it was obvious that he would be very wrong, very blameable, to condemn a lady — any lady, let alone one so singular and admirable as Elizabeth — to a lifetime in his company. Georgiana and Bingley — their miraculous regard for him — was far more than he merited, surely; and with two such friends in his life, he could not justifiably repine his want of a wife. Indeed, he felt all his luck in having those two: until Elizabeth had shown him a true vision of himself, he had never realised that his manners were in any way accountable for his having so few intimates; it had always appeared to him rather a consequence of his own taste and discrimination. Now he was forced to own that his ill temper, his overbearing manner, and his want of even the most common cordiality, would have put off all but the most congenial of individuals. Having thus injured Elizabeth especially by his incivility, was inexpressibly painful to him: that she should have disliked him so determinedly, from the first moments of their acquaintance even, when he had been so selfishly unaware of what she must feel, spoke deeply to him of his short-comings. To have wounded her so cavalierly, so callously that he had no idea just what he had done to deserve her censure — and to have inflicted such a grievous injury on himself thereby — forced him to re-evaluate all of his previous beliefs as to what constituted the proper degree of consideration due others.

As the days passed, Darcy diligently sought to accustom himself to his new expectations: to learn to be satisfied with grey, where there had been colour; to anticipate nothing more than contentment, and not happiness; and most explicitly, to give over any hope where Elizabeth, or any other lady, was concerned. His success was questionable, but he was satisfied by the strength of his efforts, and trusted that they would eventually be sufficient to his needs.

His aunt was of material use during these weeks, in turning aside Georgiana's attention whenever they both happened to be present at the culmination of one of his inner chastisements; between them they succeeded in keeping Georgiana's apprehensions from awakening. Darcy made return to his aunt for this, and for her kindly instruction and support, by his solicitude for her cares and her welfare; he continued the practice of walking with her each day, listening to her relieve her fears on the subject of the Colonel, and benefitting in his turn by occasionally receiving her sympathetic attention to his concerns; most especially did he benefit from being assured he was not the most blazingly contemptible fool in the kingdom.

Chapter Six

S o did June pass away: Darcy worrying at his faults, and his aunt worrying over the fate of her son. But the first Friday in July opened a new chapter, as the family's anticipation was finally rewarded with not one, but two letters from Colonel Fitzwilliam at once. The family gathered around Lord Andover impatiently to hear the news; in the first, dated June 14, the Colonel had to tell only of his passage, and safe arrival at Genoa on that date. This Lord Andover handed to his wife, and opened the second. As he began to read, however, his repeated exclamations of surprise aroused every one's concern and alarm, until he was forced to read it all aloud:

> HMS Kestrel
> June 19, —
>
> Father,
>
> First, I am well; please reassure Mother on that account. I write with news that will bring more pleasure to her than to yourself, I am afraid: I return to England—in fact, I shall already be in London as you read this.

At such a beginning, Lady Andover gave a cry of astonishment, joy, and relief; hugging Georgiana to her, she wept a little for the gladness of these tidings. Darcy's uncle, however, remained inflexibly grave, and continued:

> On my arrival at Genoa, I heard from the commander of the blockade that the siege there

had but lately lifted, and the French surrender accepted; but, there being plague in the city…

At this Lady Andover gave a little gasp of fright, but her husband shook his head and, with a comforting hand on her arm, continued:

…I passed it from a distance on my way north, where, I had been told, the Austrians were massed at Alessandria. Riding steadily through the day, I reached the environs of that place late in the afternoon; there, my advance was restricted perforce by growing evidence of battle; indeed, the smell of powder still hung in the air, although the guns were stilled. Not knowing whether this might betide good or ill, I became cautious; I dismounted and, removing my regalia, I approached on foot as night fell. I shall not toy with your suspense: I found the Austrians had fallen to the French, led by none other than Bonaparte; their surrender had been accepted that very afternoon at a village called Marengo. For the main part of the next two days I scouted, and I shall spend much of the voyage home writing up what I discovered; but suffice it to say that the French have secured northern Italy: an incredible and staggering turn of events.

Unharmed, even uncontested, I rode harder still back to the south, my main concern being to reach Genoa before the blockade ships might leave the area. In this I was fortunate, and I took berth aboard the *Kestrel*, bound immediately for home. We are now in the waters south of Spain, but I should expect to be in England no sooner than the 1st July: the captain will swing well out to sea to avoid the French coastline, as she is a frigate and only lightly gunned.

July 2

I have kept this open that I might include word of my arrival. We just now dock in Dover; I shall spend the night here, as it is late, and ride for London in the morning; I shall post my letters from there. Father, you will appreciate the import of the intelligence I bear, and I expect you may reach me at Horse Guards in Whitehall at any time in the next week, and well beyond.

I am, Sir, your obedient &c.,

Col. Edmund Fitzwilliam

Spectemur agendo

Dinner that evening was a joyous affair, with the ladies of the house in the highest of spirits at the safe arrival of their son and cousin back on British soil. Lord Andover rejoiced in his wife's happiness throughout the meal; when they had withdrawn, however, he turned to Darcy sombrely, saying, "This will have far-reaching consequences, I fear, and I have some concern over how the Colonel's rôle will be perceived. On consideration, I believe he acted aright; indeed, I do not know what else he might have done, but it would be possible to construe his actions as dereliction; York may try to injure me through your cousin. Beyond this personal concern, a loss of this magnitude will have a profound effect on policy, both as regards the French, and as regards our current allies. I ought to be in London; would you accompany me, Darcy? Moreover—would you accept me as your guest? I have no time to be bothering with an hotel, and there will be certain discussions requisite that should be kept from outsiders at all cost."

Darcy assured him he would be most welcome at Grosvenor Square for as long as he wished, adding, "It would be as well for me to be home, too; I have no doubt things wanting my attention will have been starting to collect, and I feel the need of looking into my affairs."

"And your sister? Perhaps she might wish to remain with her aunt?"

Darcy considered, then replied: "I imagine she would do so quite happily, but I cannot but believe my aunt will insist on going to London herself to see the Colonel, do not you think? I am sure Georgiana would be pleased to have her as her guest, or she may certainly avail herself of Grosvenor Square."

"Quite right, Darcy, of course: I was thinking only of the work to be done—your aunt dislikes being around me when I have things afoot. But you are right: she will certainly want to go up to see Edmund."

"As you seem to feel a degree of urgency, perhaps you and I might go up to-morrow, with the ladies to follow as soon as they can?" Darcy suggested.

To this his uncle agreed, and the men shortly rejoined the ladies. The evening passed pleasantly; Georgiana played to them, and their aunt could scarcely contain herself long enough to stay seated through the length of a piece, for the joyfulness of her spirits; on several occasions she pulled either her husband or nephew into an impromptu little dance, as Georgiana's lively playing caused her elation to brim over into motion.

Darcy and his uncle left for London the next day, and on their arrival the morning following, his Lordship immediately posted several letters, then left to meet with some of his associates in Parliament. He did not return until well into the evening, bringing with him some three or four others; after a late supper, he remained closeted with them in one of the smaller rooms until far into the night.

This pattern was to repeat itself for several days, until Darcy began to feel himself rather in the way, even in his own home; he saw nothing whatever of Colonel Fitzwilliam, and, having come down to breakfast one morning to find a gentleman unknown to him in evening attire just finishing having eaten, who bowed to him with utmost courtesy and left without a word, he decided that perhaps he might think of taking his aunt's advice and going on an extended excursion. There was nothing to hold him: his work caught up, he had very little to do at home aside from contemplating past errors and an empty future.

The following day he met Bingley at White's for dinner, just to get himself out of the way at home. He found his friend, though, in low spirits. When he broached his plans, Bingley replied with: "What? Oh, an excursion; certainly, that sounds pleasant. I have nothing to hold me. Of course...I shall be happy to come." All this was said with a most abstracted air, leaving Darcy almost in doubt that Bingley had even understood him.

"Bingley," he said, "are you quite well? You seem out of sorts."

"I am well enough, Darcy," was the lacklustre reply. "But, as you say, a little out of sorts. Caroline has mentioned my moods, too; perhaps I *should* go on a trip, get out of London — it might do me good, and would definitely give me occupation. Where were you thinking of going?"

"I had not got that far," Darcy told him. "Have you any thoughts?"

"No; anywhere would do for me."

"Do you have any restraints on your time?"

"No, I have nothing in front of me; we can leave whenever you like."

Darcy was troubled by this lack of animation, naturally, but it reaffirmed his intention of taking his friend away in search of diversion. After dinner, he and Bingley lost themselves for a while in cards, but neither one took much interest in the play; they made their respective ways home at an early hour. Darcy continued to revolve and refine his thinking on the excursion; at first he thought of only inviting Bingley, as his friend would clearly benefit from a change of scene, both as a relief from his sisters, and for whatever else was troubling him. But, realising that would leave Georgiana with not one, but two households with guests to be looked after, and wishing her company in any event, he thought instead of a large party, including both his sister and his aunt.

His sister and aunt arrived early that next week, and settled in Davies Street, as Lord Andover had suggested they might. Darcy discussed his thoughts of an excursion with both ladies, and readily received their approbation. In a reversal of their normal routine, Darcy began to visit his sister's establishment in the mornings, again with the idea of leaving his uncle a clear field for his activities on behalf of the nation.

Bingley was invited to a discussion of the scheme; the four of them sat comfortably in the drawing-room at Davies Street for an hour or two, discussing possibilities.

"How far shall we go?" was Darcy's first question.

"Perhaps we might go to Scotland," suggested Bingley tentatively. "It would be cooler, and we could escape from the press of people here in Town."

This was an odd thing for him to say, and Darcy noted again his friend's uncharacteristically withdrawn manner; he had never known Bingley to wish to avoid the crowds of London before.

To this Lady Andover countered: "But we should miss out on the English summer! And the heat is greatly mitigated, is not it, by the delightful breezes in the open country, and the speed of the coaches?" Bingley allowed this to be true, and sat back quietly.

To conciliate his friend, Darcy offered: "What of a little sea voyage? Well, not a voyage, perhaps, but just a day on the water. What could be more refreshing?"

"The Isle of Wight?" suggested Georgiana. "One hears of it as being a pleasant trip."

"Or Cardiff," Her Ladyship put forward. "There is really very little to see in either case, but as a destination for a day's outing either would serve."

"But where shall we end up?" asked Bingley.

"Should you care to come to Pemberley for a time, Bingley?" Darcy asked. "Let me return your hospitality of last autumn, and have you stay with me this year." Bingley nodded, but it seemed his thoughts, sent back to Netherfield by Darcy's comment, had been captured by his memories of that place, and he did not speak further on the subject; the others, however, eventually agreed on Cardiff as a destination for a day on the water.

"Might we see also your university, Fitzwilliam?" Georgiana asked hopefully.

"That would work well," concurred her aunt. "I shall need some things from Clereford, and we could take it in en route to Oxford."

To this Darcy nodded agreeably. In order to bring his friend back into the discussion, Darcy asked, "Bingley, do you recall Miss Hartsbury's ball last spring? I was thinking of asking if she would care to come along. What say you?"

"Darcy," interrupted his aunt, "is not Miss Hartsbury the one they call the rabid rabbit?"

"How on Earth could you know that, Lady Andover?" he asked, placing an emphasis on her title to accentuate how at variance her knowledge was with her dignity.

"Oh, nonsense," the lady scoffed. "The young always prefer to believe that their elders are utterly unaware of what goes on around them; we simply chose to allow you your foolishness, since to oppose it is akin to opposing the tides — or any other relentless force of Nature."

Darcy grinned and asked, "So youthful folly is a relentless force of Nature, Your Ladyship? How, then, is this force expended, that it no longer troubles the elder-ly?"

"It wears itself out on our persons; why do you think those who commit the most of them are aged before their time? And you will note that I preserve an almost pristine perfection of feature, due to my having eschewed all such taxing foolishness in my early years." Even Bingley smiled at this. "But, seriously, Darcy," she asked, "do you know this lady?"

"I do indeed, Aunt. I have found her to possess considerable character." He did not explain that he felt obliged to move her interests forward where a certain gentleman from Bath was concerned, as a sort of recompense for the unrequited interest she had shown in him.

"Is she here in Town, now?" asked Her Ladyship. "I am aware that she spends a good part of each year in Bath, that her mother may take the waters." This Darcy had not known, but it explained to him Miss Hartsbury's frequenting Bath, and Lady Andover's knowledge of her: they each were accustomed to spending time there, and in such a compressed society they could not help but have come to each other's attention.

"She is, I believe," he replied.

"Very well, I will take your word on the matter: not that you have shown yourself to be a paragon of wisdom on the subject of young ladies' characters."

Bingley chuckled outright at that, but Georgiana was rather taken aback that her aunt would make light of her brother's discrimination so openly.

"Perhaps, Bingley, as we are to go through Oxford, we might include Pender," Darcy suggested.

Bingley nodded agreeably, and Lady Andover asked, "Mr. Vincent Pender, Master of Christ Church?"

"Yes, Aunt; do you know him?"

"We have met," said she. "He will be a diverting companion for a journey."

With such observations and decisions, they came at last to agree on an itinerary that would take in a great deal of England's countryside, winding about the South and the Midlands for some two weeks, to finish at Pemberley late in the month of July.

Over the next two days, Darcy put the finishing touches on the scheme. To keep peace in Bingley's family, and to make a proper return to Bingley for his hospitality the year prior, he eventually resigned himself to inviting both Miss Bingley and the Hursts; he sent an invitation to Miss Hartsbury for her and a companion, as well as one to Pender. Discreet enquiry had enabled him to discover that Sir Neville Canham's interest where Miss Hartsbury was concerned, had, if anything, augmented, and by sending an invitation his way too, he hoped to continue the good effects he had begun at her ball.

The final plan, then, was to take Bingley and his sister, and the Hursts, together with Miss Hartsbury and her companion, to Clereford, according to Lady Andover's wishes: Darcy was sure that Miss Bingley had not forgotten her desire of seeing it, and he could thereby relieve himself of that obligation without risk of repercussion. From there they would proceed to Oxford, and add Pender to their party; Sir Neville, the last member of their entourage, was to join them in Bath. On to Bristol, a short voyage across to Cardiff and a return to Bristol, then on through Gloucester, Worcester, Derby, and, finally, arriving at Pemberley after a fortnight's travel, for an indeterminate stay, with the various members of the company invited for as long as their schedules allowed. Their departure was set for mid-July.

Miss Hartsbury, on receiving her invitation, called upon Darcy one morning not long after. Georgiana happened to be at Grosvenor Square; the two young ladies had been introduced before, but had never had the opportunity to converse at any length. Once the usual compliments had been passed, Miss Hartsbury launched immediately into her delighted thanks. "How can I *ever* thank you, Mr. Darcy! I was *so* grateful to receive your invitation—I had to come straight away to accept in person. Of course, my uncle has forbidden me to go, as it means he will have to bestir himself, and he hates to leave Town; but Mamma, bless her, is on my side. Of course, she is rather weaker than usual at the moment, which is why we are not at Bath, so she will not be able to help much with him, but I shall manage, because I am *determined* to go. What fun we shall have!"

Georgiana, blinking almost as rapidly as Miss Hartsbury in her efforts to keep up with this out-bursting of dialogue, could only smile back at the spirited, beaming face of Miss Hartsbury. Darcy said, "I am sure we shall be delighted to have you with us, Miss Hartsbury."

"Now, tell me every where we are to go," Miss Hartsbury carried on. "Your invitation mentioned Bath...well, Bristol, but of course Bath is just on the way, so I naturally assumed we would go through Bath, you know..." Here the lady coloured slightly, and her voice trailed off.

Darcy supplied her with what she hoped to hear: "We shall go through Bath, it is true. There was a gentleman at the ball I had the honour to attend at your home: a Sir Neville Canham; as he struck me as an engaging sort of fellow, I have written to invite him along, and we shall add him to the party in Bath, assuming he is able to join us."

"Oh, that is...! Well, that is to say, I found him pleasant company as well; I shall be glad to see him amongst us." She hesitated a moment, a happy sort of little smile playing on her features. Then she said, "Do you know, I have never been to Bristol? Not once. For all the times I have been to Bath, I have never ventured farther west. My uncle says he does not care for the place, but then, he never cares for anything much further away than his club. But now, do tell me every where we shall visit."

Darcy obliged with a summary of their tour, punctuated by Miss Hartsbury's exclamations of delight at the prospect of so much to please and interest. She glanced often at Georgiana to invite her concurrence of anticipation. Georgiana, who had been puzzled at first by Miss Hartsbury's manner, had come to feel a genuine pleasure in her company, as well as a slight pity for her outward demeanour; but Miss Hartsbury's enthusiasm was infectious, and in her company Georgiana could see the possibility of some one with whom to share and increase the pleasures of travel, she being a person of both taste, and eagerness in the pursuit of amusement. Moreover, there was something in her character that appealed to Georgiana, making her more comfortable in her company than was customary for her with new acquaintances. Darcy saw this, and was gratified that his thought of being of service to Miss Hartsbury and Sir Neville should bear this additional benefit.

"But you say your uncle is set against the tour?" Georgiana asked in a troubled voice, concerned that her hopes in favour of her new friend might be spoilt by Miss Hartsbury's disobliging relation.

"Oh, yes, my dear, but that will not matter; he likes to make a fuss, but I can always get him to do what I want in the end. He is a well-meaning creature, but very old-fashioned in his thinking; but, however, he can always be dragged into the modern day with a little patience and kindness. He is a great deal of help to me in handling my business; although he has no head for figures, he is very punctilious in carrying out my instructions with respect to my affairs; and, of course, I absolutely require some one to do it, you know, for no one will listen to a woman in such matters."

Georgiana, somewhat bewildered by all this, looked enquiringly at her brother; Darcy smiled and nodded reassuringly; Miss Hartsbury's eccentricities always diverted him, and he was amused by his sister's confusion in the face of such a character as Miss Hartsbury's. He was sure they would enjoy each other's company, and hoped that Georgiana might learn some of Miss Hartsbury's openness, assurance, and frank enthusiasm.

Chapter Seven

*D*arcy went to find Bingley in Manchester Square one afternoon not long after, to take him to White's again. He wished to apprise his friend of the progress of their plans, and, if possible, to delve into his friend's state of mind; he was becoming quite concerned by Bingley's prolonged low spirits.

Seating themselves comfortably away from the heat coming in at the windows, Darcy gave Bingley the news and details; Bingley remained politely disinterested. "Is there anything more that might be done for your pleasure?" Darcy asked. "I am not sure I have truly sparked your enthusiasm."

"Oh, no, Darcy; I am quite looking forward to it," said his friend, although in his accent there was little real eagerness.

Uneasy on his behalf, Darcy spoke: "You once asked me if all was well—now I ask it of you: is there anything troubling you?"

Bingley shook his head. "Nothing, really. Nothing that can be mended, at any rate."

Darcy tried one or two more oblique approaches to the question, but Bingley remained unforthcoming; Darcy finally left off, not wishing to pry; they joined some others at the card tables, and the topic was dropt. His friend's attitude, however, did not fade from his memory, and he wondered if it might still have to do with Miss Bennet. He resolved to attend more carefully to Bingley's comfort, as he had done with Georgiana; they were both deserving of his attentions, and for similar reasons. As his aunt had said, pain recognises its fellows, and he was very earnest in his wish to relieve them both and improve their enjoyment in life.

Among his other preparations, Darcy had not forgotten that Georgiana's birthday was nearly upon them. Knowing it would increase her happiness for more than just the space of a day, Darcy purchased a rather superior pianoforte to replace the one at Pemberley, and, as they would be traveling on the actual day of her celebration, he also bought a small offering to give her on their journey.

Shortly thereafter, he had the pleasure of receiving an acceptance from Sir Neville; in his letter he revealed himself to be a polite, sincere, unaffected youth, and Darcy was even better pleased with his decision to include him in their party.

Having made every preparation necessary for their comfort on their journey, he notified the others that all was in readiness. Therefore, at a comfortable hour on a pleasant Monday morning in the middle of July, the Londoners set forth for Hampshire, en route to Clereford. They broke their journey in Basingstoke, as Darcy and Georgiana had done on their way to Clereford in May.

That evening after dinner when the men were by themselves, Darcy and Bingley had their first opportunity to become better acquainted with Miss Hartsbury's uncle, Mr. Morton Hartsbury. Mr. Hartsbury was a substantial individual, both in figure and by nature: heavy in speech, and holding conservative opinions and strong Church of England views. While not a man who often opened conversations, he did not shy from discourse, and, on top of all else, he was a Cambridge man: Queens' College, in fact, making him the confirmed natural enemy of Darcy and Bingley.

"Tell me, young man," Mr. Hartsbury said to Darcy not long after the ladies had adjourned, "did I not see you dancing with my niece at her home last March?"

"I had that honour, yes, Sir," Darcy replied.

"Yes; I thought I had. One has heard of the Pemberley estates, of course," observed Mr. Hartsbury. "Your holdings in Derbyshire are extensive, I believe?"

"We are, to the best of my belief, one of the larger estates in the country," Darcy admitted; he was considerably surprised by the rather bald, ill-bred tone of the question. However, he directly found Mr. Hartsbury's capacity for asking ill-mannered and impertinent questions was not exhausted.

"Have you any shipping interests?"

Again taken aback at such a brazen enquiry, Darcy answered in clipped accents: "No."

"I am glad to hear it," said Hartsbury easily. "Too risky. Holdings in the colonies?"

Darcy and Bingley shared a look of amazement. "We have some interests in India, yes," Darcy allowed. "May I know the purport of your questions? Perhaps I can satisfy your curiosity more expeditiously."

Mr. Hartsbury did not respond to this attack on his manners, saying rather: "Hmmm; I am not curious, you must understand. As I am charged with the stewardship of my niece's fortune, it is incumbent upon me to ensure that those of her acquaintance are all that they should be. You should know, Mr. Darcy, that I was against this excursion; had my niece not insisted in the strongest terms, even threatening to accompany you unchaperoned, I should never have been able to justify the time away from my duties."

This gave Darcy a considerable insight into Mr. Hartsbury's character, given what Miss Hartsbury had said about him only the week prior, but he merely said, "No doubt. Very well, let me see if I can cut across for you: our holdings in Derbyshire were granted by King Henry VIII, and extended by grant of King James II. Our family seat will see its three-hundredth year in my lifetime, God willing, and our fortunes have improved uniformly under the stewardship of the last several generations. Will that suffice, or do you require more surety of our standing and station, Sir? Perhaps you would wish to communicate with my solicitor?"

Hartsbury was unruffled by Darcy's tone. "I am pleased to hear what you have to say; it is quite acceptable," said he. Turning to Bingley, he then asked: "And you, Sir; may I know…"

Darcy cut him off. "See here, Mr. Hartsbury! I was willing to tolerate such from you, as you are my guest, and I would go some distance to ensure the comfort of a guest; but I draw the line at such an inquisition of my other guests and friends. Mr. Bingley is my close personal friend: let that be enough, Sir."

The older man remained yet unperturbed. "As you would have it, Mr. Darcy; I believe I can depend upon your authority on this occasion."

"I am most gratified by your reliance," said Darcy sarcastically.

"You must not take offense; none was meant, I assure you: I seek only to safeguard my niece's interests. I make similar enquiries of any young man who introduces himself into her sphere; I myself, place no consequence at all in the affairs of others, or their standing."

"Of course," Darcy said in carefully detached tones; but he and Bingley exchanged another glance that spoke their mutual opinion of the gentleman. To Darcy this revealed yet another obstacle Miss Hartsbury faced in finding a beau, and more reason to be glad Sir Neville was to accompany them.

When they joined the ladies, one of the waiters from the inn was attending them, and Darcy noticed Mr. Hartsbury intently observing the waiter's careful and attentive deference towards Lady Andover; shortly thereafter he approached the fellow to ask a question in a low voice. The waiter's eyes grew round in surprise, and he quietly replied with some emphasis, and at length. Mr. Hartsbury's eyes grew round too; to another brief question, the waiter nodded very sincerely. After this exchange, Miss Hartsbury's uncle seemed to undergo a change of heart; for some time after, when he spoke, especially if Her Ladyship happened to be present, he spoke with much greater courtesy and deference.

The company reached Clereford late in the morning of the second day; Miss Bingley had her curiosity satisfied, and her covetousness aroused, by the sight of that fine estate, still delightfully maintained in the old English manner; she was profuse in her admiration of it to Darcy's aunt, which lady thanked her with distant politeness. The party spent the night, then took the time for a tour of the house and grounds in the morning; Miss Bingley was evidently so overcome by its magnificence as to be afflicted with a weakness in the knees, often requiring the support of Darcy's arm as they wandered about the place.

"Tell me, Mr. Darcy," said she as they stood viewing a charming aspect of the Andover seat from the shrubbery on its northern side, "after Viscount St. Stephens and Colonel Fitzwilliam, who is in line to inherit?"

"As a matter of fact, it seems I may have some claim to the succession; the original letters patent, while a bit hazy in their wording, seem to say that the eldest male in the closest direct line inherits," he replied. "It has never been at issue, and the current laws of inheritance put it in question in any event; but, aside from myself, there is only a second or third cousin somewhere, who went to the Americas and disappeared. But as both my uncle and my cousins are in robust health, I have no thoughts of ever succeeding to it, thankfully; the Pemberley estates are quite enough for one man to oversee: I want nothing more to occupy my hours."

"Of *course*," Miss Bingley said with the greatest sincerity, "and your uncle is very hale, certainly—for a man his age; but then, the viscount *is* looking a bit florid these days—and no wonder, if he pursues all his pleasures as vigorously as I saw him do last Christmas. And of course…the Colonel, a military man, and we *are* in a time of war…but, however, I pray they all enjoy long life and health, of *course*—and there is really no reason to expect otherwise." After this obliging observation, the lady was silent some time, no doubt judiciously contemplating the various probabilities for continued existence amongst three men whom she barely knew. She only revived when, having perceived that a part of her arm was exposed to the morning sun, she sent a footman back to the house for her largest parasol but one.

That afternoon they travelled north towards Oxford, reaching the shadows of its spires on their fourth day of travel. Darcy had written ahead to Pender, asking him to arrange accommodations for the party. Trinity term being well over, Pender had offered to put Darcy and Bingley up in college; Darcy had countered with an offer that he join them at an inn in town, that the whole company might stay together.

Their old teacher met them at the gates of Christ Church on their arrival: "Welcome, welcome, gentles all!" he cried, making a sweeping bow that would have better suited a dandy from the century prior; the lines of his bow were somewhat marred by his academical dress, as tending to tangle about the knees. Straightening, he advanced to shake hands with Darcy and Bingley. He then looked expectantly at the ladies of the company.

Darcy made the introductions. Pender bowed politely to Mrs. Hurst and Miss Bingley, and with a pleasant smile towards Miss Hartsbury; when Darcy named his sister, however, Pender drew in his breath sharply: "*Such* loveliness and grace! I am *delighted*, Miss Darcy," said he. Georgiana coloured deeply, at which Pender impishly twinkled his eyes at her and kissed her hand; she quickly withdrew her hand, blushing even more, and Darcy admonished him: "Behave yourself, you old cur!" Pender merely smiled the more brightly by way of answer.

His best efforts were reserved for Lady Andover, however. She had come upon the group rather late, having stayed behind to retrieve something from her coach. "But *this* is the meeting I have awaited!" Pender cried. "Dear Lady Andover, I am your most humble and obedient servant; I swoon to be in Your Ladyship's presence again! Nothing is so bewitching to the discerning mind, as beauty mellowed and enriched by a noble maturity." He bowed deeply to her.

"Master Pender, you antediluvian rogue, I shall have none of your impertinences on this little outing," she said sternly, and, to Darcy's very great surprise, she struck him on the shoulder. "Get up, old man, before your lumbago takes you. There; you may kiss my cheek."

Pender did so with chaste respect, then laughed delightedly. "Well, this *is* a red-letter day for these old walls. Rarely has this bastion of overweening masculinity been graced by so many lovelies at once." He led the company into the college grounds. Addressing Georgiana and passing her arm through his, he said: "You, my dear, call greatly to mind the portrait of a sixteenth century marquise, which hangs in the residence hall. I pray you will call upon me for any least service you might require."

"Pay him no mind, Miss Darcy," her brother advised her with tolerant amusement, "he is only playing. For all his overblown manners, you will not find a more proper gentleman; at least, so long as he is in college—I cannot answer for his comportment elsewhere."

"He is also aware," added Her Ladyship drily, "that I would flay him alive if he were to dally with any relation of mine."

Pender stopped and clutched his chest. "You wound me to the heart with such vile mistrust! I despise this modern etiquette, which holds that any man who so much as doffs his hat to a lady, must have designs upon her. Ah, for the days of the glorious past, when a man might be a man, without fear of Heaven knows what mis-constructions!" Turning back to Georgiana, he said, "Come, my dear, you are too young to have been jaded and jaundiced by such unworthy imaginings; the purity of youth shines in you as the beauty of the sunrise: always fresh, always new, and ever radiant; you shall revive this old man's faith that the world still has hope of correcting its ways."

Georgiana turned an alarmed glance at her brother, but he merely chuckled and said, "That well-worn expression about barking and biting was meant specifically for that old dog; do not let him see you disconcerted, however, or he will never leave off his teazing."

Georgiana hesitated, but, spurred by her brother's admonition into a rare display of courage, she turned to Pender and said, "But, as yours were the hands to raise up our new generation of young gentlemen, Master Pender, I wonder at your want of faith; for was not it under your tutelage that those responsible for the world's condition, became what they are?" There her courage failed, and she fell silent, blushing a deep crimson.

"A Darcy—by Heaven, she is a Darcy!" cried Pender. "Lord bless and keep me! —what with your brother and your aunt to contend with, must I now be tormented with yet another?" Darcy and the others laughed and applauded Georgiana, who giggled bashfully to have been so bold as to beard the lion in his very den. Master Pender, however, went on in open challenge to every one in the party: "May I point out to you all that the two young men in your company were under my particular care? Do you wish to criticise my efforts there?"

Darcy laughed again and said, "That was well done, Miss Darcy, but I warn you: he is a dangerous man to match wits with."

"Bah!" scoffed Lady Andover. "I have witnessed him nearly lose the power of speech entirely, from one well-bestowed kiss." Georgiana coloured again, and her brother laughed heartily. "I never thought to try that, I confess. To think of all the hours I wasted, trying to out-wit him!"

Georgiana shyly disengaged her arm from that of Master Pender, and repaired to Miss Hartsbury's side; Miss Hartsbury whispered in her ear something that made her blush still more, and the two of them giggle delightedly, their heads together in close feminine confederacy.

With Pender as guide and *passe-partout*, they were treated to an inside view of Christ Church Cathedral, and all over the university grounds, as well as a very complete tour of the city, including a trip to the top of Magdalen Tower, to see the city laid out before them in its bright summery glory. Georgiana was delighted, although Miss Bingley had found the prospect of climbing the stairs to the top of the tower too fatiguing for her to consider; she staid below with Mr. Hartsbury. To Darcy's surprise, Pender showed himself to be quite sprightly, leading them to the top with a very lively step. Miss Bingley later expressed to Darcy a wish of going punting on the river, but on making her application general, the company, and the gentleman himself, were against it, as the day was hot and the dinner-hour was approaching.

The morrow was to bring Georgiana's birthday, and, as the company would be traveling all that day towards Bath, Darcy had decided to celebrate it that evening at Oxford. He prepared the earnest gift he had brought from Town, a lovely necklace of gold and large, old garnets, and took it down with him to dinner.

The company dined at their inn that evening; when the men joined the ladies in the salon, he brought forth the necklace and presented it to Georgiana. As the company applauded, she coloured as prettily and modestly as only the young and truly artless of her sex can, prompting Pender to observe, "My dear, you are a young lady to make an old man wish he had his youth back: and believe me, very few things in life could tempt me to traverse those weary years over again." Georgiana blushed the more for his compliment, and her brother offered her a small glass of wine as a constitutional. Lady Andover gave Pender a reproving glance, to which he tipped his glass in toast with an eye cocked in challenge; the lady shook her head disparagingly but returned his toast, at which he beamed delightedly.

On returning to his apartments after a very pleasant evening, Darcy was startled and concerned to find Perkins seated in his chambers, glumly staring out the window in the dim glow of a single candle. As he entered, his man jumped to his feet, apologizing, "I beg your pardon, Mr. Darcy, but I was sure she couldn't find me, here."

"She? Of whom are we speaking?"

"Clarissa, Miss Bingley's maid," said Perkins in a morose accent.

"Why should you be hiding from Miss Bingley's maid?"

"She seems to have set her cap at me," replied Perkins, downheartedly.

"Oh, dear," said Darcy mildly. "I take it she is not to your taste?"

"No, Sir. She and her mistress are quite the pair...oh! I beg your pardon, Mr. Darcy, Sir," said his man, flustered.

"No offense taken, Perkins," Darcy assured him. "I should think you know my feelings on Miss Bingley by now."

"Yes, Sir. Well, Clarissa seems to have decided to make it a set...her words, Sir. The thing of it is, I've a sort of an understanding with Lara, the barmaid in Meryton who I mentioned to you; and, anyway, Clarissa is a common little thing; she sets my teeth on edge just by her talking. And, Lord, how she talks! I hate to be hard, and tell her flat out I don't take to her, but I don't know what else to do—so here I be, like a mouse in a wall, hiding from a cat."

"I had always found her to be rather a refined sort of girl; at least, she has always appeared so in my presence."

"Yes, Sir, she knows how to put on airs, and that's the truth, which makes it even harder to listen to her when she's herself, if you take my meaning. Lord help me, Sir, how can a man handle a woman like that?"

Darcy could sympathise perfectly with his man, having many times asked himself the same question regarding her mistress. "Well, I think you will find that a simple, straightforward declaration of the truth is your best friend, here, Perkins," he said.

"Yes, Sir; I'm sure you're right: but it surely is a hard thing to say."

"True enough, but just imagine how your Lara would feel if she somehow came to hear of it," Darcy advised him, speaking from his own experience. "Trust me, that is something you never want, and, no matter how unlikely it appears, it can happen."

"Yes, Sir; thank you Mr. Darcy," said Perkins disconsolately; then, seeming to put the matter behind him, almost as an aside he said, "Oh, and she says her mistress is sore put upon with how little time you have spent with her during your trip, Mr. Darcy: I thought you should know." Then he turned his attentions to removing his master's attire; on his side Darcy was pleased to know that his time devoted to Mr. Hartsbury had turned up yet another benefit, in disobliging Miss Bingley; he resolved to commit even more time to his company. But he did not forget Perkins and his difficulties, and resolved to think of a way to help him if he could.

That Saturday the party arrived in Bath late in the afternoon. There they were to be joined by Sir Neville Canham after dinner, whose addition brought a special warmth to Miss Hartsbury's smile, while at the same time seeming to ease the pace of her speech somewhat. In appearance he gave the impression of being a most amiable young man, although he was quite permanently rumpled and dishevelled; his ears, which were near-perfect semi-circles, jutted out at a considerable angle from his head, giving him something of the appearance of a round sugar bowl with two handles; and to complete the uniqueness of his person, his limbs were over-sized to his body, like those of a new-born colt. On his entering the room, Miss Hartsbury whispered in Georgiana's ear, yet again bringing colour to her cheeks; she seemed to take great pleasure in discomposing her younger friend. Georgiana glanced at Sir Neville with an embarrassed look, then hastily looked away.

Sir Neville bowed and offered his compliments to the two of them then asked with a smile, "Might I ask what you were saying, Miss Hartsbury?"

"Shall I say, my dear?" she asked Georgiana, who shook her head adamantly at this.

Miss Hartsbury said, "Very well, since you insist; although I cannot help but think it would be more amusing to tell him. You will forgive me, Sir Neville," she said to him, "but I must abide by my friend's decision." She looked at him with an inviting smile, then happened to glance down at the seat next to her; he took the hint and sat happily down, his gawky arms and legs seeming to spill out in all directions from his chair. Were he to stand to his full height, he would have topped even Darcy, but his backbone seemed never to have learnt its office, or else he spent his life trying to look at the whole of his acquaintance from their own eye level; Darcy imagined he must be the absolute despair of his tailor. He and Miss Hartsbury made quite an endearingly odd pairing, what with her eccentricities and energy, and his fledgling looks and ready grin; Darcy regretted he had not stayed long enough at her ball to see them on the dance-floor together.

After Bath, Darcy made quite a point of seeing that Miss Hartsbury had as much free time at her disposal as he could manage, that she might have as much time to dedicate to Sir Neville as possible during their trip. Out of charity to the others, Darcy kept Mr. Hartsbury to himself as much as possible; in consequence, he and Bingley were to enjoy watching Pender in many discussions with the gentleman, as the four of them were often together by Darcy's design; it did not surprise him that Miss Hartsbury was always most conscientious in taking advantage of these opportunities to draw Sir Neville's company to herself.

One noteworthy exchange between Pender and Mr. Hartsbury came the day after Bath, when they all four shared a coach to Bristol; passing a tribute to the renowned clergyman, John Wesley, Mr. Hartsbury was moved to observe: "Hmmph! That man was a scoundrel, and I see no reason he and all his kind should not have been imprisoned; he was clearly a recusant, and should have been treated as such."

"A recusant, Sir?" Pender asked mildly. "Surely not; the Popish Recusancy Act, written, as I believe, some two hundred years ago, was instigated against the adherents to the Church of Rome at the time; it can hardly have been intended to describe the Wesleyans."

"You cannot deny that the man sought to overthrow the Church of England," attested Hartsbury.

Pender looked at his travelling companion curiously for a long moment before saying, "You fascinate me, Sir: do go on. I should be glad to know how Wesley, even though a clergyman in the Church of England for the whole of his life, was intent on bringing down that institution."

"Bah!" Hartsbury replied. "A wolf in sheep's clothing, if ever there was one. Did he not ordain a "bishop" for the Americas by the laying of hands, which is a decidedly popish and uncanonical practice? Did he not ordain priests outside the Church of England, and establish his own clergy—even a cabal of men which can only be seen as apostolic? 'Pon my word, the man was practically an

Antichrist! He should have been horse-whipped, —or, better, burnt for a heretic; instead they place placards in his honour!"

"Your scholarship in this subject, I confess, Sir, is more eager than mine, and I can only admire the depth with which your mind sees into the affair," said Pender in great earnest. "But, pray, when you say recusant, do you see him as a Jacobite, then, bent on bringing Catholicism, and the Stuarts, back to their former power in England?"

"I put nothing past him, Sir; nor his followers. It is well known that the Stuarts have never given over their pretentions; the descendants of James II are always lurking, seeking a return; the Wesleyans may well be *agents provacateurs* from France," he finished importantly.

Pender pretended to be aghast: "Great Heavens, Sir! Bonaparte has sided with the House of Savoy? —who, as you surely know, are the claimants closest to the House of Stuart after the Hanoverians—and now he seeks to use their veiled allies, the Wesleyans, against England? Or perhaps you refer to those descendants of the young pretender, Bonnie Prince Charlie, under the bar sinister?"

Even Bingley, who had not an iota of interest in, nor much more knowledge of, the history of accession and succession of the Stuarts—nor much of either in the policies of Bonaparte—understood this to be an utter impossibility, politically at least, if not historically.

"They may all be in it together, Sir; I should not be surprised in the least," answered Mr. Hartsbury with weighty significance, pulling down the tabs of his waistcoat in a decisive gesture, as though to say the matter was settled.

"Marvellous, Mr. Hartsbury! —I congratulate you on the acuity of your insight," Pender assured him. "May I ask, have you communicated these deductions to the authorities? I have no doubt but what they would find them extremely noteworthy."

Mr. Hartsbury seemed pleased, and, laying a finger alongside his nose, said knowingly, "I have been waiting for events to mature, but on our return I believe I shall speak with my second cousin, who is an under-secretary in the War Office."

"I bow to your superior knowledge of the affair," said Pender, "to determine whether the matter can safely rest that long; it seems to me altogether too important to brook delay, but, as I say, your understanding of the matter is far beyond the reach of mine own, lesser comprehension."

Pender then turned to both Darcy and Bingley, saying, "There is a lesson here for us all, that one must never be too heedless and quick to judge, when considering novel theories, or the penetration some minds are capable of; and that we all may be instructed on matters of deep import." To Mr. Hartsbury he said, "May I say, Mr. Hartsbury, my opinion of Cambridge, and your own college especially, has been greatly strengthened by our time spent together."

Mr. Hartsbury nodded his thanks; Pender nodded also, and nodded again, with preternatural solemnity, to Darcy and Bingley.

Chapter Eight

*T*here is, perhaps, no need to describe all the details of the excursion: the delights of the English countryside in summer, the picturesque of the Bristol Channel, and the sleepy timelessness of the mid-countries: other authors have done so at length, and their considerable efforts are not to be improved upon. When the party reached Worcester, however, Darcy found a letter waiting for him from his steward, Stevenson, to the effect that there had recently been an incident on the estate involving James Sayers: he had discovered some poachers on the grounds, and, in attempting injudiciously to drive them off, had been injured, though not seriously. The poachers, who were not local men, had been apprehended; as a result of the injury done Sayers, who was widely held to be a thoroughly harmless individual, given he was rarely himself, the sentiment in the neighbourhood was heavily against them, and threatened violence; Stevenson requested that, as his master was soon to arrive at any rate, he might hasten his arrival to take the situation in hand. Therefore, when the party stopped early that afternoon in Lichfield, Darcy took to horse, continuing as far as Derby that night, and on to Pemberley the next morning.

Arriving home, he walked around to the front entrance, rather than wend his way through the house to reach the small office where he might expect to find Stevenson. On turning the corner of the house, he saw standing on the lawn with his gardener a small knot of visitors, most likely just come from the house and about to continue with the tour of the park; this was a not uncommon occurrence at this time of year, and he was asking himself whether his improving courtesy called on him to greet them personally, or whether he might just go on about his business, when his glance was captured by one of the party, a young lady, who brought Elizabeth strongly to mind. He was reprimanding his senses for interpreting the world according to his fancies, rather than reporting what was actually before them, when a second look corrected him: it was, indeed, Elizabeth! — she stood on his lawn, not twenty paces away! This was a development of all others most unexpected: he felt a hundred things in an instant, but they very quickly merged into a single, pressing need to show her that he had mended his ways. Abruptly awakened, his aspirations to civility did most imperiously demand that he show her a better view of himself: to demonstrate that her refusal of him, far from being a source of resentment, had been taken as instruction on how to better himself.

She, on the other hand, had turned instinctively away from him, as indeed why should she not, with her very natural distress at finding herself again in his company; what could be worse than having to see him again, and re-live all the distress and confusion he had caused her at Hunsford? The walk from where he first saw her to where she stood was the longest of his life, and he could not help observing how little she desired to be received by him: her demeanour clearly showed how much she had rather flee than accept his greeting—she looked anywhere but at him, and she had coloured noticeably on his appearance, clearly signalling her displeasure at being thus discovered by him; nevertheless, he forced his feet to carry him forward against this silent gale of disapproval, in hopes of proving to her how sincerely he had tried to correct his faults. All across the lawn to her side, he heard "a more gentleman-like manner" resounding in his mind.

On reaching her, he began, "Miss Elizabeth Bennet, this is an unexpected honour, and a very great pleasure." While he tried for a measured and open tone, he was certain that, in his discomposure, his words sounded forced and harsh. He tried again: "I hope you will allow me to welcome you to Derbyshire, and Pemberley."

The lady made a proper, yet subdued curtsey, thanking him briefly in a quiet way. Darcy then asked, "How does your family do?" —hoping by an uncommon degree of sincerity to render this most commonplace of enquiries a gesture of true concern and interest. Elizabeth was silent, looking down to avoid his eye; trying to catch a glimpse of her face, he continued, "They are all quite well, I hope? But perhaps you have not heard from them, as you are traveling. Have you been travelling long?" She remained resolutely withdrawn, answering in a short phrase spoken so low its meaning was lost to him, and barely looking his way as she spoke. Her manifest discomfort distressed him exceedingly, and all his regrets welled up within him. Still, determined to hear greater comfort in her accent, he pushed on: "But I trust they were well when you left; how long have you been in the country?"

Here her civility finally compelled her to reply in full sentences: "We have been traveling some two weeks now, Sir. We arrived in Derbyshire on Saturday." She then looked away again, but Darcy was encouraged by even this slight improvement.

"And where do you stay? In Lambton?" Receiving only a brief nod, he went on, "I often thought of Lambton while I staid in the neighbourhood of Meryton. Of course the countryside here is much different. Have you seen much of Derbyshire? When did you leave Longbourn?" Hearing himself speaking in such hasty, graceless phrases, knowing he was repeating himself, he ordered his brain to cease its idling and look to its duties; unfortunately, his brain did not seem to be attending, and he struggled to think what else might be said. It was not made easier by the fact that Elizabeth was become even lovelier during his long absence from her, and that he felt her eyes upon him as he struggled. He tried one or two topics, awkward and hurried, but when he found himself on the verge of asking how long she had been from Longbourn for the third — or was it the fourth? — time, he stopped speaking entirely, racking his brain and commanding his thoughts forward into the van, but for nought; while unbearably disappointed in himself, he simply could not lay tongue to another idea.

This left him nothing to do but absent himself, that he might spare the lady's embarrassment, as she was clearly suffering under the influence of his presence. His last, halting words were, "Well, if you will excuse me, then…. Please…," the last being accompanied by a vague gesture towards the Park. At the end, though, he was at least able to marshal his abilities well enough to produce a bow that was as courteous as he required it to be.

He moved away from this embarrassing scene with all the haste that dignity would allow, cursing himself for a callow nitwit all the way into the house. Once inside, he turned hurriedly to the nearest window to see what the visitors might do: would they continue their tour, or would Elizabeth insist on their immediate departure, now he was come? But no, they carried on with their walk; his eyes lingered wistfully on Elizabeth's features for a moment before he turned back towards the stairs to his apartments; as he began to move, though, his steps gained purpose and rapidity until he was bounding up the stairway two at a time; he called out to a footman to locate Perkins and send him up instantly. By the time his man reached him, he had largely divested himself of his soiled traveling clothes, and was opening drawers and wardrobes in search of fresh apparel. "Sir?" Perkins enquired, taken aback at this sudden fit of sartorial zeal in his master. "Miss Elizabeth Bennet: here, in the Park," was Darcy's terse reply. Perkins froze for the briefest moment, then snatched the shirt Darcy held out of his hand, dexterously plucking another out of a different drawer and opening it in the air so it settled over Darcy's head and shoulders almost without assistance; by the time Darcy had got his arms in the sleeves, Perkins was holding a clean pair of breeches for him; in next to no time, Darcy was accoutred as befitted the Master of Pemberley, set for a leisurely walk about his demesnes.

On regaining the lawn in front of the house, he paused to consider: the usual path for visitors made a circuit, crossing the stream a little more than a half-mile from the house, and returning on the opposite side. If he followed after them on this side of the stream, he would certainly be able to catch them up before they reached the house again, but if he went by the reverse path, he would probably reach them sooner, and have longer with them. He accordingly set off across the bridge and took the foot path to the right, back up the stream and into the open woods on that side. After a good ten minutes of brisk walking, long enough to begin to fear that they had decided to cut short their tour and return without coming onto this side of the stream, he saw them some little way ahead. Stepping up his pace, he reached them quite near the little footbridge they had taken across the water.

Coming up to them, he was pleased to see that Elizabeth appeared less unwilling to meet him than previously; before he had time to do more than bow, she began speaking: "Allow me to say, Mr. Darcy, Pemberley is as delightful and charming as any of the grand estates we have seen on our journey hither."

At this point, however, she seemed to undergo a change of sentiment, and, colouring, she stopped speaking and looked away. At a loss to understand how he could have offended her without having spoken a word, on an anxious thought he glanced down discreetly to make sure that, in his haste, his attire was every thing it should be; relieved to find no flaw there, he looked back up again; Elizabeth was still avoiding his eye, but, perceiving her companions standing off to one side, it occurred to him to deflect her present discomfort, whatever its cause, and show her that his "arrogant disdain for the feelings of others" was no more, by requesting an introduction.

The two were a fashionable looking couple of early middle years: the lady carried an air of elegance and sense about her, and the gentleman had an open, intelligent, and accommodating mien. On making his request there was a slight hesitation on Elizabeth's part, during which he felt her eyes on him again, before she responded, willingly enough, "Mr. Darcy, may I introduce Mr. and Mrs. Edward Gardiner; they are my aunt and uncle from London, Mr. Darcy, and have been so kind as to include me in this, their annual pleasure excursion."

That they were relations was a surprise, and a pleasant one; he thought he remembered Mr. Bennet being without living brother or sister, making one of them the relation of Elizabeth's mother—an even greater surprise; in either case, though, it afforded him the perfect opportunity to demonstrate his improved consideration for the comfort of others.

"Delighted, Mrs. Gardiner...Mr. Gardiner," he said, with as much cordiality as he could convey, aware that Elizabeth was watching him closely. "I, too, have lately been traveling for the pleasure of the season. Where have you been to, if I might enquire?"

Elizabeth's uncle, stepping slightly forward, answered: "We took a leisurely route up through the Midland counties, and have been chiefly touring the countryside about the Peaks here in Derbyshire."

"And how did you find it?" Darcy asked with interest.

"Yours is a remarkable country, Mr. Darcy," Mr. Gardiner answered with a slight bow. "I know of no other that can surpass its natural beauties; and permit me to say, your own home does not detract from its splendour." Darcy bowed in his turn, and the two set off back along the path which Darcy had but lately traversed, with the ladies trailing behind.

"How old is the house, if you will indulge my curiosity?" asked Mr. Gardiner. "My wife and I were discussing the point earlier."

"The foundation was laid in 1522, although it has undergone several expansions," Darcy informed him, "which may be the source of the confusion as to the date; various portions are from very different periods. The façade is said to be Inigo Jones, but I have serious doubts; it is, certainly, after the classical school, but it was built around 1635, at which time Jones was very much engaged in building most of London, if we may believe his legend."

Elizabeth's uncle laughed appreciatively. "If he had built every thing attributed to him, certainly, he would have impoverished every other architect in England for a hundred years, having left nothing for them to do."

Darcy nodded, chuckling in agreement. "There is a folly by Wren at the crest of the hill, though," he added. "It cannot be seen from the front of the house, unfortunately."

They walked on a bit, and Darcy noticed Mr. Gardiner often glancing down into the stream; seeing the surface roil from a rising trout, he made an admiring noise, and Darcy asked: "Are you a fisherman, then, Mr. Gardiner?"

"As a boy it was my delight; in London, I fear, I rarely find the opportunity," he replied, looking wistfully back at the spot in the stream where the fish had made its appearance.

"Perhaps, if you plan to be about the neighbourhood any length of time, you might like to try your luck on my waters," Darcy told him. "I beg you will feel free to come as often as you can; I should be happy to supply any tackle you might require, and, between us, this stretch just along here is my favourite; whenever I am home I am constantly chasing William here," gesturing to the gardener, who traipsed alongside them still, "off these holes. He and I seem to be the only ones who appreciate them." The gardener chuckled and said, "Aye," his sole contribution to the conversation since his master's arrival.

Darcy was highly pleased with this invitation: his brain had finally picked up the reins again, and was providing both the manner of discovering their immediate plans, and the means of securing one or more visits by her relation, which could not but put him in the way of more time with Elizabeth. Mr. Gardiner thanked him with great appreciation, and assured him of his willingness to take him up on the offer, further stating that they would be in Lambton for the remainder of the week. "My wife lived there for some time, and has many old acquaintances to renew," said he with a good-natured smile. "Doubtless I shall have a morning or an afternoon to myself, while she and her friends are going about the affairs so engaging to their sex, and so unavailing to our own."

Darcy smiled and nodded as well, and directly began calculating the number of opportunities to be found for visiting in a week's time; he had just reached a very satisfactory total when his attention was drawn back to Mr. Gardiner, who was looking down towards the stream's edge. "What manner of plant is that, Mr. Darcy?" he asked, pointing to a small but rather striking stalk of flowers, growing in a rocky ledge just at the water's edge. "I do not know that I recognise it."

"You have a discerning eye, Mr. Gardiner. That, though you might not believe it, is an orchid," Darcy said, "*Neotinea ustulata*." On hearing this, the ladies expressed an interest in seeing such an oddity as an orchid in Derbyshire. The gardener shook his head and muttered something about "the quality". Darcy smiled over at him, amused, saying, "William prefers the name 'burnt tip'."

"Aye—tells more than tha' frippery foreign name," muttered the gardener, shaking his head with heavy and righteous condemnation. "French, by the sound of it."

"Has it escaped your conservatory and spread?" asked Mrs Gardiner.

"No, it grows wild here, although it is not common," Darcy replied. Every one made the short trek down to the banks to see this rarity, but once the exclamations and lauds were over, Mrs. Gardiner struggled to regain the foot path. Begging her husband's arm, she remained with him thereafter, leaving Darcy to escort Elizabeth. Being the more vigorous walkers of the party, they shortly out-stripped the others; Darcy, reminded strongly of the walks he had shared with her in Kent, was momentarily confused, overcome by his memories and the reproaches attending them, and therefore said nothing; they had not gone many steps, however, before Elizabeth spoke: "Mr. Darcy, your arrival here must have surprised more than our party, for your housekeeper informed us that you would certainly not be here till to-morrow; and indeed," she added, "before we left Bakewell we understood that you were not immediately expected in the country."

Darcy felt all the humiliation contained in this tes-tament to her unwillingness to encounter him, and said in an apologetic tone: "Yes, that is quite true; it was known only to my steward and myself; a group of us have been travelling, much as you have, and word reached me two days ago that my steward had need of me earlier. I con-sequently travelled on ahead of my party by some few hours." In more positive accents, he added, "They will join me early to-morrow, and among them are some who will claim an acquaintance with you, —Mr. Bingley and his sisters." The words were out of his mouth before he remembered the association Bingley's name must have with his interference in her sister's affairs.

Elizabeth merely replied with a slight bow, and Dar-cy, embarrassed, and feeling all the more how distressful must be his company, considered again how to soften her disgust to him. The thought of softness brought Georgiana to mind, which brought to mind that she had long wished to meet Elizabeth; knowing Georgiana to be a far better person than himself, and, with no history to cloud their acquaintance, much more likely to please Elizabeth than was he, he therefore said with a most civil diffidence: "There is also one other person in the party who more particularly wishes to be known to you, — Will you allow me, or do I ask too much, to introduce my sister to your acquaintance during your stay at Lambton?"

The lady gave his request her assent, although surprise was evident on her face. This Darcy could not help but notice, but at least she did not appear displeased; indeed, there seemed to be a lessening in her aversion to his company, and, though her thoughts remained unspoken, she appeared to walk beside him in greater comfort than previously. Contented thereby, and assured that by virtue of this meditated introduction he was certain of at least one other opportunity to be with her, he walked on with her in silence as they had so often done; on this occasion, however, his understanding was better informed, and he no longer deluded himself that her silence indicated approval. He patiently waited for her recent impressions to resolve themselves, determining within him to let the lady be the first to speak thereafter, and not to thrust conversation upon her while her thoughts were occupied with, as he hoped, forming a better opinion of him.

They continued thus until they regained the house, his attentions attuned to her every step; during this time, while she was silent, there was nothing in her manner that suggested a return of her distaste to his company, and he was satisfied. They were by now several hundred yards in advance of Elizabeth's aunt and uncle, and Elizabeth and he stopped on the lawn to await their arrival. Here Darcy broke his cautious silence to invite her into the house to rest: the day was sunny, and a dry, rather warming breeze was picking up. This offer she declined, professing herself to be in no need of rest, leaving them with some little while to pass until her aunt's slowing steps should carry her to them. After having Elizabeth refuse his hospitality, Darcy was loath to thrust his attentions on her, yet to stand there in silence was worse; whilst he could instantly conjure a dozen things he wished to say about their past, and its effects on him, he laboured mightily to think of a topic of neutral character; finally the lady took pity on him and mentioned her travels in the country. Seizing on this, he spoke with a will on the picturesque of the Peaks, and the various fine houses and views Derbyshire had to offer, managing to cover almost the entire period until her relations' return with a most determinedly detached and well-judging discussion of the district.

On being joined by her aunt and uncle, Darcy again had his offer of hospitality refused; in this case, however, the excuse was a bit more supportable: "Oh, I do thank you, Mr. Darcy," said Mrs. Gardiner, "and I hope you will forgive us, but I am very eager to reach Lambton, as several old friends live there still, and I have promised myself the pleasure of renewing my acquaintance with them this very afternoon."

"But, of course, Mrs. Gardiner," said Darcy with a complaisant smile. "One's old friends must always take precedence over the new."

"It is kind in you to see it that way," said the lady, "although it must be allowed that the new hold their own special charm." Darcy bowed at this, and, handing the ladies into the carriage, he bowed as well to Mr. Gardiner and bid them adieu.

Chapter Nine

*D*arcy had much to ponder as he paced slowly back into the house. This accidental meeting — and accidental it surely was, as Elizabeth clearly would never willingly have met him again — had opened his heart up again to hope, if only the hope that, even though she would never be to him what he had once dreamt, he might at least comfort himself that she no longer reviled him — that the woman whose good opinion he valued most in the world would no longer wish to avoid him as the worst of men: "the last man I could ever be prevailed on to marry...". But now, what was he to make of her words, and her manner? It did seem as though there had been a lessening of her disapproval, there at the last — some relinquishing of resentment; his asking to introduce his sister had seemed to make itself felt, and he was sure that they would get on very well.

Darcy only allowed himself to mull these points for as long as it took to walk to Stevenson's office; he felt how remiss in him it was to have already taken over an hour away from his intended purpose. On reaching his office, Darcy found Stevenson seated behind his desk, with the air of a man waiting with as much grace as he can for an event that is well beyond its time. "I do apologise, Stevenson," Darcy said, "that was entirely unexpected."

"Of course, Mr. Darcy," said his man with ill-disguised impatience. "I have taken the liberty of having the horses saddled, as we ought to be in Lambton as soon as may be; I only hope the damage has not been done already."

Feeling properly chastened, Darcy followed him back out the front door and around to the stables. On the ride into town, Darcy asked Stevenson to acquaint him with the situation. "What exactly happened?" he asked.

"According to Sayers, there were four poachers, although there were only three when we caught them," said Stevenson. "Sayers was out in the fields; he heard them and went to investigate; there was a struggle and he was knocked down; falling badly, he managed to break his arm, and the men fled."

"Had they done any other damage?"

"None that we could discover."

"What has been done with them?"

"The three of them are in the old armoury storehouse, north of town," he told Darcy. "At night we have men take it in turns to watch, but during the day they are left to themselves. Some few of the townsmen, instigated by Sayers' friends, gather around the storehouse then, throwing things, shouting threats, and, as you might imagine, passing a bottle or two. Twice now they have come close to working themselves up to violence—it is only a matter of time before they succeed."

"Who are the ringleaders, amongst Sayers' friends?" Darcy asked.

"The most vocal, and most dangerous, is John Ferguson," the other replied.

"Ferguson? I have not run across him in years," Darcy said. "What is he like these days?"

"He thinks he is the town bull," answered Stevenson. "Not as tall as you, Mr. Darcy, but he goes eighteen or nineteen stone. He has been heard to call himself the 'best man in Lambton', the blowhard."

"I take it you do not care for the man," Darcy observed.

"He is one of the sort who always imagine themselves ill-used, whether in business or privately, and are ready to take exception to the smallest slight. And," he added rancorously, "he seems to think he has claims on every unaccompanied lady he meets." Stevenson was a bachelor, but had been known to keep company with a certain widow in town; Darcy suspected a personal interest there.

"And how does Sayers do?"

"He is well enough," Stevenson allowed. "The broken arm is mending nicely; it does not help matters, though, that he spends his time in the public house, complaining of the pain and enlarging upon the fight, in hopes of wheedling a drink. But Ferguson is out for blood, and between the two of them, they keep the others stirred up."

They were riding across the fields to Lambton in order to save time, the roads winding about considerably between Pemberley and the town; Darcy's attention was drawn off by seeing the Gardiner's coach, still about a half-mile from their destination. He hoped this trouble would not thrust itself upon Elizabeth's notice.

The two men arrived at the storehouse, a heavily built stone edifice with arrow-slit windows and a slate roof; to Darcy's knowledge, it had never before been used for this purpose. A group of five or six men stood in front of it, although several drifted off into the trees at the sight of the riders. Their leader was a bulky individual with red hair, who, though large, was quite soft about the middle, and whose legs turned in at the knees from holding up his bulk; this, Darcy remembered, was John Ferguson. He had a belligerent look to him, and set down a bottle as he turned round to face them.

"What're ye doin' here, Stevenson?" he demanded angrily.

"As the maintenance of this storehouse was given to the Darcy family by King James II, I should rather ask what you are doing here, Ferguson," Darcy replied, piqued by the man's manner, and by his addressing his steward rather than himself.

Ferguson spat. "Ye've not been doin' much *maintenance* in a mort o' years," said he in a combative manner, "so why start now? These three was poachin' your lands, and they nearly did for Jimmie Sayers; but what have ye done about it? Nought!" he spat again.

Darcy began to dismount, but Ferguson shouted: "Back on your horse, little man, and run off back t' London!" Darcy paused long enough to look the man in the eye, then very deliberately continued to dismount. As he got his feet to the ground, Ferguson came around the animal sharply to confront him, only to come up short at the sight of the master of Pemberley, who topped him by two or three inches, and stood easily before him, his hand resting in a relaxed manner on the animal's flank.

"Ferguson," said Darcy, "it appears to me that you have got too used to pushing smaller men around; if you have a mind to see the other side of that coin, I am at your disposal." Darcy was no pugilist, but the man's arrogance had raised his temper, and he was not troubled by anything like reservations at that moment; rather, he was envisioning how that ruddy face would look, if it were liberally festooned with a brighter red. He added, "If you *are* inclined to oblige me, I suggest you finish it at a blow, as too much sudden exertion can be dangerous for a man your size." Ferguson's face registered a sort of animal-like bafflement, not unlike a cat set to pounce on a canary, only to run into its mistress' broom at the last moment; like most bullies, he was completely unprepared for a composed resistance. On Ferguson's hesitation, Darcy looked around at the other men: "Any one else who feels in need of exercise?" Amongst that group there was a sudden fascination with their footwear. "No? Well, then...Ferguson," he said with an air of indifference, "take care to go back by way of the front of the horse, if you would; this animal starts easily when any one gets behind him." Unseen by Ferguson, Darcy put his thumb into a particular spot on his horse's belly, just at the top of the near-hind leg; the horse gave an obligingly vicious kick at this provocation, as was his wont: Darcy had learnt the trick from his farrier.

Ferguson stood there indecisively some moments, his fists clenching and unclenching, then he shuffled off, carefully avoiding even the horse's head. "Mind you take the bottles," Darcy called. "This is no rubbish pit." Muttering, Ferguson stooped to pick up the bottle, which he would have done in any event, as it was nearly full; Darcy's making it an order, however, made him wish very much to leave it: but his thirst and his native parsimony overcame his dignity. Gathering his followers by eye, he began shuffling back towards the town.

When the men had disappeared around the turning into town, Darcy blew out his breath, and quietly muttered an oath or two. "I see why you do not take to the man, Stevenson," said he to the other, who still sat his horse. "There is a great deal too much of him, and none of it pleasant."

"Indeed. Well, that made my day, Mr. Darcy," Stevenson admitted, "but what next? We cannot keep this lot here until the quarter sessions: they would never live that long."

"No, but we can send them down to Derby to the magistrate's court there; then they will be remanded until the next session and held there."

"Can we do that legally? Transport them to Derby, I mean."

"Who is to stop us? But it just so happens I am in possession of a writ, deputizing 'Darcy of Pemberley' as a sheriff for the county. It was my father's, actually, but I believe it will serve. Mr. Horton, of Catton Hall, is High Sheriff just now, and he is a decent sort; I do not believe he will trouble himself over the fact that the writ is ten years out of date."

Chapter Ten

*T*hat night, alone in his chambers, Darcy set himself to determine what best might be done about his feelings towards Elizabeth; he lay awake for an hour or more, pondering and weighing the possibilities, but in the end, all he could resolve on was that it still must depend upon her; if he could not convince her of his amendment, nothing would have changed between them. That must be the key and primary goal; unless and until he could lessen her disapprobation, there obviously could be no approval forthcoming.

In the morning, he dressed and wandered about, impatiently awaiting the arrival of his friends; he very much wanted to tell Georgiana of Elizabeth's being in the neighbourhood. He was certain that Georgiana's perfectly gentle manners and her good sense would make a favourable impression, and Georgiana was sure to like Elizabeth; should they take to one another, what effect might that not have on the future? He allowed his imagination to roam through many pleasing byways, at the prospects conjured up by this notion.

While he thus pondered an illusory future, he walked the grounds around the house, and was pleased to observe that the effects of Sayers' hand could be seen in the rock borders and pathways. The morning was fine: still and cool, and the dew yet to burn off the lawn and low-lying fronds; he spent the hours awaiting his sister's arrival in various minor activities about the manor and checking with the servants on how things stood about the house and estate. At length, the several carriages were to be seen descending the hill across the valley. Darcy went round to the front of the house to greet them, and to welcome every one into the house. An early breakfast had been prepared, so after a brief interval for them to find their chambers and refresh themselves, they all gathered in the breakfast-room. Every one was in good spirits, and set into the meal with energy.

"What a beautiful country is this, Mr. Darcy," Miss Hartsbury enthused. "All the way from Matlock, the views just got better and better. I cannot imagine a more picturesque locality, you know — unless one went to the Alps, or the fjords of Scandinavia, or the great Sahara of Egypt; but, of course, I mean here in England."

Pender smiled at her, and said, "Have you ever seen any of the drawings of Robert Hooke, or Anton van Leeuwenhoek? They have shown that it is possible to find great beauty in the smallest of things: in the wings of a butterfly, or in a drop of water."

"I have not, I regret," owned Miss Hartsbury, "but one could hardly call beauty on such a scale as that picturesque, could one? — pretty, perhaps, but surely lacking in grandeur."

"Which is grander," replied Pender, "the mouse or the elephant? They are both miraculous creatures."

"Yes, but one is much bigger," said Miss Hartsbury simply.

Darcy supplied, "I believe she has you there, Pender, as both the terms "grand" and "grandeur" are derived from the Latin *grandis*, meaning large, or tall."

Pender sighed and turned to Georgiana. "Could I trouble you for the honey, my dear? — the world, it seems, is turned against me, and I need something to sweeten my morning. Or, perhaps I ought to refer to it in the Latin, as *mel*, or in the Greek, as μέλι, which is the more mellifluous." Darcy smiled and bowed in his chair to his former tutor, in recognition of how neatly and easily he had turned the tables on him.

Breakfast being over, Darcy singled his sister out of the company, taking her round to the north terrace; there he told her of his meeting with Elizabeth the day before, and his seeking an introduction for her; while he did his best to remain calm during this communication, Georgiana's delight and elation made it unnecessary.

"I can truly meet her?" Georgiana asked excitedly; her eyes alight at the thought of the introduction; but they immediately fell: "What if she should dislike me?" she asked plaintively.

Darcy reassured her: "She is a lady of sense and taste; she cannot help but like you: indeed, whom have you ever met who did not like you, Dearest? You are a far better person than I, and are far better received on first acquaintance — and on the second — and the third, too, for that matter."

Georgiana smiled fleetingly at what she took to be his teazing, but her face remained apprehensive. "But she might not," she worried, "and what if her dislike of me should reflect on you?"

"You may trust me on that point: that could never happen," said he with perfect sincerity. "In fact, I confidently expect the exact opposite."

Georgiana looked at him doubtfully, unsure if he were teazing again. He nodded assuringly to convince her he was in earnest, then asked: "When should you like to go? I imagine you are too fatigued at present?"

"Now?" Georgiana said. "Yes, I could go now, certainly. But what of our guests?"

"I have given thought to that already," Darcy replied eagerly, "and now might be the best time, in fact; we could go while every one was settling and taking their ease. We should never be missed."

Accordingly, after seeing to their guests and making certain that they were comfortable, Georgiana quickly went to her rooms to change into fresh clothes while Darcy saw to getting the carriage ready; standing in the stables, watching the groom hitch the horse to the curricle, steps from behind him made him turn: he saw Bingley coming up to him. "Are you off, Darcy?" his friend asked. "I saw you from my rooms."

Darcy answered cheerfully, "Indeed I am: Georgiana and I are for Lambton, to pay a brief call—on Miss Elizabeth Bennet."

"Miss Elizabeth Bennet, here in Derbyshire! But that is admirable!" Bingley cried, "Does she expect you? Do you suppose I might go along with you?"

"No, and yes," answered Darcy. "We are going unannounced, although she has said she would be pleased to meet Georgiana; I cannot but imagine she would be happy to see you, too." Of course, Bingley's presence would remind Elizabeth of her sister, and he could not help but remember that, by taking the blame for Bingley's behaviour upon himself in his letter, he had given Elizabeth that much more reason to dislike him; this could not be altered, however—he could only try to atone for it. To Bingley he said, "I know my sister is eager to be off, so we shall not wait for you, but follow as soon as may be."

"I shall!" Bingley said, hurrying back towards the house to change. "I shall be less than a quarter hour behind you."

Georgiana appearing very shortly thereafter, and the curricle being ready, they were on their way to Lambton.

On the ride to town Georgiana was exceedingly animated: "Oh, Fitzwilliam!" she said, "I am so happy to be meeting her! Only tell me you are *sure*: she *will* like me, will not she?"

"I am," said he. "I have never been so certain of a thing in my life. On rare occasions only are the heart and mind in accord, but this is one such: both are telling me it shall all be well." Georgiana showed him a happy smile, but a something of doubt lingered behind her eyes.

As they arrived, Darcy jumped down and Georgiana asked, "Fitzwilliam, is my appearance as it should be?"

"Yes," he replied briefly, as he hurried round to hand her down. In hushed accents, Georgiana exclaimed: "Fitzwilliam, please! — you did not even look!"

With an eager impatience to be going in, Darcy told her: "I saw you at home; how much could have changed?" Relenting instantly, however, he inspected his sister's dress and features attentively. "One stray lock in back, on the left." Georgiana tucked up the offending tress as they entered; Darcy asked that word be sent up of their arrival, and very shortly they were ushered into the Gardiner's apartments; somewhere between the ground floor and the first floor landing, however, Georgiana transformed once again into the shy and silent young lady she appeared as in public.

The Gardiners apartments were spacious, with a well-appointed sitting-room at their disposal. Darcy gave the Gardiners and Elizabeth his compliments, then said, "Mr. and Mrs. Gardiner, Miss Elizabeth Bennet, may I introduce my sister, Miss Georgiana Darcy?"

The Gardiners offered their compliments to both himself and his sister; he then watched with great attention as Georgiana turned to Elizabeth, and was pleased to see that she seemed ready to receive Georgiana with an open manner, in spite of her disapprobation of him.

"Miss Darcy, I am so very pleased to meet you," said Elizabeth. "Every one of my acquaintance to whom you are known speaks very highly of you."

Georgiana curtseyed shyly, but with perfectly good form, saying, "You are too kind, I am sure. My brother has mentioned you in the highest of terms."

Elizabeth smiled at her and, stepping around to her side, escorted her some few steps away from the other three. Trusting to Georgiana's powers of pleasing, Darcy left them to themselves according to his intentions, and turned his attentions to his hosts. "I hope, Mrs. Gardiner, you have found your acquaintances well?"

"Quite well, I thank you, Mr. Darcy," she replied. "We have been enjoying ourselves immensely; I have always loved Lambton: some of my favourite memories stem from my time here."

Mr. Gardiner smiled affectionately at his wife, adding: "I can scarcely prevail upon her to be still long enough to catch her breath, before she is off again in search of another old friend."

"That is as testament to her amiability, surely," said Darcy with a slight bow in her direction. "For friendship to have lasted for years unregenerate, it must have been deep indeed before its suspension." Mrs. Gardiner bowed her head in return for this compliment, and to Darcy it seemed that she was genuinely pleased.

He next turned to Mr. Gardiner and said, "I was thinking of a scheme for a fishing-party to-morrow, Mr. Gardiner; if you care to take part in it, we should be delighted to have you with us."

"That would give me very great pleasure," answered Mr. Gardiner with enthusiasm. "What time were you planning to start?"

"We shall breakfast early, and begin shortly after," answered Darcy. "Say, about nine o'clock?"

At this point, Mr. Gardiner first thought to look to his wife for her concurrence; she, however, smiled encouragingly, and the plan was set. Whilst Mr. Gardiner and Darcy spoke of the more arcane details of angling some few moments more, Mrs. Gardiner joined the other ladies' discussion. Before long, Darcy, remembering Bingley's intention of joining them, interrupted them to say: "Miss Bennet, forgive me: I should have mentioned earlier, but Mr. Bingley is also coming to wait upon you; seeing us preparing to leave, he expressed a keen desire to see you himself. I trust this will not inconvenience you?"

"Not at all, Mr. Darcy," was her reply. "I should be very happy to see him. How long do you and your party intend to be in the country, might I ask?"

Before Darcy could answer, Bingley's briskly ascending steps were heard upon the staircase. His face appeared in the doorway and he knocked on the door-frame to announce himself, wearing that grin which Darcy had been missing in his friend. While the introductions were being made, Darcy had his first real opportunity to observe Elizabeth; he had not been wrong the day prior: she did indeed look lovelier than she had in Kent. So far he had had small chance to observe her with Georgiana, but what little he had seen was encouraging: Georgiana was, of course, her quiet self, but her open countenance and her good sense were on display, and Darcy was in no doubt that she was making a good impression on Elizabeth; on the other side, Darcy had no qualms as to how Georgiana would find Elizabeth—her wit and sense of humour, her good heart and good breeding, would win any one over, let alone one so predisposed in her favour as Georgiana. As Elizabeth turned her attentions to Bingley, Georgiana came to her brother's side, and her excited clasp on his arm confirmed what he had suspected: she was very taken with Elizabeth; he smiled down into her eager face and gave her a private wink.

Darcy was very well pleased with the proceedings generally, and with Elizabeth's looks of pleasure in particular; she appeared quite eager to be agreeable to all, although Darcy was unsure how to read her temper towards himself; but in general, certainly, she seemed anxious to please. At least she did not avoid his presence today as she had done the day before, and on those few occasions in which she joined in the conversation going forward on his side of the room, she seemed to do so with every appearance of pleasure.

Once or twice he even caught sight of her looking his way, and not with disgust or discomposure, he thought.

Plus, her ready acknowledgement of, and cordial discourse with Bingley, suggested to Darcy that she had read his letter with a degree of belief—some degree at least of acceptance and credence—else she would have been far less agreeable to the man who had disappointed her sister. What this might mean regarding her disposition towards himself he could not be sure, but it gave him reason to hope that she might at some future time come to look at him with less revulsion. His spirits rising, he joined in the discussions very happily. He soon found, however, that the Gardiners and their niece were invited to have dinner with some of Mrs. Gardiner's old friends not long hence, and he felt the necessity of their taking leave—but not before he had made them an invitation of his own; said he to Georgiana: "Would it not be a pleasure to have the Gardiners and Miss Bennet join us to dinner, Miss Darcy?"

Georgiana looked surprised at this, and faltered briefly; but, recognizing in her brother's suggestion another attempt to reinforce her standing as mistress of Pemberley, she agreed, saying, "Indeed; that would be delightful. May we ask you to join us Thursday evening, Mrs. Gardiner?"

That lady looked first at Elizabeth, who, Darcy was disappointed to see, would not acknowledge the invitation, looking pointedly away from her aunt rather than respond. But Mr. Gardiner smiled with a look of agreement, and Mrs. Gardiner accepted for the three of them; Darcy saw Elizabeth's shoulders fall a little on hearing this, but whether from relief or resignation he was unable to tell.

They took leave just after this, and Bingley rode with them back to Pemberley. On their way, they discussed their impressions of the Gardiners, and Georgiana expressed her delight with Elizabeth.

"She is lovely, Fitzwilliam," said she with open admiration. "Sincere, warm, and amiable, just as you described her."

"I am sure you would be just as pleased with the elder Miss Bennet, Miss Darcy," said Bingley, following his own thoughts. "She is charming, indeed; she is quite as lovely as Miss Elizabeth Bennet, and no angel could be more tender-hearted and pleasing than she; if only she had been with us, it would have been just like those delightful times we spent at Netherfield." In this, Darcy clearly saw a degree of unaffected regret, a longing after Miss Bennet's company that had heretofore lain mostly hidden in his friend; he could now be sure of the cause of Bingley's disheartened behaviour of late. He wished he could think of anything he might say or do that would help Bingley overcome his unhappiness, but where he had failed on his own account, he could expect no better success on his friend's behalf. That was the only reference Bingley made to Elizabeth's sister, however, and the rest of the ride to Pemberley was uneventful. Directly after their arrival Bingley excused himself and went in alone.

Once back in the house, Darcy said privately to Georgiana, "I believe I was right, was I not? Miss Elizabeth Bennet seemed rather taken with you, Dearest."

Georgiana smiled modestly, answering, "Say rather she seemed taken with you, Brother. I saw her look your way on more than one occasion while she was speaking with me. I think she likes you quite well enough."

"There, I fear, your partiality is speaking, not your unbiased observation," said he.

"I cannot speak to the depth of her sentiment," she answered, "but if I know how a lady looks at a gentleman, I believe her looks were not disapproving."

Darcy could not argue with such a pleasing misapprehension, being rather content to entertain his fancies by imagining she might be right; but it simply was not credible that four-and-twenty hours could have worked such a change as that. He was reassured, however, in that at least Elizabeth's disdain for him did not prevent her from seeing the good in Georgiana; here was still more to esteem in her character, and he felt all the warmth of his prior admiration of Elizabeth rekindling.

He then made the happiness of the day complete by showing Georgiana the other presents that awaited her. He found Mrs. Annesley, asking her to go ahead first to be sure every thing was as it should be; then he took Georgiana to the upstairs drawing-room, where both Mrs. Annesley and Mrs. Reynolds awaited.

"Fitzwilliam!" she cried, seeing it freshly laid out with all the new furnishings, and its overall lightness and elegance. "How? Have you done all this yourself?"

"No, Dearest, I cannot make that claim. I chose much of it, but Aunt Eleanor had some hand in it, and even Miss Bingley chose a few of the small pieces, as we all went out together to finish up the selections; there is quite a story there, which I must share with you one day. But, do you like it?"

Georgiana hugged him delightedly, saying, "It is altogether excellent; I shall be so snug and happy, here!"

"Mrs. Annesley," said Darcy, gesturing to that lady, "did this especially."

He then pointed to the window seat, the cushion of which had been painstakingly redone, preserving much of the original, and little pillows made from such scraps as were left over. Georgiana touched it tenderly, and tears came to her eyes. "I am sure Mother would have approved of it," Darcy said gently. Georgiana nodded through her tears, still stroking the age-softened material; at the door, Mrs. Annesley sniffled loudly and excused herself abruptly, followed a moment later by Mrs. Reynolds.

After a few moments, to distract her he said, "There is one other thing." He led her down stairs to the music room; the door, opening inward, kept the new pianoforte hidden from her view until she was well into the room; on turning to face him, her question was answered before it was begun, as, seeing the new instrument standing in the corner behind him, she hugged him again joyously.

"Oh, Fitzwilliam!" she cried again. "Is it ready? May I play it?"

Darcy waved her on towards the bench, saying, "Go to it! —Reynolds tells me he had the tuner at it for a full morning last week. Yours will be the very first hands ever to make music on it." Georgiana sat to the keyboard and played a happy little strain to test its timbre.

"It is perfect! —but I do not deserve all this," she said, looking down at her fingers resting on the keys.

"Happily for you, Dearest, I see things differently," said her brother. "I wrote you once that I would do anything necessary to bring a glad smile to your face again, and I have not forgotten. To-day, then, is my reward, for I have seen it thrice, now."

"The excursion, my necklace, meeting Miss Elizabeth Bennet, now my sitting-room and pianoforte; it is too much—far too much; you spoil me, Brother."

"Good," he said with a hug round her shoulders and a kiss to the top of her head. "I mean to."

Chapter Eleven

*L*ater that evening when the party was assembled after dinner, Darcy was thinking back over his visit to Lambton, giving special consideration to Elizabeth's treatment of Bingley. She had certainly seemed open and accepting of his company: this implied that she had believed some of Darcy's letter, but how much of what he had written had she been able to accept? He regretted now the manner of its opening, and its general tone of haughtiness — how much might she be able to forgive him, but for that? He hoped she had burnt it; that way she might be able to forget what she could not forgive. In the end, though, the preponderance of their history was so decidedly against him, he could not truly hold out much hope for any significant alteration in the nature of their relations, regardless.

He was seated off to one side, watching the others go about the evening's entertainments: Bingley was seated with Georgiana and Miss Bingley; his aunt was playing piquet with Mr. Hurst, whose wife and Mr. Hartsbury sat nearby, watching their play and offering what conversation they could; Miss Hartsbury and Sir Neville were chatting and flirting on the other side of him — he watched them with a melancholy envy, thinking how simple it seemed for them, and how complex was the path his own heart travelled. Bingley, too, he watched, marking how infrequently he entered into the conversation of the others, and how seldom his smile was to be seen.

Bingley's remark on their return from the inn had made obvious the source of his low spirits; Darcy's sympathies were awakened on his friend's behalf; he felt the two of them had both been used hard in the last year, but what could one do? Life offered no guarantees, and no apologies for disappointed hopes. All a man could do was endure, and, as his aunt had suggested, hope that an uncertain future might hold some consolation, some redress, to make it worthwhile. Bingley retired early; shortly thereafter his sister came over to Darcy.

"I understand you met with Miss Elizabeth Bennet this afternoon, Mr. Darcy; she is well, I trust?"

"She is very well, I thank you, Miss Bingley," Darcy replied.

Miss Bingley looked at him a moment, then said, "How odd that she should have arrived here on the very same day you did; *what* a coincidence!"

"Indeed it was," said he. "I was never more surprised."

She looked at him again, as though weighing the candour of this statement. She then turned from him to the company and said: "We were thinking about going on from Pemberley to take in the Scarborough Fair; I do hope you will all join us." Turning back to Darcy, she said, "You would be most welcome, Mr. Darcy, and your dear sister, of course; I do hope you will allow us to repay your kindness and hospitality, and be our guest." She smiled brightly around the room. "You all would be welcome, naturally, although, of course, not every one might spare the time."

Darcy's plans being thoroughly scattered by Elizabeth's presence in the neighbourhood, answered, "I thank you, Miss Bingley, but I had hoped for now to spend some little time at home." His saw his aunt look from him to Miss Bingley, a pensive look on her face.

"We are going, of course," Mrs. Hurst said in support of her sister; her husband looked at her in surprise, but shrugged indifferently and turned his attention back to his cards. If anything, this seemed to dampen the enthusiasm felt by the others; however, there was no shortage of congratulations on a fine idea, and good wishes for their pleasure. Darcy wondered how long this scheme had been in her mind, as it had a rather impromptu feel to it. He could not be sure, naturally, but it did briefly cross his mind that this might have something to do with Elizabeth's being in the country. He shrugged inwardly, having by now become so inured to Miss Bingley's machinations that, aside from a quick thought as to any potential liability, that he might not find himself the object of his aunt's lecturing again, he largely ignored them; he followed Bingley's lead, and retired early.

The next morning, Darcy, together with Bingley, Pender, and Mr. Hartsbury, were to meet Mr. Gardiner at the bridge; Sir Neville had begged off, citing as his reason a poor night's sleep, although Darcy was perfectly confident he was, rather, simply intent on seizing the chance to be with Miss Hartsbury for an undisturbed period of hours; and Hurst, of course, was not yet stirring.

Assembling on the lawn, they were joined very shortly by Mr. Gardiner, arrived from Lambton. After selecting what tackle they pleased, they trooped together back along the path on the far side of the stream; Bingley and Pender stopped off not far from the house, where a wide opening in the trees provided an expanse of the stream largely unencumbered by over-hanging limbs, and Mr. Hartsbury decided to join their company. However, as the water there was shallow and quick, and rather lacking in pools, sunken logs, or shading plants of interest to fish, Darcy and Mr. Gardiner continued along to Darcy's favourite spots further back into the coppice wood.

"Fly, or bait?" Darcy asked politely, once they had chosen a spot.

With a critical eye at the hanging trees, Mr. Gardiner said, "I believe I could work a wet-fly here; no room for a good dry cast."

Darcy nodded, "Quite right: just what I always use."

They spent some time selecting the proper lures and securing them to their lines, and, after one or two practice casts, Gardiner made a short, but very creditable first cast in front of a shadowed pool, just before a large rock. "Your hands have not forgotten their skill," Darcy admired. "Just luck," the other replied, but his happy smile showed that he was well pleased with himself. As the line snaked along, a large trout could be seen to dart out towards the lure, but it turned back at the last minute with a flip of its tail that raised a large ripple that spread down the stream. The two men made noises of appreciation and anticipation, and began systematically working their way around the entire stretch.

As his companion was a serious angler, Darcy was careful not to be the first to speak. After perhaps a quarter hour, Gardiner caught the first, but it was too small to keep, and, after carefully remembering to wet his hands, he released it back into the water.

"Let me thank you again for this opportunity to indulge in my favourite pastime, Mr. Darcy; and I promised my wife to remember to tell you how gratified we were by your visit. May I say, we found your sister to be a most delightful young lady."

"I thank you, Sir; I will not attempt to argue, as I am of your opinion entirely," Darcy replied.

"Your friend Mr. Bingley seems a thoroughly decent fellow," Gardiner observed, as he prepared to cast again.

"I have never met a better," agreed Darcy.

After a silence lasting several casts, Gardiner asked, "It was at his home in Hertfordshire that you met my niece, I believe?"

Darcy slowly worked his fly downstream before answering: "Yes, we were together there for the shooting; he leased it just last September."

Another cast, and Gardiner asked: "Is the family from the country?"

Darcy, having decided to change flies, was rummaging for a new one. He said, "No, they come originally from Northumberland; but in fact, he is a Town man." While tying the new fly to his line, he said, "That was another reason I was happy to leave him to that sunny spot downstream; his skills at sport in general are, I fear, somewhat limited. The company will be lively, I am sure, but the fishing will not be the best."

"Well, we all find our pleasures as we will, and I do not doubt but what they will enjoy their time," said Mr. Gardiner, intently working his line back past the rock he had first tried.

"Any one in a party uniting Bingley and Pender cannot help but be well entertained," Darcy affirmed. He made his way back to the bank and made a cast further upstream from Gardiner.

"Indeed; they both seem most agreeable," Mr. Gardiner concurred. There was a minute of silence, then he cried, "Whoops!" as a very respectable trout hit his line. Darcy courteously reeled in his line, and after several minutes of highly agreeable combat, Gardiner, grinning delightedly, landed the fish to the applause of his companion. Shortly thereafter, the younger gentleman also had the good fortune (or skill, as all staunch anglers would have it) to best a most unexceptional and spirited water-beast. The two men sat down to take their ease for a moment, and allow the stream to settle after two such fearsome battles so close together.

"Were the ladies of the house planning anything for to-day?" Mr. Gardiner enquired.

"Nothing in particular," answered Darcy. "My sister was intending to stay in with Mr. Bingley's sisters — Mrs. Hurst and Miss Bingley; they neither of them much enjoy the out-of-doors."

"That is fortunate, as I know my wife and my niece were intending to call upon Miss Darcy this morning."

Suddenly, Darcy's interest in angling fell into sharp decline. "*This* morning, you say?"

"Yes; I should imagine they are there, now." The older man gave Darcy a probing look with one eyebrow raised.

"Well—perhaps, as things are going on so well here, I might just go look in on the others," Darcy observed judiciously. "And I might as well look in on my other guests, while I am about it."

"Entirely proper," approved the other, nodding. "As host, I do not think you could very well do less."

"Quite right," Darcy agreed in a rather distracted fashion. "Are you in need of anything I might bring, or send?" Mr. Gardiner shook his head with a slight smile, and got to his feet in order to make his way back to the stream. "Then, if you will excuse me, I shall just be off, shall I?" said Darcy, laying down his rod. "I shall return...before long," he finished vaguely. Mr. Gardiner waved him on, and he made his way quickly back to the house, passing the other three gentlemen, all of whom were thoroughly engrossed in untangling Mr. Hartsbury's line from about the one solitary tree limb available for the purpose in the area, with, at least on Bingley's and Pender's part, a good deal of merriment; Mr. Hartsbury did not seem quite so well entertained.

On his arrival, Reynolds informed him that the ladies were gathered in the northern salon, and that refreshments had just been sent in. Relieved thereby of any duties as host, Darcy went on towards the back of the house. Entering, he saw all the ladies gathered around the table, with a very smart-looking presentation of fruit collected from his orchards and gardens. Mrs. Gardiner was facing the door, and so was first to notice him with a smile and a curtsey. Miss Bingley immediately turned and, smiling brightly, cried, "Mr. Darcy how delightful!" Darcy, however, had eyes only for Elizabeth; she turned round to see him and gave him a smile which, though much more reserved, was more valued.

Darcy gave his compliments to the group clustered around the table; Miss Bingley, with a great display of cheerfulness, enquired: "Was your fishing expedition successful?"

"It has been so far," he replied. "Although I would hesitate to call it an expedition. We had caught two very nice fish before I came back in to see our guests."

Miss Bingley did not seem best pleased with the latter portion of his comment, but remarked, "And do you really touch them? How ghastly that must feel!"

"Not at all," said Darcy, "and there is, of course, always ample water about for washing one's hands after."

The lady gave a visible shudder, saying, "Men are so much better at that sort of thing; I should never be able to bring myself to touch a fish: such slimy, repellent things!" Darcy was unsure how best to reply; to chide her silliness would be impolite, but to agree with her would be to encourage it, and so he decided simply to let the comment be.

Georgiana led the way back to the chairs at this juncture; Darcy seated himself next to her, and, to his delight, Elizabeth sat not far from them.

With a glance in her brother's direction, Georgiana began, "Miss Bennet, I was curious to know what types of books you favour, as my brother tells me you enjoy reading, as do I."

Elizabeth hesitated, looking faintly embarrassed, and answered: "I read many different things, but just lately I have been reading a number of novels."

"Have you?" said Georgiana with interest. "So have I!"

Being therefore given license to find novels an acceptable amusement, Elizabeth said with enthusiasm: "I have just finished a work by Miss Frances Burney: *Camilla*, which I thought very well done."

Darcy was pleased with Georgiana's trying to be more forthcoming in company, and hoped it was due to her partiality for Elizabeth. "Earlier this year Georgiana was reading *Evelina*, by Burney," he remembered. "Have you ever read it?"

"No, I have not, but I have heard well of it."

Darcy next mentioned to Elizabeth a novel of gothic horror he had enjoyed when up at university, but, to his delight, she decried what she termed the "extreme foolishness" of the heroes and heroines of such works, for being so ill-judging as to place themselves in situations which any individual with a proper way of thinking would eschew. "But one must put aside such pragmatic thoughts, in order to enjoy that *frisson* of terror which is the author's object," he protested.

"Enjoy terror?" demanded Elizabeth, "What right-minded person enjoys terror?"

"Well, it is not a true terror," he admitted with a smile, "and it might well be suggested that *Udolpho* appeals more to the immature mind, which I will admit to characterise my own; your superior taste must be the foundation for your disapproval of the *genre*. But, in reality, there must be a degree of melodrama, of foolishness, if you will, else it could not be enjoyable; that is true. The very unreality of the characters' actions, the fact that such things would, in fact, be very unlikely to occur, allows the mind to enter into the thing, and taste it just enough for enjoyment, but not so much as to cause real distress."

"I had thought it the novelist's job to make as plausible a tale as possible," observed Elizabeth.

Georgiana looked up and agreed: "I believe I feel the same on that point; the more realistic the writing, the more engrossing the story."

Her brother conceded to them both: "That, I am persuaded, is because your tastes in novels must be better than mine."

Georgiana was gathering her thoughts, and her courage, to add to this, when Miss Bingley took advantage of the momentary lag in conversation to interject in rather spiteful accents: "Pray, Miss Eliza, are not the -- shire militia removed from Meryton? They must be a great loss to *your* family." The effect of her words was like the shattering of a fallen glass; the whole room seemed frozen for an instant.

Darcy realised immediately her true object must be to start the idea of Wickham with Elizabeth; his anger flaring, he looked quickly Elizabeth's way; that Miss Bingley should dare to bring up the topic in his presence was unpardonable, but he could not but fear how Elizabeth might respond: in her pique at this ill-bred provocation, she might let slip something concerning Georgiana. However, with perfect indifference, Elizabeth directly answered: "I am sure they would be no more missed in Longbourn's drawing-rooms than in Netherfield's."

Darcy's fear subsided on hearing her cool and composed reply, but his anger at Miss Bingley grew; she looked as though she longed to say more, but a glance at Darcy's darkened countenance persuaded her to withhold her comments. Looking back at Elizabeth, Darcy realised with sudden warmth that in her guarded response she had been very careful with regard to his sister's sensibilities: had she wished, she might have engaged Miss Bingley on the topic of Colonel Forster's officers easily enough, without any reference to Wickham, or anything touching on Georgiana's involvement with the man; that she had not, must have come from her desire to spare his sister any discomfort. The next thought struck him even more forcibly: she had believed that portion of his letter concerning Georgiana's elopement! — indeed, she had, for there could be no other cause to avoid the topic than her acceptance of Wickham's guilt. At this, Darcy's sentiments underwent a profound transformation: Elizabeth had taken his side against Wickham!

Never before had any one who was not a victim of Wickham believed Darcy's representations of his evil, and now, Elizabeth had taken Darcy's side against him. The warmth of his admiration for her was instantly strengthened by this realisation, although he hardly needed such reinforcement; he looked at her with a degree of grateful appreciation which, had she noticed it, must have told her how far from extinguished were his affections.

To revive the conversation, Darcy asked what reading Elizabeth would recommend; she then asked if they enjoyed the modern poets, to which Georgiana, still in confusion from the allusion to Wickham, contributed only a nod, but Darcy had not even that much to offer — in school the only English poets he had studied were Milton, Donne, Shakespeare, and Chaucer: he knew nothing of the modern authors mentioned by Elizabeth. But he was glad to learn, and listened with interest to what she said of them; all in all, even without the pleasure of knowing how it must frustrate Miss Bingley, it was a very enjoyable discussion, but short-lived: very soon the two ladies from Lambton rose to take their leave.

He escorted them out to their carriage, mostly to prolong his time with Elizabeth, and was very politely thanked by each; as he handed them in, he was extremely pleased by the fact that Elizabeth voluntarily reached for his support, without the faintest hint of aversion. As he re-entered the house, he was in excellent spirits.

Unfortunately, this lasted no longer than his return to the salon; no sooner was he in the door than Miss Bingley, who had apparently been speaking her mind very freely in his absence, judging by the discomposed looks of his sister, turned to him and said with energy: "How very ill Eliza Bennet looks this morning, Mr. Darcy. I never in my life saw any one so much altered as she is since the winter. She is grown so brown and coarse! Louisa and I were agreeing that we should not have known her again."

All feelings of charity evaporated within him, and he directly recollected how disobliging Miss Bingley had been. In repressive tones, he disagreed: "To my eye she did not appear much changed; I perceived no difference other than that she is rather tanned—no miraculous consequence of travelling in the summer."

Miss Bingley refused to take instruction from his tone, however, and continued, "For my own part, I must confess that I never could see any beauty in her. Her face is too thin; her complexion has no brilliancy; and her features are not at all handsome. Her nose wants character; there is nothing marked in its lines. Her teeth are tolerable, but not out of the common way; and as for her eyes, which have sometimes been called so fine, I never could perceive anything extraordinary in them. They have a sharp, shrewish look, which I do not like at all; and in her air altogether, there is a self-sufficiency without fashion which is intolerable."

In her attack on Elizabeth, with her particular mention of "fine eyes", Darcy could not mistake her intention of disparaging Elizabeth to him especially. His anger grew, but he held his tongue and refused to rise to her provocation. He did not scruple, however, to allow his expression to show how little he cared for what she had to say.

Heedless, Miss Bingley sailed on: "I remember, when we first knew her in Hertfordshire, how amazed we all were to find that she was a reputed beauty; and I particularly recollect your saying one night, after they had been dining at Netherfield, '*She* a beauty!—I should as soon call her mother a wit.' But afterwards she seemed to improve on you, and I believe you thought her rather pretty at one time."

"Yes," said Darcy finally, his tone marking his anger, "but *that* was only when I first knew her, for it is many months since I have considered her as one of the handsomest women of my acquaintance."

Fixing her with a quelling look, he then walked out of the room; returning with a determined step to Mr. Gardiner, he soothed his temper by joining in mortal conflict with several more unoffending fish, and by listening to the good-natured common sense spoken by his companion.

Chapter Twelve

*D*arcy's temper had regained its equilibrium by the time he went down to dinner; Mr. Gardiner had left in mid-afternoon, and between the two of them, with some help from the gardener, William, they were able to supply the fish for the evening's meal. Darcy had sought out Georgiana on coming back in, to hear her very favourable opinion of Elizabeth and discuss their time together; he was careful, however, not to touch on Miss Bingley's disobliging remarks.

At dinner, Miss Bingley wisely seated herself at some distance from Darcy, who had Bingley to his right, with Pender next to him. Miss Hartsbury and Sir Neville were to Darcy's left. Darcy asked the two of them how they spent their day, to which Miss Hartsbury replied, "Sir Neville was kind enough to accompany me on a walk about the grounds." That gentleman looked faintly embarrassed at this, but the lady maintained a perfect composure. "We had a most marvellous walk to the folly on top of the hill; what a charming little folly, so lovely and so perfectly situated! — the view from there is exquisite. I am quite struck by how beautiful is your country, you know, Mr. Darcy; every new prospect is delightful."

"I agree entirely," added Sir Neville.

Darcy reflected that, should their relationship continue to blossom, Sir Neville would of necessity need to learn to be a man of few words. To Miss Hartsbury he said, "We must plan an excursion to the Peaks, and Dove Dale, whilst you are here. They are justifiably renowned for the picturesque of their prospects."

"You have a remarkable library here at Pemberley, Mr. Darcy," offered Sir Neville.

"Thank you. I tend to it myself: it is something of an interest of mine," answered Darcy.

"It is fine, indeed, Darcy," Pender agreed. "I felt very much at home there last evening, and found an edition of Acquinas I have not seen outside of the Bodelian."

"Yes; I am afraid the penchant for philosophy runs quite far back in our family. I, myself, have added several first editions, including one of More's *Utopia* you may want to look into whilst you are here."

Miss Hartsbury asked playfully, "Is that all you ever think of, Mr. Darcy? Philosophy? —What of more practical matters? What of the here and now?" Sir Neville smiled at her in open admiration of her gift for conversation.

"What would you have me think of, Miss Hartsbury?" Darcy asked, matching her tone.

"What of families, Sir, and the opposite sex? Is there no place for women in your philosophy?" Darcy, of course, recognised her reference to the interest she had demonstrated in him the last Season but one; he was happy that the matter was now become a subject of jest between them.

But Pender replied for him, "I fear, Miss Hartsbury, that that subject lies outside the proper sphere of philosophy."

"How, Sir?" asked she in surprise. "Are we of so little consequence, then, that we do not warrant thinking of?"

"Indeed, Master Pender," said Lady Andover, "it would be folly for any man to belittle the fair sex in my company; is that your purport, then?"

"By no means," he said firmly, dividing his deferential bow of the head equally between the two ladies. "It is the meaning of the word itself that excludes the topic from consideration." He stopped there, as though he had explained himself fully, and even Darcy had to look quizzically at him. Feigning surprise, to Darcy he said, "You do not agree?"

"I fear I can neither agree nor disagree; once again, I confess, your argument is too recondite for me."

"Yet it was the general subject of a rather lengthy deliberation we shared earlier this year," Pender teazed. Darcy shook his head, unable to penetrate his meaning. "Why, if we do but consider the meaning of the word," Pender went on, "we find that philosophy is 'the love of knowledge'; and I recollect telling you at the time that a true knowledge of women is beyond any man; therefore women cannot be considered by philosophy."

The gentlemen smiled and nodded at this. Miss Hartsbury, however, said, "With the greatest respect for your logic and erudition, Master Pender, I have to say that that is utter nonsense." The whole table sat up at this, giving Miss Hartsbury their complete attention.

"My dear child," expostulated her uncle, "have a care! You will please remember to whom you are speaking."

Pender waved aside this objection, saying with curiosity: "How so, my dear Miss Hartsbury? Might I hear your reasoning?"

"Very well; tell me — is it possible that a woman might study and comprehend philosophy?"

Pender answered, "While there *are* some who might argue their capacity, I do not count myself amongst them. There have certainly been women in history with a philosophical bent, who have reflected ably on the subject, and I myself have known not a few who could argue logically and capably."

"Well, there you have your answer," Miss Hartsbury said.

It was Pender's turn to look puzzled. "I fear, Madam, you have got ahead of *me*, there. Would you be so kind as to fill in the middle elements of your argument for this tired old brain?"

"Why, Sir, the female mind can certainly be fathomed by one of that sex, as readily as the depths of the masculine mind can be plumbed by the great male thinkers, and, if it can be allowed that philosophy can be studied, understood, and argued by a woman, the female mind is therefore no more beyond the reach of philosophical study than the male mind."

Darcy and the others applauded, and Sir Neville let his looks convey his approval; Pender stood and bowed respectfully to Miss Hartsbury. "Here is one woman, at least, who is adept at the Socratic method; I honour you, dear lady."

Miss Hartsbury beamed, and Darcy saw her dart an elated glance to his sister, who applauded again gleefully. Lady Andover said to Georgiana, "This might be a good moment, my dear, for the ladies to retire; it is always well to leave on a note of triumph." Georgiana nodded, and the ladies rose; Pender stepped over to Miss Hartsbury after she had gained her feet and kissed her hand, at which she beamed and blinked with great energy; the rest of the men also stood of course, and, with more congratulations and applause, bid the ladies a temporary adieu.

The men settled back into their chairs, and the wine was passed. After a minute or two of desultory conversation, Bingley, perhaps thinking of Pender's gallant gesture to Miss Hartsbury, asked, "Pender, back in Oxford, you said something I have not forgotten: would you truly not wish to have your youth back?"

"Not for worlds," was Pender's reply. "If I knew then what I know now, I should despise my friends for fools, and those above me for worse; yet, were I as ignorant as I was at the time, to what purpose would I return?"

"There, you speak aright," stated Mr. Hartsbury importantly. "A man ought to leave off the follies of youth, and attend to those serious matters only understood in the fullness of the mature mind."

"I fear you anticipate me, Sir," said Pender, "for I confess, the follies of youth are the only attraction youth holds for me at all; they are rapidly abandoning me, and if I were to have it to do over again, I should take care to commit a great deal more of them."

Darcy and Bingley chuckled, but Mr. Hartsbury said with weighty significance, "You are pleased to make light, Master Pender, but I am well-assured that a man of your parts would never do any such thing."

Pender returned a slight bow, then asked: "Pray, might we hear your thoughts on the matter? In your estimation, what matters of a serious nature are the proper sphere of the mature mind?"

"Those same things that have been the concern of the contemplative mind, Sir, since the Fall: God, and how best we might follow His plan."

"Ah, very good," congratulated Pender, nodding, his head drooping over his wine glass in a meditative manner; a sharp glint in his eye, however, told that he had a verbal contest in view. "There can be no doubt amongst the learned that the mere events of history count but little towards God's ultimate plan; the man of worth can do nothing to better effect than to support our spiritual leaders. You therefore have tithed the bulk of your wealth over to the Church, I presume?" he asked, lifting his eyes to Hartsbury.

Hartsbury shifted uneasily in his seat. "I regret that, personally, I have but little to give."

"Of course," said Pender apologetically, "how absurd in me to assume otherwise. A man of your deeply spiritual nature could accrue little by way of worldly goods; but you give very freely of your time, surely?"

"Ah, there again, Master Pender—my time is not my own; it is consumed nearly completely in attending to the details of my brother's estate," responded Mr. Hartsbury in regretful tones. "He left a vast fortune to my niece, who, of course, cannot manage it herself."

With some amusement, Darcy recalled what Mr. Hartsbury's niece had said on this point, and wondered that the man could ignore the evidence his niece had just given of her acuity; Pender gave Hartsbury a slow, appraising look before saying with very pronounced sincerity, "*How* unfortunate for you! To have your niece depend on your superior abilities so completely: a man of such serious learning and devout leanings, to be forced to spend all your time in pursuit of temporal gain, and languishing in the trappings of wealth! Well, Mr. Hartsbury, I am sure that all of us here appreciate your sacrifice." Nodding gravely to Darcy and Bingley, Pender leaned and patted Hartsbury consolingly on the shoulder. To Darcy he said, "And I thank you, Darcy, for having given me the opportunity to be in the company of such an extraordinary fellow." Mr. Hartsbury seemed gratified that here, at least, was one man who could understand how difficult were his struggles in life.

Shortly after this, the men re-joined the ladies in the drawing-room. Miss Bingley, of course, greeted Darcy with smiles even before he was even properly in the room; he had not forgotten that afternoon, however, and so sat down near his sister and Miss Hartsbury, knowing it would prick Miss Bingley. Sir Neville joined them, and was rewarded with Miss Hartsbury's brightest welcoming smiles.

Miss Bingley, not content to have Darcy at such a distance, and so pointedly shunning her company, came over to their little grouping. "And did you enjoy your conversation over the wine, Mr. Darcy? I fear we were a little dull here, waiting for you gentlemen."

"Dull?" interjected Miss Hartsbury. "Did you find it so? Then I am sure it must have been my fault; I know, of course, that I tend to go on and on: I do apologise."

"Why, no, my dear Miss Hartsbury," said Miss Bingley, disconcerted at being thought to have made so openly a disparaging remark. "I meant no such thing, I assure you: I had nothing in view besides the natural relief that enlarging our group must bring."

"Oh, that is all right," Miss Hartsbury assured her lightly. "I do not mind; I fear the habit goes too far back to be broken. My mother, you know, was stricken in my youth, and it is so hard on her to speak, poor dear, that I necessarily provided all of our discussion, and now, well, I just cannot seem to stop. How fortunate you are to have had both a brother and a sister growing up: what lovely talks you must have had together, especially as your brother is so affable—and your sister, too, of course." She smiled cordially at Miss Bingley, blinking at her usual rapid pace, but Darcy thought he detected some tinge of irritation beneath her words.

"Miss Bingley is a lady of vast conversational resources," he put in mischievously, glad of the opportunity to repay Miss Bingley for her very obliging remark that afternoon, "and has the ability to weigh in on almost any topic with considerable strength of opinion. In fact, I do believe my friend's amiable nature was largely formed under the influence of the lengthy addresses he often hears from his sisters in concert. Her understanding of what constitutes a well-bred, accomplished lady, is, in particular, highly developed: you must correct me if my memory is in error, Miss Bingley, but did you not hold that it was founded on a thorough knowledge of music, singing, drawing, dancing, and the modern languages?" Miss Bingley nodded to this, her smile indicating her pleasure that his memory was so exact on the point. "What say you, Miss Hartsbury?" Darcy asked. "What is your opinion of such a definition?"

That lady, still blinking and smiling, said, "I am a great advocate of accomplishment in any of those endeavours, you know, where there is either genius or application to give proficiency and enjoyment, both to the performer and her audience."

Darcy looked inquisitively at her; he asked, "You agree, then? Does this definition guarantee social ability and ease?"

"No, I cannot allow that it guarantees one proficient in these accomplishments social grace. Of course, I make no claim to it, either, by any means. Heavens, no; I am the least adept of any one I know in social settings. But I have observed those who are, and I have to say, they were not all in possession of your list accomplishments; in some cases, you know, they were not in possession of any of them."

"Without accomplishment, what character do they possess, then, to give them grace and ease?" asked Miss Bingley. "High station?"

"Oh no, not that, either," said Miss Hartsbury. "Not at all. No, every one I have known who could lay claim to social ease and ability knew the limits of their under-standing, and made no assertions on things beyond their knowledge."

"My dear Miss Hartsbury," Miss Bingley chided, "this can be no definition of social powers; a person with no accomplishment at all might understand that they know but little."

"Yes: odd, is not it? One would certainly think so, but the only people I have met who seem to know their limits are people of notable ability. Observe..." she called to her uncle, "Mr. Hartsbury! —forgive my interrupting you, Uncle, but what had one best do in the face of a query on a subject unknown to them?"

"It is my invariable habit to turn to the scriptures on such an occasion, my dear," he replied with dignity. "I can always find the sought-for guidance there, no matter the topic." His niece beamed at him. "Thank you; I know you do, Uncle dear, and I was sure I could count on your reply. Master Pender, I have a question for you, too: would you call yourself a man of great ability?"

Darcy laughed and warned, "I shall hold you to what you have told me about false modesty, Pender."

Pender acknowledged Darcy with a wry expression, and told Miss Hartsbury: "I would have to say, with all *due* modesty, that I *am* a man of great ability; however, my abilities cover only a very limited subject matter."

"And may I ask, in the face of an unknown situation outside your abilities, and requiring an expedience of action too great for study, what should you do?"

"It is my invariable habit, in such circumstances, to turn to the biggest fool present, and ask his opinion; I then do the opposite. *Ergo...*Darcy, how do you think I ought to answer this question?"

As the company laughed, Darcy cried: "Why, you old reprobate...I shall have Reynolds put nettles in your sheets! Pepper in your tea!"

Pender shook his head with a great show of sorrow. "I rest my case: you can take the boy out of Eton, but you..." Darcy finished for him by flinging a pillow from his chair at him, which Pender easily deflected, laughing. Miss Bingley, who had started it all, looked rather at sea in the midst of this sort of quick-witted banter, half play and half serious; she joined in the laughter as best she could, then went off to sit with her sister. Between Pender, Bingley, and Miss Hartsbury, with occasional contributions from Darcy and his sister, the evening passed pleasantly away; Darcy retired in a mellow mood, and thought back over the day, especially Elizabeth's visit, with a good deal of satisfaction.

The morning following, Darcy was up early; breaking his fast lightly, he took to horse well before mid-morning and rode to Lambton. His purpose in going, or so he told himself, was that it was absolutely necessary to express his thanks to Elizabeth for her very collected defence of Georgiana during Miss Bingley's baiting. When he entered the inn, the proprietor, smiling and bowing, began to come towards him; Darcy shook his head and pointed enquiringly up to the floor above; the proprietor, nodding, called for his daughter to fetch the Gardiner's manservant, who escorted Darcy to the Gardiner's apartments.

On his opening the door, however, Darcy was brought up short, and his intention of once more demonstrating his improved civility dashed, by the sight of Elizabeth standing immediately before him, just in the act of reaching for the latch, her face bearing witness to great distress and a desperate urgency. Said she in accents breathless and exigent: "I beg your pardon, but I must leave you. I must find Mr. Gardiner this moment, on business that cannot be delayed; I have not a moment to lose." As she spoke she had to support herself on the doorway, her body weakened and her face so pale as to be almost bloodless.

Darcy, alarmed by her frantic expression and frail appearance, cried: "Good God! what is the matter?" But taking himself in hand, determining that he must be more help than hindrance, he said more collectedly, "I will not detain you a minute, but let me, or let the servant, go after Mr. and Mrs. Gardiner. You are not well enough; —you cannot go yourself."

Elizabeth tried to command herself forward, but her legs began to fail under her weight, and she clung to the door-frame for support. She called to the servant: "John! John, you must fetch Mr. Gardiner immediately—make haste; oh, make haste!" Darcy, though standing nearly at her side, could scarcely make out what she said, so quick and feeble were her words. With this, all strength left her and she sank speechless into a chair, her face pallid, her eyes wandering, focused on objects far away. Under the circumstances Darcy could not leave her, whether she wished for his presence or not; in truth, however, she hardly seemed to realise he was still there. After a moment's concerned observation, he gently urged, "Let me call your maid. Is there nothing you could take, to give you present relief? — A glass of wine; — shall I get you one? — You are very ill."

Elizabeth strove to be more in control of herself, saying, "No, I thank you. There is nothing the matter with me. I am quite well. I am only distressed by some dreadful news which I have just received from Longbourn."

At this she dissolved into tears completely; Darcy, shocked and apprehensive, hating to imagine what might have brought on such affliction, and fearing he hardly knew what, wished he could do anything rather than sit by in ineffectual solicitude, waiting until she should be able to speak again; but he could bring to mind nothing profitable to the situation. He endeavoured to speak comfort, but his words tripped over themselves, and he felt the perfect uselessness of all stale, worn, trifling words, to moderate such overwhelming sorrow as this.

After giving way to her emotions for some moments, Elizabeth spoke, her voice low and despairing, "I have just had a letter from Jane, with such dreadful news. It cannot be concealed from any one. My youngest sister has left all her friends — has eloped; — has thrown herself into the power of — of Mr. Wickham. They are gone off together from Brighton. *You* know him too well to doubt the rest. She has no money, no connexions, nothing that can tempt him to — she is lost forever."

At the sound of Wickham's name, Darcy's world heaved beneath him; that devil! — still he would reach out and work ruin on every thing he touched! He stared at Elizabeth, unable to speak; he knew not whether his most exigent object should be to hunt Wickham down and prove his anger on his person, or to cast aside all personal concerns that he might marshal every relief at his command to Elizabeth's aid and comfort.

"When I consider," she said in a piteous voice that quite pierced him through, "that *I* might have prevented it! — *I* who knew what he was. Had I but explained some part of it only — some part of what I learnt — to my own family! Had his character been known, this could not have happened. But it is all, all too late now."

Darcy was transfixed with horror and guilt when he realised what she was saying: her words made it obvious that she had, in fact, given full credence to his letter, and, as he had requested, had not shared his secret, had not revealed Georgiana's disgrace, even to her own sisters; her whole family was now to pay a terrible price for her most faithful defence of his family's honour. Nor could he disregard the fact that her words might very well have been his own — had *he* but taken it upon himself to make Wickham's character known in Meryton, and even before, this ruinous misfortune could never have overtaken her family.

"I am grieved, indeed," he cried, his sense of guilt growing by the moment, "grieved — shocked. But is it certain, absolutely certain?" He vainly hoped that, somehow, some propitious error might befriend him, however hidden or improbable, and save him from the burden of guilt he presently laboured under.

"Oh yes!" replied Elizabeth. "They left Brighton together on Sunday night, and were traced almost to London, but not beyond; they are certainly not gone to Scotland."

In the time it took for her to speak this, Darcy let go his weakness, his foolish hopes and useless self-reproach, and became resolute: he would not suffer this to stand. What he wanted first was information: "And what has been done, what has been attempted, to recover her?"

"My father is gone to London, and Jane has written to beg my uncle's immediate assistance, and we shall be off, I hope, in half an hour. But nothing can be done; I know very well that nothing can be done. How is such a man to be worked on? How are they even to be discovered? I have not the smallest hope. It is every way horrible!"

Shaking his head silently, Darcy realised how true this was; in his whole life he had never found the means of curbing Wickham and bringing him to heel to face his misdeeds; short of bribery or violence, how did one check an unprincipled man? No, not even bribery, for had not Wickham reneged on their agreement regarding the living? Once the money was gone, so would be the understanding between them.

"When *my* eyes were opened to his real character," Elizabeth went on. "Oh! had I known what I ought, what I dared, to do! But I knew not—I was afraid of doing too much. Wretched, wretched, mistake!"

Her words lashed Darcy with an acute consciousness of his accountability in the business, and of his obligation. Elizabeth, who had the least reason of any one to protect him, had sacrificed her family for the sake of his—not with this outcome in mind, doubtless, but that was of no comfort to Darcy: he was responsible for this state of affairs, as surely as though he had delivered her sister into Wickham's hands directly. Her pain was his doing, and while accusation was far from her intention, Darcy could not have felt more at fault had she levelled a finger at his breast and proclaimed him villain.

This was the end, he swore to himself; he would finish this: Wickham would pay, and Elizabeth and her family would be released from his influence. This, he promptly realised, could not be done by means of the law without exposure and disgrace for the Bennets; but by any means—fair or foul—he meant to undo Wickham. The pair were in London: that would mean Mrs. Younge would likely know their whereabouts, for he knew from his dealings with her the year before that she and Wickham were close; as close as the deceitful may be, at any rate.

At this point he stopped in his deliberations and looked over at Elizabeth; she had covered her face with her handkerchief and given herself over entirely to grief.

To say that she was in distress, and that he felt for her, would do justice to neither: he would gladly have lifted this burden from her at any cost to himself, even unto his utter dissolution; and she, seeing no future but misery and disgrace for all her family, felt every thing that the worst sinner might, when facing the infernal Abyss. Darcy ached to hold her, to offer her his strength, to comfort her with the warmth of his arms when words could not avail; but he had no right, no warrant to do so—nor would she welcome the attempt, he was well assured. He therefore had to rely on words alone, no matter how insufficient they must be: "I am afraid you have been long desiring my absence," said he with gentle compassion, "nor have I anything to plead in excuse of my stay, but real, though unavailing, concern. Would to Heaven that anything could be either said or done on my part, that might offer consolation to such distress! —But I will not torment you with vain wishes, which may seem purposely to ask for your thanks. This unfortunate affair will, I fear, prevent my sister's having the pleasure of seeing you at Pemberley to-day."

Elizabeth, her emotions having been momentarily slaked by her tears, now struggled to respond with propriety: "Oh, yes. Be so kind as to apologise for us to Miss Darcy. Say that urgent business calls us home immediately. Conceal the unhappy truth as long as it is possible." Casting down her eyes, she finished hopelessly: "I know it cannot be long."

He instantly assured her: "I beg you will not distress yourself on that account—you may be certain I will honour your confidence." Conscious of his resolve, he offered her what little solace he dared: "I am so very sorry; I only wish there were anything I might offer in support of you and your family; but allow me to express my hope for a happier conclusion than we might reasonably foresee at present." So saying, he took up his hat and gloves and prepared to take leave: he had a great deal to do, if he were to be in time to stave off this latest of Wickham's outrages against decency, and certainly Elizabeth could have no wish for him to stand by, watching her suffer without having anything to offer that might comfort her pain. He turned at the door to look a last time into her eyes, to charge his resolution with the pain he saw there, and to offer her his silent oath that he would preserve her family as she had his. Many thoughts vied for expression within him at such a moment, but, with all propriety, all he could offer was: "Please, extend my compliments and regrets to Mr. and Mrs. Gardiner." With that, he left her.

Chapter Thirteen

*H*e rode slowly back to Pemberley, thinking hard; he wanted a tool—a weapon—and the truth would not serve: truth was too malleable in Wickham's hands, and would damage the very ones Darcy sought to protect. But at least in this case, his way forward had not the frustrations he had faced in his youth—he was no longer that boy in his father's study; no longer the one trying to convince those in authority of Wickham's misdeeds—it was he who now wielded the authority, and held the resources. And, he swore to himself, as Elizabeth had protected his sister from disgrace, so would he defend hers.

But there was something in that former thought—resources—that gave pause; Wickham was always profligate, always in need of funds; and, a child no longer, he had no patron to protect him from the consequences of his over-reaching. Beyond any doubt, his most vulnerable point was that of his finances: he left debts wherever he went, and no amount of charm or artifice could alter or eradicate them. Perkins had mentioned his gaming in Meryton: that meant Wickham would have accumulated debts of honour, and probably amongst his brother officers; this would deny him the benefit of their protection as well, thereby increasing his vulnerability. As long as the debts remained, Wickham's flanks would be exposed: therein lay an exceptionally durable lever for use against him, if Darcy could secure those debts to himself. Wickham was not a man to be sparing and frugal that he might reimburse his debtors. Whoever controlled those debts, controlled Wickham: the threat of debtor's prison was a powerful one, and would be Darcy's so long as he held Wickham's debts; this would be his weapon, and one that would remain useful for years. It was not, perhaps, as gratifying to his more primitive urges as contriving a quietly violent end, but it would allow him to honour his father's intentions and expectations for Wickham's future. It was sure, ready to hand, and — as a threat — quick to be enacted: he could bring it to bear almost as soon as he could find Wickham and the youngest Miss Bennet — Lydia? — yes, that was her name; and speed was of the essence if he were to save Lydia from the effects of her imprudence.

But if his weapon against Wickham were to last for years, he would need a way to keep track of his whereabouts; while it might be possible to track him down once he had fled, if he *were* to flee it would be best to know about it right away. And it would be particularly useful if whatever profession he followed involved a degree of scrutiny over its practitioners. When put in those terms, the thing was obvious: the military was the answer. But not a militia: the regular army — extensive, regulated, with stricter code of conduct, and far more likely to hunt down and punish deserters. And Colonel Fitzwilliam would be useful, both in getting him in, and in keeping him in.

On reaching home, he went directly to the library and brought out pen and paper. He wrote an express to Colonel Forster, explaining the essentials of his plan and asking him to discover and procure all the debt Wickham had left behind in Brighton and the regiment, for which he pledged himself; he asked that it all be sent to him in London, not excepting the debts of honour, additionally pledging his own honour that they should be held in confidence. It then occurred to him that the Bennet family might also look to Colonel Forster for aid, and he made it clear in his letter that their requests should be given priority over his, and asked that his efforts be kept in confidence from them especially, lest he should hinder them in any way, or they be given false hope by his endeavours. He also realised how critically important it was that Elizabeth should never be apprised of the rôle he meant to play: her sense of obligation under the circumstances must be crushing, and completely preclude any future comfort between them.

As for discovering Wickham and the Bennet girl, he would first have to get hold of Mrs. Younge; he had obtained intelligence previously that she kept a large house with rooms to let in a decent sort of neighbourhood near Deptford, out the Kent Road south of the river. He rather thought Wickham might be there; but he needed to be sure of his prey, once he had him treed. His first, unformed thought was to ask the local authorities to keep an eye on him, but this was immediately replaced with the thought of Colonel Fitzwilliam again, and some of the men he must know who were returned from the wars on the continent: they would fit in without notice, were accustomed to rough usage, and would have no other duties to distract them. He wrote to him too, asking him to name half a dozen stout fellows who knew how to be useful and were up to anything. He then went to his father's study, and retrieved from it a miniature his father had had done of Wickham some six or seven years previously; he would have it copied in London, as he had a mind to use it both as a means of identifying Wickham to his small company of men, and also of restricting Wickham's travel in future.

Giving his letters to Reynolds to post, he next went to find Georgiana: he would need her assistance to bring all this about. He hesitated only briefly over how much to tell her: he felt, however, that what she had gone through in the last year had exposed her to more of life's difficulties, and its less savoury side, than most ladies twice her age; in his estimation she had successfully overcome that assault on her sensibilities, and so he determined to hold nothing back.

"Dearest," he began, "I fear I have bad news: that…blackguard…is close to bringing disgrace down on another family, and I needs must go to London to stop him."

"Fitzwilliam, no!" she cried. "Oh, how can he be so wicked?"

"I know," he said sympathetically to ease her distress. "But at least this time I hope you see that it can have nothing to do with you."

"No...except that I thought I loved him, and now I see what he really is," she said unhappily.

"Well, yes; but...if there *is* wisdom to be learnt from our affairs of the heart, I am certain that it is the lesson of knowing who is worth loving, and who is not."

His sister looked up at him compassionately. "Is this something *you* have learnt, Fitzwilliam?" she asked him.

"For good or ill, yes, I believe I have; I trust I know better now who to love, and I am sure I know better who *not* to love," he said. Georgiana placed her hand gently on his arm.

"Who is she?" she asked. "Whose family is it?"

Darcy placed his hand over hers, then frowned and sighed. "It is the Bennet family," he told her. Her eyes grew wide with alarm and horror. "He has attached Miss Elizabeth Bennet's youngest sister; they are off from Brighton, and are thought to be in London. That is the reason I must go."

"No! You must stop him! Oh, how Miss Elizabeth Bennet must feel it!"

"Yes, Dearest, I agree, and I am sure you must feel, as I do, how much responsibility our family bears in in the matter. I have a plan, though, and one that may finally put an end to all his misdoings." He explained to her briefly what he had in mind.

"But," said she when he had finished, "will that not mean that you must keep abreast of his whereabouts? How long must that last?"

"As long as necessary: perhaps it will be a matter of some years, but certainly until he is married and settled, if that be possible. But I should have realised sooner that it would come to this, or something like it; trust me: I have allowed for all that, Dearest. He must be stopped, and if I do not stop him, no one will. And as I shall require some hold on him, this will give it to me. Can you see to our guests whilst I am absent?"

Nodding pensively, Georgiana said, "My aunt will help; we must do this for Miss Elizabeth Bennet. Unless we can prevent this, her disgrace would be unthinkable — I know very well what it would be." She lifted her eyes to his. "Very well, then: we will do what is necessary. Leave as soon as may be; I shall manage here as well as I can."

"Very well; I shall inform my aunt — but, Georgiana, for your own sake, she cannot know that you are in possession of the complete facts: I could never excuse sharing so much with one she thinks so young in the ways of the world; she can only know I have told you an affair of some urgency calls me away."

"Will you tell her whose family it is?"

"No. I would not have told even you, had I not known that your knowledge of the man would let you understand it in the proper light," Darcy replied. "I will tell her it is the family of a good acquaintance, and rest the matter on our family's responsibility where he is concerned."

And so he next spoke with his aunt and informed her of the true purpose of his journey; having seen enough of life to know the recklessness men and women are capable of, she was unsurprised and pragmatic. "Marriage will save your friends, Darcy," she said, "and nothing else. Make haste, though; the longer this goes on, the less likely you are to succeed." He nodded, but she continued seriously, "Darcy, let me counsel you: do not fail in this, for your sake as well as theirs; by failing, you will be hurt too; I have seen this, and I can tell you it is very painful to go through life knowing you might have saved a friend, but did not. I hope you will not fall into such a circumstance. Now, that said, be assured I am confident of your success."

He looked at her, considering her words carefully. Nodding, he kissed her cheek and thanked her, with his assurance that he would do his best, and that he hoped to see her before many weeks had gone.

Chapter Fourteen

*D*arcy said good-bye to the rest of his guests that evening, explaining only that business carried him back to Town unexpectedly. Bingley was concerned, and asked what he might do, to which Darcy had replied to the whole company: "Stay here and enjoy yourselves, so I might at least have the comfort of knowing my friends happy, even though I must toil. It will all be well, I am sure, and I trust my labours will not be long; I have some hopes of being back in a fortnight."

He journeyed back to London, arriving in Grosvenor Square early Saturday afternoon; having polished and refined his plans on the trip south, his first step was to see Colonel Fitzwilliam. He rode directly down to Horse Guards in Whitehall Street, and was, after waiting the proper amount of time for the military mechanism to churn its way round to movement, shown up to an office on the second floor, where one small and rather dirty window cast the light of day on stacks of letters and reports, and box upon box of maps rolled up in bundles. He found his cousin seated behind a battered desk, on which sat a single candle-holder, bearing three burnt-out stubs.

On entering, Darcy remarked, "Such imposing chambers! But, for the man who is saving the Empire, I suppose nothing is too good."

Looking up, the Colonel rose and came round the desk to greet his cousin. "Dash it, Darcy, but it is good to see a familiar face! How are you, and what brings you here?"

"Have you not had my letter?"

"Oh, I...yes, I believe I did," the Colonel seemed bewildered for a moment, charging his memory. "Perhaps…I thought I saw an envelope from you come across my desk. Honestly, Darcy, I have not had time to look about me much of late."

"Does it go well?"

"My bit does, but Bonaparte has the Devil's own luck, blast him, and we make no progress worthy of the name." He ran a hand through his hair, which showed little evidence of having been attended to in recent days. "But what is it that brings you to Town, and to me, Darcy?"

"In truth, Edders, I need a favour—well, two, in fact."

"Fair enough," replied his cousin, "I believe I have one or two hereabouts that are owing to you; what do you need?"

"First, I need to hire perhaps half-a-dozen men: rough-and-ready sorts who know how to handle themselves—and others, if it comes to that. I thought I might use some you might know of, who will recently have left the army."

"Good Heavens, Darcy: planning to turn to a life of crime, are we?" the Colonel said in jest.

"No," replied Darcy in all seriousness, "in fact, I mean to put a stop to one; George Wickham is at it again, and is bent on ruining the family of some one of my acquaintance: I intend to stop him."

"That swine! Again? Lord, but I should like to see him at the Devil! Who is the acquaintance?"

"It hardly matters: I should have done this after Ramsgate, as it was almost inevitable he should do it again. But it is probably best I keep their name in confidence, if you will not take it amiss."

"No, certainly not," Colonel Fitzwilliam said. "As you say, it hardly matters—it was always going to be some one."

Darcy, nodding in agreement, said: "Wickham has attached a young lady of good family, and has run off with her from Brighton; she is a rather silly little creature, but there are others in the family much more worth saving. The pair of them appear to be hiding here, in London. It is clearly up to me to stop him, but that I know the family obliges me that much more to take a hand."

Colonel Fitzwilliam said contemplatively, "I can see why you need some stout men; but let me be sure I understand what you are proposing." He then looked at Darcy with a rather fierce smile. "If you mean to do what I hope you mean to do, you will need only one man, but a rather special sort of man, at that."

"You mean leave him toes-up under a dock somewhere?" Darcy smiled back. "I have often contemplated it, and with considerable satisfaction, I assure you; but no—out of respect for my father, I shall stop short of that."

The Colonel snorted disgustedly. "Sorry to hear it—what is your scheme, then?"

"We know Wickham is a gamester, and is always running from debts: you recall the way he left Lambton?" The Colonel nodded. "Well, I strongly suspect he is on the run again now; I mean to run him to ground, then keep his feet nailed down while I secure all his debts. I have written to Colonel Forster to send me what he owes in Brighton, including the debts of honour I have no doubt he has incurred—at least those amongst the officers; with those in hand, I believe I can persuade Wickham that being a good little boy is better than Fleet Prison."

"It should work," his cousin allowed with a nod. "So you want the men to keep him from bolting while you put it all together?"

"Mostly, although in all probability it will go longer than that. I also mean to give him a good scare, and let him know I will brook no taradiddles."

"Can I at least hope for a bit of bastinado, or a nice, comprehensive flogging?" asked Colonel Fitzwilliam with another vicious grin.

"As gratifying as that would be, George Wickham is an abject coward; he showed us that in Ramsgate, and again in Hertfordshire: frighten him too much and he will run, no matter how many men we keep on him."

"Sound analysis and well-reasoned tactics, but utterly unsatisfying," the Colonel observed in a disappointed manner. "How do you mean to keep him under thumb, though? Will not he bolt as soon as your back is turned?"

"That is the second thing, Edmund; I wish to purchase a commission for him in His Majesty's Army."

The Colonel bridled a bit at this. "The army already has its full quota of bounders, Dirks; can we not simply throw him in prison for a lifetime or two?"

Darcy shook his head. "That would leave the family in utter ruins; the girl has been gone with him a week already, and it might be another week before I can discover them; no, marriage must be our goal."

Colonel Fitzwilliam's enthusiasm built anew: "And then we commission Wickham and send him off to the continent! If ever a man was meant for cannon fodder, it has to be George Wickham. Brilliant, Darcy! — the girl gets a husband, we get a corpse...and the world gains another young, obliging widow! — the perfect solution! Brilliant, truly — I congratulate you."

"I regret that that would not serve my purpose of honouring my father's wishes; he would turn in his grave if I sent Wickham to his death against the French."

Colonel Fitzwilliam sighed and shook his head; glancing down at the piles of papers on his desk he said, "Well, I can see you mean to pluck every shred of pleasure out of this for me, and I must get back to work. I shall look into getting you some men to-morrow: there are always a number of lads who have been mustered out attending the regimental services of a Sunday morning; there is one in particular I have in mind: a Corporal Sands. Come see me...no, never mind: I shall send them to you on Monday morning."

"And the commission?" Darcy pressed.

"Quite right; where do you want his posting?"

"In the north, near Derbyshire, if at all possible, that I might have a better chance of keeping a grip on him, and where it will be harder for him to hide if he runs."

"Well and good; I wonder if we have anything on the Isle of Man? Never mind: I should have it ready by this Tuesday week. And now, I regret I really must be getting on..."

"Of course; I am on my way. Thank you, Fitzwilliam."

As Darcy reached the door, his cousin's voice stopped him: "Good luck, Darcy," he said. "For what it is worth, I believe you are doing the right thing." Darcy turned and nodded his thanks, and left.

Determining that there was still daylight enough for a trip beyond Southwark, he rode across the bridge and down to Edwards Street, just south of Deptford. Directly after Ramsgate, Darcy had learnt of Mrs. Younge's having taken a house there, mostly because he felt the need to keep abreast of her activities; now that seemingly useless bit of information was the only thread he could see to pull at in unravelling the whereabouts of Wickham and Miss Lydia Bennet. In going there he had meant only to assure himself of the right location and to look the place over, but now, as he viewed the house, it struck him as being too prosperous, and the neighbourhood too open, for some one who wished to remain hidden; it would be an unlikely place for Wickham to go to ground in company with an unmarried woman. He stopped to consider: if Wickham were by any chance to be there, he had no reinforcements to contain him; but, whether he were or not, Mrs. Younge would still be the key to discovering him, no matter if he did flee. He determined to take the chance, and rode directly to the door. The maid answering it was new, and so did not recognise Darcy, but when he was admitted into Mrs. Younge's presence, that lady changed colour, and a sullen look of surprise crossed her features.

"Yes?" she asked insolently. "It is rather late in the day for revenge, if that is what you have in mind; but I cannot imagine you are more willing now than previously to sacrifice your sister's good name, just to injure me."

"No, not retribution, Mrs. Younge," said Darcy, ignoring her implied attack on Georgiana. "But I can offer you a chance to make restitution: tell me where George Wickham is."

"So that's your game, is it? I might've known," she said, her refinement of speech slipping temporarily. "They're not here, I can tell you that; I have a reputation to consider."

"So they did come to you," Darcy said with satisfaction. "I thank you for confirming that."

"Well, what if they did?" the woman said sourly.

Darcy shrugged, and asked, "Where are they now?"

"They're not here, and that's all I know," she said; something in her manner, however, said otherwise.

"Is it, indeed?" Darcy said. "Would you know more for ten pounds?"

"Ten pounds!" the woman said scornfully, "you carry that much in your boot! You forget, Mr. Darcy, I know exactly who you are, and how much you're worth. Try ten times that."

"And, again, I thank you for the confirmation," said Darcy. "You have the information I require, so now it is merely a matter of determining the price."

Evidently tired of losing so many tricks to Mr. Darcy, Mrs. Younge cried. "Here! — that's enough of that! You can take that on out with you — the door is just there behind you! And don't bother to come back until you're ready to talk business."

Darcy walked to the door, but warned her: "I shall leave; but I mean to have Wickham, Mrs. Younge. If not for the sake of what you owe me, then you had best think about saving your own skin in this business."

"Oh, now I *am* frightened!" said she sneeringly. "What do you take me for, an innocent?"

"Hardly," said Darcy in his driest tones. With that he left her; but he promised himself he would be back, with assistance.

Chapter Fifteen

*T*he next day was largely uneventful; while he was desperately anxious to be doing something towards saving Elizabeth from the position he had put her in, especially in view of his aunt's exhortation at Pemberley, he was not prepared to take further steps until he had heard from his cousin and Colonel Forster. He therefore took advantage of the day of rest to do precisely that, in hopes that the coming week would be more demanding.

Darcy's hopes in this respect were to be rewarded; shortly before breakfast the next morning, Goodwin came to the library to announce: "There is an individual at the door, Sir, calling himself Corporal Sands; he claims he was sent by Colonel Fitzwilliam; he has a number of rather rascally looking men with him, Mr. Darcy—shall I permit them to enter?"

"Yes, thank you, Goodwin; I shall be there in a moment. And would you have the carriage made ready? I shall be leaving directly after breakfast."

Goodwin bowed in acknowledgement and withdrew, a chill disapproval emanating from his person. Darcy smiled as he left, privately amused; he had often thought that, given Goodwin's sense of personal dignity, he ought to be no less than a duke.

Entering the hall, he found six men, somewhat scarred and battered-looking, but generally clean and upright in appearance. At their front was quite a small man, waiting patiently at a parade rest, as one who has lived through great strife and turbulence will wait; he had an enormously strong physique—one of the strongest of any man Darcy had ever seen. To this man Goodwin gestured and pronounced: "Corporal Sands, Sir."

Darcy stepped forward and said in greeting: "Corporal Sands."

"Sir," the other responded with the briefest bow.

"Goodwin, these men are here to help me in a matter of some importance; perhaps you could find something for them in the kitchen," suggested his master, gesturing towards the men who stood behind the corporal. Goodwin bowed and said, "Of course, Sir," in that resigned tone that means "On your head be it."

Corporal Sands spoke up, as though issuing an order: "Just tea and toast; no ale for these lads." To Darcy he said, "Beggin' yer pardon, Sir. I knows this lot."

From behind him one of the men muttered, "Oi, Sandy...!" Sands turned slowly to the men, who all suddenly froze, as mice will when the cat appears; while the smallest of the men by far, there was about the corporal a sense of sheer physical presence that suggested he could, should he take a mind to, tear the house—and every one in it—down with his bare hands. Goodwin turned rigidly on his heel, leading the men away, and they followed him single file, averting their eyes from Sands' face.

When they were gone, Darcy motioned his guest towards the front drawing-room. "Have you eaten, Corporal?" he asked.

"Yes...Sir," the man replied. There was *that* in his manner when he spoke, though, that made Darcy press: "This morning?"

Sands gave a faint, sheepish grin, "No, Sir."

Darcy called a footman and told him to bring his breakfast there, and to double it for the corporal. Looking about him, the man hesitated to sit on the elegant, tapestried cushions perched on the finely carved legs of the chairs placed about the room. "Oh, do be seated, Corporal," Darcy told him briskly. "I dare say they have supported less worthy hindquarters than yours. Tell me about yourself."

"Nothin' to tell...Sir," he replied.

"Where have you served?"

"Here an' there."

"Well, then, how is it you know Colonel Fitzwilliam?"

"Never claimed to…Sir,"

Darcy believed he had deciphered the corporal's code: hesitation before the "Sir" signalled prevarication. He decided two could play at this game. "Did I say you had?"

Another faint smile showed on Sands' face. "No, Sir."

"As it happens, I *do* know Colonel Fitzwilliam, and very well: he mentioned you by name, and your being here says he vouches for you. So, how does *he* know *you*?"

"I was a Corporal o' the 'Orse in the Royals. The Colonel wanted me for 'is batman, but on account of a misunderstandin' with a captain, I got volunteered to go to the lowlands last year, instead. When officers got thin in the cavalry, we was assigned to the Grenadiers, and I got blown up a little—bad knee; can't tell, normally, but I can't ride for long. They offered me reg'lar Army, but I'm Cavalry, I am. That's 'ow I'm 'ere."

"'Nothing to tell', I believe you said?" Darcy said, cocking a brow in the man's direction.

"Yes, Sir."

"I should very much like to hear what you might consider worthy of mention," Darcy said drily.

Their breakfast arrived just then: eggs, sausages, cold ham, bread, fresh muffins, two different sorts of cake, scones, butter, honey, and jam. The corporal sniffed appreciatively and gave a cheerful, two-tone whistle, but Darcy held up a restraining hand to the footman. He asked the corporal politely: "Unless you would prefer tea and toast?"

The man finally smiled openly. "No, Lieutenant, I'll make do with this 'ere."

"Excellent; I am obliged to you," Darcy said. Wondering at how the man had calculated his rank, he mentioned: "You know, I imagine, that I have never been in military life. But I have listened to what Colonel Fitzwilliam says, and he always says that feeding the men is the first, and biggest concern for any army, no matter the size."

"The Colonel's a man I wouldn't argue with, Lieutenant," Sands agreed. "Now, wot's this we're about, then?"

Darcy explained while they ate. When he had done, the Corporal, after working half a sausage around in his mouth so he could speak, said "Yer goin' through all this trouble for some article wot run off with a man...Sir?"

"Not at all," Darcy disagreed, noting that he had lost his rank again. "I know her, and, silly as she is, it would hardly be worth the attempt."

"Well then?"

"Her family *is* worth the attempt, and the man is my responsibility; he was brought up at my family's expense, and it is on me to see to it he does not dishonour that endeavour."

The corporal considered this a moment; apparently he found it satisfactory, as he then nodded, saying, "Right; when do we start?"

"As soon as we have done eating."

"I'd rather fight than eat, so let's be gettin' on with it." Prepared to leave that instant, he stood up, wiping his mouth on the back of his hand.

Darcy waved him back to his meal. "Finish your food," he told him, "we have until the carriage is ready."

"Aye, Lieutenant," said the Corporal, sitting down and tucking back into his plate.

Before leaving, Darcy made sure to give him sufficient funds for the needs of his men for a reasonable period of time. The Corporal preferring to ride with the coachman, Darcy was left to himself inside the coach during the ride back to Deptford. When they arrived at Edwards Street, Sands swung down and, clinging to the coach, said through the window, "You wait 'ere whilst I get inside their lines. Lemme 'ave three minutes, then you come in." He dropped easily off the side of the coach and walked down the street towards the house run by Mrs. Younge. Darcy asked himself when the other had taken command of this incursion, but did as he was bidden.

As he approached the door some few minutes later, the sound of a raised voice reached his ears. "Be off with you, I said," a woman's voice cried; Darcy recognised it as belonging to Mrs. Younge, but in an accent far more common that any she normally used in his presence. A man's voice, speaking too low for Darcy to distinguish, answered back. "I don't care about that: leave, I tell you!" came Mrs. Younge's voice again.

Darcy made his entrance without knocking; at the sight of a gentleman at her door, Mrs. Younge appeared momentarily relieved; upon recognising her caller, however, her high colour left her, and she cried, "Mr. Darcy!"

"Mrs. Younge," Darcy acknowledged. "Not whom you were hoping to see?"

The lady merely glowered at him spitefully. "No, I should imagine not," said Darcy. "Let me ask you again: where is George Wickham?"

"He still isn't here, if that's what you're after," she said rudely. "And I am about to call the watch on this ruffian, so if you would rather not come to their notice, I suggest you leave immediately."

Darcy ignored this. "There is only one way for this to end well for you, Mrs. Younge," he said. "Wickham is the only link left between us; sever that link, and I have neither reason, nor desire, ever to seek out your company again. Understand this, though: I *will* find him, and if that means tearing you down to get to him, I shall not hesitate."

Sands asked, "You want me to search for 'im, Captain?" Darcy nodded, gratified to an irrational degree by his field promotion.

Mrs. Younge looked from one to the other, comprehension dawning that they were in league together. "You can't do that," she cried in great indignation, stomping her foot three times on the floor in exasperation: those who make free with others' prerogatives are often quite jealous of their own. Ignoring her, the Corporal left the room. She made as though to follow, but Darcy stepped in front of her and held up a restraining hand.

"'Ere," cried Mrs. Younge, her accent reverting to one whose native haunts were closer to Manchester than Westminster, "You wouldn't 'it a lady!"

"Not on my life," Darcy agreed. "I merely wished to point out that the other gentleman might not be so nice in his manners; and as he would barely notice if you were to hit him with a hammer, I urge you to consider carefully what you expect to accomplish, before going after him."

After that Mrs. Younge merely stood without speaking, looking at Darcy with a hard and calculating eye. The sounds of Corporal Sands moving about the place could be heard; starting at the top floor, he worked his way down, stopping to open various doors, and moving methodically from front to back; back on the ground floor, as he passed the sitting-room he reported: "No one 'ere now, Captain, and only the one woman livin' in the 'ouse." Going through the kitchen, then opening the door to the cellar, Darcy could follow the sound of his steps going down the stairs; suddenly, the crashing noises of a scuffle reached Darcy and his hostess; there was a cry and a heavy thump, followed by a short, cheerful whistle and a lengthy silence. Steps approaching from that direction, Mrs. Younge looked eagerly towards the door to the kitchen, only to sink back into a chair as Corporal Sands reappeared, a satisfied smile on his face.

"'Tis a fine mornin', Captain," he observed, apropos of nothing in particular. "I found a freebooter with a very 'andy little club 'idin' down the cellar. He was 'idin' summat else, too: a big pile o' candlesticks, jewellery boxes, silk 'andkerchiefs, and whatnot. The missus 'ere 'as a side-business, seemingly; I shouldn't wonder if the watch 'ereabouts would be 'appy to know about that."

Darcy felt suddenly at peace: "It *is* a fine morning, Corporal," he agreed.

Chapter Sixteen

*J*ust past noon Darcy and Corporal Sands arrived in Whitechapel, where Mrs. Younge had supplied them a direction in George Street. As the coach could not negotiate the narrow by-ways of the neighbourhood, Darcy sent it home. They began at St. Mary's, as she had told them the address was in that parish, but they had considerable difficulty finding their way. The day was overcast, and with no sun to steer by, it was easy to get turned about in the warren-like streets; and they very soon learned that the locals' information was not to be trusted, having been sent on several detours that had ended at establishments for the entertainment of men.

From the church, they searched to the east and south along the dirty streets and alleys bordering Whitechapel Street. Darcy and the Corporal had decided to come on their own to perform the search, rather than deploy all of their men; the Corporal had felt they would be less conspicuous that way. Less conspicuous was a relative term, as Darcy, always tall, and to-day, far too well-dressed for his surroundings, drew the attention of the urchins, hawkers, and muslins at every turning. It was slow going, and they eventually took to the expediency of having him trail Corporal Sands by twenty or thirty paces, allowing Sands to progress unimpeded out in front.

They were to spend some hours in this manner, searching the close and weary dens south of the high street; it was getting on in the afternoon when they crossed Whitechapel and proceeded up Osborn. It was there they encountered their first real incident of note: as the light from the sun behind the clouds began to fade, Darcy suddenly found himself set upon by two men; the first, wielding a knife that missed being a sword by inches only, stepped right out in front of him; he was wiry and quick of movement, holding his weapon with practiced ease. The second, a hulking beast of a man, though unarmed, got between Darcy and Sands, obviously intent on delaying Sands from coming to Darcy's aid.

When Darcy had been up at Oxford, he had, along with most young men of his class, taken lessons in the sword at a *salle d'armes* in town. Darcy had enjoyed the exercise a good deal, but there had been one individual whom Darcy never could abide, who was a most devoted student of the rapier; rather than undergo the daily aggravation of practising with this disobliging individual, Darcy had turned to the single-stick. His pleasure in the art had given him application, and, by the time he left, he was more than proficient. At the time it had all been rather for his enjoyment and convenience, but now it turned to material advantage, as a walking-stick differed from a single-stick only by the lack of a guard. He had the reach on his assailant by more than a foot, and addressed his blade *en garde* in third almost with amusement.

The footpad, seeing that Darcy had no intention of yielding easily, lost a good deal of his initial enthusiasm and swagger; he began circling Darcy, looking for an opening. Darcy took a quick scan of the footing around him, and noticed too that the crowded street had become suddenly empty. From behind him, he could hear Corporal Sands giving out as good as he got; his cheery whistle told Darcy there was little to worry about from that quarter. The man before Darcy, waving his blade sinuously in front of him, made an exploratory lunge to test Darcy, but his distance was faulty, and he came within reach of Darcy's arm; Darcy took his blade in fourth with a *riposte volante* to the left, which he carried down to low-line, cutting back hard across the kneecap with the brass tip of his walking stick. As the man cried out, Darcy administered a soporific that quieted his cries: a solid *coup de taille montante* that caught the man on the left angle of the jaw, bringing his adversary an instant, alleviating sedation, temporarily putting him beyond the pain which his knee, and now his jaw, would know for weeks to come.

Darcy spun now to his rear, executing a *passe avant* to reach the other two, and finished with a heavy blow to the sinews on the back of the larger man's heel just as he took his weight on that foot to leap at Sands; while the timing of this manœuvre was entirely fortuitous, the results were both impressive and satisfying: instead of vaulting forward at Sands, the man's leg gave way under him directly; clutching at his leg as he fell, his skull came down on the curbing with a resounding crack, and suddenly all was still. Sands looked in surprise at the man on the ground before him, then at Darcy; he then looked over to the other man where he lay motionless, his knife still in his grip, and finally back again to Darcy; he gave a low-pitched whistle and rubbed his cheek in wonder. While astounded at his good luck and the ease of his victory, Darcy met the Corporal's gaze impassively — though he held his features in check with difficulty: his elation at having the whole engagement go so perfectly, as thoroughly in his favour as any he had ever imagined as "Dirks Darcy" in the woods at Rosings, made him want to dance about and wave his fists in the air. Such a very un-piratical display would, naturally, rob his performance of much of its effect, so he contented himself with a little twirling flourish as he brought his stick back to its proper place under his hand. Sands went to the smaller man and, kicking the blade from his hand, reached down and retrieved it; he offered it to Darcy, who declined with a gesture. The corporal tucked the blade into his belt at the back under his coat by way of compensation for his troubles, and, with a new respect, gestured for Darcy to precede him.

While they were able, after this, to proceed unhindered through the streets for the first time in hours, with the crowded streets parting miraculously before them, Darcy questioned the wisdom of staying on after dark; it would not do to trust his luck to such a degree twice in one day, nor did he like the attention their skirmish had given them; in addition, the Corporal, while not seeming to notice, had not escaped as easily from his struggle as Darcy had from his; he was bruised and bloodied, and Darcy thought the two of them had best be off the streets. However, just then they found the looked-for street, and the very unprepossessing inn whose direction Mrs. Younge had given them. Darcy, at a bit of a loss, said, "Corporal, you need attention and I should not be seen here; yet it goes against the grain to leave just when we have him."

"Aye, Major; just you stay put right 'ere," Sands told him, gesturing to a recessed doorway; he then slouched across the street to the inn. Darcy reflected happily on the agreeable prospect of his out-ranking his cousin by day's end, if events continued at their present pace. In a moment Sands reappeared, and, motioning Darcy to step around a corner into an alleyway, joined him there. "'E's there, right enough," he confirmed. He looked round until he spotted a ragamuffin boy with an intelligent face. "Hi there, Jonny! —come 'ere," he waved him over, some coins showing in his palm. The lad stepped over warily, one eye on the coins, and the other searching the vicinity for a trap. "You'll do," Sands drawled. "'Ere lad, see this?" he said, showing him the miniature of Wickham. "This young blood bides over in that 'ouse across the street. You seen 'im?"

"What if I 'ave?" the boy asked suspiciously.

"'E's a sharper, is what, and this gen'leman 'ere wants 'im."

"Wot's in it fer me?"

"Enough," answered Sands, "if you can stay awake long enough for me an' my mates to get back 'ere." He tossed the boy a ha'penny, who snatched it dextrously out of the air. "That's for starters, and if you and the swell are both still 'ere when we get back, there's thrupence waitin' for you."

The lad thought it over, then spat in his hand and offered it to Sands, who solemnly repeated the ritual; they shook on it.

"What are you called?" asked Darcy.

"My name is Tibbs, Mister," the youth replied, and Darcy found himself possessed of another vassal. The corporal then led Darcy back to St. Mary's and on down the high street. They took the first hackney coach they could find back to Grosvenor Square; sitting back against the seat, Sands grunted and sat forward again; reaching behind him, he pulled out the long knife he had tucked into his belt. He gave it an appreciative look, then, seeing Darcy's eye on it as well, passed it politely to him. As Darcy looked it over, he felt some qualms about his willingness to engage it in combat: it was a savage thing, and unwholesomely sharp. He looked down at his walking stick, and observed a four-inch gash marring its finish, about a third of the way up from the tip. "Blast!" he swore; the cane was a favourite, and he was sorry to have injured it. Sands, tucking the knife back behind him, settled back and closed his eyes; soon his contented snores announced he was sleeping, as any experienced campaigner will, when there is no chance of action in the offing; Darcy, however, was not inclined to join him, as the prospect of tightening the net around his quarry was too exciting to allow for repose.

When they arrived at Grosvenor Square, Darcy had the driver wait and sent Sands below stairs for some beefsteak to put on two or three beautiful bruises that were rising on his face, and to get some food in him. When he came back up some little while later, he looked well-fed and well-pleased, but rather more tattered and begrimed even than when he went down; he had applied what appeared to be a mixture of soot and grease here and there to his face and clothes. Darcy looked at him quizzically. "I can't go back there all 'igh in the instep, now, can I, Major?" he grinned. "People might come arter me with knives." Still grinning, he gave a whistle, pointing at Darcy, and swaggered off down the steps to the waiting cab. As he climbed in, he called, "You'll see me in the morning!" As the cab started to roll, Sands gave out three short, piercing whistles, and the rest of his men appeared swiftly from various positions about the house: from behind the steps, lounging by the side wall, and several came up from the space below street level that gave onto the kitchen; with four inside, one by the driver, and the rest perched on top, the hackney set off for Whitechapel.

Chapter Seventeen

The next morning, Darcy was up early, having slept but lightly; to-day was to be a day of extraordinary importance to him; it was just short of one year ago that he had found Wickham with Georgiana at Ramsgate, and five since he had quitted Lambton, leaving another stew for Darcy to settle, not to mention the innumerable lesser failures of his younger years, when he had attempted to impeach Wickham before Pemberley's master; now he was finally about to pull this thorn in his side, bringing Wickham to justice; it had been long—very long—in coming. He could almost be grateful to Miss Lydia Bennet for having brought the thing to such a point, and giving him the impetus to set it to rights at last.

Just as Darcy finished breakfast, Corporal Sands came to Grosvenor Square and the two of them went directly back to George Street. On their way thither, the Corporal explained the situation to Darcy: "Me and the lads were in and out last night accordin' to plan; I made sure each of 'em got a look at yer boy. He doesn't know we're onto 'im, and there's two of us there now; I made sure of 'im afore I come to get you."

"When we get there, I shall want you to go in first," Darcy told him. "He will likely bolt at the first sign of me; if you would be so kind as to prevent him from succeeding, I should be obliged.

"That'll be my pleasure, Major," said Sands, giving a happy little whistle.

That made Darcy advise him: "I am afraid he will offer little by way of physical resistance, Corporal; less even than Mrs. Younge, I suspect."

The corporal frowned, his forthright countenance showing deep disapprobation. "Now, that's not right," he judged. "No man should give in that easy. 'Ere I was thinkin' I'd be 'is jailor, and now you're tellin' me I'm to be 'is nanny! No, Captain, t'isn't proper."

So Darcy had once more been demoted; but, he reflected, so long as he held an officer's rank, he supposed he ought to be grateful. In general, though, the Corporal's attitude was encouraging; he was right: if Wickham was that easily cowed, and he was, this would not be a very difficult morning at all.

On their arrival in Whitechapel, the Corporal again preceded Darcy down the narrow streets, but Darcy was almost beginning to feel familiar with the neighbourhood. He let Sands have a minute or two to position himself and his men, then walked in openly through the door. The low ceiling and beams of the room were darkly stained with smoke, and the few small windows were tinged brown; most of the ground floor was taken up by a tap-room, and it was there that his quarry waited. Wickham was seated at a table to Darcy's left as he entered, and Sands was lounging by the door on that side, one hand in his coat pocket, the other holding a pipe. Squinting through the smoke, he glanced Darcy's way, then looked away indifferently; Wickham, however, looked towards the door and, starting at the sight of Darcy, gave a loud cry of alarm. Darcy thought that was going a bit far, but soon discovered it was not entirely for his benefit: from across the room, a largish man, heavy-set and very bleary-eyed, lifted his head from where it lay on his arms; with a roar he rose to his feet and charged Darcy. Many things happened all at once; Darcy took a firm grip on his stick and braced to meet the bellowing drunkard; Wickham was up and moving, making a dash for the rear as the other two of Sands' men closed in on him; as the large man charged heavily at Darcy, by his side Sands gave a contented grunt and stepped forward with a perfectly timed right hand that caught the man in the midriff, stopping his charge in mid-step and folding him over completely. As every thing slowed back down, Darcy heard the Corporal's cheery, satisfied whistle once more, and saw Wickham flanked by the other two men, looking very dispirited and rather mussed about.

"Now, that was nice an' tidy, as per plan," opined Sands. "I *knew* I could trust you, Major; bein' around a man such as yerself just '*as* to lead t' trouble. Lads, bring that rabbit over 'ere." After that, Darcy decided not to attempt to keep up with his advancements and demotions any longer; at any rate, he needed to focus now on Wickham.

He sat down at a nearby table; as Wickham was placed in a chair opposite him, Darcy reflected on how different this all was: this time, he held all the trumps; this time he need not convince any one of Wickham's misdeeds; this time Wickham was solely answerable to him: he was accuser, judge, and jury. Having devised what he hoped would be a cage strong enough to hold Wickham for years to come, he once more reviewed the scheme; he saw no flaws, and, so far, every thing was going according to his expectations. He was curiously dispassionate at that moment; he had rather thought he would be fraught with all manner of emotions when this time came, but what he felt most was caution: appreciating the need for care, lest his quarry slip free.

As he stared across the stained table top, he reminded himself that Wickham, once caught in a lie, would only offer another; therefore, rather than bother listening to him, he decided his first concern ought to be Miss Lydia Bennet.

"Corporal, do we know if the young lady accompanying him is here now?" he asked.

"Tewkes, is the piece still 'ere?" the Corporal asked one of the men behind Wickham.

"Aye, Corporal: she ain't come down at all yet."

Darcy winced at the designation: "Corporal Sands, whilst I cannot argue you are unjustly offensive in referring to her so, out of respect for the family…" at this Wickham, who had yet to speak, gave a short, barking laugh, "…out of respect for the family," Darcy continued, ignoring Wickham's interruption, "I should be obliged to you if you would refer to the lady as Mrs. Wickham." He amended her name just at the last, realising that to call her by her right name in an establishment such as this would be to ruin her as surely as ever Wickham would have. Wickham shifted in his seat, but offered no objection.

"Before we begin, Wickham," Darcy said by way of opening, "I confess myself curious: how are your present circumstances at all superior to marriage into the young lady's family? I realise her father is not quite as wealthy as you might wish, but certainly it would have to be better than this," he gestured to the sordid room, where two men, evidently deep in their cups, still snored at a corner table, oblivious to every thing that had just happened.

"Marriage? To Lydia? You must be joking, Darcy," Wickham said in casual accents. "Were her father twice — no, thrice — as well-off as he is, it would not be enough to tempt me."

"If that is how you feel, I wonder that you brought her with you; she could only have made travel more difficult, and more likely that some one would come after you. In fact, I certainly would not have troubled, were it not out of concern for her family."

"Always the honourable one, eh Fitzwilliam?" Wickham said in a sneering manner.

Wickham's insolence triggered the hot anger which had been curiously absent until that point, but he forced it down; with a hard stare, he replied, "Wickham, these men are here primarily to make sure you do not wander off. Let that tongue of yours loose again, however, and I am sure they would happily hold my hat and coat whilst

I remind you of your manners." One of the men behind Wickham muttered an appreciative "Aye!" and Wickham hunched down deeper in his chair as though to ward off a blow from that quarter. When he did not speak, Darcy prodded him with: "Why did you bring her, then?"

"I never did," Wickham said scornfully, as though the idea were absurd. "She came on her own; when I told her I was off, she was wild to come on the 'adventure'; the silly minx thinks we are on excursion."

Darcy made no comment on his ill-mannered way of speaking of Lydia, as he had a question that he very much wanted an answer to: he asked off-handedly, "Then why did you leave Brighton, if not for her sake?"

Wickham shifted uncomfortably in his seat, then, with the air of a man resigning himself to the inevitable, he said, "I was in rather deep to some of the officers; I was all done up: a string of the worst luck imaginable; when they started talking seriously of taking a pound of flesh, I thought it best to retire to a more hospitable setting."

This, of course, was just what Darcy hoped to hear, although nothing less than he expected; but, not having heard from Colonel Forster as yet, he was quite relieved to have confirmation for his suppositions. He could not forebear to ask, however: "But what was your plan?"

"I had none, really," Wickham said indifferently. "I thought perhaps an acquaintance here in Town might have something for me, or…I just had to get away—that's the whole of it. I shall, of course, resign my commission; then at least Forster will have no reason to chase after me, but as for the rest…I have no idea; something will come up."

"But her father undoubtedly could have been of *some* assistance, surely, had you married," Darcy pointed out.

Wickham shook his head dismissively. "Once I got loose, I knew I could do much better: an heiress in Bath, or perhaps Ireland—even the Americas."

"So you went to Mrs. Younge," said Darcy.

Wickham looked at him momentarily, understanding crossing his features. "She sold me to you," he stated bitterly.

"Well, I did apply to her interests, yes," replied Darcy, not untruthfully.

"I might have known," Wickham grumbled.

"Yes, you might," agreed Darcy easily, sensing things were well in hand, now he had confirmation of Wickham's debts. "But at present, the only one of your companions I have any interest in is the one staying in this…well, call it an inn, by courtesy. If you would let the lady know I shall be attending her shortly, I should be obliged. Corporal, would be so good as to make sure they do not misplace themselves before I come up?" Sands made a small salute and gestured to the men to let Wickham go. They trooped upstairs together; Darcy, left on his own, inspected his surroundings; the barman, who had been watching with a wary eye this whole time, decided things were not going to end in damage to his establishment, and went back about his business, ducking his eyes away from Darcy's gaze. The large drunkard felled by the Corporal got slowly to his feet, having been down this whole time, and staggered out into the street, holding his arms around his belly and groaning ominously, leaning against the walls to support his progress. After his inspection was complete, Darcy wisely abstained from ordering refreshment.

It was not long before one of the men came to fetch him; Darcy caught the barman's eye, and left a gold sovereign on the table. The man's eyes went round, and he made an unschooled bow, but with all the respect he could manage; Darcy was thereby assured that there would be no difficulties from that quarter, no matter what the Corporal and his men got up to.

Wickham and Lydia were lodged on the top floor just under the eaves; Sands and his men stood outside the door with Wickham. Darcy said, "Please tell Mrs. Wickham I will see her now." Wickham went in briefly, and, re-opening the door, he bid Darcy to enter. Darcy told him, "I will see her alone."

"Certainly not," Wickham objected, but not very forcibly. The Corporal turned slowly to face him...but Wickham's eyes failed to meet his, and the men escorted Wickham back down the stairs, the Corporal making a low, disgusted whistle as they left. Darcy entered the room, finding himself in a small, cluttered room in which the bed was the main article of furniture. Indeed, it drew the attention most notably because it was still occupied: the youngest Miss Bennet had disdained to bother with her toilette before greeting her guest, and was holding a sheet to her shoulders with no apparent concern for the proprieties. Darcy made a slow examination of the room before turning his attention to her; clothing cluttered the floor, and empty bottles and dirty wine glasses lined the bedside tables. At length he turned to Lydia, who had something of a smile on her lips. "What amuses you, Miss Bennet?" he enquired.

The smile turned to a pout; "Now you've spoilt it!" she cried. "You were the first to call me Mrs. Wickham, and now you've gone and ruined it!"

Darcy, rather taken aback that — under the circumstances — this should be a concern, looked at her in consternation. "Miss Bennet..." he began, but she interrupted him, insisting: "No! You must call me Mrs. Wickham!"

"That, I never shall, unless you actually be married," he informed her firmly. At this she put on a face like that of a child pouting to get its way, and Darcy was reminded of the qualities of the person he addressed. He continued, "Without any wish to dwell on your present circumstances, I have come to offer you any assistance you might require in order to be reunited with your friends. Your family, I know, is extremely worried about you, and I cannot but imagine that, by now, you have tired of this style of living, and are anxious to return to them."

"And that *I* never shall," she contradicted him. "I've never been happier in my life; we are having such fun! Dear Wickham is all I could wish for, and all I want. La! Go home? Do you expect that I should ever leave Wickham?"

Darcy, looking about the room in a pointed manner, asked: "Is this life truly preferable to residing respectably amongst your family?" He could scarcely credit such.

"We have ever so much more fun here than ever I had in Meryton," she asserted with some heat, "and I need no help of yours — nor my family's. Wickham and me are doing very well, thank you, and I certainly shall not leave him. As for respectable, we shall marry soon enough, and if I don't care, it surely can be none of your concern, so you may keep your assistance!" Darcy, quite convinced by now that respectability could not be an object with her, considered only briefly before capitulating: "Very well, Miss Bennet; please do not hesitate to call on me should you change your mind." He then turned and left her.

Wickham was back in the taproom with the Corporal and his men. "I congratulate you, Wickham," said Darcy. "I imagine few men could inspire such loyalty in a woman they do not care a fig about." Wickham shrugged indifferently; he seemed perfectly at ease, and Darcy felt he needed to give him cause for concern, if not alarm, were the negotiation ahead of them to go forward favourably. Looked at from Wickham's side, Lydia's disinclination to accept Darcy's assistance put him in a much stronger position; as Darcy had said, were it not for the need to return her to her friends, there could be no reason for pursuit. Looking at him, Darcy determined on his approach.

"Do you know, Wickham," he said reflectively, "there is one thing at which you have ever excelled, far surpassing almost any one else in the whole of my acquaintance."

Wickham looked at Darcy with polite expectation. "Lies," Darcy said distinctly. The man named Tewkes sniggered, but the other two remained impassive. Wickham, disinclined to argue the point under the circumstances, merely looked away disdainfully. "Quite honestly," continued Darcy, "you are very nearly the most accomplished liar I have ever met; a lady here in Town can best you, I own, and by a good long chalk, but you are an absolutely uncontested second." At this, the ghost of a smile appeared on Corporal Sands' face. "Well, I mean to help you to attain perfection in the art to which you have devoted yourself: from this day forward, you are going to live the lie of being a respectable husband; and, by month's end, that of being an upstanding officer in His Majesty's Army."

"Really?" Wickham smirked. "And why should I attempt such an odd thing?"

"For the same reason you do most things," Darcy said. "Money."

"Come, now, that's sounding better," Wickham brightened and sat straighter in his chair. Behind him the Corporal frowned, but Darcy's assured smile set his mind at ease. Wickham said, "Well, now…you couldn't expect me to take that on for less than…well, fifteen thousands has a nice feel to it." He looked at Darcy expectantly.

In wonder, Darcy observed, "How easily that came out! How is it you do not see, Wickham, that you are lucky not to be in prison, or dead? What makes you think it is no more than ask and have, with neither responsibility nor penalty for the damage you have done?"

"That is how it is, Darcy," said Wickham imperturbably. "Money comes to me: it always has done. I knew something would turn up, and it has; not what I expected, of course, but still…"

His assertion amazed Darcy: it was true—somehow, Wickham always managed to get by, no matter how deep a hole he put himself in; Darcy was not to forget this point in the ensuing years; at the moment, however, it elicited this response: "I beg your pardon," said he, "but you mistake me: I meant that I am now collecting and paying off all your debts, including those to the officers in Brighton; of course, so long as you do what is fitting and right, and cause the Bennets no more harm to than you already have, I shall have no reason to bother myself further in the matter. If, however, you should take it into your head to pick up where you left off with your previous life, I should be obliged to have these gentlemen collect you and deliver you to Fleet Prison...or perhaps King's Bench. What say you, Corporal: Fleet, or King's Bench?"

"Well, Major, Fleet's been re-built better, but it's 'arder; King's Bench 'as the typhus mostly, but they gener'lly treat a man better there."

Darcy smiled pleasantly at Wickham: "Fleet, it is, then," said he in a satisfied air. "And now, if you will excuse me, I shall leave you to ponder those options—but I shall be pleased to call again to-morrow. These gentlemen will stay on with you, however; I trust you will find their company agreeable."

Chapter Eighteen

*D*arcy and the Corporal went together back to Grosvenor Square; there they discussed certain strategies and contingencies for more than two hours, as Darcy was fully convinced Wickham would try an escape before much time had elapsed. Corporal Sands was sure his men could keep the two secure for the day, but he did return to the inn later in the afternoon; in addition, at the Corporal's suggestion they had agreed to keep the boy, Tibbs, on as a scout, as he would be able to blend in on the streets in a manner no adult could hope to match.

Darcy also had the pleasure of receiving an entirely satisfactory letter from Colonel Forster, detailing Wickham's debts; even without the gaming debts, there was more than enough to send Wickham to Fleet Prison for an extremely long stay. He sent a note round to his solicitor, Mr. Colster—a gentleman as ancient and dry as the books that lined his chambers—inviting him to dine that evening; then, when the Corporal left, Darcy, too, went out into town, to secure the services of a young artist of whom he had heard, who specialised in miniatures. Later, Colster came to dinner, and afterwards they spent three-quarters of an hour together in the library writing several documents, to which Colster made several important amendments; then Darcy retired early, as the morrow would be eventful.

As he lay in bed, his thoughts again turned to Elizabeth; but in this case it was with more anxiety than longing; as much as he was doing all this for her sake, he very much feared the outcome if she ever heard of it. Her mortification at the depth of his knowledge into her family's disgrace would drive a wedge between them far greater even than his interference in her elder sister's affairs. He would have to find some means of ensuring that neither of the two principals would find it useful or desirable to make his actions known.

The next morning he prepared for the day with some eagerness; he went back to Whitechapel directly he finished breakfast: there he found Wickham and the Corporal once again seated in the taproom, but now Wickham's head was bound across the forehead with a blood-stained cloth. As Darcy came into the room, the Corporal whistled a few bars of a regimental march. "'Ere 'e is, the man o' the hour!" He stood and saluted, gesturing happily to Wickham's bandaged head. "It was just like you said, Major." Darcy winked at the Corporal without answering, taking a moment to inspect Wickham's wounds: they did not appear severe. Taking his seat, he gestured to the Corporal to give him his report.

"Me an' Larsen was 'ere in the taproom 'bout an hour, might be two, past midnight, when we 'ears this fellow a-tiptoeing down the stairs. So, just like we planned, we pretends to be asleep, and, slick as you please, 'e's gone out the door. We 'adn't even got to th' door afore the lads outside 'ad 'im down and trussed like a duck."

"Did he see any of them?" Darcy enquired sharply.

"'E did *not*," gloated the Corporal. "No more than Jenny's blind mule."

"Excellent," said Darcy.

"What is all this, Darcy?" Wickham spoke at last, irritably eyeing both his jailors and his warden.

"Just a demonstration, Wickham," answered Darcy frankly. "I want you to understand just how serious I am about this, and how far I am willing to go to ensure its success. From this day forward, and for years to come, you will seldom be unobserved, and you will never know when that will be. The men I have engaged have been mustered out of the army, and are entirely at my disposal for as long as I have need; and I assure you, retaining them is far less expensive, and far more gratifying, than paying down your debts every few years. You have seen some, but by no means all of them; take a look at the faces around you. Periodically, as you go about your life, you will see one or the other of them, just as a reminder of the others, unknown to you, who will be following you as well."

Just then, a young man, thickly bearded and wearing a foreign sort of hat, came through the door, carrying with him an easel and an artist's wooden box. He bowed crisply to Darcy, checked a miniature painting in his hand, looked at Wickham, and nodded. "And zis bandage?" he asked Darcy in a noticeable German accent.

"No, no need; while it might well have to be renewed from time to time, I am sure Mr. Wickham is too intelligent to require us to make it a permanent feature."

"And this is?" enquired Wickham with some heat.

"This is Herr Grundig, Wickham; he will be doing your portrait, in miniature, to match the one you sat for to oblige my father. Miniatures are his speciality; I have commissioned him to make quite a number of copies. In fact, he need not have seen you: I have seen his work, and he could easily have made the copies directly from my father's miniature, but he thought it would be best this way."

Wickham tried to appear uncaring, but there was *that* in his eye that spoke of feelings not so wholly sanguine. "I wanted to have them ready to hand," Darcy explained, "to send to all the ports, should you turn up missing at any time." Moving along, he said: "And then there is this." He held up the letter he had received from Colonel Forster, letting Wickham see the signature. "We have here an accounting of your debts both in Brighton and amongst the regiment; I have purchased them, through Colonel Forster, and, as they are now mine, I hereby demand payment in full, before these witnesses. Corporal, how are your ciphers?"

"Good enough," the Corporal answered. "Better than most."

"Can you recognise this figure?" asked Darcy, pointing to a number at the bottom of a long list, on another document he had taken from his coat pocket.

"Aye, but it don't look quite right, Major; one pound, fourteen and five don't seem to add up, nor it don't sound like much to put a man in prison for, neither."

"No, Corporal; not pounds, shillings, pence: try thousands, hundreds, tens, and ones," said Darcy, pointing.

"You mean to tell me this sharper owes that much?" cried the Corporal, his voice rising at the end; he snatched the document from Darcy's hand and stared at it as though it were a negotiable security in that amount. Darcy nodded in answer to his question. "To 'oo?!"

"About half is owing his fellow officers in the militia regiment which has the misfortune of claiming him as their own: gambling debts. The rest is to tradesmen and shopkeepers in Brighton, so far as we have been able collect."

"You never told me 'e was in no militia," said the Corporal reproachfully, giving the paper back to Darcy. "And 'e took that much off 'is mess mates, then run off? —now, that's too bad, even for a militia man." He gave Wickham a look with very little love in it. "Coo! I sees wot you mean, Major: this bachelor's son needs watchin' and no mistake. I wonder you don't just leave 'im in a shallow grave, somewhere the crows can get at 'im; or better yet, 'am-string 'im and 'and 'im over to 'is mates."

"That would seem to be the proper military response," observed Darcy drily. "Colonel Fitzwilliam suggested much the same thing."

"I told you the Colonel's a man 'oo knows wot's wot," said the Corporal, nodding in agreement.

Turning to Wickham, Darcy said, "Well, there is another option for you to consider, Wickham; to oblige *you*, I should be happy to investigate that as an alternative."

To this, Wickham did not deign to respond.

"And of course, you may put an end to all of this at any time, simply by calling the watch; in that case, we would naturally bring charges of desertion, abduction, fraud, gambling, and various and sundry other offenses, but I assure you, neither I nor any of these men will stop you, should you be so inclined." Darcy here paused to give Wickham a chance to speak, but still he held his silence. "No? Well, any time you decide it is in your best interest. Now, this," he said, producing another paper from his pocket, "is an acknowledgement, by you, that the debt is true, and that it is now due in full. These men will witness it." He called to the barman for pen and ink; the man scratched his head a moment, then allowed as there "might be some out back".

"Tell him not to bother, Darcy: I will not sign any such thing," said Wickham.

"I rather thought you might feel that way," Darcy said, "so I shall now be sending this." He took out and showed a letter to Wickham. "It is to Colonel Forster, informing him of your whereabouts, and assuring him that my men will hold you here until he has leisure to come and fetch you. And, as you decline my offer of protection, I can have nothing to say that would stop these gentlemen from demonstrating on your person how they feel about a soldier who does his own down." At this, a feral smile split the Corporal's face, and he let out an eager whistle. The other two men made unsettlingly savage noises of anticipation as well; Wickham looked from one to another, the confidence ebbing from his features entirely. The barman just then arriving with a small ink pot and a rather dispirited-looking quill, Darcy turned an expectant face to Wickham; with an angry sneer sent in

Darcy's direction, he pulled the acknowledgement to him and applied his signature.

Chapter Nineteen

*D*arcy returned home very much pleased with the day's accomplishments; no matter how he looked at it, it appeared to him that he had stopt up all the earths his fox could run to. He sat down to write Georgiana about his progress.

Grosvenor Square
Wednesday, August 6th, —

Dear Georgiana,

Well, it has been a busy few days, but I am now able to report that we have made considerable progress, and met with good success thus far. I was able to trace Miss Lydia Bennet successfully to an inn in London, although a part of London I trust you will never have cause to visit. Unfortunately, she has attached herself to the fellow without reserve or condition, and is resolute in her intention of staying with him; I was unable persuade her otherwise. As little esteem as I have for her, I did most sincerely urge her to return to her friends, although I confess her obstinacy prevented me from urging the matter as strenuously as I might.

Her refusal leaves nothing to be done but arrange for their marriage, and I shall put that in motion shortly; I must first communicate with her family: fortunately, in the Gardiners I have a ready entrée, there. My plan, it would seem, is holding up, and I have hopes that all will be finalised before the month is out. I do not imagine I shall be needed here in London all that while, so I trust you will see me again at Pemberley before long.

In all truth, Dearest, I confess I am unsure as to which of the two principals will suffer most from these arrangements; but, as it is owing entirely to their own actions that they find themselves in this position, I cannot condemn myself for forcing its conclusion. Miss Lydia Bennet clearly expected marriage to be the ultimate outcome of this adventure, as she seems to characterise it in her mind, and, given the enormity of the damage the failure to bring about their nuptials would cause the Bennets, it seems only right to me that he satisfy those expectations. He is like a river in flood, destroying whatever is in its path, and prudence demands that that flood be channelled, lest it lay ruin to entire counties; the steps I have taken will, I hope, stem the course of that flood and, if not contain it completely, at least gentle it to the point that its damage is confined only to those attached to him.

The Bennets, I dare say, would never have compounded for such a son-in-law, but there is nothing else that may be done to save them; I pity them for what their future will hold, but, given her character, the girl would never have chosen well or wisely, so on their side I suppose all this is little more than what was inevitable; it is, at least, finished early and, I hope, quietly.

My real pity is reserved for Miss Elizabeth Bennet, as she, I know, thought well of the fellow, and now must recognise and live with the knowledge of his character, and accept him as brother. Her mother, in all likelihood, will find nothing exceptional in the match, and her father seems largely indifferent to his family's affairs;

while not a man without ability, he adopts a very sardonic outlook, and, with three silly daughters and a very silly wife, one perhaps cannot wonder.

Speaking of indifference, it is the indifference of that low person I seek to constrain, to the suffering he causes the innocent and the worthy, that angers me most. Were he to confine his misdeeds to such as his soon-to-be wife, who has not the acuity to realise she suffers, or to the miscreants who populate his world, here in his proper milieu amongst the lower haunts of London, he would be relatively innocuous. But, I shall hope that the manner in which I have him hemmed in will render him that mildly unpleasant nuisance he ought to be, and leave decent people free of his influence. I pray it may be so.

But now, Dearest, I am going to take myself off to my club, and indulge in a little celebratory dinner, and toast to a future where you and I might never need speak of the man again. Your loving brother,
Fitzwilliam Darcy

Post scriptum:
Please tell my aunt that I have taken her advice to heart, and have followed it to good effect.

Thereafter, in rather buoyant spirits, he dressed and went to White's, to enjoy an afternoon of easy company, a good meal, and a rather special bottle of wine. From time to time through the evening, he thought of Wickham in his taproom, and was at peace.

The next day when Darcy returned once more to the inn, he was surprised to find Wickham more seriously battered about than previously; there were a number of scrapes and bruises here and there on his person, and an ugly, ragged tear down one ear. The corporal and his men stood with belligerent faces, hovering threateningly behind Wickham where he was seated; Darcy looked to the Corporal questioningly.

"This monkey 'ad more fight in 'im than we thought," said the smaller man. "'E went out the window last night just as it were dark, an' climbed down the drain pipe. But Tibbs was onto 'im right smart, an' comes to fetch us. This back door boy," he said angrily, pointing to Wickham, "wasn't 'avin' any; 'e takes a knife to Tewkes — gets 'is shoulder; only missed 'is throat by inches. I were 'ard pressed to keep the lads from doin' for 'im, Major, but orders is orders."

"I am obliged to you, Corporal," Darcy acknowledged gratefully. "It might help your men to realise that their discipline has saved a family from ruin." Looking at the other two men behind Wickham, he nodded to include them in his thanks. Neither looked pleased, but they nodded back. "Will Tewkes be well?"

"Aye, 'e'll make it," said the Corporal.

"Be sure he sees a surgeon," Darcy instructed. "Have you funds enough?" The corporal nodded.

At this point, Wickham, who had yet to speak, broke in sneeringly, "Yes, he'll live; but I swear, Darcy, you may as well kill me now, if you think I am going to live forever in *either* of the prisons you have planned for me."

Darcy looked at him in surprise at such audacious language. "Well, Wickham, you astound me, I confess: where did *you* find any courage?"

"It has nothing to do with courage," Wickham said angrily. "Death would be far better than a life of poverty — either with Lydia, *or* in Fleet Prison; there could hardly be any difference; I swear to you, you will never hold me."

"Death before honour, is that it, Wickham?" Darcy scoffed.

Wickham pronounced a word well-suited to his surroundings. "If you expect me to live your lie, then you had best make the lie a liveable one," he said angrily. "Do you really expect I would throw away my life on Lydia for a lieutenant's pay?"

Darcy was unmoved: "You are to be an ensign, actually; and I suppose it would be unnecessary to mention the possibility of advancement, given time and a bit of actual work—but, yes—I should expect so, indeed, given the alternative, and the fact that you have already imposed on the largesse of my family to the tune of five thousands and more." A low growl emanated from the Corporal's throat on hearing this; Wickham glanced uneasily at him, then back to Darcy.

"'Alternative'!" Wickham spat the word. "And if I do go to prison, what becomes of the Bennets? Do you suppose I have given that no thought?"

"If you are able to see things that clearly, then if you do decide to ruin the Bennets, what do you suppose my instructions to these gentlemen will be? They had little enough love for you before, and now you have tried to kill one of them."

"I did no such thing," Wickham said heatedly, "He was about to bounce a dashed great club off my head, and I had to stop him somehow."

"With a knife," Darcy observed.

"Yes, with a knife!" Wickham argued. "Do you suppose I would use my bare hands?"

"Does it not occur to you, that by arming yourself, you forced him to use a weapon, and he chose one less lethal than your own?"

"Does it not occur to *you* that you have no right to hold me a prisoner?" demanded Wickham in mocking accents. "What *would* your dear father say to all this?"

At this, something in Darcy snapped with an almost audible report; the Corporal was standing to Darcy's right, staring angrily down at Wickham; without thought, Darcy snatched the big knife from behind the Corporal's back and, lunging across the table, swung it down at Wickham; in later years he never could be sure just how he stopped from killing him — he believed it may have been a fleeting thought of Elizabeth that deflected the blow and spared the life of his enemy; but whatever it may have been, he buried the tip of the blade two inches into the table top between Wickham's elbows, rather than his chest. "One...more...word," he ground out, "and I...*will*...kill you." His eyes blazing not a foot from Wickham's, he kept his hand on the blade, almost hoping Wickham would take up his dare.

But Wickham was no fool when it came to his own skin, and held his tongue; in any event, he looked too frightened for speech. When Wickham's terrified eyes looked away from his, Darcy felt the murderous rage leave him; he sat back, working to control his breathing. The corporal reached over to take the weapon out of the table, but it refused to yield. Grunting in surprise, he applied both hands to the task, his muscles straining; slowly the wood groaned and released the blade. All the men around the table looked at Darcy in amazement at this evidence of the force of the blow: the Corporal looked uneasily at him; he inspected the tip carefully before turning a shocked face back to Darcy.

"I do apologise, Corporal," Darcy said, passing a hand across his brow. He had almost undone the good that all their discipline and restraint had done for Elizabeth and the Bennets the night before, not to mention that one simply did not take another's weapon without permission.

"That's all right, Major," the Corporal replied, still looking at him in wonder. "I always like to know just 'ow far I can trust a blade; I guess I can trust this one 'ere with just about anythin'."

Darcy was quite overset: he had allowed Wickham to get under his skin again, something he had sworn he would not do. It was thus every time he argued with the man; immune to logic, blind to right and wrong, Wickham always succeeded in enraging him; when they were children, however, Darcy had not the ability to do the harm he had only just missed doing here. He needed to go where he could not see Wickham for a time. To the Corporal he said: "I will return," and he walked out of the inn.

Darcy walked back towards the city proper, going as far as Aldgate. He stopped at the old pump and cooled his brow, still in the grip of the savage emotions Wickham had triggered. It distressed him deeply that he had almost killed a man out of temper, but even now half of him wished he had finished it; it almost seemed that his emotions were breaking free with greater and greater frequency and strength, since his having met Elizabeth; the wounds she had received at Wickham's hands burned within him, and in great measure were driving his recent actions; yet, had he followed the dictates of that pain, he would have done far worse by her. He grimly took hold of himself and started to re-trace his steps, applying his mind to this new twist of Wickham's as he returned to the inn.

When he arrived shortly thereafter, he said in a flat voice that brooked no discussion, "I am going to settle on Miss Lydia Bennet, as dowry, enough to give you an extra eighty pounds per annum as income. Added to that which you will earn as an officer in His Majesty's Army, you should, with a modicum of prudence, be able to live comfortably; in time, with advancement, even well. The principal will also, used wisely, provide for an easier life, and allow for emergencies. The dowry will be left in your wife's name, so she, and only she, may dispose of it. Do you understand?" he demanded of Wickham. He nodded mutely.

"This is your very last chance, Wickham: have you anything further to urge? Once we are done, I will hear nothing more on the matter."

"Lydia has mentioned some money coming to her from her mother," he said, averting his eyes from Darcy's angry gaze.

"Find out the particulars," he instructed brusquely. With that Darcy left, offering no further word; quitting the inn, he stalked almost all the way to the Bank of England, seeking to clear his thoughts. It is perhaps not surprising that no one sought to interrupt his walk through Whitechapel, as his face would have quelled the most determined hawker, or put off the boldest muslin.

Darcy's next errand that day was to have been finding Mr. Gardiner in Gracechurch-Street, in order to acquaint him and the Bennet family with the current status of his scheme. However, his state of mind left him ill-suited for civil intercourse, and the time he was spending in Whitechapel lately was tending to make him feel rather coarse; he therefore decided to return to Grosvenor Square, where he spent the night quietly reading Montaigne, as one of the more cultured and enlightened authors in his collection, and trying to forget the fact that he had almost killed a man that day.

By morning he felt himself much more equal to the task of speaking with Lydia's uncle; but, on the assumption that Mr. Gardiner's days would normally be taken up with his business concerns, he determined to set out to discover him rather late in the afternoon. The majority of the day he spent quietly at home, still seeking to forget his transport of rage, and the damage he had almost done Elizabeth and her family. In the morning post he received a note from Colonel Fitzwilliam, saying that the commission was secured, and, as Darcy had requested, Wickham's posting was to be in the north, at Newcastle.

Well into the afternoon, he set about his task; he first went to Whitechapel, to hear from Wickham the details of Lydia's inheritance, and to see how things stood with the Corporal, and Tewkes, especially. He received a favourable report on the injured man; he was doing well, and sent Darcy his thanks for sending the surgeon to him. Wickham gave him the intelligence he required without offering Darcy any further aggravation. Darcy then proceeded to the Gardiner's. Gracechurch being rather a populous street, he made but little progress until he chanced to spy the postman making his rounds; he asked the man for the proper direction, and five minutes later he was knocking at the door. The girl answering it was, by her dress, a maid, and unaccustomed to the activity: seeing a gentleman before her, she dropt a quick curtsey and explained herself before he could even speak: "Begging your pardon, Sir, but Mrs. Carstairs is that busy just now. Can I help?"

Darcy, who was by habit soft-spoken with female servants, replied in well-moderated tones, "Is your master in? I was rather hoping I might see him."

"Oh, Sir, he is in, but he just this very minute sat down to dinner with his brother from Hertfordshire, and him only here till morning."

This was a situation Darcy had not anticipated; he hesitated, uncertain how best to proceed. That Mr. Bennet was with Mr. Gardiner was a bit perplexing: properly speaking, it were better for Darcy to take the matter up with him; he did not, however, think that that would be the best way forward for the enterprise he had brought thus far along. Deciding delay was to be preferred to the possible failure of the thing altogether, through an explicit ban from Mr. Bennet, he determined to return the next day. On his hesitating, the maid asked, "Is it very important, Sir? Shall I interrupt the master then?"

"No, please do not trouble him; I shall call again another time." He nodded a good day to the girl and returned to his carriage.

On the following day, he presented himself at the Gardiner's in mid-afternoon, well before the dinner hour: the woman who met him at the door this time was a respectable-looking woman of middle years, with iron-grey hair and a very proper manner. She took his card and ushered him into a pleasant sitting-room in which a number of books were distributed about, left ready to hand to be taken up again by their owners; the wide variety of reading matter told Darcy that some of the readers were quite young, informing him that the Gardiners were eager in the instruction their children. In very short order, Mr. Gardiner appeared at the door, still buttoning his coat.

"Mr. Darcy?" said he as he entered. "Is it indeed you? This is an honour as delightful as it is unexpected, Sir!"

After their bows and compliments, Darcy shook hands with him, gratified at being received thus gladly, as what he had to relate would be as unpleasant for Mr. Gardiner to hear as it would be for him to tell. The other offered him refreshment, which he declined, suspecting his welcome would be in question after his news.

"Was it you, then, who stopped by yesterday?" Mr. Gardiner enquired.

"It was," Darcy admitted. "but you were just sitting down to dinner, and I put off my call."

Gardiner air became momentarily gloomy. "Ah, yes...but I would certainly have delayed my dinner to receive you, Mr. Darcy," he said.

"I felt the matter was better put before you alone; I gathered that you were with Mr. Bennet."

Gardiner looked surprised and puzzled. "Well then, Mr. Darcy, I surmise some very particular need has carried you here," said he, "not just to my door, as it were, but to London at all; I had thought you still in Derbyshire with your friends. So: in what way may I serve you?"

"It is rather I who hope to be of service to you, Mr. Gardiner," said Darcy. "But first, I must ask your forgiveness."

Mr. Gardiner looked at Darcy with a curious and amused expression. "Before receiving a pardon from the bench, perhaps I might hear the charges laid against you?"

"I fear that I have inserted myself into your family's affairs; I have no excuse to offer other than the responsibility my own family, myself most especially, bears in the case."

Mr. Gardiner, looking at him dubiously, waved him on: "Do go on; I am all anticipation to hear what you might possibly have done to affect us, and how your family could conceivably be obligated to mine for anything at all."

Darcy gathered his resolution and stated, in as careful and unprejudiced a voice as he could command, "I have taken upon myself the discovery of Miss Lydia Bennet's whereabouts. I have seen her: she is well, but I fear she remains committed to her chosen course."

Mr. Gardiner, after looking searchingly at Darcy, rose without speaking and went to the mantel; there he pulled the bell rope and stood, occasionally looking over at Darcy, but still without speaking, until a manservant shortly appeared, whom he told, "We shall require tea, Carstairs, and we are not to be disturbed." He then resumed his seat, looked at Darcy with all interest, and waved for him to continue.

"I happened upon Miss Elizabeth Bennet at almost the very first moment she learnt of the affair," Darcy explained. "In the distress of the moment she revealed it all to me; concealment, circumspection even, could not be expected of any one under such circumstances— notwithstanding, I was honoured by her faith in discovering it to me. But, realising immediately that, had Mr. Wickham gone to ground here in Town, it would be a miraculous stroke of luck if you were to find their trail…" at this, Mr. Gardiner inclined his head in agreement; his rueful expression spoke of the efforts he been to in vain, "…I therefore set out from Derbyshire only one day later than yourselves," Darcy went on. "You are perhaps unaware that I have been associated with Mr. Wickham throughout my life; he was raised at my father's expense, and largely under his direction. This explains my family's responsibility for his actions in the present case."

"A slender reed," said Mr. Gardiner, looking at him thoughtfully, "but I will allow it in evidence. Do go on."

"More particularly, *I* have known Wickham well, and have seen him dishonour my father's efforts and esteem on many occasions, yet I failed to give warning of his ways to the world at large; I erred on the side of familial pride, not wishing to connect his name with our honour; and I erred on the side of personal pride, not wishing to admit any association with him myself; my character was to speak for itself, and he must make shift to get through life on his own: such was my thinking. But I have lately learnt that character is mute, and only one's actions speak in ways that others might hear. Had I taken the steps I ought, had I endeavoured to make his character known, he could never have insinuated himself into decent society, and this attack on your family would never have taken place. My responsibility, and my duty, was clear in the matter; and, as I know Wickham and his associates, I took those steps only I could be in position to take."

"And so you found them. How, if I might ask?"

"Knowing him as I do, I felt sure I knew where he would go first. I was correct in my assumption, and after such a beginning it was not difficult to pick up their trail."

"What are my niece's circumstances? You say she is well, but where, and under what conditions, has he kept her?"

Here Darcy hesitated. "Might I ask that I not be obliged to give a description of the place, or its direction? I have no wish to compound your concern; can we allow it to rest at the fact that she is fed, clothed," here he stumbled somewhat, remembering her state of undress when he interviewed her, "and free to come and go as she pleases? Their lodgings are such as only Wickham would dream of taking any woman, regardless of quality, but she is quite content to remain. I have offered her my personal assistance to be reunited with you, for whatever that is worth, but she is determined to stay with Mr. Wickham."

Mr. Gardiner's expression said he would have something to say on the subject of her obstinacy, were it not for Darcy's being a comparative stranger. "What does this Wickham have to say for himself?" he asked.

"George Wickham is a man utterly without conscience," Darcy told him. "Having determined to run from debts he had incurred in Brighton, he brought your niece along apparently as an afterthought, or so he says; for its motivation he imputes her own enthusiasm to be off on an adventure. He makes no apologies, and to the best of my belief, feels no guilt, let alone remorse. He never has, in the whole course of his life; never have I known any one so totally devoid of better feelings. In my anger with him at times, I confess, I have thought him something other than human, as we are by nature able to tell right from wrong—yet he seems incapable of making the distinction."

Mr. Gardiner contemplated this statement for a time, then asked: "But how, then, can he be prevailed upon?"

"Here again is why I felt compelled to take action in the case: no one else could know him well enough to work on him to effect; but the fact is that he is a remarkable compound of avarice and indolence; he is therefore always short, and open to the persuasive influence of ready money."

"An altogether exemplary young man," said Mr. Gardiner sourly. "Just the man for my niece to have attached herself to."

"Yes," agreed Darcy, "he is quite a specimen of his type; I have, however, recently met with worse among London's society."

"It can always be worse, is that it? Cold comfort, Sir," remarked Mr. Gardiner wryly.

"I beg your pardon," Darcy apologised. "My comment was more a reflection on my own amazement at finding he was not the worst of humankind, than an attempt to offer you a sadly hackneyed consolation."

"Better and better," said Mr. Gardiner sardonically, although he smiled as he said it. "For more than twenty years you believed the man of my niece's choosing to be the worst humankind had to offer? I am so relieved to know you now find yourself mistaken, and he is only the second worst."

"I do not seem to be getting much forwarder," Darcy observed, reproaching himself for not being more sensible of Mr. Gardiner's position. "Let me just move on: Wickham has agreed to marry your niece, so long as his more pressing debts be covered; Colonel Forster very honourably stands ready to accept his immediate resignation, and has further gathered together Wickham's debts in Brighton, not excepting a rather stiff accounting of gambling debts to the other officers, for the whole of which I have pledged myself. I have arranged a commission in the regular army for Wickham, upon execution of which he will be posted to Newcastle, if all goes according to plan. All this, I am sure you will readily understand, is no more than what is due from my side, having left a man raised in my family to prey upon the innocent, unchecked."

"Allowing that to stand for the moment, although I do not feel inclined to accept your position at all, what further terms does he require?"

"I am given to understand that there is an inheritance due the lady on the decease of her mother and father: she wishes to be secured of it; I have also agreed to settle two thousand pounds on her as dowry, to help them get a start and provide some additional income."

"That is the sum of their requirements?" Mr. Gardiner asked.

"It is."

After a moment's reflection while gazing over Darcy's shoulder, Mr. Gardiner looked back and said, "I see; this, then, is the case against you, and the accused stands before the bench for sentencing: I find, young man, that your actions are not satisfactory, and do not answer the occasion."

"Mr. Gardiner..." Darcy began to expostulate, but Gardiner held up a restraining hand. "You have made no allowance for any contributions from her family, no way for them to moderate their own guilt, which must be brought into account for the failings of their unfortunate offspring."

"Because I perceive none," Darcy protested. "Were it not for my nonfeasance, Wickham's malfeasance could have had no effect on the Bennet family."

"So you see no culpability on that side at all?"

"None, Sir. Every thing that has occurred would have been prevented, had I not thought it beneath me to lay the affairs of my family open to the world."

Mr. Gardiner gave Darcy another long, concentrated look. When he spoke, however, it seemed to be on another topic entirely: "It was my niece who told you of this at Lambton; do I recall correctly?"

"Yes, Sir; before you and Mrs. Gardiner were returned that morning."

Mr. Gardiner thought for a long moment. "Well," he said, "I truly have no wish to disrupt the negotiations you have been at such pains to finalise, Mr. Darcy; however, while the terms thereof may be acceptable to Mr. Wickham, *I* cannot accept them; in particular, I find it wholly inappropriate that my brother Bennet should have no hand, suffer no hardship, in rescuing his daughter from her own folly."

"What is your thought, then?" Darcy asked.

"The family must pay for the dowry."

Thereinafter the two men entered into a lengthy and hard-fought dispute; Mr. Gardiner was most determined that Lydia's family should bear the expense of the dowry; but Darcy was in a position to prevail by dint of sheer stubbornness, as without his information, Mr. Gardiner was powerless. The upshot of it all was that Darcy was to supply a dowry of only one thousand, and the family would provide an additional one hundred pounds per annum, which was more even than the interest of the original sum would have provided, and would limit the ability of Wickham and Lydia to recklessly spend the principle. Further, Mr. Bennet would be called on to clear Wickham's debts in Meryton, which Darcy believed, from comments dropt by Wickham, to be less substantive than those in Brighton.

When at length they reached this understanding, Mr. Gardiner rang for fresh tea, and the two waited in near silence during the interval until it arrived; Darcy, feeling he had imposed more than enough on Gardiner's good will, waited in a self-deprecating manner until the other should come around. But with the commonplace comfort of sharing hot tea, the contentiousness of the matter was relieved, and they revived. Reassured, Darcy brought up the more practical issue of the wedding arrangements, on a preliminary basis, to prepare him for another meeting with Wickham.

"We shall have to have Wickham take up new lodg-ings in this parish," observed Mr. Gardiner: "From your rather guarded description, I shouldn't imagine their cur-rent parish would suit."

"No, I suppose not," Darcy allowed. "But this should not go on any longer than it must; if he were to move soon into your parish, do you think you might be able to persuade the vicar to grant a license without the full four weeks residence, or must we have the banns read?"

Mr. Gardiner paused to reflect. "He is a bit of a stick-ler, but I believe he would be willing to halve it, as she is my niece," he said hesitantly. "But I will just walk over to the rectory this afternoon, to test his disposition and try to get his agreement."

"Shall I bring Miss Lydia Bennet to you?"

Gardiner thought this over a moment, then an-swered, "I think not; let her remain in her chosen circum-stance; there is no use vexing ourselves until I can discover the vicar's feelings: we may be better off simply having the banns read."

Darcy nodded his acceptance, and took his leave not long afterwards. Going back to Whitechapel, he informed Wickham where things stood, and that, to Darcy's intense disgust, the financial aspects were moving in his favour.

Chapter Twenty

*T*he next morning Darcy returned to the Gardiner's. He was quite looking forward to being in Mr. Gardiner's company again, and hoped that Mrs. Gardiner might have news to tell of Elizabeth; if nothing else, he hoped to hear that she was well, and to be assured that his efforts on behalf of her family would have the desired effect in setting her world to rights.

Mrs. Gardiner, who had arrived home from Longbourn not long after he had finished his discussion with her husband the day before, greeted him warmly, as did Mr. Gardiner. They sat down in the same drawing-room he had been in the day before; Mrs. Gardiner was exceedingly curious and quite aflame with questions, but first, however, Darcy asked to hear what the vicar had said concerning the marriage.

"He will accept their residence on the strength of my guarantee," said Mr. Gardiner, "but only if he sees them in church twice before the wedding; I fear to have the two of them walk through the doors together, though: who knows what divine retribution they might call down on our poor congregation."

Darcy and Mrs. Gardiner chuckled at this, and Darcy was relieved by the news. But then he was called on to tell his tale; where Mr. Gardiner had more wanted to hear the facts pertinent to the remedy of the situation, Mrs. Gardiner was every bit as anxious to know the parties' motivations, and would not be satisfied until she had heard every thing Darcy had to say. He was therefore obliged to relate the affair at rather greater length, from finding the trail at Mrs. Younge's through meeting with Wickham and Lydia, and on to the end of the business at the inn. In describing these events, Darcy was careful to withhold any mention of the men he had employed, and to soften any and all difficulties he had experienced — and in particular, giving no hint of his use of coercion with either Mrs. Younge or Wickham — not that he felt remorse for what he had imposed on Wickham, as what he deserved was much crueller, and so he felt no unease for the means he had been forced to use; but if Wickham was to be accepted into their family, it was best that they should remain ignorant as to the full extent of his low companions and his predilection to corruption.

As he recounted this history, Mrs. Gardiner repeatedly expressed her amazement and admiration for all he had done, as well as her deep sense of obligation. Darcy did his best to convince her that there was no need for the latter: "I assure you, Mrs. Gardiner, there can be no obligation on your side," he informed her. "It was due solely to my neglect that the situation arose at all; I only regret that it took so grave an act as his eloping with your niece before my duties became clear to me. Wickham had to be stopped, and on no one's shoulders but my own could this fall."

She looked unconvinced. "If not Wickham, it would have been another such," said she in long-suffering tones. "You have saved us from irredeemable disgrace, Mr. Darcy."

"We cannot know that," he protested, "whereas I have seen this coming for years, and ought to have taken action sooner, before your niece was drawn into his influence."

"Notwithstanding," put in Mr. Gardiner, "my wife has a point. Finance aside, as I have no wish to re-open that matter, there can be no question of our moral obligation to you. We are in your debt, whether you will or no."

"If I accept that, will you accept that I am also in your debt, for the steps you have taken to help bring Wickham to the altar? I doubt I could have managed without your help."

"The two are not of equal magnitude, but I can allow that we have been of some assistance," said Gardiner with an air of measured assessment.

"Good," said Darcy. "Then let us leave it at that, shall we?" To this Mr. Gardiner gave a grudging nod. Then, knowing what he was about to say must set off yet more contention, Darcy said with some hesitation, "Now; I believe no one but Miss Elizabeth Bennet, and ourselves, are aware that I have any knowledge of the matter: I must say I feel it ought to remain that way. I hope that we can keep my involvement from the family, as it must give them great uneasiness to know of it, which can avail no one."

"But surely, Mr. Darcy, one must give credit where credit is due."

"I appreciate your thinking, of course" he replied, "but this must place them under a terrible, if misapplied, obligation; I would not have them think they owed me anything, when it has been all my own fault." Of course Elizabeth was uppermost in his thoughts, but the battle must be fought on a larger field of interest.

Mr. Gardiner's face grew grave. "Now, Mr, Darcy, I cannot but think that, no matter how burdensome, the truth would be best; better they should know their bene-factor, surely."

Darcy shook his head: "This could only create diffi-culty and pain, with no benefit to accrue: most certainly none to my side. I do not deserve their thanks, as I feel myself to have been the offending party, and would be just as uncomfortable in receiving them, as they would be in giving them. To whatever degree it is necessary to re-veal what steps have been taken, I cannot but believe it would be best if you were to take responsibility, Mr. Gar-diner, as that way it will be kept in the family, and we might put the best face on things: specifically, we can maintain the impression that Wickham meant to marry her all the while, in order that the couple might begin to reclaim somewhat of their reputation."

"This goes too far," Gardiner began, shaking his head. "I have already felt it wrong in me to have let the money matters go…" He was beginning to work himself into a more forceful and resolute tone, but his wife hastily interceded: "Well, but this news will be *such* a blessing to the family; Elizabeth, I know, will feel it so especially," she said, directing the last to her husband; she watched him for a moment, until a change in his temper revealed itself in his face. "I can scarcely imagine how relieved they will be," she went on, still keeping a wary eye on Mr. Gardiner. "When shall we be able to tell them?"

Darcy embraced her change of subject, and looked enquiringly at Mr. Gardiner. "I should assume it will be possible to write them to-morrow with sufficient detail to ask for their acceptance and concurrence—would not you think?"

After a slight hesitation, Mr. Gardiner pursed his lips and blew out his breath. "No doubt," he agreed, finally letting go his objection. "We need only ensure that all terms are properly laid out; my man of business can draw up the settlements once Mr. Bennet has agreed to the terms, and as the vicar has agreed to the wedding after seeing them at services twice, we might have the wedding as early as Monday the 25th."

"Good Heavens," said Mrs. Gardiner animatedly. "And it will happen that soon! Mr. Darcy, really, is there no way we might repay such kindness?"

Darcy shook his head. "Indeed, it would be quite out of my power to accept any such attempt," said he.

"Well, we cannot force it on you," said Mr. Gardiner, "and it appears pointless to try to press the matter, but know that we feel it, nonetheless—and thank you." He extended a hand to Darcy, who took it gladly, expressing his own thanks most sincerely; the atmosphere cleared, and they were able to bring the discussion to a conclusion on terms of great mutual esteem and goodwill.

He was not to stay long after this, as he still had many things to see to before leaving for Pemberley on the morrow. After leaving the Gardiners, Darcy went back to Whitechapel to see how things stood, and be assured of Wickham's removal the next day to the parish of St. Clements, where he was to take lodgings in Lombard street. He also enforced to Wickham that Lydia must be restrained from mentioning anything of Darcy's involvement in the affair, pointing out to him how much to his advantage such disguise must be. "The thought we are to convey is that you were always honourably disposed towards their daughter," he said. "That, in spite of a momentary deficiency of funds, you were always intending to wed; and, thanks to some minor assistance from Mr. Gardiner, all has been made easy. For her to reveal my part would be to reveal just how far from the truth this is, which would, of course, permanently injure you in their eyes." Wickham promised to do all he could. Darcy was far from satisfied, but could think of nothing more to attempt.

Darcy then sat down with Corporal Sands, to toast their success.

"Wot now, Major?" the Corporal asked.

"I shall return to Derbyshire; but I wanted to ask, Corporal, is there any one amongst the men who could be trusted with Wickham in Newcastle? I have in mind something else for you."

"Tewkes would be my first choice, but maybe you wouldn't be wantin' the man knowin' 'oo was watchin' 'im."

Darcy said, "No, actually, we would want him to recognise a face: it would make it easier for the others, and serve to remind him; I think three men should do it: one known, and two unknown to him. But is Tewkes well enough?"

"Aye, 'e will be," nodded the Corporal. "Are you sure Colonel Fitzwilliam didn't 'ave any 'and in this? A military way of thinkin' must run in the family, Major."

Darcy smiled, and shook his head. He said, "No, I must take the responsibility for this scheme. What I wanted to ask you, though, was whether you might be interested in being constable for the towns and villages near my estate. I recently have had a bit of trouble there which suggested to me that a man such as yourself would be uncommonly useful to have on view in that part of the country. A number of the local lads seem too disposed to take matters into their own hands, and I will not have that. Besides, you would be more or less centrally located to give Tewkes whatever assistance he needed in his task."

"I might be interested, at that, Major," the Corporal said. "There's nothin' to 'old me 'ere, and I never been to Derbyshire; 'ow's the beer?"

"Good," said Darcy, grinning. "Our young women are pretty, too."

"Aye, that's it! A nice country lass to settle down wi'," said the Corporal. Whistling and rubbing his hands together, he returned Darcy's grin. "These 'ere Town girls are a bit 'ard for my tastes, if you know wot I mean," he said in a conspiratorial whisper. "Well, Major, let me just think about that, and I'll let you know."

"Do," said Darcy, "I am sure it would be to both our advantages."

The next morning the respective deliveries were made: Wickham was escorted to his new lodgings, and Darcy took Lydia to the Gardiner's himself. Darcy took advantage of that trip to emphasise once again the importance of keeping his name out of the affair when speaking amongst her family, but he was fairly sure that she did not attend.

When they arrived at the Gracechurch-Street, the look with which Mrs. Gardiner greeted her niece was quite a masterpiece of censure and condemnation; Lydia, however, gave it no notice at all, smiling and greeting her relations with great energy and evident pleasure. Darcy reminded himself never to be amazed by impudence again: Darcy would have been reluctant to show his face, but here was Miss Lydia Bennet, perfectly at her ease, as though she had not just brought her entire family, the Gardiners included, to the brink of ruin merely for her own pleasure.

He left for Pemberley immediately after dropping off the young prodigal with her family. After an uneventful trip, his sister came to meet him before he was fairly descended from the carriage, demanding that he particularise very fully on the whole affair almost from the moment his feet touched the ground. He did so at length, again being mindful to withhold those details that must have given her pain.

When he had done, she said: "Then I trust is all well?"

"I believe so," he replied. "I do not know what else I might do, short of putting the two of them in manacles for the next few weeks; the license is to be granted, and they will wed before the month is out; it helps that it is the Gardiner's parish: that enabled him to smooth things over with the vicar. Miss Lydia Bennet is with her family, my men are keeping tabs of the fellow, the Colonel has procured the commission: all we need do is wait out the residence period."

Georgiana sighed. "Does Miss Elizabeth Bennet know?"

"She must, by now. Mr. Gardiner was going send an express to her father the day before yesterday."

"Oh, Fitzwilliam, well done!" Georgiana smiled on him.

"Yes, I really believe it seems to be in hand. How do things stand here?"

"Things are quite well," she replied easily. "There has been nothing to mar the last two weeks except your absence."

"Very good. And our guests?"

"Every one is well, although Miss Bingley has daily bemoaned your absence, and cursed the Fates that led you away, and repined at length to any one who would listen; Miss Hartsbury has no patience with her."

"And how do things stand between Miss Hartsbury and Sir Neville?" asked Darcy.

Georgiana eyes widened. "Dear me! I would not be surprised if they had had the banns read, themselves! I do like Lavinia, as I now call her, but honestly, Brother, I have to say she is…" here she hesitated. In a whisper she said, "Well, she is a bit *fast*!"

"Say rather, *determined*, and I should agree with you," Darcy allowed. "I have known her three years, and this is the first time I have seen any eligible gentleman show an interest, let alone one who seems genuinely to esteem her. And given her uncle's attitude towards the young men who venture to enter her 'sphere', as he puts it, to her it must seem to be a chance sent from Heaven. I think I can forgive her for wanting to snatch at love, rather than wait for the fullness of time." Georgiana gave this consideration, and accepted it with a nod. Darcy continued, "But I am delighted to hear they are getting on well; I had a bit of a hand in it, you know."

"You did?"

Darcy told her the story of his dance with her at her ball, and the reasons behind Sir Neville's invitation on their excursion.

Georgiana laughed at the story of the ball, then told him wonderingly, "You astound me, Brother—indeed you do; I should never have imagined you would ever do such a thing."

"It seemed the thing to do at the time," he said, "but I am rather surprised at it, myself. At least it seems to have worked out well. Now, Dearest, I should like to wash this dust off, and see our guests."

Later that day, after he had had time to see every one and be welcomed back, he had the opportunity to tell his aunt how things stood in London, happy to assure her that the marriage seemed all but certain of completion; she congratulated him too, and with her he did not hold back on the various elements he had in place to control Wickham. Lady Andover seemed impressed: "Heavens, Darcy, you have gone to a great deal of trouble to make sure the thing lasts. Your friends would have been saved just as well by the marriage, even if Wickham did run off afterwards."

"True," Darcy acknowledged, "but he would only surface somewhere else, and I should have to go through all that trouble again. No, I wanted this over and done with."

"Well, I should imagine this will do it; well done, my dear," she said.

Darcy thanked her, as well as for her assistance in seeing to his guests in his absence. He retired early that evening, as it seemed forever since he had had a sound night's sleep.

The next two weeks passed quickly, with a variety of activities that Darcy had not indulged himself in for some years: an excursion to the Peaks, and another to Dove Dale, riding, and even simply having the full and unfettered use of his own library; it had been a long while since he had been home long enough to appreciate it, and appreciate it he did. Master Pender left them within a few days of his return, and Lady Andover left just after, leaving behind Bingley and his sister, the courting couple, the Hursts, and Mr. Hartsbury. The latter made several references daily to the advisability of getting back to London, but his niece was deaf to them all; to Darcy it seemed that she was very pleased with herself, nor could he blame her; Sir Neville appeared to be just the foil she needed to ease her way through life and bring her fulfilment, and he was exceedingly happy for them, feeling, as he did, a not unreasonable degree of connexion to their happiness.

The wedding between Wickham and Lydia was to take place on the last Monday of the month, so on the Saturday before, Darcy again took leave of his guests. The ceremony itself was uneventful, and barely noted by any one outside of their own family circle. Lydia was in exceedingly high spirits, smiling and waving to any and every one she passed; Wickham was more subdued, no doubt reflecting on his future state of connubial bliss. When it was all over, Darcy let out a great sigh of relief; he had always feared that something would come up and prevent the ceremony from being performed: another wife, perhaps, or an angry mob of creditors who would carry Wickham off before the parson could finish. But here they were, every thing complete, secure, and satisfactory.

Corporal Sands was there in his regimental jacket, which, while somewhat the worse for wear, nevertheless still fit him well, and was undoubtedly his best. After the service was over, Darcy asked, "Are you here on God's business, or mine, Corporal?"

"I've always had a soft spot for marryings, Major; I let the lads outside take the watch."

"Very good. How is Tewkes?"

"'E'll be 'imself in no time," the Corporal assured him. "'E won't 'ave no trouble keepin' up with this 'ere fellow in Newcastle; and you can bet 'e won't be lettin' 'im get away."

The party was just then leaving the church, and the two men followed them out. Once the newlyweds were off with the Gardiners, taking the carriage back to Gracechurch-Street, with Lydia leaning out the window and preening and waving her ringed hand at every passer-by, Darcy saw two of the Corporal's men walk off after them around the corner.

He and the Corporal watched them go, then Darcy asked, "Am I to understand, Corporal, that you have decided to take me up on my offer?"

"Well, Major, you never really did make no *offer*," said the other. "'Ow much is it worth to a man to be a constable?"

Darcy mentioned a figure that he knew to be more than the Corporal would have made in the army.

"Coo!" exclaimed Sands. "That's a nice little sum. I think a man could make do on that. Well, then, Major, you've got yourself a constable." As Darcy had seen the boy Tibbs do, the Corporal spat on his hand and held it out to Darcy; after the briefest of hesitations, Darcy removed his glove and did likewise, and they shook. The corporal then grinned and gave a cheery whistle, pointing at Darcy and wiping his hand pointedly on his breeches. Darcy laughed and with careful deliberation drew his handkerchief for the purpose, looking at the Corporal as though to say, "*This* is how a gentleman sees to such things." Then he whistled and pointed *his* finger at the Corporal; they both of them laughed at this, and Darcy departed, telling the other he would send for him from Pemberley as soon as he arrived.

The next day Darcy dined at the Gardiners; again he was glad to have come, as the Gardiners were comfortable people to be with; Mr. Gardiner's views and address Darcy found to be well-informed, pleasant, and amusing, and Mrs. Gardiner had a caring, refined nature that was at once elegant and agreeable.

Mr. Gardiner began with a toast: "To a successful conspiracy!"

The other two heartily endorsed this, Mrs. Gardiner adding, "I own that I was terrified throughout that something would come up to put it off."

"As did I!" Darcy exclaimed. "I kept looking over my shoulder to the doors, for fear he had another wife somewhere who would turn up at the last moment."

"I was thinking more along the lines of a jealous husband, and gun-fire," said Mr. Gardiner, "but the sentiment was the same."

"But here it is, done at last, and we may breathe easy," said his wife.

"I imagine the family at Longbourn has been apprised of events?" Darcy asked, hoping perhaps to hear something of Elizabeth.

"They have, indeed; and the happy couple have gone to the house of her father, there to be fêted with the fatted calf," Gardiner said sardonically. "Or perhaps a cold shoulder of mutton—no... —goat, I should imagine."

"Lydia would neither notice nor care," said Mrs. Gardiner. "I swear she cannot see anything past her own nose; she still has no more idea of having caused any trouble for the family! —I have no patience with her." She looked apologetically at Darcy for having spoken so freely, but she was determined in her anger.

"I fear I must agree with you," said he. "On the few occasions I have attempted to sway her, or even inform her, I admit I failed so completely that I wondered if she had even heard me."

"That is my niece," agreed Gardiner, "but now, at least, she has only her husband to vex with her genius for inattention."

"That, I will drink to," said Darcy. "To Wickham's lasting vexation!"

The Gardiners both laughed and tipped their glasses to this.

"The Bennets are pleased, then?" Darcy pressed, still hoping to hear of Elizabeth.

"I have heard only from Mr. Bennet himself," said Gardiner. "His letters are always brief, but his tone in the last was not what I would call conciliatory; at least where his daughter and her husband are concerned."

"I had a letter from Miss Bennet," Mrs. Gardiner told Darcy. "She was, of course, very pleased, as she can see nothing but the good in any situation; but her sister Elizabeth has been oddly quiet on the affair." She looked at Darcy here, as though expecting him to have something to offer.

"Miss Elizabeth...Miss Elizabeth Bennet is well, I trust?' he asked.

"She is quite well," Mrs. Gardiner assured him, still looking at him in that expectant manner.

Darcy nodded and waited, but nothing more was forthcoming. He, of course, had no news to supply, and was rather puzzled by her air; but he did understand by this that there was nothing to be gleaned about Elizabeth's sentiments at the moment, so his questions were answered, even though in an indirect fashion.

After a very pleasant evening, Darcy took leave, thanking the Gardiners again for their help and hospitality, expressing the hopes that they might meet again soon, and inviting them to visit Pemberley any time they might happen to be traveling that way.

His work in London having finally been brought to a satisfactory close, he left the next morning for home. On the way back to Pemberley through the fading summer colours of the English countryside, Darcy thought over the diverse and very disparate views he had had of marriage, and more generally, love itself, in the year preceding. It was just about this time a twelvemonth ago he had escorted Georgiana back to Pemberley, thus beginning a period filled with all manner of perspectives on the subject. With all the disappointments and trials, the mismatched principals and their quite impossible hope of any kind of happiness, was it all a delusion? For Mr. Collins, and for Lydia, it surely was; but was it ever real, and lasting—that eternal enchantment immortalised by Donne? Would Miss Hartsbury and Sir Neville prove the exception? Every one, it seemed, sought love most diligently, but what was it they sought after, in reality? Was it the search for the other half of their soul, as the poets would have it, or merely the blind, imperious drive to increase their kind? Why did both the wanting and the having seem to bring equal pain? Watching the miles pass by outside his coach window, he saw villages and farmhouses, churches and markets, all teeming with people who, in spite of their myriad natures and pursuits, all felt love's compulsion and power; whether living in it and for it with all the fervent sensibility of a young girl in the bloom of first love, or with the defeated, ashen yearning of the old man whose hopes had failed, no one, it seemed, escaped its pull. But to what end? — that was the point.

The answer provided by the intellect — that the end sought was a phantasm, merely a cruel will o' the wisp — was instantly and utterly rejected by the heart; to which ought one listen? Did it even matter, when each side was fraught with the potential for disappointment of the bitterest kind? But then he remembered his aunt's words: "Overmastering passions overmaster us." — Did one even have a choice, then? Absurd, Darcy thought: what is a man if not the choices he makes? But what, then, of Bingley? He was as good a man as any one could hope to meet, but Darcy would take his oath he hardly ever made conscious choices — certainly not in matters of love; he was led by the heart, not the head.

It was at that moment that Darcy came to the astonishing realisation that his touchstone and ideal, the intellect, was not the only sufficient guide through life; indeed, it was not sufficient at all: his devotion to it had not made him the better man, nor had Bingley's disregard for logic and reasoning made him the worse. Darcy's overbearing manner and arrogance in guiding his friend's choices now appeared to him to be nothing but the worst sort of pride — and empty pride, at that, as he had nothing to show that his was the superior guide in life. This revelation left poor Darcy in a pitifully confused state of mind; of a sudden, his polestar disappeared from his fir-mament, leaving him adrift and rudderless; if not to the intellect — open, logical, and long-sighted — to what did one turn, to direct one through the endlessly ramifying paths and alternatives of one's life?

It was not before many minutes, and many miles, had passed, that Darcy came to recall Pender's having once said, "Each discipline has its own tools, and its own language. One does not analyse history with the Calculus, nor does one measure a journey in iambs and anapaests." Though not within the compass of Pender's teachings, Darcy now grasped that this could be taken to mean that the heart had its own realm, too, over which it wielded its influence undisputed, and which only it was competent to rule.

Well, and what, then, did his heart have to tell? That which the intellect had fought so long to deny: that Eliza-beth, and only Elizabeth, held sway in his heart's realm. This was hardly a revelation to him, but his new view-point did allow him to admit to the depth of his attach-ment to her, and cease his attempts to hold it off. His aunt had been right about overmastering emotions, but having been overmastered did not mean that happiness was to be his. That Elizabeth was mistress of his heart could no longer be denied, but she had declined to accept it and make it her own — and their history made it all but certain she never would; that was his fate, and, if literature was any guide, he was not the first, nor would he be the last, to find himself in that situation.

Having contemplated these points for some miles, it then occurred to him to reconsider his inability to distin-guish Elizabeth's feelings for him — or rather, her lack thereof — at Rosings; he had tried his best *not* to listen to his heart in that case, so was that the source of his great misunderstanding of her disposition towards him? This thought was succeeded in time by the question: if he could so entirely mistake a character as animated as hers, might he not also have mistaken her sister's? Miss Bennet was, after all, much more composed and reserved by nature, and offered less to the observer for interpretation; he surely had not listened to his heart, or even made enquiry of it, in that instance. This brought back to mind Bingley's persistent lowness, and his comment after their meeting with Elizabeth in Lambton; he obviously still harboured a fondness for Miss Bennet. Almost as a test, Darcy asked his heart for an answer: did Miss Bennet love his friend? There was now no answer forthcoming on the point, but of his friend's continued esteem he was certain. Now that his prior conclusions were thrown into doubt, however, he was forced to acknowledge that he lacked any deep conviction of the lady's relative want of admiration for Bingley, and all his actions to separate them were rendered suspect, to say the very least. His inaction where Wickham had been concerned, he had seen as very blameworthy; what then was this very active transgression, in Bingley's case? If his faults where Wickham was concerned necessitated the efforts to which he had just put himself, what did not this injustice towards his friend positively demand? He had hoped his exertions were over, and that he might be granted a period of rest and peace at Pemberley, but he now foresaw another lengthy period of activity; he now must make sure that he had not stolen from Bingley his chance at happiness.

Chapter Twenty-One

*G*eorgiana had been listening for him all morning, and came again to meet him as the coach swung into the stable yard.

"Is it done, then?" she asked immediately as he came down from the coach.

"It is," he answered with a sigh. He drew her into a quick hug, then gave her his arm as they walked the long way around to the front hall.

"You must be happy," she said, looking up at his face.

"Yes, happy enough," he said, although with little spirit. "But, truthfully, Dearest, I hardly know whether I have done good or ill for all concerned."

Georgiana looked surprised and concerned. "What else could be done? How could you have made it better?"

"That is exactly what is troubling me: what could I have done better? It is impossible that the two of them should be at all happy, or that their marriage should be marked by any degree of warmth or steadiness; so, was there anything else that might have served better?"

"Fitzwilliam, if, after having thought of little else for a month or more, nothing suggests itself to you that would have served better, surely that must suffice."

"True, but still..." He shook his head to clear away those thoughts. "I am sure I do not know, but the doubts remain. But I now find myself plagued with other doubts, too." He quietly and briefly described to her his fears where his friend was concerned. He then told her: "I have to make certain of the thing, and so I fear I must absent myself again from Pemberley, and you."

"Oh!" she cried. "Must you? I had hoped you would be able to stay with us for a nice while."

"I had hoped so, too, Dearest. But I must revisit all my observations, for it now appears that I may have taken something from Bingley that must be returned: if I have taken him away from the lady he was intended for, it cannot be mended soon enough. This means I shall have to contrive a way to get him to return to Netherfield; but for you, anyway, there will be a choice: the Hursts and Miss Bingley will, I should imagine, carry on to Scarborough as they planned, so: should you rather go with them; return with me to London, knowing I shall be leaving for Hertfordshire shortly thereafter; or stay here at Pemberley?"

After consideration, Georgiana replied: "I shall stay here, I think. I do so love the autumn at home; and in truth, I am in need of some time to myself; as much as I love my aunt and uncle, and as greatly as I have enjoyed our travels and friends, I have been in company far more than I am accustomed to, and I should be very glad of a period of quiet."

"Yes, as would I," agreed Darcy. "But I cannot rest whilst this hangs over my head. I should like nothing better than to stay here quietly with you, but if things go as they might, I shall be able to return within a month or so. Perhaps we might have a quiet Christmas here this year?"

"I should like that very much, and I shall count on it, so you must not let your business with Mr. Bingley keep you from home that long."

"It will not; in any event, it will be resolved within weeks. I just wish I might have a bit more time here first; but if I have erred, it must be mended soonest. I shall see if I cannot persuade Bingley to go back to Hertfordshire for some hunting."

Therefore, after having spent a pleasant evening with his friends, during which nothing more telling was at issue than the best way to defeat Hurst and his partner at whist, on the next day Darcy addressed his friend in the morning, when the two were alone at breakfast.

"Bingley, I have been thinking of doing some hunting; what say you?"

"I should like nothing better," he replied. "A hard day or two in the saddle would be just what I need. Is there a chase here you favour?"

"Actually, the reports of game here in Derbyshire have been poor; I was thinking rather of Hertfordshire."

Darcy watched attentively as Bingley's face showed his conflicting emotions. Darcy said casually: "I happened to hear something in Town concerning the Bennets; actually, there has been a marriage in the family."

Bingley looked up quickly. "Who was married?" he demanded.

Darcy instantly calmed his friend's alarm with: "The youngest: Miss Lydia Bennet has married."

Bingley's features relaxed, and he asked, "To whom? Some one of our acquaintance in the neighbourhood?"

"To Mr. George Wickham," Darcy supplied.

"That fellow? Lord! Poor Miss Bennet, to have such a connexion!" Catching himself, he went on, "That is, one naturally feels sorry for the family, but Lydia always was a silly creature. I suppose we can be relieved it was not worse, and is accomplished while she is too young to have got into any real mischief."

"If we go to Hertfordshire, we could take the opportunity to offer our congratulations...or condolences, as the case might be," Darcy said with a grin.

Bingley grinned back. "Both, I should think, depending on whom one was speaking to," he said.

"Indeed. And, do you know, I rather feel that I have left some unfinished business in Meryton," said Darcy.

"You, Darcy? I confess I have never felt easy with how we left the place, and I...to be honest, I have to admit I have never completely got over my memories of ...well, I, too, feel I left some things unfinished. But what could you have left undone, Darcy?"

"In all truth, I cannot be sure; I was aware you regretted the way we left the place, nor have I been able to rest entirely easy on the point of our leaving. I can hardly tell you what I hope to accomplish, but I find the need in myself for a visit, to put the ghosts to rest; perhaps it would be best for both of us to go back, and put our minds at ease."

Bingley was looking at his friend in surprise, but immediately agreed, "Well, that would suit me; when would you like to go?"

Darcy had heard from the Gardiners that Mr. and Mrs. Wickham were to spend some time with the Bennets, but he knew Wickham had to be in Newcastle by the second week of September; he therefore said: "I should like a week or so to catch my breath, and you can send word ahead to Netherfield; we shall see the others off to Scarborough, then go straight down—unless you have something to do in Town?" Bingley shook his head, and they were agreed.

That night as he prepared to retire, Darcy chanced to observe Perkins's face, looking rather glum, reflected in the looking glass; concerned, he asked, "Perkins, if I am not prying, how have you managed with Miss Bingley's maid?"

Perkins turned a woebegone countenance to his master. "Lord, Sir, I thought that, what with the time we had been away, she might have forgot. But when I got back yesterday, there she was, same as ever. Well, I told myself while we were in London that I'd just up and tell her, like you said, and so I did. For a minute every thing seemed all right; she just stood there, all quiet, like. Then she lets out a shriek like a banshee and tries to claw out my eyes! I barely escaped, Sir! Every time I've had to go through the house my heart's been in my throat, not knowing which corner she might be around. Hadyn has been scouting for me; he's new-married himself, you know, and says he understands how mad women can be when a man makes them angry."

Darcy did not need this new example to make him wonder at the ways of men and women, but at least here he could take steps.

"I see; very well, Perkins: Mr. Bingley and I are going back to Netherfield in less than a fortnight; most of my hunting togs are still in London, I believe. You head up to Town to-morrow, if you like, and get it all down to Hertfordshire; stay—take a day in Bakewell, if you will, to see you mother. I shall make do with Reynolds during your absence."

Perkins's face spread into a wide grin. "Thank you, Mr. Darcy! You're sure you won't have need of me?"

"No, not to worry. Take it as payment for all the help you have given me with her mistress. I understand they will all shortly go off to the north, and they will not be joining us at Netherfield, so Miss Bingley's maid should have had sufficient time to recover before you have to see her again."

"I really don't know how to thank you Mr, Darcy; escape from Clarissa, and a chance to see Lara: I don't know what to say."

"Well, all it costs me is having Reynolds shave me for a time—and I am sure that he and I can manage my neck cloths between us here in the country: it seems a good return for a reasonable investment."

"Yes, Sir. Thank you again, Mr. Darcy. Oh, and don't forget, Sir, that the green coat must not be worn under any circumstances, until I can see to the rent in the seam," Perkins told him. "No, hold, Sir: I'll take it with me, and make the repairs in Town." After this, he went about his duties briskly and in much better spirits. He wasted no time in executing his instructions, and was gone before Darcy rose the next morning.

Chapter Twenty-Two

*T*he days passed easily; the Hursts and Miss Bingley left for Scarborough shortly after Darcy's return, although not before miss Bingley entreated Darcy strenuously to accompany them, and Darcy and Bingley spent a quiet interval of a week or so, shooting during the day and playing cards with Georgiana in the evening. Darcy was glad of the respite, but his feeling of having left a task undone began to urge him southward.

The second week of September, therefore, Darcy and Bingley made their way back to Hertfordshire. Since having made the decision to return to Netherfield, Bingley's fears about their welcome, after their rather hasty departure the year before, had increased, but these were somewhat diminished by the reception he got from the servants at Netherfield: there seemed to be no lingering ill feelings at their having left so abruptly, and on the first evening they dined very pleasantly on country pork, and duck with peas and onions. The gentlemen settled in, and spent the next several days finding their way about the place again, and scouting possible courses for a hunt. In Bingley's case, he was also steeling his courage for a visit he both longed for and dreaded; finally, on the third day since their arrival, he told Darcy at breakfast, "I believe I shall pay a visit to Longbourn to-day; should you care to you accompany me?"

"Certainly," said that gentleman. "We have yet to deliver our condolences," he joked. But, he, too, had some decided trepidations, thinking how he might be received by Elizabeth; he had not seen her since having left her in tears at Lambton, and moreover, as the only person outside her immediate family to know of her sister's elopement, she must necessarily view him with greatest embarrassment.

As they approached the door, his friend sent a nervous look his way. "I find my mind is more uneven than I had anticipated, Darcy," he said. "Our departure was so sudden last year, I fear we must have left hard feelings behind us."

"Possibly," Darcy allowed, "although there is but one way of knowing, and it is also the necessary first step towards effecting a reconciliation, if one is wanted. Come, now: unto the breach!" He reached past Bingley and rang the bell.

They were admitted, and, allowing Bingley to precede him down the hallway, Darcy braced himself to once again see Elizabeth: he must follow this course and weather the storm he had himself called forth; his embarrassment was acute, but against what was owing to Bingley, seeing her again was no more than what was required. As they entered the drawing-room, Bingley was greeted effusively by the lady of the house; Darcy was careful to keep his attention on Miss Bennet, who, he thought, betrayed a degree of emotion—embarrassment, or pleasure? —on Bingley's greeting her; Elizabeth he barely glanced at, although he was aware of her every least movement—quite nearly her every breath. She had merely curtsied in return to the compliments they offered, and seated herself again at the work table with barely a word. He felt this subdued welcome very much, but it did no more than confirm his expectations; so, while Mrs. Bennet went on at length on how happy she was to see Bingley again, he carefully held himself in, and tried by his behaviour to avoid causing Elizabeth any more distress than she already felt.

Only when Mrs. Bennet's unmistakably cold words of greeting to him released him to speak did he permit himself to ask Elizabeth: "Miss Elizabeth Bennet: I hope that Mr. and Mrs. Gardiner are well?" She, scarcely looking up from her work, answered in the affirmative, but in so hurried a manner that he had difficulty distinguishing the words; clearly, his reference had brought back memories of their last meeting at Lambton, which would, of course, upset her deeply. After a few minutes she did call upon her civility to ask after Georgiana, which pleased him, but, to spare her discomfort, he did not allow himself to engage her in further conversation. He seated himself at some distance from her, and gave his consideration over to Miss Bennet; that Elizabeth made no attempt to speak to him again after their brief exchange was further confirmation of his deductions, but this small triumph had little power to soothe him.

Observing Miss Bennet, the first thing to strike him about her was that she seemed to be listening to the conversation between her mother and Bingley with peculiar attention. Her hands stopped their work whenever he spoke, and once or twice he thought he saw the colour rise to her cheeks at something that was said; surely this was not a sign of indifference—whether approval or disapproval he could not be certain, but surely not indifference.

While he tried his best not to catch the sense of what Mrs. Bennet said, he could not help but hear with what pleasure she spoke of the marriage of her youngest daughter to "Mr. George Wickham, Esquire", his commission in the army, and his posting to the north. By this did he at least have the pleasure of understanding that the Gardiners had not disclosed his rôle in the matter, and that he had no reason to fear that Elizabeth might have to bear with that too, in seeing him.

Their visit was not long, but by its end he had already seen enough to begin to doubt his previous conclusions concerning Miss Bennet; Elizabeth, without question, had been frequently suffering during their time there, but her sister had shown no such signs of distress—if anything, he felt, he would have said she showed interest; nothing else described it so well. On the ride back to Netherfield, Bingley was cautiously enthusiastic: "That went well, I thought," he opined, looking at Darcy to gauge his reaction. "There surely was no displeasure evident; there did not appear to be any ill-feelings for the manner in which we left the country last time, certainly."

"True," Darcy agreed, "if we are to go merely by Mrs. Bennet's manner, there has been little change, indeed, from the sentiments of last autumn. I was not seated where I could see properly: did Miss Bennet offer any clue as to her feelings?"

"I smiled at her once, and she seemed to smile in return; her self-possession makes it hard to know for certain, but I thought I felt something, there. No ill-feelings, at any rate." Darcy nodded at this; his newly-formed sensibility to the impressions of the heart made him give this far more weight than he would have done a year prior, and he also had Elizabeth's assertion of Miss Bennet's affection for Bingley to support his observations. The two rode on, each preoccupied with their separate interpretations of what had transpired during their visit.

Chapter Twenty-Three

*T*hey were not to return to Longbourn until the following Tuesday, when there was to be a large party gathered from among the families of the neighbourhood. Bingley was eager in his preparation, being the first one down for the only time in Darcy's memory; Darcy, being himself always punctual, was therefore down in time to allow the gentlemen to be amongst the first to arrive. He was pleased, and Bingley was delighted, to see a faint blush rise to Miss Bennet's cheek as she smiled at them on receiving their compliments; and Elizabeth seemed to smile upon Darcy with more warmth than at their last meeting; yet she still had little enough to say to him. During the arrivals, they were neither one given any peculiar attention, but later, on entering the dining-room, Bingley was fortunate enough to find a seat next to Miss Bennet; luck did not favour Darcy, however, and he found himself once more adjacent to Mrs. Bennet, with Elizabeth at the extreme opposite end of the table. At least on this occasion she restricted herself to the minimum conversation required by strictest propriety, for which Darcy was thankful. Bingley darted a happy glance at Darcy as he sat down next to Miss Bennet, and Darcy returned a slight smile and a lifted eyebrow in brief conspiratorial acknowledgement, then looked casually away. All through dinner he was able to observe Miss Bennet: as before, her outward demeanour was reserved, but Darcy was now sensitive to the fact that she spoke infrequently to any one but his friend, and attended to Bingley intently, stilling her own comments when he spoke. To Darcy this again indicated a notable interest; as for Bingley, he wanted nothing more than her company to be perfectly happy.

But his friend's happiness was Darcy's only reward through the dinner; although the food was good, the company at his end of the table could not have had less to say for itself; Darcy looked forward to the time they might re-join the ladies after dinner, in hopes he might have some conversation with Elizabeth, or even just some portion of her notice.

When that time came, he entered the drawing-room and looked round, only to see Elizabeth tightly surrounded by ladies at a table to one side, where she and her elder sister were doing the honours by helping every one to tea and coffee. There being no hope for a *tête a tête*, Darcy merely helped himself to a cup of coffee from the table; Elizabeth did not even glance at him as he passed by. He drifted off in another direction, but he often looked back to where she stood, envying those to whom she spoke. He was careful, though, to pay attention to those around him, holding himself to his new standards of comportment, and not allowing himself to simply stand to one side, observing without participating.

He joined Mr. Bennet and Sir William, standing off to one side of the proceedings. "Mr. Darcy," Mr. Bennet greeted him laconically; Darcy merely bowed his acknowledgement, as he had noted Mr. Bennet was averse to unnecessary conversation. Not so Sir William.

"How good to see you here amongst us again, Mr. Darcy; will you be long in the country?"

"A few weeks, Sir William; Bingley wanted to get in some shooting."

"As my wife has given him free use of all my game, I am reasonably assured he will be pleased with his success," Mr. Bennet observed in a vexed tone. "But if memory serves where Mr. Bingley's skill with a gun is concerned, he is unlikely to thin their numbers by much," he said. "You, Mr. Darcy, are another matter: I trust my wife failed to mention you specifically; might I expect that you will limit yourself to the Netherfield coveys?"

Knowing him to be in jest—primarily at least—Darcy replied, "I fear, Mr. Bennet, that Mrs. Bennet did authorise Bingley to bring his friends, if he would; but, to oblige you, I shall restrict myself to an instructional rôle when we avail ourselves of your wife's generous offer to decimate your game."

Mr. Bennet gave him a droll look: "Of course; she would do. Very well, Sir; I thank you for your abstinence."

Darcy made an overly formal bow, and received the hint of a smile from Mr. Bennet.

He staid with them until the crowd around the table where Elizabeth stood eventually eased, and he took the opportunity to return his cup to her. On this occasion he was rewarded by the enquiry: "Is your sister at Pemberley still?"

"Yes, she will remain there till Christmas," he replied.

"And quite alone? Have all her friends left her?"

"Mrs. Annesley is with her. The others have been gone on to Scarborough, these three weeks."

Barred by propriety and a foreknowledge of failure, he could not speak of those things he most pressingly wanted to say, and, try though he might, he could find no subject for conversation which might be broached with entire safety and propriety; yet he was perfectly unwilling to leave her, and stood by her without speaking for several minutes before another young lady came up and addressed her in whispers. Darcy left her side at that, disappointed, but not surprised; he could only invite, he could not command, and if it were to be his lot to dance attendance on Elizabeth for weeks, or even years, in hopes of gaining some measure of her regard, so be it.

Meanwhile, as the evening progressed, he was able to watch his friend monopolise Miss Bennet more and more. His smiles thawed her own, and Darcy could almost see her interest in Bingley re-kindling in response to his candid warmth and very evident esteem.

For the rest of the evening, however, Darcy and Elizabeth were kept apart by being placed quite a distance away from each other at the whist tables; he tried to keep his attention where it belonged, but, as the play at his table was unrelievedly stupid, and the conversation not much better, he had a great deal of time to look Elizabeth's way, and wish they could be at the same table. And, unaccountably, Bingley's carriage was among the very first to arrive, so the two gentlemen left without any further opportunities for either to speak to the one he wished to hear from most. But on the way back to Netherfield, Darcy was pleased to see that his friend was in excellent spirits; evidence, he thought, that so far things were promising well.

The day following, Darcy and Bingley took part in a hunt hosted by the Gouldings, a family in the neighbourhood comparable in standing to the Bennets. As they lived at a considerable distance the opposite direction from Meryton, there could be no chance for the friends to be in company with the Bennet ladies; and, indeed, throughout the day Darcy was turning over in his mind a step he felt little enthusiasm for, but which he knew to be the best thing for both Bingley and himself: his removal to London. Given her obvious discomfort in his company, he could conceive of no adequate reason to trouble Elizabeth with his continued residence in the neighbourhood, and surely Bingley would do better with Miss Bennet if he, Darcy, were to take himself out of the way. He took up the topic with his friend that evening.

"Bingley, I shall be returning to London for a time; there are a few matters I should attend to."

Bingley looked at him in surprise. "But you will not be gone long?"

"I should imagine I can be back by this Saturday week."

"Very well, Darcy; I am sorry to hear it, though. You will let me know if anything changes?"

"Of course," Darcy hesitated, loath to initiate what would be a painful relation, for both of them. "To be quite honest, Bingley, something has changed, and it affects you." Bingley looked at his friend expectantly. Darcy paused again, struggling to overcome his reluctance to reveal his miscalculations to his friend; then, calling upon his sense of duty, he started in: "The truth is, Bingley, I believe the steps I took last November with regard to Miss Bennet and yourself to have been in error."

"In error?"

"Yes. At the time I was fully convinced that she held no esteem for you; I can no longer make that claim."

"You are saying that you believe Miss Bennet has feelings for me?"

"I am."

For a long moment Bingley said nothing. Then, an especially large grin split his face. "But, Darcy, this is marvellous!" he cried. "How do you know?"

"Much the same way I thought I knew before, but this time I watched with more heart than head. At a minimum, I can now make no positive claim against her having a regard for you, and am rather inclined to believe the opposite to be the case, given my recent time with the two of you in company."

"Cautious dog!" Bingley cried. "Would it do you an actual harm to just once make a categorical statement of fact on a matter of the heart?"

"That is as may be; but see here, Bingley: there is something else. I kept something from you last winter, and I will no longer be a party to deception." Darcy drew breath, then went on, "Miss Bennet was in London last winter for several months; I knew it, and I did not apprise you of the fact."

"You knew Miss Bennet was in Town? How? Did you meet?"

"No, we never met; she called on your sister; I had it from her."

"She called on Caroline! And I was not told? And you—you sided with my sister against me?" Bingley visibly quelled his rising anger, his face showing confusion instead. "I can scarcely believe this; have you any explanation to offer?"

"No; only an apology. I could see that you were not over your feelings for her, and, convinced as I was at the time that she did not return your affection, in my arrogance I decided it would be best if more time passed before the two of you saw each other again."

"And the fact that Caroline agreed with you did not give you pause?" said Bingley angrily. "What were you thinking?"

"I did feel those doubts, I confess," Darcy told him contritely. "But I forced them down in service of what I thought was the greater good of your well-being. It was no more than a continuance of that same presumption and assurance that separated you from Miss Bennet in the beginning. It was not until Lambton that I was sure your esteem for her was not extinguished, and even more recently, coming back from London, that I began to doubt my conclusions where Miss Bennet was concerned. As soon as that occurred, I suggested our return, that I might make certain, and I have now given you the results of my observations."

"That she likes me."

"Yes; well, more than that."

Bingley could not keep his grin from wiping the anger from his face. "Lucky thing for you that worked out," he admonished Darcy. "Otherwise I should be very angry with you right now."

"And you would be right to be so. I have learnt better though, now, I trust." He put out a hand with a repentant and hopeful look. Bingley, good man that he was, took it gladly, and the difficult bit was over. Darcy stood and said, "Now, I plan on leaving for London to-morrow morning. You have no need of a hanger-on to intrude on your time with Miss Bennet. I shall absent myself for a while to leave you a clear field."

Bingley stood happily and shook his hand again. "I shall be as quick as I can about the business, that you may return the sooner."

"I am confident you will; but I leave that to you," Darcy said with a smile.

Accordingly, Darcy took himself off the next day, wending a rather gloomy way back to a very quiet Grosvenor Square. He spent his first day in Town going about his affairs, but they were soon exhausted. That left him with little to do other than read, or take walks, and he divided his time almost equally between them. His thoughts passing over and over all his time with Elizabeth, he recalled her mention of the modern poets at Pemberley that day, and, charging his memory, was able to come up with two or three of the names she had mentioned; he purchased them directly; in reading them he was able to imagine himself closer to Elizabeth, and was pleased to picture the discussions they might have on them in the future.

After a day or two passed in this manner, it occurred to him he had not written to Georgiana since leaving Pemberley, and he sat down to rectify that oversight.

Grosvenor Square
Friday, September 19, —

Dear Georgiana,

I have returned to London to wait until Bingley should have had time to secure his future with Miss Bennet; I deemed it best done without the hindrance of my overbearing personality being quite so much in evidence. I doubt it will take long, however; the two principals involved seem as likely to connect as any couple I have ever witnessed, just on the strength of Bingley's esteem alone; but I am persuaded that Miss Bennet cherishes a deep regard for him, as well. Indeed, I am sure that, now the discouraging influence of my fearsome features is removed, Mrs. Bennet will be able to contrive ample time for the two lovers to be alone to get the job done with admirable efficiency.

So, I am sure the light of tender love triumphant shines by now on Bingley's schemes of domesticity; I left him yesterday, and I cannot imagine it would take him too much longer to declare himself: he was never one to be reticent in making his feelings known. I expect to hear from him almost hourly to declare his profitable addresses. In spite of my way of talking, Dearest, I am very pleased for him, and wish him every joy in his married life; I am certain he will be happy, and in their mutual goodness I see much to value, and a most favourable prophecy of felicity.

There is little going forward in Town just now, and I am catching up on some reading. After our discussion with Miss Elizabeth Bennet in July, I have been tasting poetry by our modern authors; this afternoon I read *The Castaway*, by Cowper: have you read it? It is dark, though moving: the tale of a man swept overboard at night, far out at sea; its metaphor found harbour in my heart, and I have turned to this missive, my own link to light, land, and beauty, to distract me and release me from its power. I understand the author was a man given to fits of insanity — what does this say about me, I should like to know? I shall trust your regard for me to be sufficient evidence of my being of sound mind, however.

You will, I know, wish to hear of Miss Elizabeth Bennet; she is well, and asked after you particularly, and on more than one occasion. But I confess that it is nearly as much for her sake as for Bingley's that I have removed to London—knowing of her younger sister's condition before her marriage, as I do, my presence could not but inflict some measure of discomfort on her. Of course, she knows nothing of my involvement latterly in the business, which would be much worse, but still, it must be bad enough, and so I have distanced myself from her. I can only trust to time, to let her present suffering amend itself to a degree that will allow her to see me without painful recollection. How much simpler our lives would be if we could regulate our brains to the extent that we could forget whatever we chose to: imagine the bliss of forgetting all pain and embarrassment! These are the scars of the soul, and I cannot but imagine that it would be more beautiful without them. Well, having now given that more thought, I see I am wrong; the soul of the babe is not more beautiful than that of the adult, except in the beauty of the promise it holds for the future. The soul is formed, and *in*formed, by every thing in our lives, including, certainly, all of our trials; pain and mortification must be the price of a beautiful soul: the natural trimmings and prunings, if you will, that create the majestic beauty of the mighty oak. I do not believe that an oak raised in a hothouse would be nearly as picturesque as the forest patriarch which has withstood all the tempests and droughts Nature could throw against it.

Well, there it is, I suppose; we must weather our storms, and persevere through straitened circumstances, and grow slowly into beauty. I must, at least: you, it seems, have somehow managed to by-pass the requirement for trials and travail, having arrived at perfection quite naturally in earliest adulthood. Your trials *demonstrate* the beauty of your soul, whilst those by which I am afflicted must labour still to shape mine. Perhaps that is simply the difference between men and women — those of my sex must toil, and struggle, and fight with the world, before we are moulded into our correct shape, whilst your sex finds it more spontaneously and benevolently within you. Perhaps, as you are the bearers of life, you are necessarily and innately more sacred and serene, and we men are drawn to that immaculate purity in order to soothe and correct our own great imperfections. I do not know, Dearest; but surely a man without a woman must suffer the more in this life before finding tranquillity and repose.

I do apologise; the residue of melancholy left behind by Cowper does not seem to have left me completely. Be assured, Dearest, I am not so desperate as it may sound; I find that my new susceptibility to poetry affects me more strongly than I have any idea of whilst I am reading it. Then, I am more conscious of the scansion and rhyme scheme, the author's use of diction and imagery — a dozen things. But afterwards, as I revisit it in my mind, the impact is felt the more for being free of such critical thinking.

Best I turn my attentions to something rather more mundane and purposeful; there is a letter from Stevenson, which will no doubt oc-

cupy my mind to better effect than poetry.
Therefore, adieu, Dearest. I remain,
Your affectionate Brother,
Fitzwilliam Darcy

And, as he had foretold, it was not long before he heard from his friend that his courtship had produced early and very favourable returns. An express arrived on Saturday to this effect:

Netherfield
Saturday, September 20, —

Dear Darcy,

Great news! She has accepted me! You were quite right: she had feelings for me all along. It happened this way: Mrs. Bennet invited me to go shooting with Mr. Bennet on Friday, which I was rather worried about, you know, but we got along very well, although my luck was not with me—I hardly hit a thing. When we got back I spent the afternoon with them and staid to dinner. After tea I chanced to have a bit of time alone with Miss Bennet, and I lost no time in testing your theory. Fortunately, you were correct, and I am now the happiest man on Earth, in simplest truth. She is such a perfect angel: I am sure I do not deserve her, but I am so happy to be able to give her a secure future.

Well! I went straightaway to Mr. Bennet, and I was glad to have spent a pleasant morning with him, as it rather eased the way for me. He made no objections at all, and actually seemed pleased, although he said not a word about it all through supper; he is an odd sort, but really quite a good fellow, underneath, I believe. Every one else, though, was delighted by it, and Mrs. Bennet could hardly let any one else speak, so determined as she was to sanction our happiness with her good wishes; it was all very gratifying.

That is all my news for now, and I expect I shall see you before long, as there is no need now for you to stay away, so I shall leave off; I am to meet the Bennet's after breakfast, and I still have to change.

Therefore, adieu: with warmest regards, I remain,

Your Obedient &c.

Charles Bingley

Darcy read this with a certain wistful pleasure, and wrote a reply that was, for him, quite sentimental.

Grosvenor Square
Saturday, September 20, —

My dear Bingley,

I am very heartened by your letter, and so very glad my interference had no permanent effect on your fortunes in love. I have no doubt at all of yours being the happiest marriage of my whole acquaintance, and am willing, to please you, to stipulate that you are currently the happiest man extant. With the most faithful sincerity, I am glad for you with all my heart; you have my deepest congratulations, and my gratitude for your generous clemency where my faults affected your felicity for so long.

Your prospective father-in-law is, indeed, a singular sort of man; while not without some faults, I have observed in him certain behaviours that smack of a good heart, albeit somewhat hidden and restricted in scope — but I am sure he has your lady's best interests firmly at heart; it is undoubtedly to your benefit to be on his good side, as he may then be expected to help with the management of his wife.

I still depend on returning a week from today, although I am most eager to be able to offer my congratulations to you and your Jane in person. So, until then, I remain,

Yours faithfully, &c.,

Fitzwilliam Darcy

Darcy had already determined he would stay out his time in London, in spite of Bingley's encouragement to return: there was still Elizabeth's state of mind to consider, after all; he was to have gone back on Monday week, and that still seemed the best plan.

Almost a week after these events, Darcy, having finished dinner and starting idly to think about a volume of poetry for the evening, had just reached the library when he heard an imperious knocking on the front door. There being no one in Town he could expect to visit him, he stood by the library door to hear who this importunate caller might be: he had not long to wait.

"Where is my nephew!" Lady Catherine's voice rang out through the halls. Alarmed and perplexed, he went hastily to meet her.

On reaching her, he bowed promptly, asking, "Dear Lady Catherine, welcome; whatever has brought you to London?"

An ill-tempered nod to his bow was all the answer vouchsafed him. The lady waved him magisterially into the front drawing-room and firmly shut the door behind them. She swung round to face him and cried, "You!"

"I beg your pardon?" Darcy said, taken aback.

"*You* are what has brought me here! You and that impertinent slip of a girl in Hertfordshire, Miss Elizabeth Bennet."

Darcy face froze at this; "Do go on," he said in carefully measured tones. His first, blind anger at her interference he quickly suppressed; whatever injury she had started was done, and he needed her intelligence that he might repair the damage, more than he needed to rebuke her galling invasion of his affairs; but he could not help but rail inwardly, though, at the malignant fates which provoked people and events, at every turn, to conspire against his interests where Elizabeth was concerned.

"I am just come from Meryton, in Hertfordshire; I presume you know the cause for my journey? What has compelled me to travel without rest for two straight days, in order to rescue the family's honour?"

Over the course of years Darcy had learnt the futility of contending with his aunt, so he merely said, "I fear, dear lady, you have me at a loss; how is the family's honour at risk?"

"I warn you, Darcy, do not try my patience; I have had quite enough of that already for one day."

"I assure you, Madam, I am not sporting with your patience: what is it you wish to discuss? What has compelled you to this exigency?"

His aunt looked at him with an unfriendly eye. "Very well, Darcy, if this is how you wish to treat me, I shall tell you: two days ago I was informed that, not only was your friend Bingley to be married to the eldest Bennet girl, but that *you* were soon to marry the second, Miss Elizabeth Bennet! Now, deny it, if you dare!"

Putting the sum of her statements together in his mind, Darcy asked, "Forgive me, Lady Catherine, but do I understand that you have been to the trouble of a journey to Hertfordshire, to enquire of Miss Elizabeth Bennet whether or not she has engaged herself to me? I hardly know how to express my amazement." Having had time to recover from the surprise of her attack, Darcy recalled that she herself had married beneath her, making her present impertinences even less defensible. But he wanted very much to hear what she had to say of Elizabeth, so he bit back on his ire, asking mildly enough: "What had she to say?"

"She said nothing—or nothing to the purpose! What are you thinking, Darcy, to pay your addresses to such a person? I have never been so insulted in my life as I was this morning by that girl. Enquire, you say? I did not go to enquire—to what purpose would I enquire? I went to put an end to all such disgraceful rumours and expectations, and to convince the girl she could never succeed. Now what have you to say?"

"I assure you, I have not the least idea that Miss Elizabeth Bennet entertains any intention of marrying me," he replied.

"I can scarcely credit that; whence came this report, if that be the case?"

"In strictest candour, aunt," he assured her, "you astound me quite—on my honour, I sincerely believe Miss Elizabeth Bennet has no notion whatever of marrying me; I can hardly express my surprise at what you tell me. What was the substance of your discussion?"

Somewhat mollified, Lady Catherine took a seat; Darcy took one opposite her, making no attempt to disguise his interest; his aunt, presuming his attentive expression to be due to the extraordinary nature of her encounter, told him, "First, I told her why I had come; she pretended ignorance of the affair, but I could see through her arts. I felt I could be sure of you, you realise, but I could not be easy until I knew her temper. You know not what some women are capable of, Darcy, but I am not one to have the wool pulled over *my* eyes."

"What said she?"

"Humph! She tweaked me for making the journey! —*that* is what she said: that a visit from me was more likely to confirm such a report than deny it. Then she tried to pretend that no such report was abroad, when I had had it directly from her dear friend, Mrs. Collins. I pressed her closely, but she flouted me again, refusing to answer my question."

"Forgive me: what question was that?"

"I challenged her to declare there was no foundation for such a rumour; she defied me and declined to reply, without even an attempt at civility."

Darcy saw that this was no more than Elizabeth's honesty at work; of course he *had* proposed, but he could hardly reveal this to his aunt without sparking some very heated contention, and he wished to hear more. Nor, apparently, had Elizabeth felt she was due any such frankness; and, given Lady Catherine's own want of civility, Darcy could hardly blame her.

Lady Catherine continued: "I demanded to know the truth; the girl had the impudence to try evasion—evasion, with me! I, who have ever been known for the candour of my address! As if evasions would work on *me*. Well, in her evasions I read the truth, for lies *are* the truth, to those wise enough to read them."

"What truth was that, Madam?"

"That she wishes for your addresses, of course!"

Darcy shook his head. "That simply cannot be the case, Lady Catherine; what did she say that could support such an idea?"

"It is rather what she did *not* say: she refused to satisfy me on any point regarding a potential union between you, even though I attacked her on various sides."

"Attacked her, how?"

"First, you may imagine, I told her you were intended for your cousin."

"And her response?"

"That she was aware of it, and it held no interest for her at all! Her very words were: 'If I am his choice, why should I not accept him?' Her very words! 'Because honour, prudence, nay, interest, forbid it,' said I. 'Do not expect to be noticed by his family or friends, if you act against the inclinations of us all. You will be censured, slighted, and despised, by every one connected with him. Your alliance will be a disgrace before the world and God; your name will never even be mentioned.' *That* is what I told her!"

"And what did she offer by way of reply?"

"That the wife of Mr. Darcy would be so happy in her marriage that she could not repine! Conceive the arrogance, if you can! Imagine life with such insolence, from such a near, such an inescapable source! Such as she can bear no comparison to the delicate reticence of a truly well-bred lady like Anne, Darcy; you cannot be so blind as to persist after this."

Darcy's thoughts raced at hearing Elizabeth's remark, but he cautiously said: "I am astounded to imagine the scene, Lady Catherine, I truly am. Blind I may have been in the past, I warrant you, but I believe I begin to see better, now. What said you next?"

"I was forced to remind her to whom she was speaking; when I had sufficiently made her feel her place, I pointed out the utter unsuitability of her pretentions: with no family, connexions, or fortune to her name, how could she think of ruining you before all good society? I told her she had best learn to be content within her own sphere. 'I am a gentleman's daughter,' said she then. To me! She declared herself your equal! —imagine it! Well, I had had enough, and beyond. I demanded to know, once and for all, if she were engaged to you. Finally, I was able to force her to admit she was not. But did that end her presumption? It did not! I required her promise that she would never enter into such an engagement; she absolutely refused to give it to me."

Darcy's thoughts froze: "She what?"

"She categorically refused to give me the assurance I required of her."

His heart did a revolution within him; there could be no rational motive for such a refusal: Elizabeth could have released herself instantly from Lady Catherine's impertinences simply by stating what he firmly believed to be her true sentiments; that she had not was a greater cause for hope than any he could have ever expected. When coupled with her statement about the happiness his wife must anticipate, Darcy was hard-pressed to keep his elation from revealing itself. "Said she anything else?"

"She defied me yet again!" cried Lady Catherine, whose return journey to London had seemingly given her time enough to have amplified her indignation many times over. "She called my arguments frivolous, and my intentions ill-judged! Ill-judged! She forced me to remind her of the scandalous reputation her family suffered under, and even this could not shame the girl into a proper show of respect."

"What scandal is this?" Darcy asked coolly.

His aunt eyed him. "No, I suppose you are not informed on this point; naturally she would be careful to keep it from you. Well, then, Darcy, you should know that her youngest sister has but recently eloped with that Wickham fellow. Eloped! And lived with him for months before they were married, by what I understand. I asked her how she could imagine you would ever consent to be brother to the son of your father's steward, or call such a libertine sister."

"And Miss Elizabeth Bennet's response?"

"She all but called the dogs on me! She threw me off of her property! I tell you Darcy, her final words to me were: 'Neither duty, nor honour, nor gratitude have any possible claim on me'. There's for you! Can you still conceive any regard for her? Is such a woman to be preferred to your cousin in any way?"

Darcy knew this could not be as his aunt represented it: Elizabeth could never seriously cast off all that was proper, as his aunt would have him believe. But still he forbore to argue; he knew better than to attempt to work on his aunt with anything resembling logic. "I am shocked — astounded. I should never have believed her capable of saying such a thing."

"Well... you now see her for what she is." At this the lady's demeanour softened, and she said: "Darcy, when will you put an end to all such foolishness and difficulty, and declare for Anne? How long must you cling to your bachelor ways before you see where your best interests lie?"

Darcy nodded pensively before replying: "Well, aunt, it so happens I was discussing that very topic with Lady Andover earlier this year; I can tell you, there may be hope: there may be hope indeed that my bachelor days are winding to a close."

"Well, I, for one, am delighted to hear it." She sighed and looked about her, as though uncertain of what might best be done at that point. At length she said, "And now, Darcy, I am absolutely exhausted. Please be so kind as to have my things sent up."

"Of course, Madam." His aunt began to gather her belongings, and Darcy said, "What do you require for your present comfort — have you eaten?"

"No: I was too intent on reaching you."

"Then you doubtless must be famished. Go on up, and I will have something sent up. Or would you rather dine?"

"Thank you, Darcy; I shall just stay in my rooms." So saying, she made her way up to the apartment she was accustomed to use. Darcy saw to her needs, relieved that he would not need to sit with her through her dinner, then retired to his rooms himself for some privacy; he was greatly puzzled by his aunt's information. To his wondering and painstaking enquiry into what he had been able to collect, the two most salient points were these: Elizabeth had refused to offer his aunt any assurance she would not marry him, and had declared that marriage to him was a thing to be desired. The former was the most striking: she had so little to lose by providing the sought-for guarantee, and so much to gain in being relieved from his aunt's importunities, that her refusal was very hard to understand in any way other than that she harboured some idea of marriage to him as being a possibility. The latter was more pleasing, however, in that it was such a noteworthy reversal of her earlier statements; she could now, it seemed, see some positive benefit from such a marriage. These two points buoyed his hopes to a degree he had not known since the spring. But then, when he had thoroughly reflected on what she had said, he began to look at the interview from Elizabeth's side, and was very uneasy on the point of what her annoyance must have been on being thus attacked in her own home, and on this subject particularly; once again he began to feel an almost physical distress at what she must have suffered, and how she must regard his family, and himself, after such an affront as this.

These thoughts carried him to sleep, and had not abated before morning. Lady Catherine continued on her way back to Kent right after breakfast, and Darcy set out for Hertfordshire as soon as she had gone.

Chapter Twenty-Four

On the way to Hertfordshire, however, the hopes that had fuelled his desire to return began to be challenged by the idea of the apologies due Elizabeth; his hopes were by no means lessened, but he recognised that he could not reasonably expect any favour from Elizabeth until he had made every apology in his power. Yet there were so many points on which he felt himself and his family to be at fault, he could not imagine where he might start. He told himself over and over that he must simply make his apologies, as sincerely as he could, and as often as he must, and trust to time and her goodness; as soon as he could discern any indication that her resentment had moderated, he told himself, there would be time enough to try to discover how much foundation his hopes might have. It required quite a number of repetitions of this before he could bring his mind to accept it.

When he arrived at Netherfield some little while after noon, Bingley was not at home; not surprisingly, he was at Longbourn. Darcy decided not to follow him and arrive at Longbourn unanticipated; he therefore satisfied himself by wandering about the house and grounds, dining lightly, and waiting up until Bingley came home late in the evening. Bingley came to find him on entering. "Darcy! How marvellous! When did you get in?" said he with an exceedingly generous grin: there was about his whole person a particular joy that shone in his every aspect.

"I came this afternoon," Darcy replied, "but as you were out, I staid here to wait for you."

"You should have come to Longbourn," cried Bingley.

"I could not know if you would be there," Darcy said reasonably, "or perhaps be out with Miss Bennet, and so thought better of it."

"Understandable," Bingley allowed, "and more likely than not to be the case."

"Well!" Darcy said heartily, "let me congratulate you in person; I can see by your face that you are still happy with the state of affairs."

"I thank you, Darcy, and for your letter. You were right, as I said in mine." But then his manner changed, and he became serious. He said, "But, listen here; something has come up in the interval which has surprised me greatly: I have heard from Miss Bennet that you had actually proposed to Miss Elizabeth Bennet—is this true?"

Darcy could not deny it. "It is," he said.

"But, great Heavens, Darcy; why did not you tell me?"

"What was there to say, that could be of use to either of us? You had troubles enough of your own, and there could be nothing you might say that would improve my situation. No, it was better so."

"Yet it was you who recommended a return to Netherfield. I cannot imagine what pain it must give you to be with her; what could induce you to willingly be in her company again?"

Darcy eyed his friend with mild surprise. "The need to correct my error concerning you and her sister, of course. No matter what my sentiments might be in the circumstances, I could not let my interference stand, when I could no longer be certain of my conclusions. And, as I was not unaware of your continued regard for Miss Bennet, there was nothing for it but to convince you to return."

Bingley very sincerely offered Darcy his hand; the two shook warmly without speaking.

"Have you any plans for to-morrow?" was Bingley's next question.

"I do — I owe Miss Elizabeth Bennet an apology for a visit she recently suffered from my aunt, Lady Catherine."

"An apology, Darcy? How so? I know she visited, of course, but it was merely to pass on news of the Collinses, was not it?"

"I wish it were that benign; no, she came to insist that Miss Elizabeth Bennet not marry me; a rumour, apparently promoted by Mrs. Collins, had given my aunt to believe that such an engagement was an established fact. Can you imagine the scene? You have not had the honour of meeting my aunt, so you can have no idea how insufferable she can be when she chooses, but based on what she told me, she could hardly have been more offensive without an actual attack on Miss Elizabeth Bennet's person. So now I have even more to try to live down." He could not speak of his hopes until he knew how much substance might be behind them.

"Good Lord!" Bingley exclaimed. "How disastrous! How can I help?"

"If you might just conceive a way Miss Elizabeth Bennet and I might have a word in private, that would be most helpful."

"Nothing easier: I shall propose a walk. Neither Mrs. Bennet nor Miss Mary Bennet will ever take the trouble; Miss Catherine Bennet is no walker, and usually goes to call on the Lucases; Miss Bennet and I shall be happy to lag behind for a bit of time by ourselves, and there you are."

"Excellent: I thank you, Bingley," Darcy said. But he then noted, "I see this is not the first time you have availed yourself of the idea."

Here Bingley coloured slightly, murmuring vaguely about its being "a scheme of Miss Bennet's, actually." The two retired not long after, and Darcy had only to wait until the morning.

On that morning, Perkins dressed him with exceeding care, although Darcy could not truly appreciate the results; his dress could matter but little: if one were intent on humbling oneself, it could hardly matter whether one was in the height of fashion, or not.

On their arrival at Longbourn, Darcy held himself in very carefully, uncertain of how he might be met by Elizabeth. Shortly, Bingley proposed their all walking out, as he said he would; Mrs Bennet declined, as did Mary, according to Bingley's prediction. The other three ladies prepared themselves for the out of doors, and they all set off together. Darcy paid no attention to the direction they took, being too preoccupied with what he could say to Elizabeth to begin to make amends for—well, for every thing. The burden of obligation and contrition he felt towards Elizabeth was so substantial he had no idea of how it might ever be discharged. He could but begin, and trust to time; he vowed he would commit however much time was necessary, even if it meant taking a manor in the neighbourhood, if need be.

Not far from Longbourn, Bingley and Jane slowly let the others outstrip them; shortly before they receded from view altogether, Darcy turned discreetly to tip his hat in thanks to his friend. Catherine was pleased to leave them and proceed to the Lucases, again as predicted; Elizabeth made no objection, and continued with him alone. This, to his most exacting observation and analysis, seemed auspicious, and he was preparing himself to bring up the subject which had brought him thither, when Elizabeth spoke first: "Mr. Darcy, I am a very selfish creature; and, for the sake of giving relief to my own feelings, care not how much I may be wounding yours." At such a beginning, Darcy was prepared to be amused, imagining that another of her diverting impertinences was to follow; that she should feel sufficiently at ease with him to once again favour him with her wit was very promising, and gave him hope that, sooner rather than later, she might come—

not to forget, perhaps, but to overlook: in some measure to overlook. What succeeded, however, was this: "I can no longer help thanking you for your unexampled kindness to my poor sister. Ever since I have known it, I have been most anxious to acknowledge to you how gratefully I feel it. Were it known to the rest of my family, I should not have merely my own gratitude to express."

All Darcy's hopes sank within him; all the time he had been working on the dilemma posed by Wickham, this was exactly what he had most wished to avoid: when added to their previous history and the more recent offence offered by Lady Catherine, how could she ever feel comfortable in his presence again? Annoyance heaped on top of obligation and resentment—was there a worse possible combination to foster ease or esteem? Blast! Why must every thing scheme so against him?

Wishing her to know that it had been his first object to prevent this discovery, he said with sincere contrition, "I am sorry, exceedingly sorry, that you have ever been informed of what may, in a mistaken light, have given you uneasiness." Then, realising whence this intelligence must have come, and that he must again have wholly mistaken some one's character, he said with unaffected disappointment, "I did not think Mrs. Gardiner was so little to be trusted."

But Elizabeth hastened to exonerate her aunt: "You must not blame my aunt. Lydia's thoughtlessness first betrayed to me that you had been concerned in the matter; and, of course, I could not rest till I knew the particulars." At this Darcy nodded, relieved that, at least in this instance, his judgement had not erred. How obvious that Lydia should have been the first to let loose the secret, flighty and inconstant as were her thoughts; at any rate, he now had a target for his anger.

Elizabeth, turning to face him directly, was going on: "Let me thank you again and again, in the name of all my family, for that generous compassion which induced you to take so much trouble, and bear so many mortifications, for the sake of discovering them."

Darcy was thankful that at least she did not blame him for his interference; however, the idea that her family might be indebted to him must of course occur to her, but he could not let her think her family bore any obligation; for, aside from stopping Wickham, he had thought only of her well-being: he could not let her think he had been seeking any hold or advantage, or that he had in any way intended to disparage her family. He entreated her solemnly: "If you *will* thank me, let it be for yourself alone. That the wish of giving happiness to you might add force to the other inducements which led me on, I shall not attempt to deny. But your *family* owe me nothing. Much as I respect them, I believe I thought only of *you*." While he was trying to speak nothing more than the truth, unintentionally he allowed some of the longing he felt enter into his accent.

Elizabeth looked down and would not meet his eye again; they continued their walk. But either she took a slight step towards him, or perhaps a slight unevenness in the footing impelled her gently in his direction; in either case, this minor shift brought her closer to him, and she did not directly move away. An anxious moment later, after watching intently for her to recoil to her previous distance, his desires suddenly overcame his misgivings: his newly-ascendant sensibilities insisted that this suggestion of approval from her was the sign of esteem he had been hoping to see, and suddenly he found himself once more surrendering to the demands of the heart. Almost against his will, dreading the outcome even as he spoke, he abandoned his cautious schemes and measured resolutions, and threw himself over to fate—he made his last, despairing appeal to her: "You are too generous to trifle with me. If your feelings are still what they were last April, tell me so at once. *My* affections and wishes are unchanged, but one word from you will silence me on this subject forever."

To his immediate dismay, the lady's face showed nothing so clearly as confusion; she seemed hardly to know how to respond to this fresh avowal of devotion from him; she said at once: "Mr. Darcy, I...I wonder to hear it..." She paused to choose her words, and her awkwardness told him every thing; in the space of a single step all hope within him died, as it may easily be conceived how ready was he to distrust the wisdom of the heart where his own happiness was at stake. Regret and mortification overcame him, and he was prepared at that very moment to disappear forever from her life; indeed, he wished that he might instantly be hundreds of miles hence. His application had been absurdly and senselessly impulsive, and he knew not how to censure himself enough; how could he ever expect she should make such a leap, and return a favourable reply to yet another unsuspected attack—on this subject, above all others? Fool that he was, why had he not held to his original purpose, and merely apologised? All this took but the briefest moment; he was just on the point of speaking, to release them both from further embarrassment, and her, from ever having to address him on the subject again, when, making a strong effort to speak directly and to the purpose, Elizabeth went on: "That you should still hold me in any esteem at all, is more than I could have ever hoped, and is very grateful to me; I...I cannot say how happy you make me by this assurance, as from last spring I have learnt a very different feeling for you. I can say...I can say that I return your feelings, most sincerely."

He looked down at her in incredulously, doubting his senses; she met his gaze with a warm, open, and slightly apprehensive look. Having, in his most disordered imaginings, presumed to hope for no more than a slight thawing towards him, this sudden development was stunning, unbelievable. He stopped, momentarily robbed of the capacity for movement, and stared at her in disbelief; but he knew Elizabeth would never toy with him in this way, and, as the possibility of its being true made itself felt, he stammered out: "What can this...are you saying...?" He paused, watching uncertainly; then, as he became convinced that she did speak from her heart, that it was no misunderstanding, an irrepressible exultation seized him. "Elizabeth, do you really...am I truly authorised to speak? —can you truly feel a regard for me? God in Heaven...if only you knew! —for so long have I dreamt of winning some slight approbation, but I despaired of its ever coming to pass."

Elizabeth looked down as he spoke, but made no move to step away from him, nor did she appear to wish him to stop. Her arms clasped round her middle, and she hugged them to her with a soft, gladsome little sigh; at this, Darcy's heart overflowed, and in his joy he spoke in ways he never dared imagine he might: "My darling Elizabeth! —just speaking your name is perfection, and rapture beyond all hope! No—'tis impossible to feel so much...this is beyond all understanding: it is not the stuff of mortals." Awe-stricken, carried off into an elation of spirit he had never before experienced, with an almost reverential tone he told her: "You are an angel, sent to save me—truly, you must be: from grey and barren despair you have delivered me unto lush fields of unqualified felicity, and I owe you every thing: every benefit of life I ever hope to know." His sense of deliverance was overwhelming, but at this point he became conscious of his display of emotion, and his feelings took an uneasy turn; like a child holding a prized and delicate new possession, he almost feared to move, that it all might shatter at an unwary touch. Saying that which he wished most urgently for her to hear, lest he somehow missed the chance, he continued: "You are the most perfect of women, and Heaven alone can know how much I adore you; there are no words to say how profoundly I love you."

Still she neither retreated nor retracted, and he stopped for a long moment, just to reassure himself that they were, in fact, together—now, and for the whole of their future lives.

He bent down to see her face; she was smiling winsomely, but would only meet his eye for the briefest moment. He extended his arm to her and said, "Will you?"

She now looked up at him fully, and her smile brightened until Darcy felt he could hardly bear its beauty. "Very gladly," was her reply. As her hand settled into its place, he experienced a feeling of peace and wonder unlike any other he had ever known; they began to walk together, although he had no idea of what direction they took.

"Every thing I have done since Rosings," he told her, most solemnly wanting to open his whole heart to her, "and even longer, I believe, has been to merit your good opinion—although I had no hope of ever earning it. It was your instruction at Hunsford that showed me how empty and insufficient was my understanding, how unseemly my manner. Since that time have I tried most diligently to correct my ways, and teach myself not to hope; how I have longed, with my every fibre, that I could take back the folly and arrogance of my manner towards you, to let you see that I was no longer what you had known; and now…my happiness is beyond comprehension! One thing above all else is evident: this blessing is beyond any virtue I possess—only your angelic temper and benevolence could be capable of forgiving me my transgressions, and to know it makes my love for you all the deeper. You are more perfect than any woman the poets ever dreamt of."

At length, on the lady's abiding with him through these fulsome speeches, and becoming assured thereby that she truly approved him from her heart (for only a lover can endure a lover's rantings), he learnt to trust that this miracle was not going to disappear as suddenly as it had come, and he came back to himself enough to attempt rational conversation. Putting aside his extravagant language, although not, perhaps, completely subduing the high-fountaining feelings which had led to it, he guided them along the lane once more. Trying to think of a subject that might be broached more calmly, with embarrassment to neither, he quickly arrived at that providential affront which was his aunt's visit to Longbourn.

"My aunt, you must know, was behind my being here to-day," he told her. "I came expressly to apologise to you for her behaviour. After she finished so thoroughly insulting you, trespassing so horribly on your time and patience, she came to me in London, determined to complete the set by giving me a piece of her mind as well, and to ensure that my addresses would be delivered where they properly belonged — according to her apprehension." With a smile and a shake of his head, he went on, "To that end, she retailed to me the whole of her conversation with you, most minutely, and all wrapt in a fine, high indignation. It was apparent that she believed such a relation would persuade me of what she deemed an offensive degree of assurance and impertinence on your side, and inform me of your appallingly wilful nature," he laughed and smiled at her. "But, not knowing how dearly I cherished every least particular of your character, her plan was gravely flawed: it taught me to hope, as I had scarcely ever allowed myself to hope before. I knew enough of your disposition to be certain that, had you been absolutely, irrevocably decided against me, you would have acknowledged it to Lady Catherine, frankly and openly."

Elizabeth coloured as she replied, "Yes, you know enough of my *frankness* to believe me capable of *that*. After abusing you so abominably to your face, I could have no scruple in abusing you to all your relations."

"What did you say of me," he protested, "that I did not deserve? For, though your accusations were ill-founded, formed on mistaken premises, my behaviour to you at the time had merited the severest reproof. It was unpardonable. I cannot think of it without abhorrence."

Elizabeth generously assured him that she felt her guilt over that evening's proceedings just as fully as did he; by this did Darcy first learn that she believed that she had been at all in the wrong, took any of the blame on herself for the pain surrounding the memories of that evening. She charitably attempted to deflect an equal portion of the blame to herself, but Darcy's sensibility on the point was unassuaged. He told her how much her chastisements had affected him: "Your reproof, so well applied, I shall never forget: 'had you behaved in a more gentleman-like manner.' Those were your words. You know not, you can scarcely conceive, how they have tortured me; — though it was some time, I confess, before I was reasonable enough to allow their justice."

"I was certainly very far from expecting them to make so strong an impression," Elizabeth said, shaking her head. "I had not the smallest idea of their being ever felt in such a way."

This, Darcy knew too well: what he knew she would *not* say, was that his behaviour till then had been such that no one could have thought him capable of any sensibility, civility, or policy worthy of the name — he had certainly given her no reason to esteem him — and he told her so; but the lady was still pleased to forgive him, and say again how ashamed she had been of her own contributions to their exchange that evening.

But now he wished to hear of his letter, and what had been its effect. "Did it," said he, "did it *soon* make you think better of me? Did you, on reading it, give any credit to its contents?"

"Will you think me too very contemptible," she replied, "if I say that, at first, I had no wish to think it at all reliable?" She coloured again. "It required more than one reading before I was persuaded that some parts of it could not but be true, and many more before the whole appeared so to me. I was slow, perhaps, to relinquish my misconceptions, but I hope my reproaches were no less sincere than yours."

"You were not the first to disbelieve, I assure you; but you were, I am certain, the quickest to correct your misplaced faith. What first convinced you?"

"What you had to say of Wickham and your sister: surely this could never be invention, and much of it coincided perfectly with my prior knowledge; then, where belief was once admitted, it was inevitable that I should come to allow to the truth of it all. But still, it was some time before I came to appreciate its full meaning—how far my former beliefs were mistaken. I fear I had allowed my thinking to be swayed against you almost entirely by the misrepresentations of Mr. Wickham."

"I assure you, my dear Elizabeth—how I delight in that sound!—I know very well how credible are his lies; it has been my fate to have the three I have loved the most—my father, my sister, and now you most especially—all fall prey to his mendacity."

"I fear, my dear...my dear Fitzwilliam," she stammered, blushing most charmingly on the first time of saying it, "I fear my fault lay in being too willing to believe what he had to say for himself, and ignoring what was said by others, regarding his character."

Hearing her call him so, Darcy would have forgiven her far worse than believing Mr. Wickham; so sweetly did his name sound on her lips that, by the time he was called on to reply, he had all but forgotten the sense of what she was saying.

"You must call me that again, soon and often," was all he said, smiling into her eyes.

Chapter Twenty-Five

*A*s they went on with their walk, Darcy continued to apologise, as his original intention had yet to release him that he might enjoy his good fortune; he was still concerned with his letter, and felt the need to relieve his feelings further on the subject. Try though she would, Elizabeth could not convince him that his behaviour had not been as faulty, nor hers as blameless, as he seemed to believe, and that his liberal self-deprecations were unnecessary.

"I have been a selfish being all my life," said he, "in practice, though not in principle. As a child I was taught what was *right*, but I was not taught to correct my temper. I was given good principles, but left to follow them in pride and conceit. Unfortunately an only son (for many years an only child), I was spoilt by my parents, who, though good themselves (my father, particularly, all that was benevolent and amiable), allowed, encouraged, almost taught me to be selfish and overbearing; to care for none beyond my own family circle; to think meanly of all the rest of the world; to *wish* at least to think meanly of their sense and worth compared with my own. Such I was, from eight to eight-and-twenty; and such I might still have been but for you, dearest, loveliest Elizabeth! What do I not owe you! You taught me a lesson, hard indeed at first, but most advantageous. By you, I was properly humbled. I came to you without a doubt of my reception. You showed me how insufficient were all my pretensions to please a woman worthy of being pleased."

"Had you then persuaded yourself that I should?"

"Indeed I had. What will you think of my vanity? I believed you to be wishing, expecting my addresses." His thoughts harkened back to that dreadful evening, and, indeed, their entire time in Kent, and he was pained to remember it. Elizabeth, too, had apologies to offer for the part she had played, most unintentionally, in his self-deception; but they could not dwell too long on these errors, in their first impatience to share all.

She mentioned Derbyshire: "I am almost afraid of asking what you thought of me, when we met at Pemberley," she told him. "You blamed me for coming?"

Darcy was startled by the question. "No indeed," he replied, "I felt nothing but surprise."

"Your surprise could not be greater than *mine* in being noticed by you," said Elizabeth. "My conscience told me that I deserved no extraordinary politeness, and I confess that I did not expect to receive more than my due."

Again Darcy was surprised and confused by the idea that she could feel she bore any guilt in the matter, or that any degree of consideration at all could be beyond her due. "My object *then*," he assured her, "was to show you, by every civility in my power, that I was not so mean as to resent the past; and I hoped to obtain your forgiveness, to lessen your ill opinion, by letting you see that your reproofs had been attended to. How soon any other wishes introduced themselves I can hardly tell, but I believe in about half an hour after I had seen you." On saying this last, he smiled at her again, and was rewarded with another of her lovely smiles in return.

"It was in pursuit of those wishes, I confess," he went on, "that I sought to introduce you to my sister. She is unquestionably the best of my family, and I hoped that you might see, by the rather overblown esteem she holds for her elder brother, that at least one worthy individual could feel a regard for me. I may say you won her over completely; though in all truth she was already disposed in your favour from my mention of you, in my letters from Netherfield."

Elizabeth, smiling to recall, said, "I was delighted with her; so were my aunt and uncle, although I do not recall her having had *quite* the beneficial effect you intended. Still, the afternoon was one whose memory I take a great deal of pleasure to recall."

"She was very disappointed not to have had more time with you; so few of her acquaintance offer the sort of companionship best suited to her nature, and her two meetings with you had left a very strong impression of your merits."

"And I was very sorry to go, as you know better than most," she replied, embarrassment writ broadly on her features. She directly changed the topic. "But when did you leave Pemberley? Your arrival in London cannot have been much later than our arrival at Longbourn."

"I left the day after yourselves, and arrived on the Saturday."

"So soon as that?"

"I was convinced that there was no time to be lost; I had set my plan in motion before leaving Pemberley, but it was not fully fashioned until the Wednesday following, when I finally discovered Wickham's hiding place."

"How could you know what it would require?"

"I began planning it at the inn, as soon as I recovered from the first shock of hearing Wickham's name connected with some one of your family; by the time I bid you adieu I knew how to find him; I had much of it arranged in my mind before reaching Pemberley."

Elizabeth dropt her eyes, saying: "I had thought you repulsed by what I had related, and that your leaving had no other purpose than to distance yourself from the stain."

Darcy was astounded: "But how could you ever imagine that?" he cried. "My own sister having very nearly done the same, and for the same man, how could I have been offended by *your* sister taking a similar step? I had no other thought than how best to spare you, as you had spared Georgiana. The two cases are nearly identical."

Elizabeth thanked him, but she refused to be comforted; as the pain brought on by the recollection of her family's near ruin was clear on her face; he quickly turned the conversation back to Derbyshire. "Well, then...when we met at Pemberley, confess: you were very loath to see me, were you not?"

"Not as you seem to suggest it, no — I feared to have you find me there."

"But why?" he asked.

"I feared what you must have thought of me," she said with the air of a governess correcting a wilfully obtuse pupil. "To have appeared at your doorstep — indeed, in your very hall — after what had passed between us; what would you not think?"

Darcy was quite candidly perplexed: "I had told you I loved you: how could you fear my opinion of you?"

Elizabeth fixed him with a stern eye. "Mr. Darcy, do you ask me to believe that, after having had your addresses spurned so bitterly, so unfairly, your regard for me remained undiminished?"

Darcy confusion only grew. "Of course; how else should I be here, now?" he pointed out. "Why should your well-merited refusal have lowered my esteem? Angry, I was, yes — at first — but anger is fleeting, and when it has passed, what is sound remains. And to realise that, even under the distress my behaviour must have occasioned, you would still speak the strict truth as it was known to you, with admirable forbearance and decorum, I may say, could only increase my esteem for your character."

"You never stopped loving me?" the lady asked, her manner much softened.

"Never," he swore. "Even on that very first night, sitting alone at Rosings through the height of my most intemperate resentment, I realised that I had lost something precious and irreplaceable; I was certain that I should never feel whole again."

Elizabeth offered no reply; she hastily looked down so he might not see her tears, but she stepped next to him and slipped her hand under his arm, and he was very glad to have it there; they continued for quite some little way along their walk without the need for speech.

Some while later, Darcy's thoughts going back to Hunsford, he asked, "When did your own, very natural resentment at my proposal at Hunsford Parsonage begin to decline?"

"It was not immediate, I confess," said Elizabeth. "It was much lessened by time and your letter; and surely it was done away entirely when I heard from my aunt what you had done for Lydia."

"I have regretted that moment in my life, deeply and unrelentingly, since its occurrence," said he. "Will you understand if I still feel the need to apologise for it, from time to time? I had persuaded myself that nothing but years of contrition could atone for it, and such firmly held beliefs are hard to let go."

Elizabeth told him, with an indulgent, forgiving smile, "If you insist; but you will please remember that to hear your apology is to re-live the event, and I had rather not be reminded of my own part in it; so I beg you will restrict yourself to the absolute minimum number of apologies required for your own peace." She smiled again, then went on, "And, if we *are* to speak of faults, how can I ever apologise enough for my reprehensible defence of Wickham?"

"There is not the slightest need," he answered. "I swear it to you, on my honour. In truth, it almost seems more my fault, when one realises that any one I love is bound to fall prey to Wickham's lies. It is my fate, I am convinced it is. But I have hopes that he will now no longer be able to impose so freely on others."

"Do you think, then, he will be genuinely steadied by his marriage to my sister?" she asked, her surprise but poorly concealed.

"No, not precisely," he admitted. "I have taken certain steps to ensure he will do right by her, and by your family…" he smiled and said with a certain satisfaction, "now *my* family, too—although at the time I had no idea of that ever being possible. It gives me even more reason to be pleased with the measures I have put in place."

"Whatever have you done?" asked she.

Darcy supplied a summary of how he had managed Wickham, omitting entirely the violence associated with the campaign, emphasising the financial arrangements, and the provisions for keeping track of him. Elizabeth was aghast. "You have done all this! I heard from my aunt that you had paid his debts and purchased his commission, but I had no idea of the extent of it! How can we ever repay you?" She seemed quite seriously distressed.

Darcy took her hand in his, saying, "First, bringing Wickham to justice was something I was going to be forced to do at some time or other; this merely provided a sufficiently exigent reason to do so. And second, *we* is now you and me, Elizabeth; had I had any inkling that the one would lead to the other, I would have stopped at nothing to bring it off, and I would have been a hundredfold more eager in the pursuit of its execution. And," he went on more practically, "in all honesty, I seriously doubt it will be necessary to keep the men on too very long; I shall have one of them, Corporal Sands, at Lambton from now on as constable, and after a time, a periodic foray to let Wickham catch sight of him as a reminder, should be all that is required."

They carried on in this manner for miles, drawing forth all their transgressions for the mutual benefit and pleasure of being forgiven and of being able to forgive. Which one felt the most culpable for their history of mischief and misconstruction might be argued, but by the time the afternoon was gone, they had forgiven each other every misunderstanding several times over, and laughed over most of them.

Chapter Twenty-Six

O n their return to Longbourn, Elizabeth went to directly her room to change, leaving Darcy in the drawing-room with Bingley and Mr. and Mrs. Bennet. Mr. Bennet was silent, as was his wont, although he glanced curiously in Darcy's direction. Mrs. Bennet was engrossed in conversation with his friend, so there could be no occasion for Darcy to speak to Bingley about what had transpired. When Elizabeth came down with her elder sister, her father asked quite pointedly where she had been, and the query was echoed by the rest; Darcy saw her conscious blush as she made her halting excuses, but no one else seemed to notice it, or to be overly concerned by their long absence; it was a delicious sensation to share her consciousness without any one else being the wiser. As they all sat down to dinner immediately though, the topic was soon forgotten.

Later that evening, Darcy sat quietly in a corner in a highly bemused state, trying with little success to bring some degree of tranquillity to the great perturbation in his mind, and to accept his astoundingly good fortune. He glanced often Elizabeth's way, and was rewarded more often than not by a secret smile, and a long, warm, open look. The room before him was full of light and colour, in a way he had never before experienced; he was in a mood of charity and sympathy with each and every member of the company, rejoicing most especially in the good humour and happiness of his friend—soon to be his brother! —and Miss Bennet. Often he found himself wanting to smile: a foolish, befuddled, euphoric smile; but each time he satisfied himself by merely looking in Elizabeth's direction again.

On the ride back to Netherfield that night, he broached his news with his friend in the following manner: "Bingley, tell me: having now enjoyed the prospect of your nuptials for going on a fortnight, how do you regard the thing?"

"How do you mean, Darcy?"

"Does it strike you still as being a sound notion? Given your history of falling in love with some regularity, have you had any thoughts of leaving off?"

"Do not joke about this, Darcy," Bingley warned his friend. "I was pleased to forgive, but I have not yet forgotten, I assure you; this is dangerous ammunition for your wit."

"No, no," Darcy asserted jovially, "I have no intention of sporting with your devotion, on my honour; I am well assured of your constancy towards Miss Bennet. It is only that I have since committed to joining you in the matrimonial state, and wished to know how I could expect to regard the decision in the fullness of time."

"Darcy!" cried his friend. "Are you in earnest?"

"Indeed I am," said he. "I hope I may count on your blessing, brother dear?"

Bingley let out a whoop of delight, leaning across and alternately pumping Darcy's hand, and thumping his back. "This is excellent! I cannot say how delightful this is! But is it done, really? How on Earth did you win her over? Jane and I have said how we wished it might be so, but her sister's dislike of you was so marked that we believed it impossible."

"As did I," Darcy admitted. "In all honesty, I do not know myself how it all came about. But she has forgiven me the past, it seems, and has made representations of esteem for me that I cannot but believe sincere. I know not why or how it should be so, but she has convinced me, on my oath she has. I made such a lovesick fool of myself this afternoon that I am wholly convinced that she is sincere, for she did not laugh at me—not once." Bingley did laugh at this, but Darcy went on: "My primary purpose, as you know, was to apologise; but somehow, I am not sure how, it all changed: instead of apologising, I proposed, and, miraculously, she accepted."

"It does not sound like your famous logic was of much effect," Bingley teazed.

"None whatever," Darcy said wryly. "If I had trusted to logic, I should never have said a word. I swear, I feel I should be apologising to her still; in my wildest imaginings, I was absolutely certain that nothing less than a decade's worth of penitence would suffice: but here I am, happily engaged to be married."

"Only think — it was quite nearly a year ago that we first came: that first assembly was Tuesday, October 22nd. Imagine, all this time gone, and here we are, back at the beginning; I was right, was I not, when I said we should meet some one special that night?" Darcy could do no more than nod his head in wonder.

Back at Netherfield, he could not retire without sending off an express to his sister to announce the news.

Netherfield
Sunday, September 28, —

My dear Georgiana,

I have to write you straight away regarding the most wondrous and amazing news; Miss Elizabeth Bennet has agreed to be my wife! Yes, quite true, I assure you. How or why I have been so blessed is still a mystery to me, but I wanted to share it with you as soon as possible.

I returned to Netherfield, you must understand, to apologise to Elizabeth (as I am now admitted to the honour of calling her) for a visit she received from Lady Catherine. That good lady had heard a rumour that Elizabeth had agreed to marry me, apparently based on the assumption that, as her sister was to marry my friend, naturally she would be next, and I was fixed on as the lucky man. However it may have come about, Lady Catherine went to Hertfordshire to forbid the banns, as it were, and gave Elizabeth quite a substantial piece of her mind. She then proceeded to Grosvenor Square to give me one, too. The upshot was, I left for Meryton yesterday, intent on making every apology in my power to Elizabeth, and determining whether I might ever have a chance to succeed with her. This, I know, will surprise you, but now I must tell you something that will surprise you even more: I had actually proposed to her before, when we were together at Rosings. She turned me down in a decided fashion, for which I was solely to blame, I admit. It was this that was troubling me throughout the spring; I could not bring myself to tell you of it, Dearest, as I knew it must pain you, too—and there could be no point in upsetting you with what could not be mended. So, when my aunt's retailing of her interview with Elizabeth gave me some suspicion that she might not be as resolutely set against me as she was before, I was compelled to return, both to apologise and to see what hope I might ever have.

Arriving at Longbourn last night, and contriving, with Bingley's connivance, to be alone with Elizabeth this morning, before I could so much as mention my aunt, let alone my more pressing interests, Elizabeth gave me to understand that she knew of my involvement in her younger sister's elopement and marriage—imagine my horror and chagrin! But somehow, I know not just how, my apologies and expressions of contrition turned into a declaration of

my continued regard for her. And, miraculously, Elizabeth made representations to me of her
own regard, and is now to be my wife, and your
sister. Is that not a wonderful and staggering
piece of news? I would stake anything that you
had no more idea of it than myself. I could wish
for a more imaginative word, but I am absolutely dumbfounded; I am constantly having to
stop myself from grinning in the most idiotic
way. There: I have just had to stop it again. I am
persuaded that those men who declare themselves the happiest in the world must know
nothing at all of the matter, as, in the main, on
the point of their ladies' esteem they are moved
no farther than from near-certainty, into certainty — which surely can be no great source of exceptional wonder or joy — whereas I was
transported from despair to amazement and
bliss in the space of a few heartbeats. To have
scaled such heights from so great a depth is to
truly know happiness.

It is already late, and I wish this to go out
tonight, so I will leave off here, Dearest. I expect
to hear from you soonest.

Your affectionate, and bewildered brother,
Fitzwilliam Darcy

Chapter Twenty-Seven

*D*arcy and Elizabeth's second day together began with the gentlemen's arriving at Longbourn just after breakfast. Miss Bennet smiled warmly at Darcy, and laid a hand on his arm in welcome as she gave him a gentle "Good morning," letting him know that Elizabeth had shared the good news with her. Bingley again suggested a walk, and this time he neatly cut out every one but the two courting couples. Darcy could see his own lady blush at such bare-faced design, which brought another fatuous grin to his face. He quickly smoothed his features, however, patiently and quietly waiting while Elizabeth went to get her things for a walk. Once free of the house, the two couples soon took different paths, and Darcy allowed Elizabeth to lead him into distant lanes and fields until they were quite alone. They stopped by a hedge-row, where he once more admired her as she was framed with green in the morning sun, as he had done in the grove at Rosings; and there he received his second real kiss, although it could certainly be maintained that it was more accurately his first, as it was so much sweeter and more affecting than even fond reminiscence could render the other, as to displace it forever from his memory. When they resumed their walk, Elizabeth asked, "Did you *truly* never stop loving me?"

"Not for an instant," he replied with conviction. "No sooner had my anger passed than I realised you had been entirely right, and I, entirely wrong. And even in the midst of my bitterest recriminations, I never stopped thinking of you — never really stopped regretting you."

"You have a remarkable ability, Mr. Darcy," said she, "of answering questions with the most singularly disarming replies! How fortunate for me that you keep it so well hidden, or some Town-bred lady would surely have taken you by now."

"And would I have had nothing to say in the matter?" Darcy wanted to know. "If it were as easy as ask and have, then I dare say some one might have done; but by that same token, I should have been rewarded with your hand much sooner, as well."

"Are we to congratulate ourselves, then, on our mutual obstinacy?" asked Elizabeth. "Is the source of our present delight the fact that we are both ungracious, unfeeling beasts who turn our noses up at others' hearts? After all, I have turned down two-thirds of the offers I have received — and what, pray tell, is your tally?"

"I shall compose a singularly disarming and very cautious reply to that presently; who was the other one you refused?"

Elizabeth, colouring, answered, "My cousin, Mr. Collins."

"Ah!" cried Darcy. "I feared as much! One of the visions that plagued me, last year when I quitted Netherfield for London, was that you might, for the sake of your family, be persuaded to accept him. Having seen him married to his present wife, however, had driven it from my mind. Good Heavens, what a job *he* must have made of a proposal."

"Yes," said Elizabeth with a heavy sigh. "It was quite nearly the worst proposal I ever received."

Darcy brought both hands to his chest. "Oh! — you pierce me to the heart! But, as you have accepted me now, I shall endeavour to forget what an awkward fellow I was then."

"I envy you the compliancy of your memory, Mr. Darcy," said she. "Not every one is privileged to be able direct their recollections with such exactness. Would that I were so fortunate, that I might forget what a clumsy fellow I have attached myself to." So saying, she gave him a playful push that nearly made him miss a step. Laughing

first, he then gave a growl like a bear and reached out
with both hands as though to seize her, to which she responded by lightly springing out of reach with a joyful
shout of laughter. He dropt his threatening attitude,
tipped his hat and bowed, then offered her his arm again.
She hugged his arm to her, and they walked on together
in harmony and contentment.

A little while later, after wandering and talking over
several back lanes, Darcy's curiosity was again awakened
on a point that he had longed to know in the months between his devastating awakening at Clereford and the
present: "When you told me that you had formed your
initial disapproval of me in the first moments of our acquaintance..." Here the lady stopped him, exclaiming,
"You really *must* not dwell on past offenses! I beg you
will not pain either of us by intruding these recollections
on our present contentment."

"But I must know," he insisted, "if you happened to
overhear that which I have been most ashamed of; and, if
you did, well...I therefore beg you will tell me quite candidly: there was a moment that first night, at the assembly in Meryton; Bingley insisted I should dance, and out
of a momentary ill-humour, I made a most disobliging
comment; did you happen to overhear us?"

Elizabeth did not speak, but her colour rose, which
answered for her. "You did!" cried he in an absolute fever
of distress and shame. "Oh, dear God above! Shall I grov-
el? Here and now — say the word and you shall have me
at your feet. Most gracious woman! Even this you have
forgiven me?"

"I have; but remind me of it again, Sir, and I shall not
be so merciful," she said sternly. Then, with a smile to
confer absolution, she tugged on his arm to emphasise
her words and told him: "We have both learnt better of
each other, surely."

"As you would have it," said he, shaking his head in amazement at the flawless excellence of her temperament. How he could ever deserve her, he could not conceive.

The topic was dropt, and they spent the afternoon thus, wandering about and talking; the only thing they resolved on, however, was that he should approach her father that evening after dinner. They returned to Longbourn, where they spent the time until dinner in pleasing and easy conversation in the little hermitage to one side of the greensward.

In accordance with their plan, that evening after dinner, when Mr. Bennet retired to his library, Darcy shortly rose to follow him; as he left the room he offered Elizabeth a reassuring smile, as she appeared rather apprehensive at his going. He knocked on the library door, and Mr. Bennet bade him enter.

"Mr. Darcy," said he, rising from his chair, "are you in search of a book, or is there anything I can do for you?"

"In truth, Sir," Darcy began, "I have come to speak to you on a matter of some consequence: I wish to ask you for the hand of your daughter, Elizabeth, in marriage."

Mr. Bennet sank slowly back into his chair, his face showing a rare discomposure. "Elizabeth? Surely you cannot...that is, this seems rather sudden, Mr. Darcy, and you catch me unawares...I do not wish to suggest you do not know your own affairs, but are you quite certain you have the lady's approval?"

"Indeed, Mr. Bennet, I do not wonder at your surprise: I share it, in fact. I do not blame you for doubting, but I am quite certain of having reached a proper and complete understanding with your daughter. You will wish, of course, to speak with her before making any final determination, but, on the assumption the situation is as I represent it, may I count on your consent to court her?"

Mr. Bennet, still looking alarmed and puzzled, very shortly replied: "Of, course, Mr. Darcy. We are, naturally, honoured by your interest. Now, Sir, as I presume you to be going back to the drawing-room, might I ask you to send my daughter to me?"

Darcy said tentatively, "I am prepared, Sir, to discuss a possible settlement, if you wish."

"Eh? Oh…the settlement; not just now, Mr. Darcy; after I have spoken with my daughter, perhaps…."

"Of course, Mr. Bennet," Darcy replied. He took his leave directly, and found Elizabeth still at her needlework in the drawing-room. She looked anxiously his way, and he smiled again to communicate his successful application; he had no doubt of Elizabeth's endorsement of their engagement, and that Mr. Bennet would be satisfied thereby. After a few moments' pretence of examining a picture hung behind her, he went to her and, bending over to express his admiration of her work, he whispered, "Go to your father, he wants you in the library." She was out of the room without a backward glance at him.

He sat down by a table and lifted a newspaper, but his eyes were not on the words. Having Mr. Bennet's consent had been a subject of some trepidation, as he knew him to be of uncertain humour, and could not be confident just how his application might be received. Now that that was past, provisional though his consent had been, Darcy had little to fear; on his side, based on how his aunt had spoken at Clereford, and the questions his uncle had asked in London when he first mentioned the matter to him, he was now reasonably sure he could count on their support; and, while she could certainly be obstreperous, Lady Catherine could hardly forbid his marriage. He therefore saw little to concern him, and sat back in the delightful conviction that his marriage to Elizabeth was nearly assured. The second or third time his absurd grin made its appearance, he laid down the paper and went to where Bingley sat with Miss Bennet.

Elizabeth's sister smiled warmly on him, and he told them in a low voice what was going forward. Miss Bennet started to rise, then sat back down. "I feel as though I ought to do something, but I hardly know what," she said.

"Give your sister what time she needs," said Bingley. "She will come to us when she feels able." She placed her hand on Bingley's arm and smiled. "You always seem to know what others need most," she said in warm admiration.

"Yet I hope, Miss Bennet, that yours is a more practical turn of mind," Darcy teazed, "as my friend here is somewhat lacking in that area."

"Please, you must call me Jane now," she told him.

"Jane," he acknowledged with a bow from his seat. "Has he ever told you how long he deliberated before taking Netherfield?"

"Yes," she replied, "but perhaps that was again an instance of the wisdom of his heart, as it has brought so much happiness to every one."

When he paused to consider, Darcy could not argue the point.

Chapter Twenty-Eight

*T*he next day was marked by rather a different beginning: when the gentlemen arrived at Longbourn for their morning visit, they already found the house abuzz with activity. In the hall, Darcy could see the door to Mr. Bennet's library firmly shut, which was unusual for this time of day; Mrs. Bennet's sister, Mrs. Phillips, was at the house, and Mrs. Bennet was flying about in quite a state; on their appearance, all her energies and attentions switched to them: "Oh, Mr. Darcy, good morning, good morning! I am *so* pleased you are come!" Mrs. Phillips, whom Darcy had found to be rather simple woman, was simpering in a most unbecoming manner and echoing her sister's sentiments in her rather shrill voice. Mrs. Bennet gushed on: "We are so honoured! So happy! Please tell me what dish you most like, and I will have cook see to it for tonight. Oh, good morning, Bingley; how d'ye do? Please, Mr. Darcy, do sit here."

At this point Elizabeth entered the room and, seeing her mother's attack under way against Darcy, immediately effected a rescue. Taking him by the arm, she told her mother, politely but firmly, that they would be out for a walk around the grounds, bid her aunt good morning, and escorted Darcy out of doors.

Darcy began chuckling as they rounded the corner of the house, headed for their favourite seat in the hermitage. "Hush!" cried his saviour, giving his shoulder a light slap.

"No, no—I am all gratitude," he protested, still laughing. "The stories have it all wrong, with knights rescuing maidens! —I know no more delightful experience than to be rescued from the Termagant by a maiden fair."

He kissed her hand in thanks, then led her by it to their bench.

When once they were seated, in softer tones he said, "Good morning, Miss Bennet."

She smiled warmly at him, replying, "Yes — good morning to you, Mr. Darcy. Did you sleep well?"

"How can I tell?" he said, shaking his head. "It feels as if I have been dreaming these last two days."

She squeezed his hand. "Is that real enough?"

"It will do for now," he said. She coloured, but held his eye, and they sat quietly for some time, wanting nothing more than to be holding hands and watching the morning open into day.

"But, now," said she after some little while, "I have been thinking: tell me, when did it occur to you that your first proposal was at all flawed? Was it while you were still at Rosings, or later?"

"Much later, I fear. It was over a month gone before I gained sufficient distance to look at it from your side; and even then it took my aunt's guidance before I became aware of just how poorly I had represented my wishes."

"Your aunt?" asked Elizabeth in surprise. "Lady Catherine?"

"Oh, no: there, I fear, we still have a good deal to overcome. No, it was my other aunt, Lady Andover. It was she who first told me what a fool I was, and how thoroughly I had insulted you."

"I am in her debt, then," said Elizabeth with impish good humour. "Shall we meet?"

"Yes, certainly; I trust that you will like each other very well. I believe she will be every bit as taken with your wit and address as was I. Perhaps we can go down to see them at my uncle's seat, Clereford, in Hampshire, although they are in Town just now."

Elizabeth looked a bit concerned as she began to adjust to the stature of her relations-to-be: "You are the

grandson of an Earl; I had never fully made that association before."

"Yes, I fear there is no escaping it. But do not trouble
yourself: most of my relatives are fine people; and I certainly will not bother with any of them who cannot see
your qualities."

"I hope you will forgive me if I worry just a little,"
she answered in a light tone, although her eyes were sincerely doubtful. "I have never tried teazing an Earl before; I am not entirely sure I am up to the task."

"You have already got a good start on his son, Colonel Fitzwilliam, so you are well on the way," he smiled at
her. "Continue to practice on my cousin until you feel
comfortable: it will be good for both of you." They both
laughed, and Elizabeth was reassured.

Darcy returned to a thing that had puzzled him.
"But I should like to know: when did you learn to feel
anything for me? I detected little warmth at Lambton, and
when I brought Bingley back to Meryton, we barely
spoke; what could have altered your heart so completely
with so little going forward between us?"

Elizabeth looked up at him askance. "Perhaps you
recollect a set of particularly fine Queen Anne chairs, that
sits in your entrance hall?" she asked.

"I do; is that in some obscure way responsive to my
question?"

"It is," attested Elizabeth. "It was the chairs."

"The chairs made you love me?"

"Indeed," said she positively. "It was seeing those
chairs, so casually disposed amongst the very first impressions your home offers, not treasured away in some
secret corner, that made me realise how sinfully rich you
were, and I decided I loved you at that very moment."

Darcy sighed; the only trying thing about a lively intellect was when one wanted a straightforward answer.

"But now it is your turn," said his lady. "What set
you off? How could you begin? I can comprehend your

going on charmingly, when you had once made a beginning; but what could set you off in the first place?"

"I cannot fix on the hour, or the spot, or the look, or the words, which laid the foundation. It is too long ago. I was in the middle before I knew that I *had* begun."

"My beauty you had early withstood," she gave him a piercing glance at this, to which he responded with an apologetic wince, "and as for my manners — my behaviour to *you* was at least always bordering on the uncivil, and I never spoke to you without rather wishing to give you pain than not. Now be sincere; did you admire me for my impertinence?"

"For the liveliness of your mind, I did."

"You may as well call it impertinence at once," she told him. "It was very little less. The fact is, that you were sick of civility, of deference, of officious attention. You were disgusted with the women who were always speaking, and looking, and thinking for *your* approbation alone. I roused, and interested you, because I was so unlike *them.* Had you not been really amiable, you would have hated me for it; but in spite of the pains you took to disguise yourself, your feelings were always noble and just; and in your heart, you thoroughly despised the persons who so assiduously courted you. There — I have saved you the trouble of accounting for it; and really, all things considered, I begin to think it perfectly reasonable. To be sure, you knew no actual good of me — but nobody thinks of *that* when they fall in love."

Darcy smiled through all this, and they bantered a bit before Elizabeth returned to her original topic: "What made you so shy of me, when you first called, and afterwards dined here? Why, especially, when you called, did you look as if you did not care about me?"

"Because you were grave and silent, and gave me no encouragement."

"But I was embarrassed."

"And so was I."

"You might have talked to me more when you came to dinner."

"A man who had felt less, might."

"How unlucky that you should have a reasonable answer to give, and that I should be so reasonable as to admit it!" cried Elizabeth in mock displeasure. Darcy reflected happily that he might already have determined the best way to manage her teazing: the simple truth, always his trusted friend, seemed to be all that was required.

They then drifted off onto various other matters, until Lady Catherine's name came up again; Elizabeth asked, "Shall you ever have courage to announce to Lady Catherine what is to befall her?"

"I am more likely to want time than courage, Elizabeth. But it ought to be done, and if you will give me a sheet of paper, it shall be done directly."

"And if I had not a letter to write myself, I might sit by you and admire the evenness of your writing, as another young lady once did." Darcy laughed at the memory. "But I have an aunt, too," Elizabeth went on, "who must not be longer neglected." They went back into the house, to attend to their separate correspondence. Darcy's letter ran thus:

Longbourn, Herts.
Tuesday, September 30, —

Dear Lady Catherine,

I should like, dear aunt, to apprise you of the fact that my bachelor days are, indeed, at an end. On the strength of your information to me in London, I became convinced that I might, after all, have a chance to persuade Miss Elizabeth Bennet to accept me, which I was perfectly sincere in protesting to you as being completely impossible, according to my understanding at the time. I therefore returned to Hertfordshire the day following your own departure, where I was fortunate enough to have my application for her hand be received with favour. As I owe my present happiness to you, I wished to give you my thanks at the earliest possible moment. Please give my regards to my Cousin Anne, and accept my thanks and very best wishes.

Your obedient servant, &c.

Fitzwilliam Darcy

He wrote also to Lord and Lady Andover, in rather a different tone and at much greater length. To the Colonel he wrote:

Dear Edmund,

I have news that will shock you, but I hope it will bring some satisfaction, as well: I am to be married, to Miss Elizabeth Bennet. This must give you considerable surprise, but I assure you, your surprise can be no greater than mine. Through a most fortuitous and wholly unwarranted intervention by my Aunt Catherine, I got wind of the possibility that Miss Elizabeth Bennet might not be totally opposed to me, after all. I therefore hastened to Hertfordshire where, in very short order and through no merit of mine own, the lady accepted me. So, I have taken your advice to "marry and be damned," although I trust that I may be excused the latter, at least until my lady sees fit to release me from her service.

I shall reserve full particulars until we meet, but I felt I had to give you earliest news of my happiness. I note in passing that Bonaparte is still at large; I recommend plenty of sleep, good meat, and strong ale, that your *forces vitales* might be equal to his—I had rather ex-

pected you would have the matter in hand by now.
My very warmest regards,
Yours &c.
Fitzwilliam Darcy

That same day, Miss Darcy sat in her cool yellow sitting-room at Pemberley, watching the afternoon shadows lengthen over the lawn and stretch down to the river. A footman at the door arrived with an express from her brother; as unusual as this was, she anxiously tore open the seal.

My dear Georgiana,
I have to write you straight away regarding the most wondrous and startling news; Miss Elizabeth Bennet has agreed to be my wife!

On reading those first words, Georgiana nearly lost hold of the letter as she gave out a small shriek. She clutched it hard and read through it twice. She could scarcely contain her joy; she did not know whether to jump up and dance, or fall back in a swoon in the true style of a novelist's heroine. After some minutes, she sat down to write her reply:

Dearest Fitzwilliam,
I have just received your news and I cannot say how happy it makes me! But this is so sudden, how can this be? Your news has left me so bewildered I hardly know what I should say...

After four sides of paper filled with exuberant and heartfelt wishes for his, Elizabeth's, and her mutual happiness, she left off to post it. She very nearly decided to journey immediately to Hertfordshire herself, but even all her joy was insufficient to permit her to take such a liberty as that; she determined to wait to hear from her brother, although it cost her a good deal to rein in her rampant desire to be there with them, and to express directly her great happiness, and her esteem for her sister-to-be. She read and re-read his letter until she was in a fair way to knowing it by heart, and still she read it again. In her short life she had been subjected to many emotions and transports, but few had ever affected her as strongly as this. To her it seemed that this was the repayment of all the previous year's trials, and the beginning of many years' delight. Such was her joy that she barely slept that night, and in the morning her first object was to read her letter once more; she spent the day going about the house, thinking how it would be, when Elizabeth was there, and at last she would have the sister she had always wanted; at that point, it seemed as though all of life's greatest gifts were hers, and she felt herself to be the luckiest creature on Earth.

Chapter Twenty-Nine

*T*hat same morning, as Perkins was readying his master for the day, with an exceedingly diffident manner he asked, "Mr. Darcy, Sir, I was wondering if I might have a moment?"

"Of course, Perkins; what is on your mind?"

"Well, Sir, I know that you have been more than generous already, but I was hoping , Sir, that I might have the morning off to-morrow."

"This is rather an unusual request from you, Perkins; might I ask why?"

"I am to marry to-morrow, Sir."

"What! Why have you not mentioned it, man?"

"Well, Sir, your time being so taken up with your own plans, I didn't want to intrude my business."

"Nonsense, man! Congratulations! And I take it the happy lady is your Lara?"

"Yes Sir," Perkins grinned, unable to hide his happiness.

"When is it to be? I shall certainly attend."

"Oh, thank you, Mr. Darcy, but it won't be much; Lara has no family, and of course, my mother couldn't be here."

"But who is to give the bride away, then?" Darcy asked.

"Well, John Barman was to have done that, but he has to be over to Welwyn to-morrow."

In the charity of his feelings, the result of his own happy state, Darcy said, "I should hate to intrude myself, but it does seem a shame that a girl should have no one to give her away; I would be honoured to stand in for her absent family."

Perkins was very affected, but said, "You have already done too much, Sir; I couldn't ask that of you."

"Well, but you did not ask: I offered. Why not broach the subject with your young woman, and see what she says; and you certainly have my blessing, and all the time you wish, Perkins." A dark thought broke in on him. "I trust this does not mean you will be leaving me?"

"Oh, no Sir; I never would," Perkins hastened to assure him. "We only thought, it wasn't likely we'd have another chance for a long while, so best to go ahead; at least we'd be sure of each other, that way; the money will come some time, and until then...well, it's no worse than sailors' wives, is it, Sir?"

"Well, we shall be in the country for at least the rest of the month, so you will be together for a time," Darcy said.

"Yes, Sir," Perkins said happily. "We had that same thought." Darcy clapped his man on the shoulder, but could think of nothing more to say.

In the evening as he prepared to retire, Perkins said to him, "Mr. Darcy, Lara wants you to know she would be most pleased if you were to give her away, Sir."

"Are you sure? I do not want to make any difficulties."

"Yes, Sir: she cried; that is her way. Seems she was pretty torn up about walking up the aisle alone, but didn't want to say so."

"She sounds like a fine person, Perkins: again, you have my congratulations."

"Yes, Sir; thank you, Mr. Darcy."

So it was in the morning, after carefully reviewing his man's attire and very precisely adjusting his neck cloth, Darcy carried Perkins in his coach to pick up his bride; she was dressed in a neat, immaculately clean frock, and had two flowers done up in her hair. She waited for them on the steps of the inn, and seemed almost overcome at the grandeur of the coach when Perkins clambered down to hand her in. As Perkins got down, Darcy replaced his hat, just so he might take it off to her when she entered. Red faced, Perkins introduced them: "Mr. Darcy, may I introduce Miss Lara Brawley?" Darcy removed his hat, saying, "I am delighted to meet you, Miss Brawley; and I am honoured to be allowed to stand up for you this morning. I know what a good man you have here in Perkins."

The unfortunate girl began to cry, sobbing, "Y-y-yes, Sir, I know he is, thank you." That was as far as she could speak, and the rest of the short trip to the church was occupied by Perkins in trying to calm her.

When they reached the church, the bride was at first almost afraid to take Darcy's arm, but her own emotion made his support more or less a necessity, and he thought at one point they might have to stop in one of the pews to let her compose herself. "I'm so sorry Mr. Darcy, Sir," said she through her tears.

"It is quite all right, my dear; you are just happy."

"Oh, Sir, I'm so happy I think I might die."

Darcy smiled at her in amusement. "Oh, please do not,'" he said. "Perkins would be so very disappointed." He gestured up the aisle to where Perkins waited; the bride seem to take courage from the sight of her groom waiting for her, and, in a more resolute manner, she finished the remaining steps to his side.

The ceremony was soon over, as they always are; the happy couple, under Darcy's direction, took the coach back to her rooms while Darcy himself began the walk back to Netherfield, feeling well-pleased with life in general. He had not got too far before the coach came by to gather him up; he was in an exceedingly fine mood all the way back to Netherfield.

In the afternoon Darcy entered into consultation with Elizabeth, Jane, and Bingley, to decide their own plans. They determined that they would be married by special license on a Friday, three weeks hence, with the two couples returning to London together for their honeymoon. Unfortunately, this left Darcy with much to do, and little time in which to do it, but Bingley was positively set against waiting longer, pointing out that he had had to wait nearly a fortnight longer than Darcy already; this robbed Darcy of much of the season of courtship; he had the settlements to see to, he must acquire the license, and it was absolutely necessary to go home for Georgiana — she would never forgive him, nor would he forgive himself, if she were not at the wedding. His plan was to spend a week or so in Hertfordshire, run up to London to pick up the license and settlement papers, then go on to Derbyshire to retrieve his sister. That would put him back at Netherfield with no more than days to spare, but it seemed the most reliable means of ensuring the weddings would be on time. The Reverend Mr. Hershey, vicar of the parish for Meryton, was perfectly willing to write to the Archbishop on their behalf for the special license, but felt it would be more timely for Darcy to pick up the papers, and be on site to certify the information if need be. In the most exigent case, Darcy felt he could depend on his uncle's good offices for expedition of the matter, as he was, of course, personally known to the Archbishop.

It was not many days after their engagement that Elizabeth's friend, Mrs. Collins, and her husband arrived in the neighbourhood. Darcy immediately learnt that Lady Catherine, on receiving his letter announcing his engagement, had promptly abandoned all moderation of speech and temper, and, in consequence of Mrs. Collins' close friendship with his betrothed, had levelled much of her spleen at that unfortunate lady. She had therefore retreated to the house of her father until Lady Catherine's ire might dissipate. Elizabeth was very pleased at her arrival, although it brought Darcy back into company with her husband, which pleased no one but Collins himself. Darcy, however, was bent on making the most of his time with Elizabeth, and so had little to say to the man; nor had he much to complain of, as his lovely Elizabeth was always present to ameliorate the effects of the parson's presence. In truth, Mr. Collins was considerably less offensive than St. Stephens, as he was at least deferential and readily silenced; he was also easier to ignore than Sir William Lucas: in his courteous benevolence, that gentleman oft-times repeated how he hoped they might all meet at St. James's, and teazed Darcy for having stolen away the "brightest jewel in the country". True to his resolution, however, Darcy forbore to show any disgust to these displays, and tried to take them in the amiable spirit in which they were meant.

The most difficult to bear, perhaps, was Mrs. Bennet's sister, Mrs. Phillips: her assertive lack of refinement wore on Darcy's best efforts to be cordial. But he soon learnt that putting up with ignorance and a want of grace was very similar to putting up with arrogance and a want of tact, and the forbearance he had learnt in dealing with Lady Catherine stood him in good stead with this other aunt at the opposite end of the spectrum of social standing.

He left Elizabeth early on a Friday in the middle of the month, having stretched his time with Elizabeth as far as he dared; arriving in London that afternoon, he went straight to Doctor's Commons and was relieved to find that all was in order: he was allowed to take both his and Bingley's licenses. The next day he went to see Mr. Colster, to review and sign the settlements; to his shock and amazement, this document, the instructions for which had taken no more than four paragraphs, extended to thirteen pages of tightly-worded legal verbiage, whose meaning was all but lost in the convoluted language of the law. After questioning Colster very minutely over each section's meaning, and satisfying himself that the document was not, after all, an attempt to re-define the laws of the land, and in fact did no more than it was intended, he signed it and took his leave, with a most cordial shake of the hand from Colster.

He dined that evening with Colonel Fitzwilliam, who made quite sure to keep their wine glasses full, and who chafed him humorously almost without pause through the entire meal: "Well, Darcy, they say that a husband is living proof a woman can take a joke, and Miss Elizabeth Bennet is to be congratulated on her most extraordinary sense of humour. To Miss Elizabeth Bennet!" Poor Darcy, who was never adept at this sort of game, always came out the worst when his cousin goaded him in this manner, but it had been a part of their friendship for so long, and was always conducted with such wit and affability, that, in truth, he quite enjoyed the experience; this time, making it even more difficult for him, with nearly every jibe the Colonel followed with a toast to Elizabeth, leaving Darcy little chance for a retort, and none at all for any clarity of thought with which to compose one.

"I agree with Socrates," said the Colonel, a bit later. "He said: 'By all means marry. If you get a good wife, you will be happy. If you get a bad one, you will become a philosopher.' And we already know your penchant for philosophy, Darcy, so you are well ahead, there. Though, perhaps in this case we should turn it on its head, as I have no doubt Miss Elizabeth Bennet will need the advice more than yourself. I give you Miss Elizabeth Bennet!"

After drinking the toast, Darcy was pleased on this occasion to be able to reply, "Yes, I know that one, but Hesiod said, 'Whoever, fleeing marriage and the sorrows that women cause, does not wish to wed, comes to a deadly old age.' So unless you plan on dying in battle, for which your mother would never forgive you, I suggest you re-think that position. To a happy old age!"

Towards the end of a most entertaining evening, the Colonel said, "As my final warning, let me remind you: weddings are at the root of every unhappy marriage, so have a care with this one," to which Darcy could offer no reply. But, having been so well accustomed to this sort of sportive *repartée* since childhood, he was actually quite gratified by the efforts his cousin went to, whereby he assured Darcy of how satisfied he really was with their union, as demonstrated by the length and originality of his raillery.

Edmund's final toast of the evening, however, was the most heartfelt: "In utmost sincerity, Darcy, may your union combine great strength of body and spirit, and may you both live long into a splendid maturity, graced by love, and with all your children and loved ones about you. To you, and your Elizabeth." Darcy thanked him warmly, deeply affected, as both the words and the wine were strongly felt. The two friends helped each other out to the carriage, and Darcy took his cousin back with him to Grosvenor Square, to rest the better after a rather bibulous evening.

The next morning he spent the early hours drinking coffee and writing to Elizabeth, his very first such letter; he was quite astounded at how much he missed her, having only been admitted to the privilege of loving her so very lately.

Grosvenor Square
Saturday, October 18, --

My dearest Elizabeth,

It hardly seems possible that only two days have passed since we parted, although I still feel your lips on mine from your farewell kiss — an ethereal reminder of your love. Last year when I left you, your sweet smile gently haunted me wherever I would go, but now, having held you in my arms, your absence is an almost tangible punishment to me; I am amazed by this, as only a week ago I despaired of ever knowing the touch of your hand on my cheek, or the smell of your hair against it. I miss you so deeply that it feels a lifetime we have been apart; suddenly, you are become home and haven to me, and I feel rootless and alone when I am from you. All my sensibilities reach out toward you: I feel you still, here with me in my heart—your love calls to me, like a symphony whose notes come from far away; straining to catch its sweet intensity, it is all I listen for, the only sound I seek to hear.

Occupation is my only defence against the pain of your absence, and I have contrived to remain active on our concerns, that I may return to you the sooner. The licenses are in my possession, as are the documents for the settlements, so there is only the retrieval of my sister to achieve before I can be with you again. I leave directly after breakfast, and I hope to see what speed can be made, using hired teams of six when I can find them: if it can be done, I mean to be back with you on Tuesday. I regret having to subject Georgiana to such challenging travel, but I will trust that she will not suffer greatly, as the generally dry weather has kept the roads in reasonable condition.

That I may accomplish that goal, I shall leave off, and be on my way.

May God protect you till my return; I am, I hope you know, your own, adoring,

Fitzwilliam Darcy

When his letter was complete, to his cousin he left a note of thanks, and consolation for the state of his head, and immediately began the trip back to Pemberley. The autumn colours were strikingly lovely, and the trip on this occasion seemed less lengthy than previously. Arriving on the following day, Georgiana ran to him before he could turn into the stables. He hugged her and swung her about for joy, and they neither one could talk fast enough to say half what they wished to say. As they entered, the servants were arrayed inside to greet him, and to offer their collective congratulations; he shook hands with Reynolds and Mrs. Annesley, and Mrs. Reynolds welled up with tears; Darcy kissed her cheek, which forced her to hastily excuse herself. Georgiana smiled in a pleased manner during all this ceremony and pomp, then dragged him by the arm directly to her drawing-room, where she demanded that he immediately satisfy her curiosity. He did his best, but it took the rest of that day, and most of their trip south, before she could be content that she had heard it all. Using the hackney teams of six or four, renewed at two-hour intervals, they made exceedingly good progress, arriving before dinner time on Tuesday.

Although the Bennets had invited Darcy to make their home his own, he decided it best that they remain at Netherfield; Georgiana would not even stay to see her things unpacked; she freshened up very briefly, and the two of them went to Longbourn. As they approached, she said stoutly, "It is not large, but it looks well-kept and comfortable."

"Indeed," Darcy agreed, "comfort is, I believe, one of the governing tenets of Mr. Bennet's life. No, I should not be harsh; he is a good man, even though an indifferent father to three-fifths of his children. You will find him a bit sardonic at first, but I do believe he loves Elizabeth from his heart, and would do anything he could for her happiness. What I recommend is to try to stay close to Elizabeth, and let her tend to the rest. You will like Miss Bennet very much, I think, and of course Bingley will always be about, so you will never want for company."

"I keep reminding myself that it does not matter if they like me, as you will marry, regardless," she said worriedly.

"Dearest!" Darcy protested, "You know Elizabeth likes you already, and Miss Bennet sees nothing but good in every one she meets, so I do not know what it is you fear."

"What about Miss Elizabeth Bennet's parents?"

"Frankly, her mother cannot distinguish good from bad, and judges almost exclusively by the most superficial of criteria; as you are well looking and well off, she will approve of you. And as for Mr. Bennet, he values quiet, good sense, and good manners, all of which you have in abundance. It will all be very well, trust me."

Elizabeth made the introductions, and so kept the formalities to a minimum; and, by intentionally introducing her father after her mother, she was able to cut short those enthusiastic expressions of approbation her mother had treasured up for the occasion. Mr. Bennet said more than usual, for him, but still little enough that Georgiana had no time to become uncomfortable by it. Miss Mary Bennet paid her compliments with quiet propriety, but Catherine seemed in awe of Georgiana's dress and manners, and barely spoke, for which Darcy was grateful. Elizabeth and Jane took their new sister out to the hermitage to get better acquainted, and the other ladies went about their business, leaving Bingley and Darcy with Mr. Bennet.

"Well, Mr. Darcy," Mr. Bennet said, "you have made very good time; you were successful in London?"

"I was, Sir. I sent word of it to Elizabeth before leaving Town; perhaps my letter failed to arrive?"

"No, I had heard it; I was rather inviting a more complete history."

Darcy was becoming more accustomed to Mr. Bennet's odd manners of speech: half jesting, half testing, he was quite conversible unless in the presence of folly or ignorance. Darcy obliged him with a short recital of his time in London. Mr. Bennet was amused by his description of Colster's grand manuscript, and declared himself most pleasantly amazed by the smooth delivery of the licenses at Doctors' Commons. He shuddered delicately at the idea of traveling at speed, with four horses, all the way to and from Derbyshire, but congratulated Darcy on having the "fortitude of youth". This recital and exchange having exhausted his social powers for the time being, Mr. Bennet excused himself to go to his library, leaving Darcy and Bingley by themselves.

"This had been an extraordinary month," said Bingley.

Darcy shook his head wonderingly, "Lord, yes; but a good one, all the same."

"Indeed; the very best."

"Where does one go from here, I should like to know?" Darcy mused aloud. "Does having the hand and heart of one's lady mark the heights of happiness, or is there more to hope for?"

"Darcy," Bingley reprimanded him, "I should have thought that by now you would have stopped trying to analyse your emotions: when has it ever served?"

Darcy ruefully admitted, "Never; but I suppose it is rather like expecting you to read leases and such; we all have certain restrictions in our thinking, I suppose, that cannot be overcome, for all our best intentions."

"But, between us, we manage quite well," Bingley grinned.

"Between us," Darcy agreed, grinning back, "we manage *very* well, indeed."

Chapter Thirty

*O*ver the next two days both Darcy and Georgiana were subject to a whirlwind of social obligations; every one in the entire neighbourhood, it seemed, came to call, either at Netherfield or Longbourn, or both, to wish the two couples joy.

On Wednesday evening, Bingley had a large party planned; every one Darcy had met before, and quite a number of others unknown to him, were there to add their good wishes. Darcy stood with Elizabeth and his sister as the guests swirled around them; Georgiana was behind Elizabeth to one side, doing her best to remain unnoticed; she had taken Darcy's advice and staid fixed to Elizabeth almost wherever she went, and Darcy was pleased to see how happy Elizabeth appeared to have her by her side. Elizabeth spent almost as much time talking with Georgiana as she did with her neighbours.

As Jane and Bingley were acting as hosts, greeting the arrivals, it fell to Darcy and his bride-to-be to attend to the general conversation and comfort of their wellwishers. As every one stopped by to offer their felicitations, Darcy found that, with Elizabeth next to him, his tolerance for sociable nothings was greatly augmented.

Early amongst the arrivals were Sir William and Lady Lucas, who largely set the tone for the day: "Well, Mr. Darcy, you have succeeded at last, have you? I always knew you meant to. I congratulate you, Sir, but I must say," and here Sir William could not forbear to trot out his most cherished platitude, "it is hard on the rest of us to have you take away the brightest jewel of the country!" he smiled genially at Elizabeth and shook Darcy's hand with great warmth. Darcy returned his smile, but only because Elizabeth was blushing at hearing the compliment again, which was amusing to see.

But the next one to raise a blush on her cheeks was her aunt, Mrs. Phillips; after prattling at him about her own happiness at the union, she told him, "I'm sure Elizabeth will make you happy, Mr. Darcy; rich as you are, she would be a fool to turn into one of those disobliging scolds, you know." Elizabeth, her cheeks positively on fire, took Darcy's arm and led him firmly in the opposite direction.

It was not all mortification, of course; Mrs. Collins joined them some while later, and Darcy had always found her a person of sense. She, it turned out, had lately discovered she was with child, however, and as the conversation began to turn in that direction, Darcy allowed himself to wander off in search of Bingley; he was pleased, though, that his sister chose to stay with Elizabeth, and take part in her discussion with her friend.

He found Bingley with Mr. Bennet and several other men standing off to one side of the room. "Come to find relief, Mr. Darcy?" asked Mr. Bennet. "Have you tired of female conversation already? Woe betide you, if your endurance is exhausted so soon." The others smiled and laughed, and Darcy noted Bingley's wide grin especially. Bingley was happier than Darcy had ever seen him, and that reflection gave him almost as much satisfaction as his own present good humour.

"I found myself superfluous, in a discussion of exclusively womanly concerns," he replied. "I could think of nothing to contribute to Mrs. Collins' discussion of her condition."

Mr. Bennet smiled with a nod of perfect understanding. "Well, I understand you have a rather remarkable library; I recommend you avail yourself of it on all such occasions; or, should you be here in Meryton, you may always take refuge in mine." He turned to Bingley with an exaggerated frown and said, "Unlike your friend, here, you seem capable of maintaining twenty minutes' silence." Bingley returned a good-natured smile in response to this impeachment, at which Mr. Bennet smoothed his brow and gave a slight smile of his own.

Just then Mr. Phillips, who was standing in the group with a rather vacant smile on his face and was finishing a cup of punch, looked around to see his wife coming up to him; she cried in tones that carried half-way across the room, "Mr. Phillips! We've not been here half an hour, and that is your second cup!" His smile changed to a look of guilt, and he looked about him, trying to determine what might be done to hide the offending cup in his hand. Mr. Bennet's smile fled, and he shortly did the same, seeking to distance himself from his sister-in-law.

It was not long before Elizabeth came in search of Darcy; taking his arm, she walked over to where Georgiana was seated with Jane; naturally, Bingley drifted over to them shortly thereafter. They were not long left to themselves, as the two couples were sure to draw others to them. Lady Lucas, with Mr. Collins in tow, came up to them with her good wishes and prognostications of happiness. but then she said, in accents alive with curiosity, "I do hope Lady Catherine won't stay angry *too* long: I should imagine you have had word from her, Mr. Darcy?"

"I have not," Darcy allowed.

"But you will naturally wish to make amends," interjected Mr. Collins anxiously. "I should never dare to judge your actions, Sir, but I'm sure that, as you will naturally want to make your apologies to your noble aunt, I should be happy to carry them to Her Ladyship on your behalf."

Darcy felt Elizabeth take hold of his arm, and he took pause to reconsider the heated words he was about to utter. He gave a curt nod to Collins by way of acknowledgement, thanked Lady Lucas for her good wishes, and led his little group away. Aside from these few moments, though, the afternoon went well; indeed, Darcy had need of little besides Elizabeth at his side, and with Georgiana, and Jane and Bingley, he could not ask for a more comfortable, congenial party.

The weddings took place on that Friday afternoon, with a small but lavish dinner to follow; Mrs. Bennet had been in a torment of indecision over holding the dinner at Longbourn, for the delight of having such an entertainment in her own home, or having it amidst Netherfield's grandeur, that her daughter's new station might be properly admired by all who attended. The two gentlemen wished to hold it at Netherfield, and their ladies wisely withheld their opinions, not wishing to intensify the uncertainty in their mother's mind. It was finally resolved by Mr. Bennet, whose well-balanced judgement—and thrift—combined to favour his son-in-law as host.

Meryton parish had not seen such a wedding-day in living memory, and nearly the whole town turned out to greet the couples as they emerged. Perkins and his wife were amongst those nearest the door, smiling and applauding, with, in Mrs. Perkins' case, just one happy tear to show the sincerity of her good wishes.

The Gardiners were not in London that week and could not make the trip, but Darcy and Elizabeth had invited them instead to dine at Grosvenor Square on the following Thursday. Their evening party that night at Netherfield was mostly a family affair, with a few good friends and neighbours to round out the gathering and increase the joy of the event; it was quite splendid, indeed—well beyond what was normally seen amongst even the best families of the neighbourhood—but still marked by Bingley's friendly ease and hospitality; so delightful was it, that even Mr. Bennet was in a sufficiently mellow mood to essay one or two good-natured *bons mots* for the benefit of the company. The servants of Netherfield and Longbourn held their own modest celebrations, and it was an evening altogether remarkable for a nearly universal sense of well-being in the little community of Meryton. On Saturday morning, after rather a late start, the two couples and Georgiana took to their coaches, and once more followed the road to London.

Of course, Georgiana was with Darcy and Elizabeth; the ladies were both tired from the week's activities and a late night, and slept a good part of the journey. Darcy, sitting cradling Elizabeth against him as she dozed, looked out over the scenery with a drowsy sort of be-musement; this was, he calculated, the sixth time he had passed along this road, yet with such a vast contrariety of thoughts and emotions as to quite amaze him, looking back over the year. Extraordinary — astonishing — that so many things had changed in his life during that time, and what this stretch of road through the English countryside would always mean to him; such things as held more im-port than the wealth of nations and the rising and falling of empires, all comprehended and brought to completion by the surpassing peace and ease of holding Elizabeth asleep in his arms.

Epilogue

*E*lizabeth left her chambers after dressing for the day and went in search of her recent acquisition; she found him seated in the breakfast-room, quietly reading the paper along with her Uncle Gardiner. The two men rose as she entered, and she was kissed first by her uncle, then more spiritedly by her husband. When she was seated, Reynolds brought her a cup of tea.

"Good *morning*, Reynolds. Is your back at all better?" she asked with concern.

"Yes, thank you very much, Madam. That plaster was a vast help, and I slept well for the first time in weeks; amazing."

Elizabeth patted his arm, smiling up at him. "I am so glad; it always worked for my father."

"Yes, Madam; thank you again." He smiled at her in an almost paternal manner before turning back to the side-board.

On her arrival in Derbyshire some four weeks earlier, Elizabeth had been pleasantly surprised at how smoothly Pemberley was run; her day-to-day responsibilities were minimal: but she recognized how invaluable Reynolds was to its operation, so when she had heard he was losing sleep with a bad back, she had instantly thought of the soap-and-salt plaster her father used on his back when it seized. She and Jane had been making it for years, as her mother could never quite remember the recipe properly.

"Where is my aunt?" she asked Mr. Gardiner.

"She is somewhere about," he said. "She finished breakfast and, tiring of watching the two of us read and dawdle, she went off in search of occupation."

"It will be time for services before too long," Elizabeth pointed out.

"Yes, my dear; I am sure she will not have forgotten Morning Service on Christmas Day," Mr. Gardiner said, amused.

"Gardiner," Darcy spoke up from behind his paper, "have you any idea where my wife got this notion that no one is capable of running their lives without her help?"

"Certainly not from my side of the family," he said. "Yet it seems unlikely to have come through my brother Bennet: it almost makes me wonder if my sister had outside help."

Elizabeth gasped. "I shall throw something at you in a moment!" she warned him.

"And where did she acquire that habit?" queried her uncle.

"Ah...that comes from my side," Darcy admitted with some embarrassment. "I throw things: pillows, and rolls and such; and my aunt has been known to throw a spoon with deadly accuracy."

"Charming," said Mr. Gardiner dryly.

"Is not it?" put in Elizabeth with pleasure. "I do adore these little customs of the *ton*; they give one so much more latitude of expression in daily life."

"Are you saying I belong to the *ton*?" Darcy asked in an injured voice. "I hope I am not so trifling a person as that."

"Oh, my dear!" Elizabeth jumped up and soothed him with caresses, at which her uncle rolled his eyes and shook his paper, lifting it even higher in front of him. Darcy, mollified, put his arm around his wife and said, "You look well, my dear; am I fit to accompany you to church?"

"You look very well, indeed," she told him gently. "Blue becomes you exceedingly," she said, smoothing his lapels with the palm of her hand.

"Did Perkins shave me properly?"

Elizabeth ran the back of her hand delicately across his cheek. "Umm, perfect," she said softly. As the two of them seemed to have no immediate inclination to disentwine, Mr. Gardiner said pointedly, "I *beg* your pardon! Do you mind? Elizabeth, finish your breakfast, and have some respect for an old man's feelings: poor Reynolds hardly knows where to look." That worthy changed a laugh into a cough, turning away to the side table and adjusting the placement of the tea service quite unnecessarily.

Georgiana came in to join them at this moment, and Elizabeth ran to greet her; the sisters embraced, and walked together to the table arm in arm. Georgiana was also in looks, and, whether by design or coincidence, her frock went very well with Elizabeth's.

The two ladies breakfasted lightly, chatting about the plans for the day's activities; Mrs. Gardiner came in just as they finished, dressed for the out-of-doors and pulling on her gloves. "I have been outside," she announced, "and the mist is clearing, but it will be a raw day; we shall need our coats. Darcy, do not forget you are to read the Lesson; the vicar's asthma is bad and the curate is gone to Lambton for the early services."

"Yes Ma'am," Darcy said with a smile. It had been quite a while since he had found himself being shepherded to church by an older female relative, and he found the experience amusing. To Mr. Gardiner he said, "It strikes me, Gardiner, that perhaps managing men is just what women do; it seems to be quite a wide-spread practice amongst them." Mr. Gardiner chuckled and nodded his agreement.

Ignoring this, Mrs. Gardiner said, "Come along; we must not keep the congregation waiting on such a day as this." Darcy reflected that his new family had a remarkably well-developed sense of what was due one's dependents, and honoured them for it.

The ride to Kympton was over in short order, and Elizabeth found herself once again seated in a place of prominence in the Darcy family pew; it was not an entirely new sensation to her to be shown respect by the villagers—it was so even at Longbourn—but she had to own it was done to a much different degree here at Pemberley. It had come back to her on more than one occasion that the villagers and tenants were glad to see the pew occupied, and that they were pleased that the estate had a new mistress at last. As mistress of Pemberley, one of her larger tasks up till now had been preparing for Boxing Day, with all the gifts for the many dependents of the estate. As it was to be her first real introduction to those she would live amongst, and would reflect strongly on her husband, she had taken the task very seriously; it had occasioned the early arrival of her aunt and uncle, Darcy having encouraged her to invite them to support her in her efforts, as she adjusted to her new rôle as patroness for what seemed to be half a county. Stevenson had made out a list of those to be included, and Elizabeth had consulted with him at length, as well as with her husband and the Reynoldses; it had taken quite a few shopping trips to Kympton, Matlock, and even Derby, to fill out the list, but it was done at last.

During services, Darcy was pleased to note that the congregation was quiet and orderly; this, he thought, must be out of respect for his new lady: she was as yet an unknown quantity to them; although, he had to admit, the glances towards him and his family were not anxious, or even curious—rather they reflected a sort of unobtrusive contentment, or so he thought; this could be merely a reflection of his own contentment, though, he supposed. When it was time for the Lesson, he rose and went to the lectern. There was a creak and shuffle as the congregation adjusted their seats and readied themselves to listen to him. The reading was out of Isaiah, for which Darcy was grateful; he had once had the rather wearisome task of recounting the nations of Abraham in Genesis, and had also once been thrust into a variety of particularly ferocious beasts in a gloomy section of Jeremiah. But to-day he found a particular meaning in the reading: "...The people who walked in darkness have seen a great light..."; this could certainly pertain to him, and the light Elizabeth had led him to. He scolded his mind back to his reading, and, up until "Here Endeth the First Lesson," he kept his mind resolutely on the page before him.

Back in his pew, Mrs. Gardiner leaned over and whispered, "That was very well read, dear; you have a very nice voice for reading."

He smiled his thanks, and turned his attention back to the vicar, who wisely spoke very little before calling for the *Te Deum*. Darcy led his family out down the aisle, and waited for the vicar to come out. As the rest of the congregation filed out, Darcy was pleased to see Corporal Sands, wearing his uniform jacket as usual, saunter out and join a small family gathering off to one side; one of the family members was a young woman of perhaps five-and-twenty, who, Darcy thought, showed more than a passing interest in the Corporal.

Darcy and his family staid just long enough to hear that the vicar's affliction would not keep him from attending dinner that afternoon, and returned to Pemberley House, for there were still a number of preparations to be made. The carriage went through Lambton first, as Darcy had an errand to attend to, then on to Pemberley; the ride was soggy, but they made good time.

Elizabeth disappeared below stairs on their return, and Mrs. Gardiner set about putting the final touches on the decorations, including the placement of the mistletoe ball. Darcy saw with amusement that his sister was careful to adjust her path so she might never find herself under it, even though there were as yet no young men about.

"Who is it you wish to avoid, Dearest?" he teazed her. "That new curate, or young Horton?"

"Both, thank you, Brother," said she with just a hint of asperity.

Darcy smiled at her in an apologetic way to show he was only playing; he rather suspected he was right about a tentative interest from the two young men, though; but knowing Georgiana, he was certain she did not return it: otherwise he should never have mentioned it. But he did enjoy sporting with her in this mild way, and was pleased that she allowed herself to show some slight pique; he hoped that, over time, such little ploys, in conjunction with Elizabeth's example of liveliness and wit, might help increase her equanimity and assurance in company.

Mr. and Mrs. Bingley and the Bennets had, of course, been invited to spend the holidays at Pemberley, but Jane had expressed a wish to spend their first Christmas in their own home, and naturally Bingley would deny her nothing, although it must be admitted that he, too, enjoyed his new rôle, as one of the principle figures in the neighbourhood, to no small degree. And with the Bingley's decision to stay at Netherfield, nothing could have torn Mrs. Bennet away from the chance to display her daughter's circumstance and comfort, with great parade, to all their acquaintance in and around Meryton.

Through the afternoon the preparations continued, but all was in readiness well before the guests started arriving; the halls were covered in greenery, and gilded decorations adorned every corner. When the guests first began to arrive, Elizabeth went with Georgiana and Darcy to greet every one as they came in; Elizabeth smiled charmingly at her new neighbours, and Darcy found himself relaxing in a manner he never had before in such circumstances; being sensible that Elizabeth was there to support him — or rather, that he had only to support her —

allowed him to greet his guests with a degree of welcome new to him. Georgiana, too, seemed more comfortable as the arrivals filed past, and added her voice to the greetings as well; Elizabeth had a pleasant word for every one, and had a knack of making each welcome seem very personal; perhaps, Darcy hoped and believed, because she truly enjoyed being mistress of Pemberley, and could not help but show it in the performance of her duties.

Dinner was a pleasant affair, marked by excellent food, quiet comfort throughout, and the occasional outburst of laughter. Afterwards, there were games and cards, and, while Georgiana carefully avoided it, the mistletoe ball had to be replaced twice. Darcy was fairly certain he could distinguish an understated interest from the curate, a young man new to the neighbourhood, but from a good family to the south, and also from young Alistair Horton, heir to Catton Hall; Georgiana, however, remained near her sister's side, often with Elizabeth's arm around her waist, leaving little opportunity for the two gentlemen to speak with her.

The vicar left early, and Elizabeth made sure he was well supplied with heated bricks for the carriage ride back to Kympton. Their revels lasted well into the evening, with a small ball and a supper to follow. However, Darcy had, for the health of his family and servants, determined not to let it go more than an hour past midnight, as the next day was also to be a tiring one.

On this Boxing Day Pemberley held open house, starting after breakfast and lasting through the afternoon; the many dependents of the estate were greeted with thanks, gifts, and food; the visitors included one hardy company of mummers, arrived from Lambton; Darcy was pleased to see Corporal Sands was amongst the company, assuring him thereby that the Corporal was fitting in well here in Derbyshire.

Drawing him aside, Darcy was pleased to give the Corporal a new, very fashionable coat to replace his uniform jacket. "I like the other well enough for your official duties as constable," he told him, "but I suspect that you will soon have need of another, for a different sort of official ceremony."

Sands whistled happily, saying, "I thank you, Major. You might just be right, at that."

Darcy said, "I have had a note from Tewkes, you know; he says that things in Newcastle are quiet."

"Aye, yer boy won't be goin' anywheres this winter," the Corporal said complacently. "Come spring I'll take a jaunt up there meself, an' see if we can't remind him wot's wot."

"How are your duties here?"

"Nothin' to it, Major; I feel like I'm stealing your money."

"What about Ferguson?"

"Aye, Ferguson," the Corporal said ruminatively. "'Im I will 'ave to keep an eye on: one of us isn't long for this part of the country."

"He does have some size on him," Darcy observed noncommittally.

"That's all 'e 'as: 'e's all sound, no sand."

"Well, I trust you to handle it," said Darcy. "Just do try to stay within shouting distance of the law, and even closer to what is proper."

"Aye, Major, that I will," said the Corporal with a whistle. Clapping him on the shoulder, Darcy wished him a Happy Christmas and returned to his other duties as host.

For Perkins, he had prepared a very special gift; in the morning as they were in his dressing-room, he had given him a new watch and fob, but, a coach arriving from Lambton mid-morning, he called for his man; leading him to the front hall, he was very pleased to watch Perkins's face as his Lara, weeping happily, descended from the coach; this had been Darcy's errand in Lambton the day before, to ensure that Mrs. Perkins had been properly settled at the inn for the day. Darcy had brought her up from Meryton, Mrs. Reynolds having assured him that a place might be found for her in the household. Mr. and Mrs. Perkins were both in tears on this occasion, and Darcy was not above feeling a little constriction in his chest; his own lady coming up and taking his arm to view the happy couple, she squeezed his arm and whispered, "You are a good, just, and honourable man, Fitzwilliam Darcy."

"I simply do what I am able," he said practically.

"You do what very few of your standing would think to do," she pointed out.

"That does not make me better," he said. "It only points out their failings."

Elizabeth patted his arm, and did not argue under the circumstances. Perkins led his wife, still crying and smiling, past them with a grateful smile of his own, to show her to their room.

At the end of an extremely long day, during which a seemingly endless procession of folk filed through their doors, up stairs in their chambers Darcy asked Elizabeth: "I am sure it has been a very trying two days for you, my dear; would you rather I sleep in the other room?"

"You *are* a good and just man," she said, smiling as she took his hand and drew him into her chamber.

"It would seem goodness is its own reward," he observed to the world at large, closing the door behind them. Elizabeth was pleased to reinforce her opinion of her husband's character at some length; and it might be deemed that, of all those under that roof, those with the greatest comforts enjoyed the least slumber.

Correspondence

EDITOR'S NOTE
N.B.: It is not necessary to follow the correspondence in its entirety to understand or appreciate the history contained in the body of the work; when important to the movement of the story, the letters, either in part or in whole, have been included in the text. As the written word was so important a means of communication during the time before the advent of electronic communication, though, the letters, even those with no part to play in the story, are included separately rather to give the reader a chance to follow the story from a different, and perhaps even deeper, perspective, and at a pace more consistent with that experienced by the story's characters.

The correspondence between Mr. Darcy and his sister is given in chronological order by correspondent. The various threads interweave in time, making it all but impossible to follow each thread individually with a proper chronology; it is necessary therefore to separate them in this way. References are given to the appropriate replies, where applicable, to facilitate following the chain of correspondence correctly.

Letters from Miss Georgiana Darcy

*****

*Pemberley
Monday, September 22, --

Dear Fitzwilliam,

I trust this finds you well, and that you have fully recovered from the images and impressions created by Mr. Cowper. I am so happy to hear what you relate about Mr. Bingley's prospects; have you heard anything? Is he engaged to Miss Bennet? I have to say, I have always thought him quite the most affable man of my acquaintance, and I am so pleased he has found his some one. But do you really think he would not succeed if you were present? This cannot be true, if the two of them hold the regard for each other your seem to believe. Is it then primarily on behalf of Miss Elizabeth Bennet that you are gone to London?

It is the second half of your letter that struck me most: I am so sorry you are troubled by how Miss Elizabeth Bennet must see you, with your intimate knowledge of her family's affairs. Imagining myself in her place, though, I cannot but agree that such knowledge must be felt strongly by her. I am very glad to know she thinks of me; I, too, have often thought of her, and have found no reason to change my high opinion of her, which, I confess, was formed

C1

largely before I ever met her. And, in light of that opinion, I have reason to hope that she might come in time to see that her sister's error has not affected your esteem for her, and be more comfortable in your company; and, of course, you can have no ill opinion of her sister's frailty, in view of you own sister's misdeeds. If you can forgive the nearer source of shame (a circumstance that humbles me still, more than I can say: and given subsequent events, your rescue means all the more), then that of a comparative stranger can require no great stretch of mind. So, as I was once told by a most trusted authority, time will heal these feelings, and bring about the correction of her manner, which you presently feel so acutely.

How you can imagine my soul to be free of the need for amendment, or that I do not undergo the same trimmings and prunings as you, must stem from your extravagant regard; surely I do not see myself so. I am flattered, although somewhat surprised, by such a significant impairment in an otherwise remarkably clear vision. But I am so pleased to be of use, as your "connection to light and land," even though I know full well I do not merit the office.

We are quiet here, Mrs. Annesley and I, which is a great relief to me; I have been making a habit of walking to the folly each day to spend some time alone—well, hardly alone, as nature has populated the season with so much to see and hear. But I catch the breezes, and the scent of summer fading, and I find a peace I despaired to hope for a year ago; I have you to thank for that, Brother. I pray, and trust with all my heart, that you will find the same.

Yours, most sincerely,

Georgiana Darcy

*For reply, see Darcy, September 25.
*****

*Pemberley
Monday, September 29

Dearest Fitzwilliam,

I have just received your news and I cannot say how happy it makes me! But this is so sudden, how can this be? Your news has left me so bewildered I hardly know what I should say. But from what you say it is not sudden; it has been many months, even a year almost, in fact, that this has been coming on. Whence came this rumour that sent my aunt to Hertfordshire? Was it anything to do with you? And poor Elizabeth! (I hope I may call her so). I should never wish to be on the wrong end of Lady Catherine's tongue, especially as there was no justification—or was there? I am so confused I hardly know how to think on the matter; you had proposed to her, she had refused you, there was a rumour, and on Lady Catherine's interference, it came out that, while the rumour was unfounded, Elizabeth was no longer so completely opposed to you—there, I think I have it right. In light of the event, she must have been *very* well disposed towards you. I will congratulate myself on having told you something to the effect in July when she was in Lambton.

Oh, Fitzwilliam, my heart will not stop racing! Elizabeth will be part of our family! I love her already, just from the little I have seen of her, and for her love of you. I do so hope she truly approves of me, and not just in the way one approves of some new acquaintance who, while pleasant, is not destined ever to be more than just an acquaintance. I keep thinking back to your list of her qualities: sincere, charming, warm, and amiable—that is how you described her last year in your letters, and every thing I have seen agrees with it, so I flatter myself she would not show an interest she did not feel. Bur why should she like me? I have no conversation or charm; in what way would she form an attachment to one so limited in abilities? And how will some one of such high merit view one such as myself over the course of time? You, too, of course, are a person of highest abilities and worth, and I can almost hear your words of assurance, but you are the closest family I have, and we cannot escape the bias that brings, and must discount your feelings on that basis.

Goodness, we have to determine where your chambers will be! Oh, but you have probably made that decision already. You will be coming here, will not you? Or will you stay at Grosvenor Square? You will send for me, I hope? I do so wish I could be at the ceremony, but I suppose that cannot be; there are so many things to see to other than making arrangements for me to travel south. But surely you will come here soon; Elizabeth will wish to see it more fully, of course, and I hope she will like it well enough to wish to stay here at least part of the year.

Am I at liberty to tell people? I hardly know how I could keep such a secret as this. You must be sure of the event, else you would not have written, but I will try to hold my tongue until I hear from you again. Do write soon! This is just the most splendid, exciting news! I know she will be good for you, Brother, as she is so easy, cordial, and amiable; she will be the perfect mistress for Pemberley—much better than I ever would have been.

We can have Christmas here, as you and I planned! Oh, please do say we can, Fitzwilliam; that would be such a delight! A long, lovely, family Christmas, just the way we talked of it, but now with my new sister. My new sister! —I do so like the way that sounds. I am listening in my mind to all the times you have told me she cannot help but form a regard for me, and am trying my utmost to have faith that you are correct. But I do not wish to be selfish, of course; perhaps Elizabeth prefers Town, and then I would naturally understand your wishing to gratify her wishes in every respect.

And we are to be related to Mr. Bingley! How lovely! I have always had a regard for him, and of course you must be exceedingly pleased that he will be your brother. I have heard very little of Miss Bennet, but surely she must be amiable and pleasing. This is all so perfect and fitting, it is wonderful how it has all come together. How happy he must have been when you told him your news. But I have just thought what Lady Catherine's response must be when she hears of it; Heavens, …well, I shall not dwell on is yet to occur, especially as the present holds such joy.

I am sure I must sound half-distracted, but I cannot help it: my thoughts will not be still; what is more than dumbfounded? Now, you say Elizabeth had learnt of your interference in her younger sister's marriage? How could that be? And, that being the case, how could the subject of your continued esteem ever come up? How could you have ever been able to speak of that, with the consciousness of your involvement hanging over you both? Oh! —how I wish that I was there amongst you, and on the spot, that I might understand it all! Miraculous, as you put it, must be the very word; and like all miracles, it is a source of exceeding awe and joy.

I have hoped and prayed you might find some one worthy of you, dear Brother, and in all of your letters last autumn I saw evidence that Elizabeth might be the right one, irrespective of any feelings I have come to feel for her during our short acquaintance. Based solely on your letters, I was ready to accept her as my sister, and the deeper knowledge I have gained of her character since, has only strengthened that conviction. I will certainly do all I can to ease her way as Pemberley's new mistress and your helpmate. Now I have calmed down somewhat and can think on it, the joy you express in your letter, unparalleled in all the letters you have ever written me, says all that needs to be said about her, and is the surest guarantee of your future happiness. I know you well enough that such joy is very telling, and I know her well enough to be sure that your joy is not misplaced. I await your next letter very anxiously.

Your amazed and devoted sister
Georgiana Darcy

*For reply, see Darcy, October 1.

*****

Letters from Mr. Fitzwilliam Darcy

*****

Grosvenor Square
Wednesday, August 6th, —

Dear Georgiana,

Well, it has been a busy few days, but I am now able to report that we have made considerable progress, and met with good success thus far. I was able to trace Miss Lydia Bennet successfully to an inn in London, although a part of London I trust you will never have cause to visit. Unfortunately, she has attached herself to the fellow without reserve or condition, and is resolute in her intention of staying with him; I was unable persuade her otherwise. As little regard as I have for her, I did most sincerely urge her to return to her friends, although I confess her obstinacy prevented me from urging the matter as strenuously as I might.

Her refusal leaves nothing to be done but arrange for their marriage, and I shall put that in motion shortly; I must first communicate with her family: fortunately, in the Gardiners I have a ready entrée, there. My plan, it would seem, is holding up, and I have hopes that all will be finalised before the month is out. I do not imagine I shall be needed here in London all that while, so I trust you will see me again at Pemberley before long.

In all truth, Dearest, I confess I am unsure as to which of the two principals will suffer most from these arrangements; but, as it is owing entirely to their own actions that they find themselves in this position, I cannot condemn myself for forcing its conclusion. Miss Lydia Bennet clearly expected marriage to be the ultimate outcome of this adventure, as she seems to characterise it in her mind, and, given the enormity of the damage the failure to bring about their nuptials would cause the Bennets, it seems only right to me that he satisfy those expectations. He is like a river in flood, destroying whatever is in its path, and prudence demands that that flood be channelled, lest it lay ruin to entire counties; the steps I have taken will, I hope, stem the course of that flood and, if not contain it completely, at least gentle it to the point that its damage is confined only to those attached to him.

The Bennets, I dare say, would never have compounded for such a son-in-law, but there is nothing else that may be done to save them; I pity them for what their future will hold, but, given her character, the girl would never have chosen well or wisely, so on their side I suppose all this is little more than what was inevitable; it is, at least, finished early and, I hope, quietly.

My real pity is reserved for Miss Elizabeth Bennet, as she, I know, thought well of the fellow, and now must recognise and live with the knowledge of his character, and accept him as brother. Her mother, in all likelihood, will find nothing exceptional in the match, and her father seems largely indifferent to his family's affairs; while not a man without ability, he adopts a very sardonic outlook, and, with three silly daughters and a very silly wife, one perhaps cannot wonder.

Speaking of indifference, it is the indifference of that low person I seek to constrain, to the suffering he causes the innocent and the worthy, that angers me most. Were he to confine his misdeeds to such as his soon-to-be wife, who has not the acuity to realise she suffers, or to the miscreants who populate his world, here in his proper milieu amongst the lower haunts of London, he would be relatively innocuous. But, I shall hope that the manner in which I have him hemmed in will render him that mildly unpleasant nuisance he ought to be, and leave decent people free of his influence. I pray it may be so.

But now, Dearest, I am going to take myself off to my club, and indulge in a little celebratory dinner, and toast to a future where you and I might never need speak of the man again. Your loving brother,
Fitzwilliam Darcy

Post scriptum:

Please tell my aunt that I have taken her advice to heart, and have followed it to good effect.

*****

Grosvenor Square
*Friday, September 19, —

Dear Georgiana,

I have returned to London to wait until Bingley should have had time to secure his future with Miss Bennet; I deemed it best done without the hindrance of my overbearing personality being quite so much in evidence. I doubt it will take long, however; the two principals involved seem as likely to connect as any couple I have ever witnessed, just on the strength of Bingley's esteem alone; but I am persuaded that Miss Bennet cherishes a deep regard for him, as well. Indeed, I am sure that, now the discouraging influence of my fearsome features is removed, Mrs. Bennet will be able to contrive ample time for the two lovers to be alone to get the job done with admirable efficiency.

So, I am sure the light of tender love triumphant shines by now on Bingley's schemes of domesticity; I left him yesterday, and I cannot imagine it would take him too much longer to declare himself: he was never one to be reticent in making his feelings known. I expect to hear from him almost hourly to declare his profitable addresses. In spite of my way of talking, Dearest, I am very pleased for him, and wish him every joy in his married life; I am certain he will be happy, and in their mutual goodness I see much to value, and a most favourable prophecy of felicity.

There is little going forward in Town just now, and I am catching up on some reading. After our discussion with Miss Elizabeth Bennet in July, I have been tasting poetry by our modern authors; this afternoon I read *The Castaway*, by Cowper: have you read it? It is dark, though moving: the tale of a man swept overboard at night, far out at sea; its metaphor found harbour in my heart, and I have turned to this missive, my own link to light, land, and beauty, to distract me and release me from its power. I understand the author was a man given to fits of insanity — what does this say about me, I should like to know? I shall trust your regard for me to be sufficient evidence of my being of sound mind, however.

You will, I know, wish to hear of Miss Elizabeth Bennet; she is well, and asked after you particularly, and on more than one occasion. But I confess that it is nearly as much for her sake as for Bingley's that I have removed to London — knowing of her younger sister's condition before her marriage, as I do, my presence could not but inflict some measure of discomfort on her. Of course, she knows nothing of my involvement latterly in the business, which would be much worse, but still, it must be bad enough, and so I have distanced myself from her. I can only trust to time, to let her present suffering amend itself to a degree that will allow her to see me without painful recollection. How much simpler our lives would be if we could regulate our brains to the extent that we could forget whatever we chose to: imagine the bliss of forgetting all pain and embarrassment! These are the scars of the soul, and I cannot but imagine that it would be more beautiful without them. Well, having now given that more thought, I see I am wrong; the soul of the babe is not more beautiful than that of the adult, except in the beauty of the promise it holds for the future. The soul is formed, and *in*formed, by every thing in our lives, including, certainly, all of our trials; pain and mortification must be the price of a beautiful soul: the natural trimmings and prunings, if you will, that create the majestic beauty of the mighty oak. I do not believe that an oak raised in a hothouse would be nearly as picturesque as the forest patriarch which has withstood all the tempests and droughts Nature could throw against it.

Well, there it is, I suppose; we must weather our storms, and persevere through straitened circumstances, and grow slowly into beauty. I must, at least: you, it seems, have somehow managed to by-pass the requirement for trials and travail, having arrived at perfection quite naturally in earliest adulthood. Your trials *demonstrate* the beauty of your soul, whilst those by which I am afflicted must labour still to shape mine. Perhaps that is simply the difference between men and women—those of my sex must toil, and struggle, and fight with the world, before we are moulded into our correct shape, whilst your sex finds it more spontaneously and benevolently within you. Perhaps, as you are the bearers of life, you are necessarily and innately more sacred and serene, and we men are drawn to that immaculate purity in order to soothe and correct our own great imperfections. I do not know, Dearest; but surely a man without a woman must suffer the more in this life before finding tranquillity and repose.

I do apologise; the residue of melancholy left behind by Cowper does not seem to have left me completely. Be assured, Dearest, I am not so desperate as it may sound; I find that my new susceptibility to poetry affects me more strongly than I have any idea of whilst I am reading it. Then, I am more conscious of the scansion and rhyme scheme, the author's use of diction and imagery—a dozen things. But afterwards, as I revisit it in my mind, the impact is felt the more for being free of such critical thinking.

Best I turn my attentions to something rather more mundane and purposeful; there is a

letter from Stevenson, which will no doubt oc-
cupy my mind to better effect than poetry.
Therefore, adieu, Dearest. I remain,
Your affectionate Brother,
Fitzwilliam Darcy

*For reply, see Georgiana, September 22.
*****

Grosvenor Square
Thursday, September 25, —

My dearest Georgiana,

I have received yours of the 22nd, and let
me tell you first that Mr. Bingley has indeed secured his future. I received word of it on Saturday last, via express. He is, predictably, quite
overcome with happiness, and I cannot say that
his hopes of felicity are ill-founded. Miss Bennet
is certainly one of the sweetest creatures I have
ever met, and her quiet obligingness could not
be better suited to Bingley's open and voluble
bonhomie.

Insofar as my response to poetry is concerned, I wanted to assure you that, although I
may often find myself sitting to one side and
"seeing into the life of things" (to paraphrase
Wordsworth, another of those authors mentioned by Miss Elizabeth Bennet at Pemberley)
without really partaking in life, this is just my
way, and should not trouble you when it appears. We are connected to life, quite literally,
through our connections to the lives of those we
love; it has been apparent to me for some time
that I am not meant for many such ties, and so
my connection to the world at large must be
lighter than those with more congenial and

C13

amiable (in both the English and the French meanings) natures, who would, of course, be drawn into life to a much greater degree. This does not reflect any disgust for life on my part; no, it is only that I must often find myself an observer, not a participant, when I am not in the company of those I love. Those such as my friend Bingley can find wherewith to join themselves to their company in almost any circumstance, but I am not gifted that way; I suppose I ought to envy such abilities, but, in truth, I cannot: I do not form such bonds myself because I do not feel the need, and so cannot repine their absence.

In some instances, it can even be of use; in the case of Miss Elizabeth Bennet, for example, such observational detachment can establish a reasonable distance from the emotions that might have been more troubling to me than to her, were I to feel that sort of bond my friend is wont to forge. Distance from vexatious emotion must be seen as a degree of contentment, so I find I can be content as I am, and not wish to emulate Bingley.

I envy you your time at home: London is hot, close, and uncomfortable; the closest thing to the "scent of summer fading" is when a wind from the north drives off the smell of the Thames for a brief respite. Some wag in Town called the London summer "a state of continual inelegance"; I do not recall who it was, but it is surely true. I went for a ride in the Park the other day, which was a great refreshment, but my poor mount required buckets of water thrown over him on our return. Town is still quiet; the Little Theatre is open, but I have not had any great need to venture out: I am content to remain comfortably in my library, and continue my introduction to our modern poets. I am even toying with the idea of reading *Camilla*, the novel Miss Elizabeth Bennet mentioned to us there in July.

I had dinner last evening with the Colonel, who sends his best; he has been rather distracted lately, as his work, while evidently well received at the War Office, has not succeeded in stopping Bonaparte, and he has begun to take this as a personal affront. He mentioned he had been thinking of simply tracking the French general down and challenging him to a duel, as he is convinced that while he lives, the French will remain victorious. He jokes that he believes the man has a pact with the Devil that guarantees a miraculous stroke of luck whenever needed to turn the tide of battle. I asked why he did not make a pact in his own right, and he replied that his superiors would object to his stepping over them in the chain of command.

Well, as I am now certain that I have corrected my error of last year, and all is well with Bingley, I shall return home the sooner. I expect to return to Meryton on Saturday (I wish to give him a bit more leisure to enjoy his time with Miss Bennet, and not trouble himself playing host to me), and I shall not stay long, I should not think. I can hope, therefore, to see you at Pemberley within the fortnight. I look forward to that, and to spending a solid period of time at home, where the world cannot reach me, and I can share in your peace.

I remain,
Your affectionate brother,
Fitzwilliam Darcy

*****

*Netherfield
Sunday, September 28, —

My dear Georgiana,

I have to write you straight away regarding the most wondrous and amazing news; Miss Elizabeth Bennet has agreed to be my wife! Yes, quite true, I assure you. How or why I have been so blessed is still a mystery to me, but I wanted to share it with you as soon as possible.

I returned to Netherfield, you must understand, to apologise to Elizabeth (as I am now admitted to the honour of calling her) for a visit she received from Lady Catherine. That good lady had heard a rumour that Elizabeth had agreed to marry me, apparently based on the assumption that, as her sister was to marry my friend, naturally she would be next, and I was fixed on as the lucky man. However it may have come about, Lady Catherine went to Hertfordshire to forbid the banns, as it were, and gave Elizabeth quite a substantial piece of her mind. She then proceeded to Grosvenor Square to give me one, too. The upshot was, I left for Meryton yesterday, intent on making every apology in my power to Elizabeth, and determining whether I might ever have a chance to succeed with her. This, I know, will surprise you, but now I must tell you something that will surprise you even more: I had actually proposed to her before, when we were together at Rosings. She turned me down in a decided fashion, for which I was solely to blame, I admit. It was this that was troubling me throughout the spring; I could not bring myself to tell you of it, Dearest, as I knew it must pain you, too — and there could be no point in upsetting you with what could not be mended. So, when my aunt's retailing of her interview with Elizabeth gave me some suspicion that she might not be as resolutely set against me as she was before, I was compelled to return, both to apologise and to see what hope I might ever have.

Arriving at Longbourn last night, and contriving, with Bingley's connivance, to be alone with Elizabeth this morning, before I could so much as mention my aunt, let alone my more pressing interests, Elizabeth gave me to understand that she knew of my involvement in her younger sister's elopement and marriage—imagine my horror and chagrin! But somehow, I know not just how, my apologies and expressions of contrition turned into a declaration of my continued regard for her. And, miraculously, Elizabeth made representations to me of her own regard, and is now to be my wife, and your sister. Is that not a wonderful and staggering piece of news? I would stake anything that you had no more idea of it than myself. I could wish for a more imaginative word, but I am absolutely dumbfounded; I am constantly having to stop myself from grinning in the most idiotic way. There: I have just had to stop it again. I am persuaded that those men who declare themselves the happiest in the world must know nothing at all of the matter, as, in the main, on the point of their ladies' esteem they are moved no farther than from near-certainty, into certainty—which surely can be no great source of exceptional wonder or joy—whereas I was transported from despair to amazement and bliss in the space of a few heartbeats. To have scaled such heights from so great a depth is to truly know happiness.

It is already late, and I wish this to go out tonight, so I will leave off here, Dearest. I expect to hear from you soonest.

Your affectionate, and bewildered brother,
Fitzwilliam Darcy

*For reply, see Georgiana, September 29
*****

Netherfield
Thursday, October 1, —

Dearest Georgiana,

You will forgive me, but I had to laugh over your letter, although I certainly do not blame you for your confusion: indeed, I still question as I wake each morning whether it all might be a dream that disappears in the light of day; so far, however, it has withstood the test. Your letter reminded me very much of my own bewilderment that first evening, sitting at Longbourn and trying to understand it all; and do you know, I had that same thought about our chambers? What a thing to think of at such a time! — but there you are: we both had it.

But let me tell you straight off that I am coming for you to bring you to the wedding; I would never think of leaving you out of such an event in my life. There: now I hope you will finally believe how much I value you, you dear, silly creature. And since you have already heard my assurances on Elizabeth's regard for you in your mind, perhaps there is no need to repeat them here, but I shall: she holds you dear already, and I would stake my life she will come to love you the more as she knows you better. This, I think, may answer half the questions in your letter, and "I do not know" is probably the answer to the other half. Almost all of you questions as to the hows and whys of her accepting me I have no answer for. I am myself still trying to understand it all, but I hope that by the time I come to bring you here I shall be able to give you more particulars.

But on to the more material items: I shall be home early on Sunday the 19th, and spend the night; we shall leave for Hertfordshire in the morning. We will spend one night somewhere on the road, and be at Netherfield on Tuesday. I recommend an early dinner on the day I am home, and early rest, as our travel will be wearisome.

That is all my news for now; it is not enough, I know, but the rest I will share when you see me: we shall have ample time at home and on our trip to make it all as clear to you as it is to me, which is to say, not clear at all; but perhaps by then it will all make sense. Until I see you, I remain,
Your loving brother,
Fitzwilliam Darcy

*****

Books by Stanley Michael Hurd:

Made in the USA
Lexington, KY
14 October 2014